PENGUIN BOOKS

THE PREDATOR

D1430997

ABOUT THE AUTHOR

Michael Ridpath spent eight years working as a bond trader at an international bank in the City of London. He is the author of four other novels – *The Marketmaker, Free to Trade, Final Venture* and *Trading Reality*. He grew up in Yorkshire and now lives in north London with his wife and children.

If you'd like to know more about the author and his work, log on to www.michaelridpath.com

The Predator

MICHAEL RIDPATH

PENGUIN BOOKS

PENGUIN BOOKS

Published by the Penguin Group
Penguin Books Ltd, 80 Strand, London WC2R 0RL, England
Penguin Putnam Inc., 375 Hudson Street, New York, New York 10014, USA
Penguin Books Australia Ltd, 250 Camberwell Road, Camberwell, Victoria 3124, Australia
Penguin Books Canada Ltd, 10 Alcorn Avenue, Toronto, Ontario, Canada M4V 3B2
Penguin Books India (P) Ltd, 11 Community Centre, Panchsheel Park, New Delhi – 110 017, India
Penguin Books (NZ) Ltd, Cnr Rosedale and Airborne Roads, Albany, Auckland, New Zealand
Penguin Books (South Africa) (Pty) Ltd, 24 Sturdee Avenue, Rosebank 2196, South Africa

Penguin Books Ltd, Registered Offices: 80 Strand, London WC2R 0RL, England

www.penguin.com

First published by Viking 2001
Published in Penguin Books 2002

1

Copyright © Michael Ridpath, 2001

Set in Monotype Garamond
Printed in England by Clays Ltd, St Ives plc

For my mother, Elizabeth, who liked to read

PART ONE

Chris pulled the yellow note off his favourite coffee mug and read the familiar loopy writing: *Gone to Prague. Back Wednesday. Maybe. Love L.*

He sighed and shook his head. It was Monday morning, the first day back after ten glorious days skiing in the French Alps. He had been in the office since half past seven, refreshed, eager to sort out whatever tangles Lenka had made of their firm while he had been away. As he had expected, there were quite a few. The computer was down, there was a letter from the fund's auditors about a problem with the accounting of accrued interest, and she had bought a pile of bonds issued by an extremely dodgy-sounding Polish mobile telecoms company.

And now there was this note.

She knew he would be angry. She must have left it on his mug in the kitchen so that he would have a few minutes to settle in before he found it. How thoughtful. She could at least have stayed a day in London to brief him on what had happened since he had been away. This was the first holiday he had taken since he and Lenka had set up Carpathian Fund Management the previous year and he had expected things to fall apart without him. But, as he closed his eyes and remembered the feel of the fresh crisp powder under his skis, he knew it had been worth it.

The phone rang. He carried the mug of coffee back to his desk and picked it up.

'Carpathian.'

'Good morning, Chris! How's your tan?' He recognized the hoarse, exuberant voice immediately.

'Lenka! Where are you?'

'Didn't you get my note? I'm in Prague.'

'Yes. But what are you doing there? You should be here, telling me what's been going on.'

'You're a clever boy, Chris. You'll figure it out. Anyway, I've got some great news. I've found us an office!'

'In Prague?'

'Yes, of course in Prague. Remember, we discussed it?'

It was true. They had discussed gradually opening up small offices throughout Central Europe. But not quite yet, Chris had thought. The idea of all the admin involved in opening and running one made his heart sink.

'What's the matter, Chris? It's in a great location. And I think I've found the right person to run it. Jan Pavlík. You'll like him. Come over and have a look.'

'When? How can I do that? There's too much to do here.'

'It'll wait,' said Lenka. 'This is important. And we have to move fast to get this office. Come on. I don't want to take these decisions without you.'

It seemed to Chris that that was exactly what she was doing.

'But what about the computer? And what on earth are we doing with twenty-five million euros of Eureka Telecom?'

'Don't worry. Ollie has got a man coming in this morning to fix the computer. And I'll tell you all about Eureka Telecom when you get here. There's a story.'

'There'd better be,' he said.

'Oh, Chris, you sound so fierce,' Lenka said in mock awe. 'Look, the office is right across the street from the Golden Bear. It's a great pub. It serves Budvar. You'll like it, I promise.'

He hesitated. He glanced out of the window at the upper branches of the oak trees reaching up from the square below. The din of London traffic drifted up to the fifth-floor office, pierced by the cries of a taxi driver hurling abuse at a bicycle courier. It was true, they had promised their investors that they would open up in Central Europe. They had said it was essential to have a local presence to understand the market properly. Well, it was about time they did something about it.

'Oh come on, Chris,' Lenka said. 'If you want to give me a hard time about it, you can do it here.'

As usual, Lenka was getting her way.

'All right,' he sighed. 'See you tonight.'

The taxi nosed through the cars parked haphazardly in the small snow-covered square and pulled up in front of the Hotel Paříž. Chris paid the driver and checked in. He called up to Lenka's room; she told him she would meet him in the lobby in ten minutes. It took him less than that to dump his case, change into some jeans and get back downstairs.

Lenka, of course, made him wait. The lobby was dripping with accoutrements from the beginning of the twentieth century: ornate chandeliers and elevator doors made of brass, a Rodin-like sculpture of a nude, and art-nouveau posters advertising everything from Czech chocolate to French plays. Lenka always stayed in the Hotel Paříž; she said it was one of the few hotels in the city that still had style. She had grown up thirty kilometres from Prague, and she had spent her student days there. She loved it. Chris wasn't at all surprised that she wanted to open an office there.

And Chris wasn't going to stop her. Although technically they were equal partners in Carpathian Fund Management, the fund had been her idea, and he still considered himself lucky that she had asked him to join her. They had first met ten years before, when they were both eager participants on the training programme of Bloomfield Weiss, a large New York investment bank. They had become friends and had kept in touch as they went their separate ways: he to Bloomfield Weiss's London office and she to their Emerging Markets group in New York. Then, when he was holed up alone in his flat recovering from a stomach bug he had picked up in India, fired in disgrace from his job, abandoned by his girlfriend, his self-confidence demolished, she had called him. She was leaving Bloomfield Weiss to set up her own fund. Would he like to join her?

She had saved him. Of course, he had refused her offer at first, saying he was the wrong person, that he would be a hindrance rather than a help. He had believed this, but she had not. With her encouragement, he pieced together the fragments of his shattered self-esteem. It turned out she was right: they made a good team.

Carpathian was a hedge fund investing in the government and high-yield bonds of Central Europe. Or at least that was the way they had described it in their marketing literature. In reality, 'hedge fund' meant high risk, 'high-yield' meant junk bonds, and Central Europe meant the old Eastern Europe less the basket cases, like Russia. The investors knew what they were doing, though. They wanted to make as much money as possible from the integration of the old Iron Curtain countries with the rest of Europe. They wanted Lenka and Chris to take big risks, and make them big bucks, or to be more precise, big euros. Lenka, with some help from Chris, had raised fifty-five million euros, and borrowed more to maximize the return on investment.

So far, all had gone well. They had achieved a return of twenty-nine per cent in their first nine months; in January alone they had made six per cent. Chris had been a trader long enough to know that some of their success was down to luck. But he knew how to trade government bonds well and she knew the high-yield market. She had the vision to see the big play; he got the details right. She wowed their investors; he made sure they received high-quality reports on time. She had found the office in Hanover Square at a bargain rent; he had negotiated the lease. And now she had found an office in Prague, the first step towards making them a truly European fund manager.

But Chris knew from painful experience that in the bond markets things could change in an instant. His skiing holiday was the first time in over a year that, for a few short days, he had not been worrying about Carpathian. Now he was worrying again.

Ollie, their young analyst, could sort the computer out. He

and Tina, an even younger receptionist-cum-assistant, would cope for a couple of days. But a bigger concern was the Eureka Telecom holding. Twenty-five million euros was a large position for a fund of Carpathian's size. Chris knew little about Eureka Telecom, except that it intended to build a mobile telephone network across Central Europe, and that the bond had been issued during the week he was skiing. Bloomfield Weiss, his old employer, was the lead manager. He couldn't help it, but he still found it hard to trust any bond issue that was led by them.

He was studying a poster advertising a play starring Sarah Bernhardt when he heard a familiar voice. 'Chris! Nice of you to show up. You're late!'

She smiled and kissed him on both cheeks. She was a tall woman, with white-blonde hair, angular cheekbones and wide, almond-shaped brown eyes. She was wearing tight jeans, a leather jacket and boots. She looked stunning. Had Chris been meeting her for the first time, he would have gaped. But this was Lenka, and he was used to her by now. Everywhere she went men turned to get a second look at her, and that was just how she had always liked it.

'I sat on the tarmac at Heathrow for three-quarters of an hour,' he said. 'Can we get something to eat? I'm starving.'

'Didn't you eat anything on the plane?'

'I was saving myself.'

'Well, good,' she said. 'Let's go to The Golden Bear. We can have a beer or two and I'm sure they'll still do some food.'

'Are we going to see the new office?' Chris asked.

'Only from the outside. We'll look at it properly tomorrow morning.'

'So, what's this Golden Bear like?'

'It's a dive, Chris. Just your kind of hole. Come on.'

As she pushed past him, he smelled the expensive perfume she always wore that had become so familiar. Annick Goutal, he had discovered. He followed her out of the hotel and into the night air. It was cold, a penetrating cold that bit straight through Chris's London coat to his bones. He wished he'd brought gloves.

'Come on,' Lenka said. 'This way,' and she set off down a quiet snow-covered street.

'Is it far?'

'Ten minutes' walk. It's just off Příkopy, where most of the big banks are located. It's a good address without being too expensive.'

'What about this Jan Pavlík? Do you think we can persuade him to come on board?'

'Yes, as long as you like him. We'll be meeting him tomorrow. He's good, I think.'

'Have you spoken about a package?'

'Of course not,' Lenka said. 'I wouldn't dream of doing that without asking you, would I?'

Chris just looked at her.

Lenka laughed. 'We can discuss it when we get to the pub, if you like. There's some other stuff I want to talk to you about as well.'

'I'm all for that,' Chris said. 'But I need food first.'

'OK, OK,' she said. 'I'm sure they'll do some goulash and dumplings. That will fill you up.'

They turned a corner and emerged into the Old Town Square. Chris stopped and stared, overcome by the magic of its subtly illuminated fairy-tale buildings glowing in the snow. The medieval town hall rose above brightly painted baroque merchants' houses, and a monument to someone or other lurked darkly in the centre. The rich notes of a saxophone drifted out of one of the bars around the square's rim.

'Come on,' said Lenka, tugging Chris's arm, 'I thought you said you were hungry.'

Chris knew that she had brought him this way deliberately, that she wanted to show off the city she loved so much, but he followed her as she led him down a series of ever smaller streets.

'I hope you know where you're going,' he said.

'Of course I do,' said Lenka, and turned under an arch into a tiny alleyway

An occasional lamp lit up quiet doorways and a couple of closed-up crystal shops. Chris could smell coal in the air. The snow still lay on the road here, gleaming in the lamplight, only slightly compacted by the few cars that must have passed by since it had fallen. All was quiet, the din of the city's traffic muffled by the walls and the snow.

Suddenly, Chris became aware of soft rapid footsteps behind them. As the sound came nearer, he turned. Lenka had just begun to say something. A man was striding rapidly towards them, only a couple of paces away. He was holding something in his hand, and making straight for Lenka.

For a fragment of a second, Chris didn't react: he was too surprised to take in what was happening. Then, when he realized what the man was holding, he shouted and dived at him. But he was too slow. In one swift movement, the attacker grabbed Lenka by the collar of her coat with his left hand, yanked her backwards and raised his knife to her throat with his right. Her eyes were wide with fear and shock, steel glinting against the paleness of her neck. Her breath came in short, sharp bursts. She stared at Chris, her eyes imploring him to do something, too scared to struggle, or even to speak.

'Steady,' Chris said, slowly raising his hands towards the man.

The man grunted. Chris saw steel flash and heard the gurgle of Lenka's attempt to scream. He dived forward, but the man pushed Lenka into him and turned and ran. Chris caught her and hesitated, unsure whether to go after him. But he let the man go and lay Lenka gently on to the pavement. Blood poured out on to the snow and all over her prized leather jacket. Chris tore off his own coat and tried to hold it against her throat.

'Help!' he shouted. He didn't know the Czech for help. He tried the Polish instead. '*Pomocy! Policja! Pogotowie! Lekarza!* Oh, come on somebody, help me!'

Lenka was lying still beneath his hands. Her face was already

9

pale, her eyes open and limp. Her lips moved as she tried to say something, but they made no sound.

Desperately, Chris pushed down hard on her throat with his coat, as though by sheer force of will he could stanch the flow. Within seconds, his hands and arms were covered in her blood.

'Please, Lenka!' he urged her. 'Come on, Lenka! Stop bleeding. You must stop bleeding! For God's sake, don't die on me. Lenka!'

But it made no difference. Beneath his hands, her eyes fixed into a stare and her breathing stopped. Chris lifted up her blood-soaked head to his chest and held it, running his fingers through her short white hair.

'Lenka,' he whispered one more time, kissing her forehead. Then he lay her gently back on to the snow and wept.

Shoulders hunched, Chris trudged through the urban snow, eyes down, scarcely noticing the city around him going about its morning business. He needed air. He needed to try to calm the tumult of emotions boiling within him. He needed time.

He felt strange. After his initial tears, a coldness had crept around him. Outwardly, he felt numb, impassive. He had slept poorly the night before. Images of Lenka's panic-stricken eyes pleading with him to do something to save her, and her pale face pressed against the blood-spattered snow, intruded into every spell of drowsiness. His brain was tired, stunned. But underneath, underneath there lay a turmoil of emotions churning away inside him. There was the horror of her death, fury at whoever had killed her, guilt that he had been able to do nothing to stop it, and the knowledge that he would never see her again, or hear her laugh, or argue with her, or tease her, or celebrate Carpathian's minor victories with her. All these emotions lurked there, waiting to burst out in a prolonged scream. Somehow, though, the brittle exterior held, keeping it all trapped inside. His face was stiff with the cold air on his cheeks, an icy membrane encasing the loss within him.

The police had come quickly. They asked Chris questions about Lenka, about the attack, about the man with the knife. Chris hadn't seen the man's face clearly. Medium build, wearing a dark jacket and a dark woollen hat, was all he could manage. Useless. And a moustache. He remembered a moustache. Still useless. The Czech police said that the man must have been a trained killer. Apparently, it is difficult to cut someone's throat efficiently. No, Chris said many times, he had no idea who might have wanted to kill Lenka.

Her parents had come that morning. Small, mild, humble people, they were totally unlike Lenka. He was a country doctor, she a nurse. They were crushed. Chris had done his best to comfort them, but their English was rudimentary. Their grief tore into his heart. He had left them, feeling once again useless.

He made his way to the street where she had said their new office was to be. She hadn't told him the number, but he saw the tavern with the sign of a yellow bear holding a mug of beer outside it. Opposite was a cream three-storey building with an ornate wooden door. Chris looked more closely and saw five steel nameplates bearing the logos of international lawyers, accountants and consultants. That must be the place. A Prague office would have to wait now. So would Jan Pavlík. Chris realized the man must be expecting to talk to him that day. Chris would have to call him to let him know what had happened.

He hesitated, tempted for a moment to go into the tavern and drink an early beer. But he turned away from its warmth. He wanted to walk, to feel the cold air on his face, to feel Lenka's death.

He wandered aimlessly through the old town, with its little squares, its churches, and its buildings of orange, yellow, cream and green, each one exquisitely decorated, all of them mocking Lenka's death with their beauty.

He found himself at the Charles Bridge and, hunching his shoulders deep within his overcoat, he strode out on to it. He stopped in the middle and turned to look back at the city. Lenka had spent many years here as a student. He could imagine her during those heady days of the Velvet Revolution, shouting with the loudest of them. A young, idealistic woman looking forward to a life of freedom ahead of her. Or only half a life.

An iron-grey cloud pressed down on the town, threatening to engulf Prague Castle on the opposite bank. A viciously cold wind whipped off the Vltava, its waters churning swiftly downstream. The chill bit through his coat, and he shivered. What about Carpathian? Forget expansion, it would be difficult to keep the firm going at all without Lenka. But he was determined to do it. She was his partner, she had trusted him, and he wouldn't let her down.

He leaned over the parapet of the old stone bridge and stared down at the angry river. He remembered the first time they had met, ten years before in New York. And, with a shudder, he remembered that other death.

PART TWO

I

The crowded train pulled into Wall Street subway station, and a twenty-two-year-old Chris Szczypiorski fought his way on to the platform, followed by two other young British bankers. Fresh faced, they looked out of place in their suits; they gazed about them with the curious bewilderment of tourists, rather than the determined blank stares of the other commuters on their way to work.

'I never thought we'd get here in one piece,' said Chris. 'I can't believe what you did back there, Duncan.'

'I swear, I saw them do it on TV,' the tall red-haired young man behind him protested in a mild Scottish accent. 'It's a tough place, New York.'

'You know, Duncan,' drawled Ian, the last member of the trio on to the platform, 'I wonder if that was Tokyo you saw?'

'It wasn't,' said Duncan. 'You didn't see it. How do you know?'

'I bet it was,' Ian repeated with confidence, grinning.

Duncan frowned. 'Oh,' he said, doubts flooding in.

When they had changed subway trains at Grand Central, Duncan had decided to push the jammed commuters further into the crowded carriage so that there would be room for the three of them. Chris and Ian had had to pull him back, and if the doors hadn't shut at that moment, Duncan would have been lynched.

'Anyway, let's not try that again, shall we?' Chris said, as he pushed his way through the exit turnstile. 'I agree with Ian. I'm pretty sure the locals don't like it.'

They climbed out of the subway station into Wall Street, descending like a narrow ravine down the hill from the blackened façade of Trinity Church at its head. They threaded their way through the hot-dog and pretzel stands, past the classical columns of Federal Hall and the solid entrance to the New York Stock Exchange, until they came to an alley, darkened by the great buildings looming on either side. There, a little way up the street, was a sleek, black block, with the name Bloomfield Weiss written in neat gold letters above the entrance lobby. A line of office workers filed into the building, like ants returning to their nest.

They introduced themselves to the squad of security guards at the front desk and headed up to the twenty-third floor. That was where Bloomfield Weiss housed its world-renowned training programme.

Chris had joined Bloomfield Weiss's London office six months before, in September of the previous year. He had arrived straight from university, as had most of the nine other graduate trainees. Seven of them had left immediately to go to New York, and they were just coming to the end of their stint on the programme. Chris, Ian Darwent, and Duncan Gemmel had been shipped out in April to join the second programme of the year. Young bankers from Bloomfield Weiss's offices all over the world would be gathered there to spend five months of their lives on the toughest training programme on the Street.

Although they were very different, the three Brits had developed a kinship during their six months rooting around at the bottom of the London Office food chain. It was in Duncan's nature to be friendly, but Ian's attitude surprised Chris. Chris had known of him at university, they were at the same college, but their paths had scarcely crossed there. Ian was an Old Etonian, the son of a junior cabinet minister, who belonged to a string of dining clubs with obscure classical names. He was frequently seen around the college with a different blonde double-barrelled girl on his arm. Chris came from Halifax. Although Ian had spent three years barely acknowledging the very existence of the likes of Chris, he seemed to realize that now they were on the Bloomfield Weiss payroll, all that was in the past. Chris wasn't about to bear a grudge: they needed each other.

As they disembarked from the elevator on the twenty-third floor they were met by a small blonde-haired woman wearing a severe suit, her hair scraped back in a bun. She didn't look much older than them, but then she didn't look like one of them, either.

She held out a hand. 'Hi. My name's Abby Hollis. I'm the programme coordinator. And you are?'

They gave her their names.

'Very good. You're almost late. Your desks are through there. Drop your stuff, and go through to the classroom. We're about ready to get started.'

'Yes, Miss,' said Chris with a wry glance at Ian and Duncan. Abby Hollis frowned, and turned to the next group emerging from the lift.

The classroom was a large, circular auditorium, with desks rising in five rows from a central space in front of an array of teaching aids: a computer, a large projection screen, a flip chart, and even a twenty-foot rolling blackboard. There were no windows, just the gentle whir of air-conditioning bringing in oxygen from the outside world. Above and below them toiled hundreds of investment bankers turning money into more money. Here, at the core of the building, almost exactly half way up it, were the trainees, protected for now from the dangers and temptations of the billions of dollars swirling around the street outside.

The room was already full of men and women of all shapes and colours. Chris scanned the nameplates. For once, his own name blended in with its exotic neighbours. Szczypiorski was no odder than Ramanathan or Ng or Nemeckova. He took his seat between a tall, fair-haired, obviously American man named Eric Astle and a black woman named Latasha James. Duncan was seated directly behind him, Ian on the other side of the classroom.

'All right, everybody, listen up!' announced a gruff voice. They fell silent. A large middle-aged man with black hair gelled back over his balding scalp was occupying the empty space at the front of the class. 'My name is George Calhoun, and I'm responsible for the training programme here at Bloomfield Weiss. It's something I'm very proud of.'

He paused. He had their attention.

'Now as you know, Bloomfield Weiss is the most feared and respected investment bank on Wall Street. How have we achieved this? Why do we lead more equity and bond issues year in and year out than any of our competitors? What makes us the best? Well, one of the answers is right here. This programme.

'This is the toughest programme on the Street.' He pronounced it '*Schtreet*', in what Chris already knew as the true Bloomfield Weiss tough-guy fashion. 'We're not just going to teach you all the tools you'll need – the bond math, the corporate finance, all that good stuff. We're going to teach you that the guy who tries hardest, who works hardest, who refuses to come second, he's the winner.' Calhoun's voice dropped to a whisper, his eyes glinting. 'Wall Street is a jungle and you're all predators. Out there,' and at this he waved his arm vaguely towards the outside world somewhere beyond the windowless walls, 'Out there are the prey.'

He paused, took a deep breath and tucked his stomach into his trousers. 'Now, I have good news and bad news. The bad news is, you're not all going to make it. We're introducing a new policy from this programme on. The weakest among you, the bottom quartile, will fall by the wayside. I know you've all worked your asses off to get here, fought your way through the best schools, beaten a hundred other candidates for your jobs, but you're going to be working harder in the next five months than you've ever worked in your lives before. And the meanest, the toughest among you, will go on to build Bloomfield Weiss for the future.'

He stopped and looked round the room, checking for his effect on the audience. They were all stunned.

'Any questions?'

Silence. Chris looked round at his fellow trainees. They seemed as nonplussed as he felt.

Then a lone hand was raised. It belonged to a tall, striking woman with short white hair. Her name card said Lenka Nemeckova.

Calhoun turned with a frown towards the hand, a frown that softened almost into a leer when he saw to whom it belonged.

'Yes, er, Lenka?'

'I understand the bad news,' said the woman in a hoarse East European accent, tinged with American. 'Now can you give us the good news?'

Calhoun was momentarily confused. The class could see him trying to remember, with all of them, just what the good news was. Chris heard a laugh behind him he recognized as Duncan's. It rippled round the auditorium, dispersing the tension that had been so carefully nurtured by Calhoun's speech.

Calhoun was not happy 'The good news, ma'am, is that you'll be eating, sleeping and dreaming nothing but Bloomfield Weiss for the next five months.' He stuck his jaw out towards her, defying her to answer back.

Lenka smiled sweetly. 'Oh, yes, that *will* be nice.'

The day was spent describing how much work they would have to do and then giving it to them. The sixty trainees emerged, reeling, at five o'clock, clasping the assignments that would have to be completed over the following week. Abby Hollis met each of them with three hefty books on bond mathematics, economics and capital markets. She also provided canvas bags, with *Bloomfield Weiss* written on them in discreet lettering. There was too much material for the slim designer briefcases most of the trainees had bought during their first few months in the job.

'Whew!' said Duncan, looking shaken. 'I need a beer.'

That seemed a perfectly good idea to Chris and Ian. Duncan, ever friendly, turned to a pudgy man with a long, pointed nose who was neatly stacking the assignments into his bag. His name was Rudy Moss. 'Want to come?'

Rudy glanced down at his bulging canvas bag and shook his head pityingly. 'I don't think so,' he said, and drifted off.

'Mind if we join you?' asked a voice behind Duncan. It was Eric Astle, the American who had sat next to Chris, and with whom he had exchanged a few incredulous glances during the afternoon. With him was a small, dark man, with a thin shadow of bristle over his jaw. Eric introduced him as Alex Lubron.

'Of course,' said Duncan. 'Do you know anywhere to go round here?'

'There's Jerry's,' said Alex. 'Come on. We'll show you,' and he led the small troop towards the elevator.

They passed Lenka, standing tall and alone, the hubbub of chattering trainees breaking round her, as though nervous of engaging her in conversation.

Duncan hesitated. 'Fancy a wee one?' he asked, overdoing his Scottish act.

'Excuse me?'

'Would you like to come for a drink with us?' he said, with a friendly smile. Lenka returned it. 'Why not?' she said, gathering up her stuff. 'Let's go.'

'Jesus, can you believe that stuff about the bottom quartile?' Duncan asked the group crammed round a small table, as a waiter distributed cold beers. Jerry's was a basement bar round the corner from Bloomfield Weiss. It was heaving with beefy traders reliving their exploits of the day. 'They can't be serious. Can they?'

'They can,' Chris said.

'But we've worked so hard to get this far, it seems completely stupid to throw anyone out now,' said Duncan.

'It is. They won't. Don't worry,' said Ian, lighting up a cigarette.

'That lower-quartile stuff is just a way of getting rid of people they don't like. We'll be OK.'

'You might be. I'm not so sure about me.'

Ian shrugged, as though Duncan might have a point but it didn't bother him too much. Ian was polished and self-confident, the cream of the annual milk round. He had dark, fine, dangerously good-looking features. He wore the best suits of the three of them, shirts with cufflinks, and ties that didn't seem to get stains on them. Unlike Duncan, his shirt tails never hung out. He was the nearest any of them had managed to come to looking and sounding like a real investment banker. The only detail that spoiled the image was his bitten-down fingernails.

'Can I have one of those?' Lenka asked Ian, pointing to his cigarette packet.

'Oh, I'm sorry. Of course.' Ian offered her one and she lit it with obvious pleasure. 'Anyone else?'

Alex, too, lit up.

'Your country is barbaric, the way you don't let people smoke,' Lenka said. 'I don't know how I'm going to get through the day.'

There was a no-smoking policy in the training programme offices. Smoking had not quite been totally stamped out in Bloomfield Weiss. Some traders held out, still managing to smoke fat cigars on the trading floor, but its days were numbered.

'That's right,' said Ian. 'Don't the people have a right to bear cigarettes? Or is it machine guns? I never can remember.'

'We used to,' said Alex. 'But Big Government is taking it away from us. What we need is a smoker for President, don't you think, Eric? Eric's our political activist. He was single-handedly responsible for getting Bush elected.'

'Thanks, Alex,' said Eric. 'I did work for the Bush campaign when I was in College,' he explained to the others, 'stuffing envelopes for the cause.'

'Oh, it was much more than that,' said Alex. 'George has been calling him on a regular basis asking him what he should say to Gorbachev.'

Eric rolled his eyes.

They made an unlikely double act. Eric was tall, upright, with a square jaw, a neat haircut, and a smile that showed the gleam of perfect teeth. Alex was six inches shorter, wiry, with curly hair, and stubble that suggested he hadn't shaved that morning. His tie was lopsided and the top button of his shirt was undone. His brown eyes twinkled with humour and intelligence under thick dark eyebrows. Chris found himself warming to both of them.

'I didn't like the look of that Professor Waldern,' said Duncan, bringing the conversation back to what was worrying him.

'Nor me,' said Chris. A lithe, intense man with a greying beard and bright beady eyes, Waldern had seemed to take real pleasure in outlining how much work they would have to do, and how hard he would be on those of them who failed to do it. He was supposed to be on the faculty of a fancy business school, but it seemed to Chris that he must be spending most of his time teaching bond mathematics and capital markets to Bloomfield Weiss trainees. The pay was probably excellent.

'He's supposed to be tough,' said Eric. 'They say he can make a grown man cry.'

'I can believe it,' said Duncan. He turned to Eric and Alex. 'You must have a better idea how the programme works. Is it really going to be that bad?'

'Probably,' said Eric. 'Calhoun took over the training programme about six months ago. The scuttle is he wants to change things. Make it more Darwinian. The idea is to weed out the losers before they even start real work. Apparently, the Management Committee discussed it and decided to go with him. I guess we're the guinea pigs.'

'I wouldn't worry too much,' said Alex. 'Like everything, it all depends who you know. If there's a managing director who wants you in his department, no one will can you. Stay cool.'

'And is there?' asked Duncan.

'I was working in mortgage trading for my first six months,' said Alex. 'The guys there like me. I'll be OK.'

This made Duncan even more worried. 'And you?' he asked Eric.

'Oh, I'm not sure where I'll end up,' he replied. 'We'll just have to see what happens.'

'You'll go wherever you want to go,' said Alex. 'They love you.'

Eric shrugged. 'There's the next five months to get through first.'

None of this was pleasing Duncan. 'I don't think there's anyone in London who gives a toss what happens to me.'

Chris knew the feeling. The three of them had been passed round the office like unwanted lost children, while the other London trainees were doing their stuff in New York. They were the lowest of the low.

'Oh come on, chaps,' said Ian, in his best public school accent. 'Let's not panic here. That's what the bastards want us to do. We're in New York for five months on investment bankers' salaries. Let's have some fun.'

'I'll drink to that,' said Lenka. She lifted her glass, which was already nearly empty. 'Cheers!'

They all raised their glasses to her.

'Duncan,' said Lenka. 'If ever things get really tough, you know what you do?'

'What?'

'You come down here and drink beer with us. It's the Czech way. It works.'

Duncan smiled and drained his glass. 'You've convinced me. Let's get some more in.' He physically grabbed a passing waiter, who scowled at him, but took his order for refills.

'So you're from Czechoslovakia?' Chris asked. 'I didn't know Bloomfield Weiss had an office in Prague.'

'Yes, I'm Czech. But I'm a New York hire. Now the Iron Curtain has lifted, the investment banks want Eastern Europeans.

And so they asked me if I could tell them all about Eastern Europe. They said they would pay me a lot of money. Actually, I know all about Keats and Shelley, but I didn't tell them that.' Her English was fluent and confident, but she had quite a strong accent.

'You're an English major?' Alex asked.

'I studied English and Russian at the Charles University in Prague. Then I went to graduate school at Yale. But all this structuralist bullshit became too much for me. America's all about money, and so I thought I'd better find out something about it. I only joined Bloomfield Weiss two weeks ago.'

'Don't you have any econ at all?' asked Alex.

'I don't think the kind of economics they teach in my country would impress Bloomfield Weiss very much. But I've read a couple of American books on the subject. I'll be OK.' She turned to Chris. 'What about you, Mr Szczypiorski? Are you Polish?'

Chris smiled as she pronounced the unpronounceable so deftly. 'No,' he answered. 'My parents are from there, obviously. But I come from Halifax in the North of England. I've only been to Poland once. And I speak Polish with a Yorkshire accent.'

'Ee by gumski,' said Duncan.

Chris smiled thinly. Jokes about his accent, or his Polish name, had ceased to amuse him years ago.

'That is quite a name you've got there,' said Alex. 'What is it . . . Zizipisky? That's a mouthful even by American standards.'

Chris didn't bother to correct the pronunciation. 'I know. I've thought about changing it to Smith or something, but it's all too complicated.'

'That's what we had Ellis Island for,' said Alex. 'Throw in a couple of vowels, lose the zees, and you've got a name as American as apple pie.'

At university Chris had become so fed up with having to spell his name twice at every bureaucratic opportunity that he had gone as far as gathering the forms required to change it by deed poll. But he had stopped at the moment of filling in the new name: 'Shipton' was what he had actually chosen. Szczypiorski was his father's name and he didn't have enough of his father left. He would just have to tolerate it. At least he was able to shorten his first name from Krzysztof to Chris easily enough.

'Who is this bloke, Rudy Moss?' Duncan asked. 'Did you see the look he gave me when I suggested going out for a drink? It was as though I'd told him his sister was a lesbian.'

'He's an asshole,' said Alex. 'There are a bunch of people like that on the programme. He's just the worst. Don't take any notice of him.'

'What do you mean?' asked Duncan.

'We've spent six months with them,' said Alex. 'A lot of them are brown-nosers. They think if they kiss the right ass, they'll get the best job. And it's not just that, they want to be *first* to kiss ass. That's Rudy's specialty.'

Duncan grimaced.

'There's a culture of competition here,' explained Eric. 'We're all supposed to be competing against each other for the best jobs and the best scores on the programme. Guys like Rudy Moss have bought into all that.'

'But not you?' said Chris.

'I guess I'm a team player. I like to work with my peers rather than against them.'

'So what on earth are you doing at Bloomfield Weiss?' asked Ian. 'That hardly seems the company line.'

Eric smiled, and shrugged. 'Calhoun was right. Bloomfield Weiss is the best on the Street. I'll go with the best, but I'll do it my way.'

They all nodded solemnly, apart from Alex, who laughed. 'Don't give me that bullshit. "Doing it your way" means coming home blasted at three in the morning, and not getting up till noon the next day.'

'I like that attitude!' said Lenka enthusiastically.

25

Eric grinned. 'Hey. You're talking about a Bloomfield Weiss investment banker here.'

Duncan finished his beer. 'Well, I suppose we'd better be going if we're going to make a dent in all that work they gave us.'

And so they headed uptown on their different coloured subway lines. Chris, Ian and Duncan made their way back towards the apartment they shared on the Upper East Side, Duncan being very careful this time not to assault a whole carriage full of commuters. But he did spend most of the journey speculating on Lenka's charms. She had clearly made an impression. Chris could understand Duncan's point of view, but he was determined to remain faithful to Tamara, his girlfriend back in London. Idle lusting after Lenka wouldn't help.

The cold night air bit into Chris's cheeks, and helped clear his brain of some of the jumbled financial concepts he had tried to cram into it over the previous three hours. It was early April, and it was supposed to be spring, but it felt to Chris as though there was a frost in the air. He hunched into his old leather jacket and headed along a cross street towards Fifth Avenue and Central Park. On either side of the street awnings reached out from the warm yellow glow of marble lobbies, where uniformed doormen stared blankly into the night.

Already the work was piling up, and he was finding it hard to make sense of it. He had tried to dust the cobwebs off the maths he had learned at school, but that wasn't enough. Discounted cash flow, modified duration, internal rate of return, what did they all mean? And how could he possibly figure it all out by Wednesday?

He had done his best to keep quiet when Duncan had spoken anxiously about the training programme. He had his own fears, but he felt it was better to keep them to himself. Ian had perfected the art of confidence, and from what he had seen so far of the world of work, he was sure that that was one of the keys to success. If you didn't know it, pretend you did, and hope no one found out.

But on the training programme, they would find out. Professor Waldern would find out the next morning when he asked Chris to explain modified duration. Or Calhoun would find out after the exams he had promised them. Duncan was right. It would be a hell of a shame if after all this struggle he was kicked out.

Chris had worked hard to get to New York. Bloody hard. It had started at eleven, when, with long hours of help and encouragement from his mother, he had scraped into the local grammar school. He had struggled through O- and A-levels, and had surprised himself with the grades he had achieved. He had applied for a place at Oxford to read history. He hadn't wanted to do it, he thought it was a waste of time, but Tony Harris, his history teacher, had persuaded him. Much to his surprise, the Polish boy with the Yorkshire accent was offered a place at Lady Margaret Hall. His mother was overjoyed. She had said that she had always known he could do it, that he had his father's brains. He knew that wasn't quite true, but he felt that his father, wherever he was, was proud of him. And that made Chris feel very good.

Oxford, and more work. Then the big problem of finding a job afterwards. The recession was beginning to bite: employers were slashing their budgets for graduate trainees. Some regular employers didn't even bother recruiting.

The competition was intense. Chris knew little about the companies who visited the university, but he applied to fifteen of them, including Bloomfield Weiss. Most rejected him, many without even offering him an interview. In his darker moments he blamed Szczypiorski for that, although he didn't have the string of extra-curricular activities, the carefully constructed CV, of someone like Ian Darwent. But at Bloomfield Weiss he went all the way. Eventually they asked him to the firm's smart offices in Broadgate, in the City, and he was grilled by five different bankers. They all liked him, he could tell. They liked the fact that he came from Halifax, they liked his Polish name, and they liked the determination that they knew breathed within him. When one morning he had gone to the porter's lodge and found the letter with the words *Bloomfield Weiss* engraved on it, he had known what it would say. They wanted him. And he wanted them. Although it was the only job offer he received, it was the one he most desired.

Now he was one of sixty overachievers. Sixty men and women who had come top of their class in whatever had been thrown at them. Sixty winners. Winners like Ian Darwent, Eric Astle, Alex Lubron, or the dreadful Rudy Moss. And from those sixty winners, the training programme would squeeze fifteen losers. One of them might well be Duncan. Another might be Chris.

He reached the low wall on Fifth Avenue that bordered Central Park. He looked over it into the gloom and mystery of the park, ringed with the bright lights of Manhattan's tall buildings. He should go back and get some sleep. There would be a lot to learn the next day. With a sigh he realized that there would be a lot to learn every day for the next five months. Well, he would keep his doubts quiet and his head down, and do his damnedest to make sure he wasn't one of those fifteen losers.

2

The work was hard. They used the 'case method', which had been invented at Harvard Law School and adapted by business schools around the country. It involved reading a 'case', which was a detailed account of a realistic problem faced by a business, chosen to illustrate a particular financial concept. This was then discussed in class. The professor would pick on some poor individual to start off the discussion and then bombard him or her with follow-up questions. At its best, this could be a fascinating way of examining the issues. At its worst, it was a series of public humiliations for those involved.

The difficulty wasn't just getting through the cases the night before. In order to understand them, the trainees had to plough through pages of heavy textbooks. They were expected to grasp at least one complicated concept each night.

Professor Waldern oversaw two of the courses in the early months of the programme: Capital Markets and Bond Math. These also happened to be the two most important subjects. A good understanding of bond mathematics was vital if you were going to trade or sell the things later on. Waldern was an excellent teacher: he could make the most mundane financial principles seem interesting and exciting. He would tease out glimpses of the solution of a case from different members of the class, and then, under his guidance, the concepts would seem to fall into place. Chris found his sessions intellectually stimulating and exhausting.

But Waldern was also a bully. Duncan was petrified from the outset that he would be called upon to start the class off, and indeed it happened, on the third day. Chris knew that Duncan had spent hours on the case the night before, about an airline deciding whether it should borrow through a fixed-rate bond issue, or a floating-rate loan. But Duncan just hadn't understood it. He started off waffling, repeating the introduction to the case itself, and Waldern sensed blood. He spent twenty minutes proving to Duncan, himself and the rest of the class, that Duncan had not grasped the most basic principles of how a fixed-rate bond worked. Needless to say, Duncan was a wreck. Some of the trainees, such as Rudy Moss, tittered at the spectacle. Chris was furious. He tried to call out some of the answers, but Waldern was having none of it.

Professor Waldern wasn't the only tough guy on the programme. Abby Hollis was a little Hitler. She was always to be seen scurrying around before and after class, nagging people left and right.

Lenka's distrust of Abby turned to contempt after an incident in the second week of the programme. Lenka dressed dramatically. She eschewed the boxy suits of most of the American women; she wore stylish dresses, short skirts, tight blouses, cashmere sweaters and elegant silk scarves. She looked more like a Parisienne than a New Yorker. The men on the programme all loved this, of course, but many of the women were intimidated, and Chris overheard some of them speculating on how she could have amassed such a wardrobe on a trainee's salary.

One morning she was chatting to Chris and Duncan in the hallway by the classroom when Abby approached. Lenka was wearing a trouser suit. It was an inoffensive light grey, and perhaps the most conservative outfit she had yet tried.

'Lenka, a word,' Abby said, taking her by the arm.

Abby murmured something to her that Chris and Duncan couldn't quite hear. But they could hear Lenka's response: 'My clothes are inappropriate! What do you mean, they're inappropriate?'

Abby glanced at Chris and Duncan. 'I feel you ought to know that it's just not appropriate to wear pants at Bloomfield Weiss,' she said.

Lenka snorted. 'That's absurd! Look at Chris and Duncan. They're wearing pants. Most of the people on the training programme wear pants. Sidney Stahl, our Chairman, wears pants. Why shouldn't I?'

'You know what I mean,' said Abby. Her face had turned red, but having gone this far she wasn't about to back down. 'It's inappropriate for *women* to wear pants.'

'So it's OK for men, but not for women, is that it? And whose idea is that? I bet it was a woman's.'

'I don't know whose idea it was,' said Abby. 'But women just don't wear pants around here.'

'Well, they do now,' said Lenka, and marched off into the classroom.

During the break she joined Chris and the others at the coffee machine. 'I can't believe that woman,' she said. 'And did you *see* the suit she was wearing, and that horrible little ruffled blouse. *That* should be banned.'

'You know she was one of us last year,' said Alex.

'What do you mean?'

'She was a trainee, just like us. Apparently, she didn't do too well. She couldn't get an assignment after the programme so she ended up as programme coordinator. The theory is that she has to prove herself to George Calhoun to escape from here and get a proper job.'

'Oh, God,' groaned Duncan. 'What if that happened to me? I couldn't face it.'

They were all silent for a moment, thinking of the fate that would befall those among them who didn't make it out of the bottom quartile.

'It's OK for most of these guys,' said Alex. 'They've all got MBAs; they've done a lot of this stuff before. But I've got to admit I'm finding it pretty tough.'

'You're telling me,' said Duncan.

'There's just so much of it,' said Chris, glad that Alex had admitted what he hadn't been prepared to. 'I mean, the second you understand one concept, they throw another two at you.'

'Look, do you guys want to come back with us this evening? Maybe if we help each other out we can crack this.' Alex glanced at Eric who nodded his encouragement.

'Sounds good to me,' said Chris.

'I'm up for it,' said Duncan.

'So am I,' said Ian.

'Do you allow in women wearing pants?' asked Lenka.

'Not usually,' said Alex. 'But in your case, we can make an exception.'

Eric and Alex's apartment was a long way up the West Side. It was large, but in bad repair. Apparently it was rent-controlled, and therefore not in the landlord's interests to look after. The furniture was basic and there was plenty of student clutter about the place. But what struck them all as they entered were the walls.

Four or five large canvases hung about the room, each one depicting petrochemical plants or oil refineries at different times of day and night. Pipes, gantries, cylinders, towers and chimneys were displayed at odd angles, forming intricate geometric networks. Orange glows, bright red flares and piercing white halogen lights added to the mystery of the massive chemical processes taking place within. The overall effects were unexpectedly beautiful.

'These are amazing,' said Lenka. 'Who did them?'

'I did,' said Alex.

'You?' Lenka turned to him, her reappraisal obvious. 'I didn't realize you were a painter.'

'I spent a couple of years after college trying to make it as a professional artist. I had a couple of exhibitions, sold some paintings, but I could barely make enough to live on. I didn't like the idea of a life of poverty. So here I am.'

'That's a shame,' Lenka said.

Alex shrugged. 'That's why we're all here, aren't we?' There was a defensive edge to his voice: Lenka had obviously touched on a sore point.

'I'm sorry, I guess you're right. But it's an odd subject. Why these?'

'I come from New Jersey,' said Alex. 'We have a lot of oil refineries. When I was a kid I used to stare out of the car window at them as we drove by. I was fascinated. Then later, at college, I thought, why not paint them? It became a kind of obsession.'

'They're stunning,' Lenka said. She moved round the room. 'Don't tell me this is New Jersey?'

She was standing in front of a dramatic picture of an installation rising out of the sand, throwing its flare into a wide desert sky. The contrast of the hostile rugged terrain with the dramatically engineered structures, and the variations in the natural and man-made light, produced an effect that was startling in its beauty.

'That's the Industrial City of Jubail in Saudi Arabia,' Alex said. 'A chemical company saw my work and sponsored me to go over there. I sold every painting I did there, apart from this one.'

'I'm not surprised,' said Lenka.

'I wish I'd kept more of them.'

'In the meantime, I feel like I'm living in a goddamn factory,' said Eric. 'What's wrong with sunflowers, for Christ's sake?'

'Bourgeois philistine,' muttered Alex.

'I like them,' said Duncan. 'Have you ever painted a brewery?'

'Not yet,' said Alex. 'But I take it that means you'd like a beer?'

'I thought you'd never ask.'

So that evening, and several evenings a week over the following months, the six of them studied together, usually meeting at Eric and Alex's apartment. It quickly became clear who knew how much. Eric seemed to take in everything that was thrown at him, and to understand it instantly. For Duncan, it was all a struggle. Alex and Chris got there in the end, Chris with more work than Alex. Ian acted as though he understood everything, and indeed he was quick to grasp the principles. But when it came to the nitty-gritty of number work, he was hopeless. This was a secret he somehow managed to keep from everyone in the class outside the study group, who did their best to cover for him. Lenka seemed to have almost as good an understanding as Eric, although she had a tendency to throw in off-the-wall solutions to what seemed to the rest of them to be simple problems. The group helped each other out and, with the exception of Duncan on that third day, they got by.

Alex wasn't alone among the trainees in having an unusual background. While there were a number of white male Anglo-Saxon MBAs, Bloomfield Weiss was careful not to recruit exclusively from that pool. There were women as well as men, Indians, Africans and Japanese. Quite a few were about Chris's age, twenty-two, but most were a couple of years older: some were in their thirties. Amongst the Americans was a professional gambler, a woman who had started and sold her own mail-order business in designer computer accessories, and a professional football player with a limp. Amongst the foreigners was an ex-submariner from the French navy, a super-cool Japanese man who liked to be called Tex and wore his shades at every opportunity, a Saudi who knew he was unsackable and hence did nothing, and an older Italian woman who struggled to understand the English spoken rapidly around her, and did her best to keep up with the course while looking after her three-year-old daughter.

Everyone was treated equally, whatever their background, everyone except for Latasha James, the black American woman who sat next to Chris. Professors, even Waldern, were careful to deal with her with respect and politeness at all times. This drove Latasha crazy. The firm wanted to place her in the Municipal Finance department, where she could sell Bloomfield Weiss to black civic leaders. She just wanted to be treated like everyone else.

Eric and Alex were proved right; there was lots of brown-nosing. The sixty trainees, who cowered behind their desks when Waldern was teaching, suddenly leapt into action whenever one of the managing directors came to talk to them. These people were in charge of the different departments of the firm, and they gave talks between the more formal classes, explaining what their departments did. They were the ones who would be hiring the trainees out of the programme. They were the people to impress. The sight of sixty young investment bankers all trying to make an impression on one human being at the same time was sickening. Chris knew he should join in, but couldn't quite bring himself to. Ian asked the odd question, in his laconic, casual style, which had the virtue of being memorable. Eric restricted himself to single immensely perceptive questions directed to managing directors in the key departments of the firm. Duncan blabbered occasionally. Lenka didn't have to thrust herself forward; they asked her questions. It was pitiful to see so many different middle-aged men pick her out, supposedly at random, to emphasize a point they wanted to make.

The worst of course, was Rudy Moss. Rudy, on a bad day, could make the rest of the class retch. The worst day was when Sidney Stahl came to talk to them.

Stahl had just acceded to the post of Chairman of Bloomfield Weiss. He was a tiny man, with a gruff voice, bright red braces and a huge cigar, which he cheerfully smoked while talking to the group. Chris found him inspiring. He was clearly a doer; he had little time for bullshit. When he said that he didn't care who you were or where you came from as long as you made money for the firm, Chris believed him. He had just finished his speech about how Bloomfield Weiss could only remain the best firm on the Street if it was the most nimble, when he asked for questions. Chris groaned inwardly as Rudy Moss put up his hand.

'Mr Stahl, Rudy Moss.'

'What have you got, Rudy?'

'Yes, Mr Stahl. I was listening to what you were saying and

wondering what skill set provides the core competencies that give us the edge against so many new entrants?'

Stahl just looked at him, taking a long pull on his cigar. Rudy smiled hopefully. Stahl smoked. Rudy reddened slightly. Stahl didn't move. Sixty trainees squirmed.

Rudy cracked first. 'I mean, the oligopoly among the major bulge-bracket firms is breaking down, barriers to entry in our business are lower, and we're going to have to survive by relying on our core competencies. I was just wondering what you would say those are?'

Stahl's eyes gleamed. So did the end of his cigar.

'Son, I'll tell you how we'll survive. Most of you kids are gonna make me money. A lotta money. I'll keep you. Some of you kids are gonna bullshit me. You're outta here. Now, which are you gonna be, Rudy?'

Smiles broke out all round. 'I'll make you money, sir,' squeaked Rudy.

'Good. Now, any more questions?'

Funnily enough, there weren't any.

3

The Bond Math exam was in the fourth week of the programme. It was one of the most important tests of the whole course – George Calhoun had made sure they all understood that. Chris worked until nine o'clock revising for it, but by then he felt his tired brain had had enough. He felt like calling Tamara in London, but he had woken her up once before at two in the morning and it wasn't a good idea. He decided to ask the other two out for a quick beer at the Irish bar on First Avenue that they had taken to frequenting. He needed to unwind before bed.

He knocked on Duncan's door. No reply. He knocked again. 'Come in.'

Duncan was lying on his bed staring at the ceiling. His desk looked like a bombsite, covered in notes and open textbooks.

'You're not doing any good here,' Chris said. 'Let's get a beer.'

'I . . . no, I mean . . . Oh, Jesus . . .' Duncan stuttered, and to Chris's amazement, he began to sob.

'What's up, Duncan?'

'What do you bloody well think is up? It's this fucking exam.'

'It's only a test.'

'It's not a test. It's my whole career. It will all be over tomorrow. They'll ship me back to London and I'll be behind a till at Barclays.'

Chris sat on his bed. Duncan's cheeks were red. His hands covered his eyes, but a single tear escaped and ran down his cheek.

'No you won't,' Chris said gently. 'You've done the work. You'll pass the exam.'

'Bollocks, Chris. I don't know a bloody thing. My mind's a

total blank.' He sobbed again and sniffed. 'I've never failed an exam before.'

'And you won't now,' Chris said. 'Look, you've got this totally out of proportion. All they're trying to do is check whether you know how to work out bond and option prices. It's no big deal. The bastards are just trying to pile on the pressure to see whether you'll crack.'

'Well, I'm cracking,' sniffed Duncan.

'Of course you're not,' said Chris. 'Now sit at this desk and we'll go through everything you don't understand until you get it right.'

They sat there for over two hours, as Chris tried to explain concepts that had only dawned on him the week before. He was patient, and his calmness did eventually work its way through to Duncan. By midnight Duncan could finally price a simple option. That would have to be enough.

As he left Duncan, Chris was exhausted. He was heading for bed when he heard music coming from the door to Ian's room. He put his head in. Ian was sitting in an armchair, a half-empty bottle of whisky beside him, smoking a cigarette and listening to UB40.

'I've just been with Duncan,' Chris said. 'He's panicking about tomorrow.'

'That boy worries too much,' said Ian.

'He has a point, though. I took him through a lot of the option theory. He'll be lucky to pass.'

Ian shrugged. 'Some people will fail tomorrow, and there's really nothing you or I can do to help them.'

Chris stared at Ian. That wasn't true. He wanted Duncan to make it, and he had done his best to help him. He hoped it would be enough.

'Will you be all right?' Chris asked. It would be hard for Ian to hide his innumeracy in a test devoted to bond calculations.

Ian looked up and smiled thinly. 'Me? Oh, I'll be fine.' He

refilled his glass with whisky and stared at the wall somewhere to the right of Chris's head. Chris left him to it.

Duncan passed, and so did Ian, but only by the narrowest of margins. To his surprise, Chris did rather well. But the big excitement was the exposure of two trainees cheating. Abby Hollis caught Roger Masden showing his paper to Denny Engel, the ex-football player. They were both marched out of the classroom, and no one saw them that afternoon. Neither did they appear the next day. Before class, George Calhoun gave the rest of the trainees a lecture about Bloomfield Weiss's high standards and how they would all be expected to meet them. He warned everyone to pay close attention to the ethics course that would be taught the following month. He didn't once mention Roger and Denny by name.

But everyone else did. The fate of the two trainees was the sole topic of conversation all day, taking some of the pressure off the four poor unfortunates who had failed the exam.

'There go the first two,' said Duncan at lunch in the cafeteria.

'It's pathetic,' said Ian. 'Complete hypocrisy. Bloomfield Weiss should be the last people to complain about cheating. They're notorious for it. I saw them ripping off their customers left and right when I was in London.'

'They're overreacting,' said Alex. 'It must have something to do with the Phoenix Prosperity investigation last year.'

The year before, Dick Waigel, an employee of Bloomfield Weiss, had been arrested and charged with operating a complicated scam involving offshore trusts and a bankrupt Savings and Loan in Arizona. The press had been bad.

'And remember those guys in equity sales who were caught supplying cocaine to their customers?' said Duncan. 'Let's face it, our employer does not have the purest of reputations.'

'Which is why Calhoun is making such a fuss,' said Eric. 'It's all part of his strategy of making the programme much tougher than it needs to be. By demanding high standards and putting pressure on us, he'll make the firm a better place.'

'That may be true,' said Alex. 'But I hear it's pissing some people off.'

'Good,' said Duncan.

'Why?' Chris asked Alex.

'The firm spent a lot of money hiring those two guys. Roger's smart, and you can bet there are some people on the trading floor who'll be disappointed not to have a pro footballer buddy to go drinking with. Bloomfield Weiss is full of guys who'd have done the same in their situation. They'd fit right in. It was dumb to fire them.'

'All you have to do is explain that to Calhoun,' said Duncan.

As they made their way back to class, Duncan pulled Chris to one side. 'By the way,' he said. 'Thanks for the help. I would never have passed if you hadn't picked me up the night before.'

Chris smiled. 'You'd do the same for me, mate.'

Spring did arrive eventually. One day they were wrapped up in their new city overcoats, leaning against a bitter wind that whipped round the tall buildings, and the next the sun was out, the trees were bursting with blossom, and the park turned green. The tempo of the programme slowed after the Bond Math exam and they were even given a couple of afternoons off. A number of non-Americans started a Saturday soccer game on the large lawn in the centre of the park. The three Brits were regular participants. Duncan was a good sportsman, well coordinated, and even in a pick-up game a tireless runner. It was a noisy event, Faisal, the Saudi, and a couple of Brazilians made sure of that, and it was fun. Eric and Alex also played, as did Lenka and Latasha James. Latasha was good; she had played soccer at college. Lenka wasn't, but no one complained. The men were queuing up to pass her the ball and then tackle her.

After one game, Lenka and Latasha persuaded Duncan, Chris,

Ian and Alex to join them for a trip to Zabar's, a delicatessen on the West Side. They bought several carrier bags of goodies: breads, pâtés, cheeses and an exotic fruit salad. Lenka became quite excited by the food she recognized from home and insisted that they load up with some Hungarian salami and pickles: lots and lots of pickles. She was also fascinated by Zabar's collection of dried mushrooms; she claimed that all Czechs were mushroom experts and she had spent most of her childhood scrambling through forests looking for them. Eventually the others pulled her away, stopped off in a wine shop round the corner to pick up some bottles and sauntered back towards the park. They walked slowly, enjoying the spring sunshine and watching the joggers, roller-bladers, cyclists, lovers and loonies that thronged New York's playground. As they passed under the statue of King Jagiello riding his horse and waving two swords over his head, Lenka paused.

'Isn't it nice to see one of your kings in the middle of the big city?' she asked Chris. 'It's as though he has ridden here directly from the Middle Ages.'

'One of my kings?' said Chris.

'Oh, come on. The man who beat the Teutonic Order at the Battle of Tannenberg? Don't tell me you have no Polish left in you at all?'

Chris smiled. 'You're right. My grandfather would be standing here saluting him. But my father would be looking the other way. I suppose I just take the easy way out and pretend I'm English.'

'I thought Poles were the most nationalistic people on the planet,' said Lenka.

'My grandfather is,' said Chris. 'That's my mother's father. He escaped to England in nineteen thirty-nine. He was a fighter pilot, a hero. He fought in the Battle of Britain. He'd give his life for Poland, as he has told me on many occasions. But my father didn't believe in any of that. He was a socialist. Not a communist, but a true socialist. He believed that nationalism divided people. He didn't like kings. I'm sure he wouldn't have approved of this one.'

'What was he doing in Britain if he was a socialist?'

'He hated Stalinism. And Britain didn't seem a bad place to go. It was nineteen sixty-six and the Labour Party had just won the election. He thought Harold Wilson was a better socialist than the Soviet apparatchiks in Warsaw. He was a chess player, an international master. He defected at a chess tournament in Bournemouth. He had cousins in Yorkshire, he moved up there, met my mother, and here I am.'

'I bet her father didn't think much of him.'

'You're absolutely right.' The rift between Chris's mother's family and his father had upset him as a boy. In fact, the whole Polish community in Halifax seemed suspicious of his father. Although he had defected, he was from the new regime, and therefore not quite to be trusted. He didn't even go to church on Sunday. Even though he was young, Chris had felt this mistrust and had resented it.

'You talk about your father in the past tense?'

Chris sighed. 'He died when I was ten.'

'I'm sorry.'

'Don't be. It was a long time ago.'

'I'm still sorry.' She smiled. 'Well, I think it's wonderful that there's a Slav hero here. Maybe they'll put up a statue to Václav Havel one day.'

'Now that would be good.'

They found an empty patch of ground near the small boat pond. They broke open the wine, ate, drank, and whiled away the afternoon. Lenka had bought far too many pickles for them all to eat, so Duncan and Alex started throwing them at her, and soon a pickle fight began. It was all quite childish, and Chris didn't have the energy to join in, but it was good to see everyone forgetting about being investment bankers for a while. Chris lay down on the grass and stared up at the blue sky, edged with the tall buildings of Fifth Avenue. He felt the pressures of the programme lifting away from him. It was actually quite nice in New York, he decided.

The wine made him sleepy, and he closed his eyes. He was disturbed by a drop of water on his face. Then another. The sun was still shining, but an inky black cloud had placed itself over their corner of the park. It opened, and they scurried around, gathering up the remains of the picnic. Latasha, Eric and Alex managed to jump into the only empty cab on Fifth Avenue, but Chris, Ian, Duncan and Lenka hurried back to the shelter of their apartment, Duncan shielding Lenka from the downpour with his coat.

When they arrived, soaked through, Chris made some tea. Lenka had a shower first, and borrowed some of Duncan's dry clothes to change into. Then Chris and Ian took their turns in the shower. Somehow, in all the toing and froing, Duncan and Lenka slipped away by themselves to go off for a drink somewhere.

Chris and Ian exchanged glances as the door slammed behind them.

'What do you think?' said Chris.

'No way,' said Ian. 'She's out of his league.'

'He's quite good-looking,' Chris said, 'in that giant puppy kind of way.'

Duncan wasn't classically handsome, but he had a large, freckled face with curly red hair, blue eyes, and a winning smile that seemed to say, 'be my friend'. Chris had seen it working on some of the women at Bloomfield Weiss in London. He could imagine Lenka preferring it to, say, the clean-cut good looks of Eric.

'She's much older than him. She's got to be twenty-five at least,' protested Ian.

'That's not much older,' said Chris. 'You fancy her, don't you?'

Ian shrugged. 'Not really,' he tried to say casually. 'She looks OK, I suppose.'

Chris laughed. 'Poor woman. To have the whole class drooling over her.'

'She loves it,' said Ian.

'You're probably right.'

Duncan returned to the apartment at about half past eleven that evening. Chris and Ian just happened to be still awake.

'Well?' said Chris.

Duncan pulled a beer out of the fridge and leapt on to the sofa, resting his legs on the armrest. 'She's gorgeous,' he said, grinning.

'And?' Chris asked.

Duncan opened his beer and took a swig. 'We'll see.'

4

'Carla, have you been listening to anything I have been saying over the last two weeks?'

'Yes, Mr Professor, I have.'

Waldern was in a bad mood. He had laid into Ian at the start of the class, but Ian had stood up to him well. So Waldern had turned on Carla Morelli, an easier victim.

'Then you should be able to tell me what a repo is.'

'OK, OK,' Carla said. She swallowed. The rest of the class waited. Waldern's beard was thrust forward, his eyes boring into her. There was silence for several seconds.

Carla mumbled something.

Waldern put his hand up to his ear. 'I can't hear you.'

'I'm sorry,' said Carla, her voice cracking. 'I'm sorry,' she said, her voice louder. 'A repo is when the client gives a bond he does not have to Bloomfield Weiss.'

'Gives a bond he does not have? What does that mean?' Waldern said, looking round the class in incredulity. 'How can you give someone something you don't have? And in finance no one gives anybody anything. They buy, sell, lend, borrow.' He was pacing up and down now, enjoying himself. 'Market participants make money, they invest money, they never give it away.'

Carla reddened. Chris felt sorry for her. Lenka had told him how Carla was finding things very tough. She had had to fire the nanny who was looking after her child, and was at her wits' end trying to find a replacement. She only understood fifty per cent of what was said in class, and needed to refer constantly to a dictionary when going through the evening's reading.

'I'm sorry,' she said. 'I try again. A repo is when the client sells a bond he does not have short –'

'No, no, no, no, no!' Waldern's lips pursed in frustration. 'Now I'll ask you my question again. Have you been listening to a word I have been saying over the last two weeks?'

'I have, Mr Professor,' said Carla, her lip trembling. 'But for me it is difficult. My English is not so good.'

'I will not accept that,' said Waldern. 'This is an American bank. If you want to be a professional here, you have to speak English well enough to understand the concepts. It's a precondition of coming on the training programme. Now, what is a repo?'

Carla sniffed. She opened her mouth. A tear ran down her cheek.

'A repo is a sale and repurchase agreement,' said a voice from the other side of the room. The class turned round to look. It was Lenka. 'One counterparty sells a bond to another counterparty, and agrees to buy it back at a specified future date at a specified price.'

Waldern glowered at Lenka. 'I was asking Carla here. Please don't interrupt me.' He turned back to Carla, whose cheeks were glistening with tears. 'Now, Carla, why would anyone want to enter into a repo?'

Before Carla could speak, Lenka had answered. 'It's a cheap way of borrowing money to finance a holding of bonds. The repo rate is usually lower than money-market rates.'

Waldern spun round. 'I asked you not to interrupt me. I want Carla here to answer my questions.'

'You can see she's in no fit state to answer your questions. So I'll do it for her,' said Lenka. 'What else would you like to know?'

'I am trying to make a point,' Waldern muttered through gritted teeth. 'The point that I expect my students to listen to what I say in class.'

'You're trying to make the point that you have absolute power in this classroom and Carla has none.' This comment came from the back of the class. It was Alex. The class went absolutely still.

Waldern's face reddened, and he opened his mouth as though

46

to shout, but he thought better of it and closed it again. 'I decide what happens in this class. And I will not tolerate any questioning of my authority.'

'That's clear,' said Alex. 'But if you use your power to bully rather than to teach, then your authority loses its legitimacy.'

The accuracy of the statement pierced all of those sitting in the room.

Waldern took a deep breath. 'Lenka. Alex. Come with me now.'

There was a pause as Lenka and Alex glanced at each other, and then they both stood up and followed Waldern out of the room. As the door closed behind them, the class erupted.

Lenka and Alex were allowed back into the class for the afternoon session, which was a talk by the precious metals group. But they were supposed to see George Calhoun in his office at five fifteen.

The others waited for them in Jerry's.

'That was a brave thing they did,' said Duncan.

'It was stupid,' said Ian.

'No it wasn't,' said Chris. 'Someone had to stand up to Waldern. What he was doing to Carla was unforgivable. They treat us like children, but we're not. We're professional people, for God's sake. It was right that Alex pointed that out.'

'That was standard Bloomfield Weiss stuff,' said Ian. 'Carla's got to get used to it some time. May as well be now. If she can't hack it, then she's better off out of it. Sooner rather than later.'

'No,' Chris shook his head. He felt the heat rising to his cheeks. 'Waldern's supposed to be teaching us, not insulting us. Alex was right: when he treats people like that, he loses all respect. He's certainly lost mine.'

'Then why didn't you say anything?' Ian asked.

Chris was silent. He should have said something. He should have supported Lenka and Alex. But he hadn't. He thought of telling Ian he was too stunned to speak, but he held back. He knew that wasn't quite true.

'You didn't say anything because you didn't want to risk your job,' said Ian with a gloating smile.

'That's bollocks!' Chris snapped. But he knew Ian was right. Ian's smile broadened. 'You're a cynical bastard.'

Ian shook his head. 'I just don't want to lose my job, the same as you.'

The truth of this remark hurt Chris. He turned to Eric. 'What do you think, Eric? Should we have said anything?'

Eric paused. 'Waldern was wrong to do what he did, but challenging him directly like that in class was never going to change the way he behaves. Calhoun will always back up Waldern. He has to.'

'So Alex should have kept his mouth shut?' Chris asked.

Eric shrugged. 'The rest of us did.'

'Well, I wish I had said something now,' said Chris.

Duncan raised an arm and waved. 'Here they are.'

Lenka and Alex saw Duncan's arm, and threaded their way through the crowd to the table where the others were sitting. They both looked tense.

'How did it go?' Duncan asked.

'We got a grade-A bawling out,' said Alex. 'Especially me. But we keep our jobs.'

'How did you manage that?' asked Chris.

'Tom Risman was coming out of Calhoun's office as we were going in.'

'The MD of mortgage trading?' Chris asked.

'That's right,' Alex said. 'Calhoun said that Risman wanted me to stay. But I got a severe warning. "Any more of that and you're outta here."' He did a passable imitation of Calhoun's voice.

'And what about you?' Chris asked Lenka.

'I told him we were right and Waldern was wrong,' she said. 'I said it was him they should be getting rid of, not us. He told me to shut up and get out.'

'I think Calhoun was after me,' said Alex. 'Waldern made a big deal of the way I had questioned his authority.'

'Well, I'm glad you're both still here,' said Duncan, raising his beer bottle. 'Let me get you one.' He turned to look for a waiter.

'It's lucky Tom Risman found out about what happened, or I wouldn't be,' Alex said. 'How was that, by the way?' He looked round the table. Eric was smiling quietly. 'Was it you?'

Eric nodded. 'Risman said he's always hated Waldern. He was glad to help.'

'Thanks, buddy,' said Alex. 'Now, where's that beer?'

Newark Airport was crowded. It was Friday evening, and everyone wanted to be somewhere else for the weekend. Chris had escaped the instant class had finished, and had fought his way there by subway and bus. He needn't have rushed. He had been waiting three-quarters of an hour and she still hadn't come through customs. Her flight was half an hour late and she was presumably still waiting for her baggage.

'Chris!'

Somehow he had missed her. She dropped her bag and gave him a warm hug.

'Tamara! It's great to see you.'

She kissed him quickly on the lips and nestled into his chest. He ran his hands through her blonde hair. It was great to see her again.

They broke apart and headed for the exit.

'Hey, where are you going?' she said.

'The buses are this way.'

'And the taxis are that way.'

'The bus is easy enough.'

'Oh, Chris, you're so mean. I'll pay,' and she marched towards the queue for the taxis.

Chris followed, and they were soon crawling towards the Holland Tunnel and Manhattan.

'Well, what are we doing tonight?' Tamara asked.

'I thought we could go out for dinner. And then we could go on to a party.'

'A party! That sounds fun. I can meet all your nice new friends. Oh, but will that dreadful Duncan be there?'

'He's not dreadful. And yes, he will be there. You know we share an apartment, so you'll just have to put up with him. Ian Darwent will be there, too, though. You like him, don't you?'

'Oh, yes. He's yummy. I suppose there will be lots of Americans?'

'New York is in America, Tamara,' said Chris, smiling. 'I expect there will be one or two.'

Tamara sighed. 'They're not all bad, I suppose. I shall just have to be patient with them.'

'You'll like Eric and Alex, the guys having the party.'

'Good. Now, come here.' She snuggled up to him, and ran her hand inside his shirt and over his chest. 'This is going to be a very nice weekend.'

The taxi battled across Manhattan and eventually reached Chris's apartment. The fare was huge, and somehow Chris ended up paying it.

They talked a lot at dinner, Chris about the training programme and Tamara about her wide circle of acquaintances in London. They had known each other at Oxford, but had only got together after the exams in the final year. Tamara was thin, blonde and sophisticated. Chris had always fancied her, but had never thought he had a chance. He was surprised when they had ended up in bed together after a party in the last week of term, and even more surprised that she still wanted to see him after they had both moved on to London: he to Bloomfield Weiss and she to Gurney Kroheim, a very British merchant bank. The relationship had developed over the following six months, although not quite to the point where they had moved in together. But she was enthusiastic about visiting him in New York, and for that he was grateful.

They arrived back at the apartment at about eleven. Loud

music was coming from Ian's room. He had been out when Tamara and Chris had changed earlier in the evening, so Tamara hadn't yet seen him. She barged straight into his bedroom without knocking, Chris following. Chris wasn't too worried that she would interrupt Ian changing. It wouldn't bother Ian and it would give Tamara a minor thrill.

Ian was fully clothed, but he was surprised. He was bending over a small mirror on the desk, on which was arranged a thin line of white powder. He turned towards the intruders and his face reddened instantly.

'Ooh, Ian, just getting ready for the party, are we?'

Ian looked from Chris to Tamara. 'Um . . .' was all he could say.

'Hello, darling,' said Tamara, clearly enjoying his discomfort. She presented her cheek to him for a kiss, licked the tip of her finger, dipped it in the powder and rubbed it on her gums. 'Yum. Can I have some more?'

'Er . . . hi, Tamara. Yeah, yeah, sure,' said Ian, glancing at Chris uncertainly.

Tamara laughed. 'Come on, Chris. I'm sure Ian can spare some for you, too.'

Chris stared, unsure how to react. After a couple of seconds, he turned and left the room. He shut himself in his own bedroom and looked out of his window at the busy street twelve floors below.

He was angry. He didn't take drugs and he assumed that his friends didn't take any either, especially his girlfriend. What was Tamara thinking of? Taking drugs was what stupid people did. Ian was a surprise, but understandable if Chris thought about it. But how could Tamara be so stupid?

The trouble was, he was the one who felt stupid, and that made him angrier still. Of course he knew people took drugs. Occasionally, at university, he had seen people slipping away together for that purpose. And, from reading the press, the financial world was full of it. But he had always avoided drugs, or to be more accurate, drugs had always avoided him. And that was what made him feel stupid. He was an unsophisticated Polish hick. What else did he expect before a party in New York City of all places?

Get a grip, he told himself. Stay cool. He took a few deep breaths and left the bedroom. Tamara emerged from Ian's room giggling. She stopped when she saw Chris.

'Oh, Chris, you look so shocked.'

'I didn't know you took drugs, Tamara.'

'I don't. Not really. Just every now and then. I'm hardly a junkie, Chris, am I?'

Chris shrugged. He couldn't help it, but he looked for signs that the drug was having an effect. Tamara's eyes looked normal; in fact they looked exactly the same as they had a few minutes ago. Of course they did: he was being stupid again.

'You're so uptight,' she said. 'You should try some.'

Chris shook his head.

She pulled him down to her and kissed him long and deep. 'Better?' she said, when they broke away. 'Look, I wouldn't have done it if I knew you were going to get so upset. Let's go, shall we? Are you ready, Ian?'

They took a taxi over to the Upper West Side. Chris sat in silence as Tamara talked animatedly to Ian, who charmed her back. When they arrived, the party was in full swing. Eric greeted them at the door. A girl was with him, whom Eric introduced as Megan. Chris was curious. This was the mysterious girlfriend who lived in Washington, or somewhere, and whom Chris had not yet met. Not surprisingly, she was attractive, but not in the striking way he might have expected of Eric's girlfriend. She had long frizzy black hair, a pale intelligent face, freckles, a snub nose and bright blue eyes. She looked very young, barely eighteen, but there was something about her that seemed wise beyond her years. Chris instantly liked her.

He introduced Tamara, and after a little small talk, Eric sent them into the crowd, telling them the beer was in the bath.

'Now, he's nice,' said Tamara as they made their way through the crowd to the bathroom.

'He's taken,' said Chris. 'That woman is his girlfriend, I think.'

'Oh, really? I assumed she was a younger sister.'

''Fraid not.'

'No need to be jealous, Chris,' said Tamara, squeezing his hand. 'I'm quite happy with what I've got.'

Chris smiled. She was clearly trying to make amends; he didn't want to ruin the weekend by being surly.

'Besides, I don't like his taste in art,' Tamara said, frowning at Alex's painting of the petrochemical plant in the desert.

'I do,' said Chris.

'Oh, Chris, you're so *industrial*.'

They found the beer. It was indeed in the bath, which was full of ice.

'How very quaint,' said Tamara. 'This must be an old American custom.'

'And a very practical one,' said Alex, who had emerged from the crush of bodies. 'But I know you Brits like your beer warm. I can put yours in the oven if you like?'

Tamara smiled thinly. 'I think I'd like some white wine,' she said in her most cutting voice. Chris winced.

'Sure, there's some in the kitchen. I'm Alex Lubron, by the way.'

'How do you do?' said Tamara, looking over his head.

'This is Tamara,' said Chris.

'I've heard a lot about you,' said Alex, with a smile.

'Mm,' said Tamara.

Alex paused and narrowed his eyes. 'All right. Enjoy yourselves.' He turned away from Chris and Tamara to Tetsundo Suzuki, who had just arrived. 'Hey, Tex, how's it hanging?' he cried, giving the Japanese trainee a high five.

'Who was that little man?' said Tamara with a shudder.

'Alex is a friend of mine,' Chris said. 'He painted the picture you didn't like.'

Tamara caught the tone in his voice. 'Look, I'm sorry, but that stuff about English people liking warm beer is such a *cliché*. Now, can you get me a glass of wine?'

Chris didn't enjoy the party. He had wanted to show his new friends off to Tamara, but now he felt awkward at every introduction. After half an hour, she mellowed under the effects of alcohol and the drug she had taken, and was probably having a better time than he was. He tried to forget about the cocaine, but he found he couldn't.

'Hey, Chris, there you are!' Lenka's hoarse voice rose above the din.

She and Duncan fought their way towards Chris and Tamara. Lenka put her arm round Chris and kissed him. She was pretty drunk. 'So, this is Tamara? Hello, Tamara. Welcome to New York.'

She smiled down at Tamara, who was at least nine inches shorter.

'Hello,' said Tamara, coldly.

'You've come to relax Chris. He needs relaxing, don't you, Chris?' Lenka said, squeezing him. 'He works too hard, you know.'

'I'm sure he does,' said Tamara. 'You American bankers are all so serious about work. I prefer the British approach. We don't go in for all this financial analysis stuff. But we get by.'

'It's useful,' said Duncan, earnestly. 'I think the merchant banks should have their own training programmes. I don't see how they can survive in the modern world without them. At some point it's what you know as well as who you know that counts.'

Tamara's cheeks went ever so slightly pink. Chris recognized the symptoms, and winced.

'That's not quite fair, Duncan,' she said. 'Gurney Kroheim have some very good people.'

'Oh, I'm sure they have,' said Duncan. 'I just think those people would benefit from some formal training.'

'Just as you have,' said Tamara, with a glint in her eye.

'Yes,' said Duncan, suspiciously.

'You don't think the Bloomfield Weiss training programme's too tough, then?'

'Well, no,' said Duncan, uncertainly. 'I mean, it is difficult, but I can handle it.'

'That's not what I heard.'

'What do you mean?' Duncan looked from Tamara to Chris, who shifted uncomfortably.

'Just that a system which pushes some of its trainees so hard that they crack under the pressure seems less than ideal to me. But I'm sure you'll pull through.'

Duncan was about to say something, but then bit his lip. He knew Tamara didn't like him, and he wasn't drunk enough to pick a fight. Lenka was, though.

'How can you be so rude to my friend?' she said.

'I'm not being rude,' said Tamara. 'At least, not intentionally. Duncan started it. I was just carrying on the discussion.'

Lenka swayed. 'Chris. This woman is awful. I can't believe you can have such a horrible girlfriend as this.'

Chris, who had been watching this exchange with dread, knew that the time had come to intervene.

'Lenka,' he said firmly. 'I know you've had a lot to drink. But you shouldn't say things like that.'

'I should,' said Lenka. 'Because it's true. You're a very nice person, Chris. You deserve someone much better.'

'Chris!' gasped Tamara, shocked. 'Make her apologize.'

The bodies surrounding Tamara and Lenka were all quiet now, all watching Chris.

'Lenka, I'm sure you didn't mean what you just said. Can you please apologize?'

'No way,' said Lenka, staring at Tamara.

'Here,' said Duncan, pulling at her arm. 'Come here. Let's get some air.'

Lenka hesitated, and then allowed herself to be pulled back

by Duncan. The crowd watched in silence as they left the room, and then exploded with chatter.

'We're going,' said Tamara, firmly.

'Let's just say goodbye to Eric and Alex,' said Chris.

'No. We're going now.'

So they left. As they spilled out on to the quiet street, they saw the figures of Lenka and Duncan disappearing round the corner. Chris hailed a cab, and they rode back to the apartment in silence.

'Bye, Chris. It was fun. I'll miss you.'

They were standing outside the gate to Departures at Newark Airport. It was Sunday evening; the weekend was over.

'Thanks for coming all this way,' Chris said.

'It was worth it.'

'Do you think you'll be able to come again?'

'I'd like to,' said Tamara. 'Perhaps the bank holiday at the end of May. If I can get a cheap ticket.'

'They'll probably put the fares up that weekend,' said Chris. 'To take advantage of people like us.'

'I'll try, anyway,' Tamara said. Chris pulled her tightly to him, they kissed, and then he let her go. He watched her as she stood in the queue to go through the metal detector. She turned as she set off down the long corridor towards her gate and waved. He waved back, and she was gone.

Chris took the bus back to the Port Authority. It was dark outside, and the orange lights of New Jersey's oil refineries glowed through the windows of the bus. The twin towers of the World Trade Center peeked over the twisted braids of a turnpike interchange. It reminded Chris of one of Alex's paintings.

Although it had started off disastrously, it hadn't been a bad weekend. Tamara had realized she had upset Chris and had done her best to make up for it. They had spent Saturday and Sunday away from the apartment. The weather had been glorious: they'd walked through the Park, visited the Frick and the Museum of Modern Art, and also spent an hour or two in Bloomingdale's and Lord and Taylor. The sex had been great, too. But the sour aftertaste of Friday night remained in Chris's mouth.

Tamara could be rude; everyone knew that. But she was usually funny as well. She had a wit that could be cutting, but she didn't really mean the things she said. Or at least that was what Chris had assumed. But she should have been nicer to his friends; she could have made an effort.

And they were his friends. He liked Duncan. And although he hadn't known Alex and Lenka for more than a few weeks, he liked them, too. Of course, he had known Tamara much longer, and he knew he had been right to defend her against Lenka. But he hadn't liked to choose between these new friends and his girlfriend, and he resented Tamara for making him do it.

He remembered Lenka's words, that Tamara was not good enough for him, and smiled. He was sure Lenka believed it, but he knew she was wrong. He was lucky to have someone like Tamara. She was attractive, she was fun, she had class. And she was good in bed. Chris was not as experienced as he would have liked to be in that regard, but he knew sex with Tamara was great. He hoped she would come over to New York again.

When he arrived back at the apartment, Duncan was waiting for him. Chris hadn't seen him since Friday evening, and for the first time he wondered how Duncan had managed to avoid him so successfully all weekend.

'Fancy a wee bevy?' Duncan said nervously.

Chris smiled. 'OK.'

They went to the Irish bar around the corner. They avoided anything but very small talk until the Guinness was on the table in front of them.

Duncan took a deep breath. 'I'm sorry,' he said.

'No, I'm sorry,' said Chris.

'I shouldn't have mouthed off that stuff about British merchant banks. It was stupid. I knew it would wind up Tamara.'

'And it did.'

Duncan coughed. 'Yes, it did.' He drank some more of his beer. 'Look, I know Tamara doesn't like me, and I don't suspect she ever will, but you've been a good mate to me, especially here, and I don't want to mess that up.'

Chris smiled. 'Don't worry about it, Duncan. Tamara can be awkward sometimes. I'm sorry you had to take that shit from her. I shouldn't have told her about the Bond Math exam.'

'The sad thing was, what she said was true,' said Duncan. 'I can't hack the training programme.'

'Now, no whining, Duncan. Anyway, where were you all weekend?'

Duncan sipped his beer. He tried to suppress a grin, but he failed. In the end, he gave up.

'You didn't?' asked Chris.

'I did.'

'What, after the party?'

'Yep.'

'Wow.'

'Yep.'

'Don't look so smug,' said Chris. 'I want details. I want details.'

'Well, after we left, Lenka was pretty upset. In fact, we both were. So we just walked in silence for a while. Then we started talking about you and about Tamara. And then we were talking about other things.' Duncan paused, a faint smile on his lips. 'We got to Columbus Circle and started looking for a cab, and then I said I'd walk her back to her apartment.'

'In the Village?'

'That's right.'

'But that's miles!'

'Yes. But it didn't seem like it. I mean, it seemed to take for ever, but we didn't get tired or anything. It was very romantic. Then we got to her street and she asked me up to her apartment. She said I couldn't just turn round and walk all the way back.'

'And then?'

'And then . . .' Duncan smiled.

'You have to tell me.'

'No, I don't.'

'OK, I suppose you don't,' admitted Chris. 'But presumably you spent the weekend at her place?'

'It seemed safer there than in our apartment.'

'That's true.'

'Didn't you notice I wasn't there?'

'No, I suppose I didn't. I just thought you were skulking in your room, or something.' Chris took a gulp of beer. Duncan and Lenka. He liked that. 'Congratulations,' he said.

'Thank you. We'd better keep it quiet from the others on the programme, though. You never know what Calhoun would think.'

'Sod him,' said Chris. 'But all right, I'll keep it quiet. Ian's got to find out, though. And Alex and Eric.'

'If they do, they do,' said Duncan. 'Oh, by the way, Lenka says she's sorry. About what she said to Tamara.'

'That's OK.'

'She says she stands by what she said, she just shouldn't have said it.'

Chris smiled. 'Tell her that's OK, too.'

Summer came. It was hot in New York in June and July, so hot that it was unpleasant to venture outside. The Brits were not dressed for it: their Marks and Spencer wool suits were the wrong clothing for the climate. The humidity was so bad that after walking more than a block they would find themselves drenched in sweat. The classroom was deliciously cool, but the subway was a sweltering hell. The air-conditioning on the Lexington line wasn't up to a carriage full of sweaty commuters. Sometimes Chris, Duncan and Ian would bail out at Forty-Second Street and grab a cold beer in a nearby bar, before returning below ground for the second leg. Of course, Lenka managed to stay cool at all times, in outfits that Abby Hollis eyed suspiciously, but couldn't quite bring herself to comment on.

The work kept coming. In addition to Waldern's Capital Markets, which seemed to be a never-ending subject, they were given courses in Corporate Finance, Accounting, International Economics, Credit Analysis and Ethics. They were spoken to by people across the length and breadth of Bloomfield Weiss, from Tokyo to Chicago, from Global Custody to Equity Derivatives. The pace came in fits and starts, but the pressure never let up, George Calhoun saw to that.

Much to his surprise, Chris found that he actually enjoyed the course. As the concepts became clearer to him, and linked together to form a coherent whole, his interest grew. He particularly liked listening to the traders talking. These were popular sessions with the trainees: if Bloomfield Weiss was anything, it was a trading house. The staking of billions of dollars, the big men with big mouths, the macho language of violent sexual acts and physical disfigurement, all attracted a certain type of trainee. But that wasn't what appealed to Chris. He was fascinated by the shifting relationships of markets, how supply and demand fed through to price movement, and how risk capital was managed so that losses were cut and profits allowed to run. He was less interested in the tall tales of Cash Callaghan, a top salesman from the London office, who bragged about 'whippin' and drivin' those bonds', and more interested in the quiet deliberations of Seymour Tanner, a twenty-nine-year-old star of the Proprietary Desk, who was rumoured to have made the firm two hundred million dollars the year before. For the first time, Chris was beginning to feel at home at Bloomfield Weiss. There was a job there that he could do, if they would let him do it.

George Calhoun was eager to crank up the competition. He wanted to fire up his trainees, make them hungry, give them something to aim for. So he put up a table of rankings, from one to sixty, or rather fifty-eight, following the departure of Denny Engel and Roger Masden. The rankings were based on the amalgamated scores from the various tests that were given out during the course. To add a bit of spice, he had drawn a big red line between number forty-five and number forty-six, the infamous bottom quartile. And he also announced that the top three trainees would receive a bonus at the end of the programme.

At number one spot was Rudy Moss. At number two, Eric Astle. And at number three, much to Calhoun's fury, was Lenka. At the other end, Duncan was hovering around fifty; in other words in the bottom quartile, but within striking distance of escaping it. After his poor showing in the Bond Math exam Ian was at forty-two, but rising strongly. Alex was two places higher at forty, and Chris, to his surprise was at twenty-five. Despite the disparity in abilities, or perhaps because of it, the study group continued to work together. Eric and Lenka's success was a source of pride for them all, and they all wanted to ensure that Duncan and Alex ended the course above the cut-off line.

There was one course, though, that Chris didn't enjoy. Ethics. Ian called it Corporate Hypocrisy, and the name stuck. It was a cynical attempt to deal with the repercussions that Bloomfield Weiss had suffered both from the Phoenix Prosperity scandal and the prosecution of the drug-dealing salesmen. The contrast between Martin Krohl, who took the Ethics course, and the succession of managing directors who described in great detail how they ripped the faces off their clients would have been funny, if it was not so seriously pursued. Ian came top in the exam, which wasn't really a surprise. He was an intelligent man, Ethics had not a number in sight, and Ian's innate cynicism was perfectly suited to the subject as taught at Bloomfield Weiss. Lenka failed. She explained that she had needed to 'clarify' some of her answers and she suspected that Krohl hadn't liked that. The irony of Ian coming top and Lenka coming near the bottom of a Bloomfield Weiss Ethics exam was not lost on Chris and Duncan, who both felt slightly ashamed at how well they had done.

Duncan and Lenka's relationship prospered. They were very professional about it. There was no hint of anything in class or in front of the other trainees. Even when they were with Eric, Alex, Chris and Ian, they behaved more like good friends than a couple. They would often sit next to each other in a bar or restaurant, and there was a lot of good-natured teasing, but there was none of the all-exclusive inward-looking intimacy with which a couple can sometimes disrupt a group of friends.

But they did spend a lot of time together. Duncan usually stayed with Lenka in the Village, often arriving back after midnight, or at weekends, not at all. They went away for the Memorial Day weekend together, to Cape Cod. Duncan wasn't getting much sleep, but he was thriving on it. He was happy, and the self-pity about his work, which had begun to irritate Chris and Ian, disappeared. Lenka, too, seemed happy with life, although for her this seemed a much more usual state of affairs. Ian would occasionally wonder what on earth she saw in Duncan, but even he couldn't complain at Duncan's good spirits.

Besides, Ian was enjoying himself. He would often venture out alone around nine or ten in the evening. Occasionally Chris would be startled on the way to the bathroom the following morning by a strange woman. During the course of the summer, he saw four or five of these. Most were American, but one of them was an au pair from France. She was the only one who Chris saw more than once. They were all attractive.

Chris wasn't surprised that Ian's success with women, which had been marked at Oxford, was even more apparent in New York. He made full use of his accent, and for some reason that Chris couldn't fathom, women seemed to find his arrogance attractive rather than off-putting. None of those who came back with him in the middle of the night thought they were at the beginning of a beautiful relationship. But, Chris reasoned, perhaps that was why they were there in the first place. Ian's success was all the more remarkable because the AIDS scare was still very much alive in New York at that time. Ian thought the risk to heterosexuals was overrated and presumably his new friends agreed with him. Duncan became extra careful with the washing up.

Alex was struggling. His mother was ill. Very ill. She had leukaemia, and it was getting worse. He had kept it quiet from everyone apart from Eric, but when her condition changed from stable to deteriorating, Alex felt he had to spend as much time with her as he could. She was entombed in a hospital near her home in New Brunswick. He went there every weekend and often after class in the evening. He took as much time off as he could but, not surprisingly, Calhoun was unsympathetic. Alex pushed it as far as he dared, but eventually Calhoun made it clear that one more day off, and Alex was out.

Alex's father had died three years before, and his brother had taken off around the world soon afterwards. He was now working as crew on a sailing boat in Australia. To Alex's disgust, his brother said he wouldn't be able to make it back to the States to see his mother. So the burden of responsibility fell on Alex, who took it hard. She was in pain whenever she wasn't pumped up with drugs, and Alex felt her pain. It was difficult flogging out there so often to see someone who could barely speak and who was obviously in such agony. He hated being with her and he hated being away from her. Lenka accompanied him on a couple of these visits and that seemed to cheer him up. But his work suffered, and he slipped to take Duncan's place in that fourth quartile.

Tamara made it over to America one more time. She came for the Fourth of July weekend. This time, she flew direct to Washington, and Chris took the Amtrak to meet her there. They had a great weekend. They saw the fireworks on Capitol Hill, listened to the 1812 Overture, and explored the sweltering city and its restaurants. Chris felt much more relaxed: Tamara was able to make unkind comments about Americans without anyone he knew hearing her, and he didn't have to worry about her insulting his friends.

Duncan's happiness didn't last the summer. It was shattered on a hot and humid Saturday night, two weeks before the end of the programme. Chris was sleeping fitfully, entangled in a single sheet on his bed, when he was awakened by the crash of the apartment door slamming. He glanced at the alarm clock. One fifteen a.m. He heard a grunt. Duncan. He rolled over. Duncan was usually quiet when he came back from Lenka's. As he surfaced from sleep, Chris realized something else was odd: Duncan usually stayed at Lenka's on Saturdays. There was no reason for him to come back to their apartment in the middle of the night.

A loud bang. Duncan swearing. Another grunt. A crash of a chair falling over. This did not sound good. Chris crawled out of bed and pulled on his dressing gown. Duncan was in the hallway, swaying. His face was white in the bright hallway light.

'Are you OK, Duncan?'

Duncan blew out his cheeks and focused on Chris. 'I've just had a wee drink,' he said slowly. 'Going to bed. Don't feel too good.'

He was smashed out of his brain. Chris didn't like the way Duncan's chest was heaving, as though he were trying to keep something down.

'Let's go to the bathroom, Duncan,' said Chris, grabbing hold of him.

'No. Bed,' said Duncan, but he allowed himself to be led away by Chris. As soon as he saw the lavatory bowl, he lunged at it. Chris held on to him as he emptied his stomach.

He heard Ian behind him. 'Jesus,' he said. 'Stupid bugger. I hope he's going to clear that up.'

'I don't think he'll be able to.'

'Well, I'm not doing it,' said Ian, and he retreated to his room, shutting the door firmly.

Chris cleaned up the lavatory, and Duncan. He pulled off most of his clothes and laid him on his bed. Duncan fell asleep instantly.

Late the next morning, Chris looked into Duncan's room. He was lying on his back with his eyes open. The room stank of old alcohol.

'How are you feeling?' Chris asked.

'Horrible,' said Duncan in a cracked voice. 'You couldn't get me some water, could you, Chris?'

Chris returned with a large glassful, which Duncan drank. 'God, my head hurts.'

'I've never seen you that drunk before,' said Chris.

Duncan shook his head. 'I don't even remember coming back here. Did you help me get into bed?'

Chris nodded.

'Thanks.' Duncan ran his tongue round his mouth. 'Yuk. I threw up last night, didn't I?'

'You did. What happened?'

'We had a row.'

'You and Lenka?'

'Yes.'

Chris waited. He knew Duncan would tell him.

Duncan sighed and winced. 'This headache is horrible. It's over, Chris.'

'No! Are you sure?'

'Am I sure? Of course I'm sure.'

'Why? What happened?'

Duncan paused. 'It's my fault. I pushed her too hard.'

'About what?'

He sighed. 'I suggested we live together. The programme finishes in two weeks, and I couldn't face the thought of going back to London and leaving her here. I realized that she's the most important thing in my life. My career at Bloomfield Weiss is screwed, that's obvious. So I told her I'd quit and live with her in New York. It should be easy enough to find another job on Wall Street. Or else she could live with me in London. Or we could both go to Czechoslovakia. I didn't care. I just didn't want to leave her.'

'And what did she say?'

'Nothing at first. She went quiet, as though she was thinking. But I knew right away that I'd blown it.' Duncan paused, and winced again, whether from his head, or the memory of his conversation the night before, Chris couldn't tell. 'Then she said she'd been thinking about the end of the programme too. She said she liked me, but she didn't want the kind of commitment that went with living with someone. She said it would be better for both of us if we split up now.'

'Oh, dear.'

'You're telling me. Then I lost it. I told her I loved her. I do love her, Chris. And I thought that if I told her that, and really meant it, she'd have to say she loved me. But she didn't. She just went completely still. She didn't say what she thought about me. She just said that it'd be best if we didn't see each other any more.'

Duncan took a sip of his water.

'I couldn't bear the thought of that. I only have two more weeks in New York; I want to be with Lenka for that whole time. So I told her we should keep seeing each other and forget about the future for now. But she wouldn't have any of it. I kept telling her, but she wouldn't listen. In the end she more or less threw me out.'

'And you went drinking?'

'I couldn't believe what had happened. I still can't. We have something very special, she and I. She's the most marvellous person I've ever met. I'm not going to meet anyone else like her again, am I?' He looked at Chris, demanding an answer.

'Lenka is unique,' said Chris carefully.

'Of course she is,' said Duncan. 'One moment, I think we're going to live our lives together, and the next . . .'

'It must have been tough.'

'It was. It is. Oh, God.' To Chris's embarrassment, tears began to run down Duncan's face. Chris had no idea what to say. Lenka knew her own mind, and if she had called it off, it was off. Duncan would just have to get over it. But that would be no easy matter, Chris knew.

'When you feel up to it, we'll go for a walk in the park. We can talk about it,' said Chris.

'That would be good,' said Duncan. 'I'll be up in a minute.'

Chris went through to the living room. Ian was reading the Sunday *New York Times*.

'What's up with him?' Ian said, his eyes on the paper.

'Lenka chucked him.'

'I knew she was out of his league.' He put down the paper and groaned. 'I'm not sure I can face the moaning. It's going to be pretty bad.'

It was pretty bad. Duncan was inconsolable. He didn't sleep. He drank Ian's whisky late into the night, and when he'd finished that, went out and bought some of his own. He called Lenka at odd times during the day and night, until she stopped answering the phone. He was an embarrassment in class, conspicuously moping in front of her, and refusing to tell anyone what was wrong. Some of the other trainees were worried and asked Chris and Ian what was the matter with him. Chris and Ian felt they had to deny any knowledge of Duncan's problems, something Ian found easier to do than Chris.

Chris tried to be as sympathetic as he could, but even he was exasperated by Duncan. The programme was hotting up. The final exam would be a four-hour test on Capital Markets, and everyone knew that Waldern wouldn't make it easy. The whole class revised hard, with the exception of Duncan. This worried Chris. Duncan was in forty-first position, only five above the dreaded bottom quartile, and the Capital Markets exam had a large weighting. When Chris and Ian were sweating away in the evening, Duncan was either out in a bar somewhere or, even worse, in his room with a bottle of whisky.

The study group still met regularly at Eric and Alex's apartment, but Duncan never showed. Although the others were worried about him, they were glad to avoid his poor humour. Lenka still came. She seemed a little more subdued than normal, but otherwise she seemed to be in much better shape than Duncan.

Chris was leaving a session early, the Thursday evening following the break up, when Lenka rushed out to catch him up. They walked down Columbus Avenue together.

'How's Duncan?' she asked.

'Not good.'

'Oh.' They walked on in silence. Then Lenka spoke. 'I like him, you know. And I'm worried about him. You will look after him, won't you?'

'I'm trying,' said Chris. 'But it's difficult.'

'The problem is that if I try to be nice to him myself, it only encourages him. I need him to know that it's finished. We must make a clean break. Otherwise, he'll be hurt much more later on. Do you understand?'

'I think so.' Chris didn't want to take sides, so he was trying to be as non-committal as possible. But he thought that Lenka was probably right; with Duncan, a 'maybe' would be fatal.

'I didn't mislead him, you know,' said Lenka. 'We were just having fun. I didn't think it was particularly serious; I thought we both understood that. Then, when he said he wanted to give up his job to live with me, I realized he saw our relationship very differently from me. So I ended it. It would have been wrong to let it go on.'

'Couldn't you see Duncan was head over heels in love with you?'

Lenka sighed. 'No. I always have this problem with men. I start a relationship with a nice man, we have fun, and then one day they go serious on me. I thought that Duncan would be different; after all, the training programme is finite. It should have had a built-in break-up date. But Duncan won't accept that.'

'So what's wrong with a serious relationship, anyway?'

'I had one. In Prague. We were engaged to be married. He was a medical student, and I loved him. But after the Velvet Revolution, when I had the opportunity to get out of our boring country and see the world, he wouldn't let me.'

'Wouldn't let you? How could he stop you?'

'He had a fixed idea of our relationship. Czech women get married much younger than Western European or American women. His idea was that we would get married, he would qualify as a doctor, and I would follow him wherever the job took him. Just like my mother did with my father. You know he is a doctor?'

'No, I didn't.'

'Well, I thought I had two choices. I could experience the new life of the West, or I could be a boring Czech wife and mother at twenty-five. It was a difficult decision, I did love Karel, but in the end there was only one choice that was the right one for me. Go to the United States.'

'And since then?'

'The last thing I need now is a serious relationship.'

'Why?' asked Chris. 'That's all a lot of people are looking for.'

Lenka thought carefully before answering. 'I guess I don't know who I really am, or who I want to be. It's hard for you to imagine what Czechoslovakia was like under the Communists. America is so different; and most of the differences I like. I know I'm changing, but I don't quite know how. I won't become an American, even if I live here for a while. I will always be Czech, and one day I will go back to my country and do something for it, perhaps using the skills I'm learning here.'

'I see.'

'So, I'm totally unsuited to a long-term commitment with Duncan or anyone else for that matter. For one thing, Duncan wouldn't know who it was he was committed to.' Lenka bit her lip. 'I know I've hurt Duncan, and I didn't mean to. But I hurt Karel, and myself, so much more. I don't want to do that again.'

'I understand,' said Chris.

'Do you?' asked Lenka, looking at him closely. 'Do you really?'

'I think so.'

'Can you make Duncan understand that?'

Chris paused. 'I don't know. Probably not. Duncan is not very rational at the moment.'

'You can say that again. I tried to talk to him again a couple of nights ago and I still got nowhere. But this can't go on. He's acting as if we're married and I've run off with another man. He calls me at any time in the day or night, he makes a fool of himself in front of me in class. He follows me. He sends me letters I never read. He whispers things to me about how his life isn't worth living. I have to make him realize it's over.'

'I'll do what I can,' Chris said.

'Thank you,' said Lenka. 'Because I've had enough. Someone has to get the message through to him.'

Chris decided to try to talk to Duncan about Lenka the next day. They had lunch together in the cafeteria on the twelfth floor, and Chris suggested a quick walk down to Battery Park. They left their jackets behind and strolled the couple of blocks to the park. It was another hot, humid day. Tourists drifted lazily amongst the souvenir sellers and the office workers eating their sandwiches. Only the seagulls were active, investigating every piece of picnic debris as it hit the ground. The city dust hung hot and heavy in the air. Out in the harbour the Statue of Liberty pointed upwards into the shimmering haze.

'I spoke to Lenka yesterday,' Chris began.

'Oh, yes?' Duncan's interest quickened.

'She says there's no chance of you two getting back together. She says she doesn't want a committed relationship with anyone.'

The glimmer of hope in Duncan's eye disappeared instantly, to be replaced with bitterness. 'So what?'

His response confused Chris. 'So, there isn't much point in chasing her.'

'I know that's what she says,' said Duncan, sounding frustrated. 'That's the whole point. But she's wrong, and I have to show her that. If I stop chasing her, that's hardly going to work, is it? I need to show her how much I love her, and make her admit to herself that she loves me. I know she does, whatever she says. I just know it.' He glared at Chris, defying him to say otherwise.

'Did she tell you about the guy she was engaged to in Czechoslovakia? About how she broke away from him? She didn't want to be tied down then, and she doesn't want to be tied down now.'

'That was different,' said Duncan. 'He wanted her to give up everything for him. I want to give up everything for *her*.'

Chris held his tongue. He had known it would be useless to attempt to persuade Duncan. He shouldn't have even tried. Then, out of the corner of his eye, he saw two figures he recognized. They were walking towards Chris and Duncan from the direction of the War Memorial, deep in conversation. Lenka and Alex.

'All right, do what you want,' said Chris, grabbing hold of Duncan's arm. 'Let's go back to the office.'

But Duncan had seen them too.

'Jesus. Look over there.'

'Duncan,' Chris said, tugging his sleeve.

Duncan shook him off. 'I can't believe it. Look what they're doing.'

'They're talking, that's all. They're friends. They're our friends.'

'Yes, but look at the *way* they're talking,' said Duncan as he walked rapidly towards them.

Lenka saw him. She frowned, and stopped still, facing him.

'What are you doing?' demanded Duncan.

'Talking to Alex,' said Lenka quietly.

'How can you do that? Why can't you talk to me?'

'Duncan.' Chris had a hold of his sleeve and was pulling him backwards.

Lenka exploded. 'I can talk to whoever I want to, Duncan. I can walk with whoever I want to. I can sleep with whoever I want to.' She took a step towards Duncan and jabbed a finger in his chest. 'I used to like you, Duncan. We had a good time together. But I don't have to put up with all this shit. You can't tell me what to do, do you understand me? We're finished, Duncan. Finished!'

Duncan was so taken aback by this outburst that he was speechless. Chris finally managed to pull him away. Duncan looked over his shoulder. 'Bitch!' he cried.

'Bastard!' came the reply from Lenka. Chris and Alex exchanged glances, and then Chris pushed Duncan firmly back in the direction of Bloomfield Weiss.

During a break in class that afternoon, Chris grabbed Lenka. She still looked angry.

'That was pretty unpleasant,' he said.

'Did you talk to him?'

'Yes.'

'And is he going to give up?'

'No.'

Lenka sighed. 'I thought so. But do you see what I mean when I say he acts like he owns me? The fact is, he doesn't, and I have to make him see that. I do like him, despite all this stupidity, but if the only way he can get it through his skull that we're finished is by me calling him a bastard, then that's the way it's going to be.'

'He's jealous. He thinks there's something between you and Alex.'

'Maybe that's a good thing. At least then he'll realize it's over.' Lenka saw the doubt in Chris's face. 'Have you got any other ideas?'

With that she stalked off back to the classroom.

6

The week before the final exam was hell. Everyone was tense. They all knew that Waldern would set a tough one. It was a four-hour paper on Capital Markets, although Waldern promised he would throw in strands of everything else they had learned on the course as well. So they had to revise everything. Fear of coming in the bottom quartile had grabbed the majority of the trainees. The rest were worried about coming top. Rudy Moss was still in first position, with Eric second. Latasha James was third; Lenka had slipped to tenth after her disastrous Ethics exam. Duncan was just above the cut-off line, Alex just below it. Even Chris, at twenty-six, felt that the bottom quartile was in his reach if he panicked. So, as Ian put it, he panicked about panicking.

Alex worked hard, with a lot of help from Lenka. The others were all determined that he would make it. They had more or less given up hope on Duncan, though. Chris tried everything: encouragement, scolding, nagging, sarcasm, but to no effect. Duncan was bent on self-destruction.

The exam was a bastard. It was about a fictitious US cable television company with dodgy accounts that wanted to issue junk bonds to finance an acquisition in France. Chris had to admit that it was clever: you needed to understand accounting, credit, cross-border mergers and acquisitions, and of course, capital markets to structure the deal and describe how it might be sold. The case took three-quarters of an hour just to read.

Chris slogged through it, and after three hours he had the bulk of it cracked. His head buzzed with fatigue and adrenaline. One more hour. He would make it. He reached the end of a page, and sat up and stretched. The classroom was silent except for the rustle of paper and the scratching of pens. Abby Hollis was staring dully at the class from her position in the centre.

He was just about to get back to work when Eric, who was sitting next to him, gathered up his papers and marched down the aisle to Abby Hollis. He'd finished already! Abby looked as surprised as Chris and began a murmured conversation with Eric.

Chris heard a whisper from behind. He stiffened.

'Chris.'

It was Duncan, who was sitting right behind him.

'Chris. Nod if you can hear me.'

Chris's eyes darted to Abby, whose head was bent next to Eric's.

He nodded.

'Let me see your paper.'

Chris remained motionless.

'Push it to one side.'

Chris didn't move.

'Oh, come on Chris. I need the help. Please.'

Chris felt a rush of anger. He was going to pass this exam now. He knew it. And he had worked hard to pass it. Why should he let Duncan have a look at his paper? Duncan knew that Denny and Roger had been kicked out for doing just that. If Duncan was in a mess, it was entirely his own fault.

'Come on Chris. Let's see the first page.'

Slowly and deliberately, Chris picked up his pen and hunched over his paper. Duncan could fend for himself. He had an exam to finish.

'Chris! You bastard!'

This time Duncan's whispering was too loud. Abby heard, and snapped her head towards Duncan. Chris dropped his eyes to his own paper.

'Fucker,' hissed Duncan a few seconds later, when Abby had turned her attention back to Eric.

*

George Calhoun was waiting for them as they trooped out of the exam, shattered. He told all the US-hired trainees to take a quick blood and urine test for their medical insurance. Chris, Duncan and Ian were too tired to notice. They just wanted to get out of the building as quickly as possible.

'Coming to Jerry's?' said Ian to Chris.

'Yes, definitely.' Chris turned to Duncan. 'You want to come?'

Duncan was pale and near tears. He ignored Chris and headed for the elevator.

Ian raised his eyebrows. 'What was that about?'

Chris sighed wearily. 'Forget it. Let's get a beer.'

It was early, and Jerry's was almost empty. But sitting there, guarding a table and a pitcher of beer, was Eric.

'How come you left early?' asked Chris.

'I'd finished. I couldn't stand it in there any more. So I came down here and got an early beer.'

'That's sickening.'

'Never mind,' said Ian. 'Just pour me one.' He loosened his tie and downed his beer in one. Eric poured him another one.

'So how did you do?' asked Chris.

Eric smiled. 'Let's not ask those questions. It's finished. It's all over. Let's just get drunk.'

So they did.

The end of the programme was an anticlimax. There were four days of agony while they waited for the Capital Markets papers to be marked and the Americans to be given their job assignments. Chris was amazed that Waldern could mark so many lengthy papers so quickly: Ian's theory was that he got his graduate students to do it.

After his initial anger at Chris, Duncan forgave him. He knew he had messed up; he admitted that it was his own fault that he hadn't been properly prepared. But the guilt still weighed on Chris. It wasn't that he felt he should have helped Duncan; Duncan had no right to expect Chris to cheat for him, and he knew it. What troubled Chris was his motivation for ignoring Duncan in the exam. The Bloomfield Weiss philosophy of look after yourself and leave your colleagues to sort out their own problems had finally got through to him. He had wanted to do nothing to jeopardize his own chances of passing; in his darkest moments, he thought that he had wanted Duncan to fail. This bothered him. Bloomfield Weiss was changing him, and having seen dozens of successful Bloomfield Weiss investment bankers, he wasn't sure he liked that.

Alex was unusually subdued. He wandered around with a grim expression on his face and hardly spoke to any of the others. They assumed that he knew he had done badly, but didn't want to talk about it, and so they left him alone.

The exam results were added to the results of all the other tests during the programme to make a grand total. This was pinned up on the wall outside the classroom at ten o'clock on the Thursday morning of the last week. The trainees crowded round Abby Hollis to look. Eric had made first place, Rudy Moss second, and Latasha James third. Lenka was fourth. To his great satisfaction, Chris squeezed into the first quartile at four-teenth. Ian was thirty-second and Alex just scraped above the cut-off at forty-second. Duncan had failed resoundingly at fifty-seventh. Only one person was below him, Faisal, who didn't care.

An hour later, there was another list to look at: job assignments for the American trainees. Eric had been given the job he had asked for in Mergers and Acquisitions. Although in theory Alex was safe, he had no job assigned to him. He seemed to take this badly; the strain of the programme and his mother's illness appeared finally to be getting to him. Rudy Moss got the assignment he wanted in the Asset Management Division, but, despite her high place in the programme, Latasha ended up in Municipal Finance. The trainees from the foreign offices would have to wait until they returned home to discover what jobs they had been given, or in cases like Duncan's and Carla's, for official confirmation that they had been given none.

The rest of the day was taken up with meetings, form filling, and further presentations by insignificant departments. The gossip and chatter was incessant. Most people were happy to scrape through. Those that had failed had different responses. Some took it stoically, some tried to joke about it, some, like Duncan, looked angry, and some, like Carla, just wept quietly. No one knew what to say to these unfortunates. The likes of Rudy Moss ignored them. They were history at Bloomfield Weiss, they were failures, they had zero networking value. Why waste time on them?

The fragile sense of community that had formed among the sixty young bankers over the previous five months was falling apart, as each looked forward to new lives either inside or outside Bloomfield Weiss. There was no farewell party, only snatched conversations as people made arrangements, the Americans to find out about their new jobs, and the foreigners to make their way home.

Eric and Alex had originally planned another party of their own for all the trainees. But, as the end approached and the programme disintegrated around them, they changed their minds. They decided to invite the three Brits and Lenka to join them on Eric's father's boat, which was moored on the North Shore of Long Island. Everyone thought this a great idea, even Duncan. So, after the last class of the programme, they all took the commuter train out to Oyster Bay, full of excitement for the evening ahead, an evening that would change their lives for ever.

7

The boat cut slowly through the sheltered waters of the bay, expertly guided by Eric. It was a sleek white sports fishing craft, about thirty feet long, with a cockpit aft, a raised bridge and a foredeck. Eric steered towards the sun, slowly sinking behind the wooded ridge of Mill Neck. The evening was lovely, the freshest for weeks. There had been a storm the night before that had cleared the muck and humidity out of the air, leaving a clear sky with little puffs of cloud and a gentle breeze. The end of the sweltering summer was near; September was only a week away.

The tensions of the training programme were gone, as everyone tucked into the alcoholic supplies they had brought with them. There were coolers of beer, and Lenka and Alex had managed to bring the ingredients for margaritas. Everyone had changed into jeans and T-shirts, and left their suits down below. Even Duncan was relaxed, and while he and Lenka didn't talk to each other, they didn't actually scowl at each other, either.

Chris took three bottles of beer up from the cockpit to the bridge, where Eric was at the wheel. Megan was sitting next to him, wearing faded jeans and an old blue sweater, her dark hair blowing over her face.

Chris opened the bottles and passed them round. Megan made room for him to sit with them. It was a peaceful evening. Cormorants darted low over the grey water, streaked with reds and orange from the setting sun. This finger of Oyster Bay stretched a couple of miles inland; on all sides were quiet low hills covered with trees, and secluded mansions with the occasional dock reaching out into the bay. Boats big and small were moored all around, from tiny fishing vessels to ocean-going yachts.

'This was a great idea,' Chris said.

'I hope so,' said Eric. 'I like it out here.'

'Do you do this with your father?'

'I used to, a lot. Less so now. I'm busy. He's busy. You know how it is.'

'Where do your parents live? In one of those?' Chris gestured towards one of the many enormous houses nestling along the shoreline.

Eric laughed. 'No. They have a small place in town. Oyster Bay used to be where all the tradesmen who served the big estates lived. It still feels a bit like that.'

Chris was surprised. He had assumed that Eric's father was one of the gilded rich. 'Will you move back here one day?' he asked.

Eric shrugged. 'I don't know. I'd like to, maybe, when I'm older.'

'In one of these?'

'Here, I'll show you where I'd really like to live. It's just around this corner.'

They motored on for a couple of minutes, and Eric brought the boat in quite close to the shore. There stood a modern white house, with curved elegant lines and large windows. In front of it lurked a pool, and a lawn that dropped down to the water. It wasn't quite to Chris's taste, but it was certainly startling.

'Too modern for you, huh?' said Eric, watching Chris's reaction.

'I know nothing about architecture.'

'It was designed by Richard Meier.' That meant nothing to Chris, and Eric saw it. 'Well, anyway, I like it,' he said.

Chris looked at the mansions all around him, built far enough apart that each was secluded from the other, but close enough that every stretch of water was spoken for. 'Who lives in these places?'

'Pop stars, mafia dons, investment bankers.'

For the first time it hit Chris that, for some, investment

banking was not just a passport to a good salary, it was the key to serious wealth. He couldn't quite believe he would ever live anywhere like that house, but he could believe Eric would. He realized that he was standing next to someone who would one day be a very rich man.

'Are you serious about politics, Eric or was the Bush campaign just a one-off?'

Eric glanced at Chris and smiled. 'I'm serious.'

'But you can't be a politician and an investment banker at the same time, surely?'

'That's not my plan. We do have professional politicians in the States. They go to law school and then spend their time knocking around Washington getting to know people. But I have a different strategy.'

'What's that?'

'These days you need money to get to the top in politics. And it'll only get worse. Campaign spending is rising and rising. So I figure I'll make a ton of money first, and then go into politics. Bloomfield Weiss seems a good place to start.'

'Makes sense.' And it did, for Eric. Trust him to have it all worked out. Chris found it impossible to make plans more advanced than being grateful he had a job at Bloomfield Weiss and doing his best to keep it.

Eric turned the boat around and drove it back along the channel, the way they had come. Lenka's raucous laugh floated up from the cockpit beneath them. 'Can you take over, Megan?' he asked. 'I'd better go down and see the others.'

Megan took the wheel and Eric climbed down the ladder to the group below, who were quickly getting drunk. Chris stayed on the bridge.

'Are you an expert pilot?' he asked.

'No,' Megan smiled. 'Eric and I have been out here a few times together. I can do the easy stuff.'

'How long have you known him?'

'Four years. We were at college together at Amherst. We've

been going out for the last couple of years.' She saw the look of surprise on Chris's face. 'You thought I was still in high school, didn't you?'

'Oh, no, no,' Chris said.

'You're blushing,' Megan said. 'You're a lousy liar.'

It was true. Chris could feel the heat in his face. 'All right, I admit it,' he said. 'You don't look twenty-two, or whatever you must be. But that's a good thing, isn't it?'

'Maybe, one day it will be. Right now, it's a pain in the ass. Nobody takes me seriously. And people like you wonder why Eric's going out with a schoolgirl.'

'Oh, no, I can see why Eric would want to go out with you,' said Chris, without thinking.

Megan glanced at him quickly to check whether this was just a smooth remark, but then she smiled. 'You're blushing again.'

Chris took a swig of his beer to hide his confusion. He really did find her quite attractive. She had a softness and a kind of calm composure about her that made him want to talk to her more.

'Eric's very ambitious, isn't he?' he said.

'Oh, yes.'

'He did brilliantly on the training programme. The way he always seemed to understand everything instantly on the course was amazing. I think he will go far.'

'I'm sure he will,' said Megan.

'But he manages to be a nice guy with it,' said Chris. 'He spent a lot of time on the course helping the rest of us out. He didn't need to do that.'

'But it didn't harm his career, did it?' Megan said.

'It could have done.'

'But it didn't?'

'No, it didn't.'

Megan looked ahead as she guided the boat round a buoy. 'Sorry. That was unfair of me. Eric is very kind, and generous. But he'd never let anyone get in the way of his ambition.'

Chris raised his eyebrows. 'Do you think he really will go into politics?'

'Oh, yes,' said Megan, still concentrating on steering the boat. 'Do you think he'll get anywhere?'

'Oh, yes,' she said again.

A thought struck Chris. 'Not all the way? Not President?'

Megan smiled, as though Chris had just discovered a secret. 'What Eric wants to do, he usually ends up doing. Never under-estimate him.'

'Wow.' She couldn't be serious. But someone had to be President, and Eric had as good a chance as anyone of being that person.

'Don't tell him I told you that,' said Megan.

'You didn't tell me anything,' said Chris. 'But you sound . . .'

'Yes?'

'I don't know. Unhappy with it.'

'I like Eric. Very much. In fact I . . .' She paused. Chris knew very well that she wanted to say that she loved him, but couldn't, at least not to a stranger. 'I like him,' she said again. 'But, please don't take offence, I'm not wild about investment banking. Eric has real talent, and I wish he'd use it for something more useful.'

'Going into politics can be useful. If he's honest. Which Eric is.'

'Possibly. The trouble is that Eric's a Republican, and I'm not.'

'Oh.'

Megan sighed. 'Anyway. Things are going quite well at the moment. He likes what he's doing, and I like what I'm doing, and although we don't get to see each other as much as we'd like, it's great when we do.'

It was beginning to get dark. Lights seemed to emerge all around them from buoys, boats and the houses on the shoreline. Megan switched the boat's own lights on.

'You look too nice to be an investment banker,' she said.

'It's not that bad.'

'It sounds awful. Eric told me how they decided to fire the bottom quarter of the programme. And actually discouraging teamwork makes no sense to me.'

'Bloomfield Weiss is a bit over the top,' Chris said. 'And, if I'm honest with myself, I try to ignore all that stuff. It's a tough place. But I think I can handle it, and that gives me some pride.'

'But don't investment bankers just speculate with other people's money and pay themselves obscene salaries with the profits?'

'It's not quite that simple.' Megan gave him a look like she'd heard that before. Which she probably had, from Eric. 'No, really. Investment banks provide the world with capital. The world needs capital to create wealth and jobs.'

'So all those Wall Streeters are fighting world poverty every day?'

'Not exactly.' Part of Chris saw her point of view. His father would certainly have agreed with her. But if he was to do well at Bloomfield Weiss, and he did want to do well, then he would have to ignore that kind of thinking. Anyway, he didn't want to argue with her. 'What do you do? You live in Washington, don't you?'

'I'm at graduate school at Georgetown. Studying medieval European history. And before you say it, I know that's not going to save the Third World, either.'

'You like it, though?'

'It's fascinating. It truly is. But it's one of those infuriating situations: the more I read about it, the less I feel I understand it. We can try to know the world as it was a thousand years ago, but we'll never quite manage to understand it completely.'

Megan told Chris all about Charlemagne and his court of scholars and sycophants, and he listened. He had studied history himself, but had avoided the Middle Ages as too alien to the world he understood. Megan made it sound real. And Chris just liked to talk to her.

As they approached the mouth of the bay, Eric came up again

to take over. He warned everyone that it would get a bit choppy once they were out in the exposed water of the Sound, and it did. The aftermath of the previous night's storm still disturbed the sea. Eric opened the throttles and the boat speeded up, heading for the lights of Connecticut on the other side of the Sound, lurching up and down in response to the power of the engines and the movement of the waves.

It was now dark, but there were lights in all directions: white, red, green, flashing, constant, moving, still, solitary and in groups. Eric could obviously make sense of them all. The moon was up, three-quarters full, transforming the dull grey of the sea to silver and leaving the shoreline in black silhouette. The odd cloud drifted across, causing a cloak of a deeper darkness to descend fleetingly over the water.

Chris climbed down the steps to the cockpit, where the others were all quite drunk. While he had only got through a single beer since they had set off, Lenka, Duncan, Ian and Alex had downed several margaritas. Although there was plenty of laughter in the air, Chris could feel the tension. It was too loud, the insults that were traded were too direct, there was an hysterical edge to it.

It didn't take long before it all boiled over.

Inevitably, it was a squabble between Lenka and Duncan that did it. Duncan was looking around him into the darkness. 'This reminds me a little of Cape Cod, don't you think, Lenka?'

'Don't be ridiculous,' she said, her voice slurred. 'It's nothing like Cape Cod.'

'Yes, it is,' said Duncan. 'It's just like it.'

'But it's dark, Duncan. You can't see anything. And there aren't really any beaches. And there are all these giant mansions everywhere. Even the sea looks different.'

'No, no it doesn't. Remember that place in Chatham we stayed in? That B&B where we lay in bed all Sunday morning just looking out of the window at the sea? You can't pretend you don't remember that. You were there, Lenka.'

Lenka exploded. 'Will you shut up!' she shouted. 'It's over.

Don't you get it, Duncan? It's over. You can't keep talking about it as though we're still together.'

'But we had a great time that weekend. You can't wipe that from your memory.'

'I can and I will!' said Lenka, a touch of cruelty in her voice.

Duncan just looked at her. Then he grabbed a bottle of beer and crept round the bridge to the foredeck.

'Careful, Duncan!' shouted Eric from above. The boat was bucketing around in the waves, and it would have been easy for Duncan to lose his footing.

Ian, Chris, Alex and Lenka all sat in awkward silence in the cockpit. Lenka had gone too far. She probably knew that, but she was defying any of them to say so.

After a minute or so, Chris grabbed a couple of bottles. 'I'll take these up for Eric and Megan,' he said.

'I'll come up with you,' said Ian.

They all crowded on to the bridge. Duncan was sitting on the foredeck in front of them, drinking his beer, staring at the lights of Connecticut, which were getting closer.

'Duncan and Lenka have a fight?' asked Eric.

'Yes,' said Chris.

'I could see it coming.'

'You shouldn't have invited him,' said Ian. 'He was bound to cause trouble.'

'We had to,' said Eric. 'We couldn't leave him out.'

'Besides,' Chris added. 'It was Lenka who was out of order there. She's pissed.'

'So is Alex,' said Ian. 'What's up with him, anyway? He's been moody ever since the exam.'

'I don't know,' said Eric. 'His mom, maybe.'

'Or his job,' said Chris. 'Does he know why he wasn't assigned anything? He did well enough in the exam and I thought the mortgage guys were looking out for him. Do you know why, Eric? Have they just forgotten about him?'

Eric shrugged. 'He doesn't know what's going on. His

mother's not doing very well. I guess it's all finally gotten to him.'

'Look,' said Ian, in an urgent whisper. He was pointing down into the cockpit behind them. Lenka and Alex were locked in a deep alcoholic embrace.

'Oh, shit,' said Chris.

They all turned towards Duncan. He had stood up, and was making his way unsteadily aft. He paused, and tossed the empty beer bottle into the sea. He couldn't yet see what was happening in the cockpit; the bridge was in the way.

'Lenka!' shouted Chris.

Lenka didn't look up, but just raised a single finger.

Chris turned to Duncan. 'Duncan! Wait!'

Duncan looked up and wobbled as a wave hit the boat, almost falling in. 'I need another beer!' he growled, and continued on his way. Then he saw Lenka and Alex. 'Hey!' he shouted and scrambled down into the cockpit. 'Hey!'

He grabbed Lenka's shoulder and pulled her back, away from Alex.

'Don't touch me!' she cried, pushing him in the chest.

'What the fuck do you think you're doing?' Duncan shouted, pushing her back.

'Leave her alone,' said Alex straightening up. He shoved Duncan away from Lenka.

Duncan took a step back and swung. Alex was too drunk and too slow to react. The blow caught him cleanly on the chin. Alex staggered. Duncan hit him again. This time Alex went crashing back against the railing, just as the boat pitched on a wave. He tipped backwards and disappeared over the side.

Chris found it difficult to piece together exactly what happened next. He could remember Lenka screaming, Duncan staring open-mouthed at the point where Alex had been standing, Eric bounding down from the bridge and diving over the side of the boat.

Then Ian tumbled down after him and threw his own shoes

off. 'Don't!' cried Megan as he, too, jumped into the water. The boat was still speeding forward through the waves. Megan, who had been at the wheel, was slow to react, but now cut the throttle. A cloud passed over the moon. Chris could just make out Ian splashing in the water, but there was no sign of the other two.

'Oh, Jesus,' said Duncan, as he struggled to take his own shoes off.

'Stop him!' shouted Megan. 'For God's sake Chris, keep him in the boat!'

Lenka was screaming at Duncan in a mixture of Czech and English. Chris jumped down into the cockpit to try to catch him, but he was too late. 'I've got to get him. I've got to get him out,' mumbled Duncan, as he went over the side.

Lenka threw herself into Chris's arms, sobbing hysterically. He tried to push her to one side, but she wouldn't let go of him. So he slapped her hard across the face. She looked at him in shock, and he pushed her down on to a seat in the cockpit.

Megan was turning the boat around. 'Chris! Come up here!'

Chris scrambled up to the bridge, but even there, several feet higher up, he couldn't see any of them. Both he and Megan scanned the dark churning water in front of them. Out here, in the middle of the Sound, the wind was stronger. Tufts of spume flashed off the crests of waves, as though a hundred tiny swimmers surrounded the boat. With the moon behind a cloud, it was suddenly very dark. They seemed to be about half way between Long Island and Connecticut, and although they were surrounded by the lights of boats, none was close enough to help.

Megan held the throttle right back and motored slowly back to where she thought they had been when Alex had fallen in. But with the turn, and the wind, and the current, it was difficult to be sure exactly where that was. There were four of them in the water, and Chris and Megan couldn't see a single one.

'There!' said Chris. 'Over to the right!'

It was Duncan, splashing clumsily. Megan steered the boat over towards him. Chris leapt down to the cockpit and grabbed the lifebelt. Duncan had seen them and was waving. It was quite difficult to manoeuvre close to him, and it was a precious minute or so before Chris had tossed the belt to him and he had grabbed it. Chris pulled hard, dragging him through the water, and hauled him in. He left him, cold and gasping, in the bottom of the boat, and dashed up to the bridge to look for the others.

'I think there's someone over there,' said Megan, and she pushed the throttle forward, accelerating towards something bobbing in the water.

It was Eric. Within five minutes, he too was in the bottom of the boat, panting and shivering.

'Did you find him?' he asked, between breaths.

'No,' said Chris. 'Ian jumped in, too. We've got to find both of them.'

By this time, Lenka had got a grip on herself, and she was up with Megan on the bridge. Chris and Eric joined them. They drove the boat around in ever-increasing circles from the point where they had picked up Eric.

'Is Ian a good swimmer?' asked Megan.

'I think so,' said Chris. He remembered Ian used to go to a pool after work in London sometimes. 'What about Alex?'

'No idea,' said Eric.

'Did you see him?' Chris asked.

Eric was still gasping for breath, but shook his head. His teeth were chattering. 'Jesus, it's cold in there.'

The circles became wider, until Chris wasn't sure they were still anywhere near where Alex had fallen in.

'The coastguard!' exclaimed Megan. 'Shouldn't we call the coastguard?'

'Haven't you done that yet?' asked Eric.

'No,' Megan stammered. 'I didn't think of it.'

'Channel sixteen,' said Eric. 'Here, I'll do it.' He grabbed the mike for the radio that was just by the wheel and put out a

Mayday call. He looked around him. 'There's nothing else near to us,' he said.

'How long will they be?'

'I don't know. Ten minutes? Half an hour? No idea.'

'There!' shouted Lenka, pointing ahead and slightly to the right of the boat.

Chris peered into the gloom, and could just see an arm waving. Megan steered towards it. Just as they approached, the cloud at last drifted away from the moon. It was Ian. He was moving feebly, but still floating. They tossed the belt towards him, and he barely had the strength left to swim the few yards to grab it. Chris and Lenka hauled him into the boat. He was exhausted.

'I saw you pick up Eric,' he mumbled. 'And I tried to wave and shout. But you didn't see me.'

'We've got you now,' said Chris.

They continued the search with increasing desperation. There was no sign of Alex. About ten minutes after Eric's Mayday call, a fast police boat sped towards them. After quickly ascertaining that someone was still in the water, the police told Megan to take the boat back to shore so that she could get the others warm and dry. Megan argued that they should stay and continue the search, but police insisted. They said an ambulance would be waiting for them at Oyster Bay.

Ian and Eric changed into their dry suits, which were still below. Duncan refused. They all huddled together on the bridge in silence, as the boat hurtled back to shore, with Megan at the helm. Now that the frantic activity had finished, the same thought bore in on all of them. Alex was gone.

Duncan was slumped in a damp crumpled heap on the floor of the bridge. Lenka had her head in her hands next to him. Ian looked exhausted, staring vacantly into space. Chris felt stunned, in shock, unable to believe what he had seen over the previous half hour. It had all been a dreadful mistake. It must be possible to get Alex back, it simply must. Now that the coastguard were there, the authorities, the adults, they'd find him. Chris couldn't quite believe that he was an adult, that this wasn't a children's game, that he had witnessed one man knock another into the sea, and that that other, his friend, was probably now dead.

'They're going to ask us how Alex fell in,' said Eric.

'I'll tell them,' sobbed Duncan. 'I'll tell them I hit him.'

'No, it was my fault,' said Lenka. 'I made you do it. I wanted you to get angry with me. With him.'

Duncan shook his head. 'I killed him,' said Duncan. 'I killed him.'

'They still might find him,' said Chris, feebly. But no one believed that. Even Chris didn't even believe that.

'This could be very serious for Duncan,' said Eric.

'I know it could,' said Duncan. 'I deserve it.'

'I don't think you do,' said Eric. 'You were provoked. You didn't mean to kill him.'

'I said it was my fault!' said Lenka. 'And I'll tell them that.'

Chris saw what Eric was thinking. 'There's no need for anyone to get into trouble. We all know it was an accident. All we need to say was that Alex was drunk and he fell in.'

'But I punched him,' said Duncan.

'You know that and I know that,' said Chris. 'But we also know you didn't mean to kill him. For whatever reason, you were provoked. But if we tell the police, they might arrest you for manslaughter, or murder or something.'

'He could be charged with second degree murder, I think,' said Eric. 'Whatever the charge, it would be serious.'

'I can't believe you can talk like this,' Duncan said. 'Alex is dead! Don't you understand that? Alex is dead.'

Lenka had stopped crying. She moved closer to Duncan. 'Alex might be dead. But Chris and Eric are right. This could ruin your whole life.' She touched his arm. 'I don't want to be responsible for that, too.'

They were silent, crouched together in the crowded bridge.

Eric spoke. 'What do you say? We have to decide in the next couple of minutes. Chris?'

'I say it was an accident. Alex was on the foredeck, he came back for another beer, he slipped and fell in.'

'Lenka?'

'I think so, too.'

'Duncan? It's your life.'

'It was Alex's life.'

'Yes, but it's yours we're talking about now.'

He bit his lip and nodded. 'OK.'

'Ian?'

Ian was still in a trance. He didn't move, just stared up at the sky.

'Ian? If we're going to use this story, we all need to go along with it.'

Ian's stare snapped to Eric. Chris suddenly wondered how selfish Ian was. Would he risk lying to the police to help Duncan? It looked as though this was something Ian was trying to decide for himself. Eventually he nodded. 'All right.'

'We're all agreed, then.'

'No, we're not.'

It was Megan.

Eric turned to her in surprise. 'Do you have a problem?'

'Sure, I have a problem. We should tell them the truth.'

'But you don't think Duncan pushed Alex in on purpose?'

'No. But that's not up to me to decide. That's up to the police.'

The boat was approaching Oyster Bay. They could see the flashing lights of at least two vehicles waiting at the waterfront.

Eric spoke to Megan softly, as she cut back the throttle. 'I know you hate to lie. I can't force you to lie. But this is a friend of mine. Can you do this for me?'

They all watched her. It was clear in Chris's mind that it was best to claim that Alex had fallen in by accident. He didn't like to lie to the police, but there was nothing to be gained by telling the truth apart from throwing Duncan into the jaws of the American criminal justice system. The result would be impossible to predict. As it was, he knew Duncan would suffer for the rest of his life for what had happened. Lenka probably would, too. Chris respected Megan for taking the honest line, but he hoped she would change her mind. As Eric had said, Duncan was their friend.

Megan watched Eric, took a deep breath, and nodded. 'OK. But I'm not making anything up. I'll just say I didn't see any of it.'

'That will do fine,' said Eric. 'Now, let me steer the boat into the dock.'

The first blow had hurt Alex. The second damaged something in his brain, some mechanism of the nervous system that kept him upright and balanced. He felt his legs buckling underneath him, as he was forced back by the power of Duncan's punch. He felt his thighs touch the railing, and he tried to lean forward, but whether because he was drunk or because the boat was lurching at the most impossible of angles, he couldn't manage it. He felt his body spill backwards, and a second later he was underwater.

The water was very cold, and it seemed to squeeze the breath out of him, but somehow he managed to retain something in his lungs. It was dark, and the weight of his clothes was pulling him down, so he couldn't tell which way was up. He kicked his legs in panic and waved his arms. His lungs hurt, but somehow he managed to keep his mouth closed and the water out. Then, somehow, his face emerged into the open air and he took a large gulp, just as a wave broke over him. The seawater stung his lungs and made him choke. He kicked frantically with his legs and managed to keep his face above water long enough to cough and splutter the water clear of his airway. He took another gulp of air, and was submerged briefly under another wave.

He could just keep himself above the water if he worked hard with his arms and his legs. His clothes were so heavy, and it was so cold. He looked around him, and caught a glimpse of the bridge of the boat speeding away through the waves. He raised his arm to catch their attention, and promptly sank, swallowing more water. More choking.

He was in big trouble; he knew it. He wasn't a strong swimmer, and he knew he was drunk. The boat was impossible to see in the waves.

Alex didn't want to die. He was too young. He had so much more he wanted to do with his life. He wasn't going to die.

He struck out towards the direction he had last seen the boat. He tried to keep his strokes steady, but it was difficult. He was swimming too fast, tiring himself. Slow down. Swim slowly. As long as he was afloat, they would find him. Already they would have turned back. They'd be with him in a second.

He saw something dead ahead! Someone was swimming towards him. Alex raised a hand, shouted, pulled harder.

The swimmer came closer. Thank God, thought Alex. 'Here!' he shouted. 'I'm over here!'

He grabbed the arms as they reached out towards him. He tried to hold on to the sleeve. He wanted to cling on and never let go. He couldn't believe it! He was safe!

Suddenly he felt strong hands on his head, pushing him downwards. He was so surprised he failed to take a breath before he went under. What the hell was happening? He was too weak. He couldn't fight. He reached out to grab the swimmer, to pull him down with him, but already his lungs were filling with water. He could feel himself slipping into the darkness, into the embrace of the cold, cold sea.

Alex's body was found the following morning, dashed against some rocks a few miles further along the coast near Eatons Neck. Chris, Ian and Duncan were delayed in New York for a week to talk to the police and attend Alex's funeral. Questions were asked, lies were told. Then the Brits flew back to London, Eric and Lenka went on to their jobs at Bloomfield Weiss, and Megan returned to Washington.

But Alex was still dead. And the memory of how he had died would stay with all of them.

PART THREE

I

Chris returned to Carpathian's office in London determined to ensure that the firm survived. It would be difficult: Carpathian was much more Lenka's creation than his. He knew all the details: the administration of the funds, the individual securities in the portfolio, the accounts, the computer maintenance contracts, the people who managed the building and so on. But the vision was Lenka's. And so were the relationships with investors.

Lenka's murder had torn at Chris from many different directions. There was the horror of the act itself. Every time he closed his eyes, he saw her pale face beneath him on the street, felt the warmth and stickiness of her blood on his hands, watched her die. Then there was the guilt that he hadn't been able to stop it. In his waking moments, he replayed the attack again and again. If only he had reacted a second sooner to the sound of footsteps, if he had grabbed the arm half a second earlier. He fantasized about how he could have caught the attacker, thrown him to the ground and overpowered him. All pointless, he knew. If he had been quicker, he would probably have been stabbed too.

There was also straightforward grief at the loss of a friend, of someone who had helped him when he really needed it, of someone to whom he owed a debt, of a genuinely good person. He missed her laughter, her hoarse voice teasing him, the immediate rush of vitality that she brought to a room when she entered it.

And lastly, there was the worry about her company, their company. She had put so much of her energy into Carpathian over the last couple of years. It had become the most important thing in her life. He found, after the initial shock wore off, that Carpathian became the focus for all his feelings about her. He couldn't prevent her murder, he couldn't bring her back, but he could make sure that her creation survived.

First, he had to deal with the two remaining members of the team, Ollie and Tina. Ollie was a wreck. Chris and Lenka had picked him the previous year from the collapsing investment-banking arm of a British bank. He was twenty-four, very bright, but very shy. He seemed to live his life in permanent terror. Lenka, in her more wicked moments, had taken cruel advantage of this. But both she and Chris had liked him, and thought that he would mature into a real asset. In the meantime, he didn't cost much, and he made the coffee without complaining. Until that week, Ollie's worst nightmare was screwing up on the settlement of a trade and having Lenka scream at him. But this was so much worse than that. He seemed incapable of the simplest task; he was barely able to speak. When Chris talked to him about Lenka's death, he cried. Chris felt sorry for him, and in a strange way he was pleased that Lenka had meant something to Ollie, despite her occasional mocking of him. Chris let him collapse for five minutes, but only five minutes. Chris needed Ollie: he was bright, he was familiar with how Carpathian worked, there was no one else. Ollie was going to have to grow up. Immediately.

Tina was made of sterner stuff. She was a fiercely competent nineteen-year-old from Ongar who could fix the photocopier when Ollie broke it, and who would not stand any nonsense from pushy brokers. During the couple of days Chris had been away, it was she who had fielded calls from the market. She had little experience or knowledge of finance, but Chris had to rely on her too. She seemed to sense his determination to ensure Carpathian's survival, and to share it.

The four of them all sat in an open-plan room, with Lenka and Chris's desks overlooking the square outside. The entire office consisted of this room, a reception area, a boardroom, which doubled as a conference room, a kitchen, and an alcove for photocopier, fax machine and computer equipment. It wasn't large, but it had been nicely designed by an American friend of Lenka's, and it was airy, light and professional. The work hadn't cost much, except for a sweeping curved wall in the reception area, which sported a mural of swirling blues. Chris and Lenka had argued about it: Lenka loved it, but Chris had objected that it was too frivolous.

We'll keep it, Chris decided.

Chris gazed at Lenka's desk. Dramatic orange and purple flowers leaned out of a tall crystal vase. 'Birds of paradise' she had said they were called. She bought a new bunch of exotic flowers every week from the florist round the corner. Chris hesitated, and then dumped them into the bin. It seemed wrong that they should be so bright and alive, as though they hadn't heard the news. But he left the vase there, empty. Under her desk were four pairs of scuffed shoes. Lenka said she thought best in bare feet, and she would even occasionally meet visitors shoeless. It had taken Chris a couple of months to work out how she had accumulated so many pairs at work; surely even Lenka wouldn't go home in bare feet. The answer was, of course, that when the markets were going against her she would nip out to Bond Street and buy a new pair, which she promptly took off when she returned to the office.

But Chris couldn't afford to waste the day wallowing in thoughts of Lenka. He checked the prices of their portfolio. The market was weak. The Russian Finance Minister had resigned in the midst of a corruption scandal, and Eastern Europe was looking jittery. The big Eureka Telecom position was down five points. Chris would have to work out what Lenka had had in mind when she bought that. But that, too, could wait. He didn't intend to trade at all if he could avoid it over the next few days.

He spoke briefly on the phone to Ian Darwent. Ian was still at Bloomfield Weiss; he was now a European high-yield bond salesman. It was from him that Lenka had bought the Eureka Telecom bonds.

The conversation was awkward. Ian had turned his back on

Chris when Chris had left Bloomfield Weiss, and Chris couldn't quite bring himself to forgive him. Ian clearly felt just as uncomfortable with Chris, especially since Carpathian was now a purchaser of European high-yield bonds. So they had come to an unspoken agreement that Ian would speak to Lenka. That would have to change. Tina had told Ian about Lenka the day before, so for now they exchanged shallow commiserations about her death. Chris was sure Ian was genuinely sorry about what had happened, but he wasn't about to help Ian overcome his public-school reticence to discuss it. They rang off with a promise to talk about Eureka Telecom the next day.

Chris also spoke to Duncan at the sales desk of Honshu Bank, the second-tier Japanese firm where he now worked. Chris had called him from Prague to tell him about Lenka. The conversation had been brief; Duncan had been too stunned to say much of anything. Now he had lots of questions. Chris agreed to meet him in a pub after work to answer them.

The next task was to inform the investors in Carpathian's fund. There were eight of them and they had invested a total of fifty-five million euros. They were mostly based in the US, and they were nearly all Lenka's contacts from her days at Bloomfield Weiss in New York. The largest was Amalgamated Veterans Life, where Lenka's contact was none other than Rudy Moss. He was the only investor Chris really knew. The rest had met Chris, but it was Lenka they trusted. Still, he and Lenka had managed to provide them with a twenty-nine per cent return in the first nine months, so they ought to be happy.

Chris decided to send them all an e-mail, which would be ready for their opening, and follow it up with a phone call in the afternoon. They were difficult calls to make. Everyone was shocked by the news. Most of them seemed to think of Lenka as a personal friend. None of them mentioned rethinking their investment in Carpathian, much to Chris's relief. The only person he couldn't get through to was Rudy, who didn't return his call. Chris wasn't concerned by this: not returning calls was a macho thing with people like Rudy, and since they knew each other, he was the investor Chris was least worried about.

Ollie seemed to pull himself together as the day wore on. Chris had him talking to the market to find out if there was any risk of the latest Russian crisis spreading in a serious way to the Central European countries in which Carpathian invested. This was the kind of thing that was usually left to Lenka and Chris, but Ollie didn't do a bad job. Chris left the office at eight that evening feeling that perhaps they could keep Carpathian going after all.

By the time Chris arrived at Williams, Duncan had already sunk a pint or two. Williams was a dark pub in a small lane off Bishopsgate. They had first drunk there ten years before. It was close enough to Bloomfield Weiss to be convenient, but far enough away to avoid colleagues or bosses. So far, it had managed to escape the frantic redevelopment that had overtaken the area, and it had become the natural place for them to meet over the years.

Chris bought himself a pint and Duncan a refill and joined him at a small table in a corner. The pub was full of sleek men in their twenties unwinding. The pissed, overweight old farts in their baggy double-breasted suits who had inhabited the place ten years before had moved on. Chris sometimes wondered what they were doing now they had been elbowed out by his generation. Perhaps he'd find out himself in ten years' time.

'Thanks,' said Duncan, draining his previous pint and pushing it to one side to make room for the new one. 'Cheers,' he said without much conviction.

'Cheers.'

'I can't believe it,' said Duncan. 'I just can't believe it. What happened?'

'Someone came up behind her and slit her throat,' Chris said, as matter-of-factly as he could. He didn't like going into the details of that evening.

'And you were there?'

Chris nodded.

'Who was it?'

'I have no idea. I couldn't see much of him – he was wearing a dark jacket and a hat.'

'What about the Czech police? What do they think?'

'Well, their first guess was a mugger, a drug-addict desperate for cash. That's an increasing problem in Prague, apparently. But by the way it was done, they think the killer was a professional. He knew how to use a knife.'

'But who the hell would want to kill Lenka?'

Chris sighed. 'I have no idea.'

'I suppose it must have been some kind of mafia hit,' said Duncan. 'There's all kinds of organized crime in Eastern Europe, isn't there? Didn't I read about some American banker being shot in Russia last week?'

'I don't think the Czech Republic is quite as dangerous as Russia. Although the police say there is a Ukrainian-run mafia. That's their best guess at the moment. But I can't see how the kind of companies we invest in would be involved in that sort of stuff.'

'You never know,' said Duncan. 'I mean, it's all junk over there, isn't it?'

'It's technically junk, yes, but that just means that the bond issuers are rated below investment grade. It doesn't mean they're crooks.'

'Yeah, but you can't always be sure who's behind them, can you?'

Chris drank his beer thoughtfully. 'No, you can't,' he admitted. It was true that by the time Carpathian invested in a company it had been sanitized for Western consumption. In the anarchy that had marked the transition from communism to capitalism in all of these countries, there had been greed, corruption and violence. Even Lenka couldn't always get to the bottom of it. That was one of the reasons why she had been so keen to open offices in places like Prague. 'Maybe it *was* something to do with one of our investments.'

'It doesn't much matter, anyway,' said Duncan.

They sat in silence, thinking of Lenka.

'You know she was the only woman I really loved,' said Duncan.

'What about Pippa?' asked Chris. Pippa was Duncan's wife. They had been married three years and separated for six months.

Duncan shook his head. 'I liked Pippa. I was attracted to her. But I never loved her. That was the trouble.' He drank his beer. 'I've been thinking about Lenka a lot recently, ever since things went wrong with Pippa. Although I've never really been able to get Lenka out of my mind. I know we were only together for a few months, but those are the only months when I felt truly alive.'

Chris thought Duncan was exaggerating, but he didn't want to argue with him. 'She was a special person,' he said.

'She was, wasn't she?' said Duncan, smiling for the first time. 'She was so warm, so generous, so full of life. And she was the sexiest woman I've ever met. What she saw in me, I don't know. I'm not surprised she got rid of me.'

'It was a long time ago,' said Chris.

'But it seems like yesterday to me,' said Duncan. 'I can remember her touch, her smell, her laugh so clearly. You know that perfume she wears? What is it, Annick Goutal? There's a French woman in the office who wears it. Whenever I smell it, I think of her. It brings her back.' His eyes misted over, and he looked down. 'We had something back then. I'm sure she felt it as well as me. If we'd stayed together after the programme, my life would have been very different now.'

Once again, Chris wanted to argue, to point out Duncan's inconsistency. But he didn't. No doubt Duncan's life would have been different if he and Lenka had stayed together. And Duncan had not had a good last ten years.

Alex's death had nearly destroyed him. Duncan had been so

filled with guilt that it seemed to ooze out of every pore. It ruined what little self-confidence he had, it made him bitter, angry, full of self-pity. The naïve puppy-like innocence had disappeared. His fresh face became lined, jowls appeared under his chin and a small paunch emerged above his trousers. The winning smile disappeared completely. He lost most of the friends he had, driving them away with complaints and bitterness. Chris had stuck by him. It wasn't just that he felt loyalty to a friend. The cover-up of Alex's death made Chris feel not exactly guilt, but complicity. He couldn't abandon Duncan. Ian could, though, and had.

As expected after his performance on the programme, Duncan had been fired from Bloomfield Weiss on his return to London. Over the next few years, he limped from job to job as a Eurobond salesman at minor foreign banks in the city. The big bonuses of the boom years passed him by; he was one of the foot soldiers in the struggle to spread bonds to the four corners of the globe, a cheap body for a new boss of a revamped sales desk to call upon in his efforts to meet a headcount target. Duncan wasn't necessarily bad at his job. He was honest, he could be reasonably personable when he tried, and some customers bought bonds from him. But he had about him an air of defeat, so that when the reorganizations came, as they did on an almost annual basis at every bank in the City, his was always the first head to roll.

After several years of this, things started to look up. He met Pippa, a straightforward trading assistant a couple of years younger than him. They married. He held down the same job at an Arab bank for nearly four years. They bought a house in Wandsworth. He became good company over a pint again.

Then it all went wrong. Pippa threw him out, Chris was never clear exactly why. The Arab bank fired him, and it took him four months to find another job. And now Lenka.

Duncan was down and out again. This time, Chris wasn't sure he could face picking him up.

'How's the new job?' Chris asked, in an effort to change the subject.

'It's a job. They've given me a list of accounts to contact who never return my calls. Same old story. We've got no product to sell, and no customers to sell it to.'

'What's your boss like?'

'He's a decent enough bloke. Ex-Harrison Brothers originally, although he's been around since then. I'm not complaining. They pay me.'

'That's good,' said Chris lamely.

Duncan's eyes flicked up to him. 'There's something I wanted to ask your opinion on.'

'Oh, yes?'

'One of my Arab clients wants to invest in some European high yield. He doesn't know anything about it, and all the big investment banks assure him that their deals are the best and the competition's are all crap. We haven't got anything we could give him, but I'd like to help him out. You couldn't give me some ideas could you?'

'Lenka was the expert on high yield, but I've picked up a little bit,' said Chris. 'I can try. It'll all be Eastern European stuff, though.'

'Go on then,' said Duncan.

Although he was slightly irritated to have his brains picked for free, it was a relief for Chris to talk about something other than Duncan's misery. He listed four issues that he and Lenka liked. Duncan dutifully jotted them down on the back of one of his business cards.

'What about Eureka Telecom?' he asked, when Chris had finished. 'My client said that was strongly recommended. Very cheap, he was told.'

Chris grimaced. 'I'm not at all sure about that one. We own some, but I fear it might be a Bloomfield Weiss special. I'd say it's better to start off with the expensive stuff the brokers want to buy. Avoid the cheap stuff they're desperate to sell.'

Duncan smiled. 'Sounds good advice. So Eureka Telecom is one of Ian's, then?'

Chris nodded. 'Yes. I'm going to talk to him about it tomorrow.'

'Jerk,' muttered Duncan.

Chris shrugged and looked around the gloomy pub. The three of them had had many a long evening in there, many years before. 'It's a pity,' he said.

'You're getting sentimental,' said Duncan. 'Ian Darwent has always looked after himself. He could be perfectly charming when he thought we might be useful, but as soon as he decided we were no good to him any more, he couldn't be bothered to give us the time of day.'

Chris sighed. 'Perhaps you're right.'

It was sad. Ten years ago the six of them had seemed to have such a bright future. They were going to be the humane investment bankers of the twenty-first century. But it hadn't quite worked like that. Duncan was a wash-out. Chris had lasted longer, but he had been fired from Bloomfield Weiss as well, and more spectacularly. Ian hadn't really fulfilled his potential, and, as Duncan said, he was a jerk. Alex, and now Lenka, were dead. Only Eric was doing well, in some high-powered corporate finance job at Bloomfield Weiss in New York.

Chris shook his head and glanced at his empty glass. 'Your round.'

2

Chris could tell it was bad news just by looking at Tina's face, and the slight tremble with which she held the fax. His heart sank. He had had enough bad news, surely.

She passed it to him wordlessly, and he laid it on the desk in front of him.

To: Chris Szczypiorski, Carpathian Fund Managers
From: Rudy Moss, Vice President, Amalgamated Veterans Life

Subject: Investment in The Carpathian Fund

I am writing to inform you that Amalgamated Veterans Life hereby gives 30 days' notice of its intention to redeem its €10 million investment in The Carpathian Fund.

   With best wishes

   Rudy Moss, Vice President

Chris exploded. 'With best wishes! Jesus Christ! No mention of Lenka. Nothing about how sorry he is to hear of her death, about how he wants to support us in this difficult time.'

Tina shook her head. 'Wanker, innee?'

'Yes, Tina, he is.' Chris grabbed at the phone, ready to scream at Rudy.

'Tell you what, Chris,' said Tina as Chris jabbed out his number.

'Yes?' said Chris, putting the receiver to his ear.

'Why don't you ring him in five minutes, eh?'

Chris heard Rudy's voice at the other end of the line. He glanced at Tina. She was right. Yelling at Rudy was not the best way to get him to keep his money in the fund. He replaced the receiver, and gave her a quick smile. 'Thank you.'

Tina left him alone. Chris stood up and looked out of the window at the neat square below. Despite the cold, there were several well-wrapped office workers finishing late lunches on the benches, watched by clusters of rat-grey pigeons.

This was serious. Ten million euros was almost twenty per cent of the fund. What was worse was the signal that Rudy's move would give to the other investors. The rest had held steady, waiting to see how Chris coped. To some extent, all investors, even the biggest, are like sheep. The easiest decision, the lowest risk, is always to do what everyone else is doing. Yesterday, everyone was sticking with Carpathian. Tomorrow?

Why had Rudy decided to redeem? He knew Chris. They had been on the programme together, where Chris had performed reasonably well. Chris remembered disliking Rudy, but he couldn't remember falling out with him. He took some deep breaths, counted to ten, and dialled Rudy's number again.

'Rudy Moss.'

'Rudy, it's Chris from Carpathian.' Chris used his surname as little as possible. It just caused confusion.

'Oh, hi, Chris,' said Rudy neutrally.

'I received your fax.'

'Uh-huh.'

'And, frankly, I was a little surprised. All our other investors have decided to stick with us, and I had expected Amalgamated Veterans to do the same.'

There was a pause at the other end of the line. 'Well, Chris, I'd like to stay with you, but you must understand this is quite a material change in the management of the fund we're talking about here. Depth of management is always important to us. We thought just the two of you was a little thin, but now it's only you . . . I'm afraid we just can't live with that.'

Be reasonable, Chris told himself. Be calm. Find out what's really bugging him.

'I can understand your concerns, and I respect them. In fact, I'm planning to find another experienced investment partner as soon as I can.' He hadn't been, but he was now. Anything to keep Amalgamated Veterans in the fund. 'But I can assure you the fund will be perfectly safe in my hands. We're fully invested. The market looks a little weak in the short term, but we're confident it will recover. We'll make you good money, Rudy, I can assure you of that.'

'We?' There was the slightest of sneers in Rudy's voice that raised Chris's hackles immediately.

'Yes, myself and my colleagues.'

'Who are?'

'I have two assistants here with me.'

'But it's basically just you running things?'

'Yes, it is,' admitted Chris. 'But I'll find someone to join me shortly.'

'I know your record,' said Rudy, an unpleasant tinge creeping into his voice.

'What do you mean?' Chris snapped.

'I mean, I know your history.'

'Are you talking about when I left Bloomfield Weiss?'

'Yes, I am.'

Chris was silent.

'I figure it's best to be straight with you,' said Rudy. 'That way we know where we stand.'

'You know it wasn't me who was responsible for that loss.'

'If you say so. I wasn't there.'

'Damn right you weren't there!' Chris snapped, and then instantly regretted it. He had to keep his cool. 'Lenka knew I wasn't responsible. She trusted me.'

'Lenka was a smart woman. I don't mind telling you it was she I was backing when we put money in Carpathian. Now she's gone . . .'

Chris took a deep breath. 'Is there any way I can persuade you to change your mind?'

'I don't think so.'

'What if I came to see you in Hartford?'

'That won't be necessary.'

Chris came to a decision. 'I'm coming to Hartford. We can discuss this further then.'

'I said, I don't think that will be necessary,' said Rudy with impatience.

'Look, Rudy. You taking your money out of the fund is what you would call a "material change" for me, and it's a material change I can do without. You owe me an hour so we can discuss it.'

Rudy paused. 'All right. If you insist.'

'I do insist. I'll see you next Thursday. Shall we say two o'clock?'

'I'm busy all next week.'

'What about Friday?'

'I said I'm busy all week. I'm in California Wednesday through Friday.'

'OK, what about the following Monday? I'll be there at nine o'clock.'

'I can't make nine o'clock. We have a morning meeting.'

'Ten? Come on Rudy, I'm going to your offices and there's nothing you can do to stop me.'

Rudy sighed. 'OK, ten thirty.'

'See you then,' said Chris and rang off. 'Bastard,' he muttered.

The worst thing was that not once in the whole conversation had Rudy shown the slightest regret that Lenka had been killed. Not once.

He put on his jacket and grabbed his coat from the stand. 'I'm going for a walk,' he told Tina and left the building.

He crossed Oxford Street, and soon found himself striding up the broad avenue of Portland Place. The wind cut damp and cold through his clothes. Although there was no snow on the London streets, it felt colder than Prague.

He couldn't believe that the Bloomfield Weiss cock-up had

come back to haunt him again. Why couldn't the world just forget it? He had tried to obliterate it from his mind, with limited success. Now he realized it would never go away. Someone somewhere would always remember what had happened and use it to undermine him.

The injustice of the whole affair once again rose up inside him, warming his body with anger. He now realized the attraction of litigation. Despite its huge cost and unpredictability, it provided a judge for you to plea to, a chance that your version of events could be publicly upheld. He had considered suing, even spent a few hundred quid discussing it with a lawyer, but his chances of a clear victory were small, while his chances of running up large legal bills were almost a certainty. A bad trade. Now he wished he had done it.

He had become a good trader at Bloomfield Weiss. Traders come in two sizes: the gamblers and the percentage players. The gamblers like to take big risks, with big payoffs. The best of them can make stunning profits, but all of them are capable of making big losses too. The percentage players like to take smaller risks, which they can understand and control. They tend to make small but frequent profits. Chris was one of the latter types. He made profits month in and month out, he rarely had a negative month. It did wonders for the desk's P&L and for the budget. Good old Chris could always be relied on to lob in a few hundred thou to the bottom-line.

The bosses loved it. His immediate boss, a wiry, hyperactive American named Herbie Exler, was a gambler. He encouraged Chris to do his trades in larger and larger size. The logic was sound. If Chris could make two hundred thousand dollars on a hundred million dollar position, why not give him five hundred million, or a billion? With trepidation, Chris increased the size of his trades. And it worked.

Chris traded European government bonds. He did things like buying a hundred million Deutschmarks of German government bonds and selling an equivalent number of French governments, betting that the relationship between the two would change. Chris had an excellent feel for how the relationships between the European markets moved, and he understood the way the weight of money of the major global investors, most of whom were Bloomfield Weiss's clients, sloshed from one country to another.

As Economic and Monetary Union approached, one trade dominated all others. It was known as 'the convergence trade'. The theory was simple, too simple. The idea was that when the currencies of France, Italy, Spain, Portugal, Germany and the rest were all rolled into the euro, and when the interest rate for the whole euro currency zone was set by the European Central Bank, then the interest rates on these countries' government debt would be broadly similar. So if Italian government bonds yielded two per cent more than German bonds, you bought Italy and sold Germany, confident that you would have a nice capital gain on the euro's birthday, when Italian bond yields would fall to German levels, and Italian bond prices would rise.

It was a no-brainer. Chris did the trade in large size, and so did everyone else on the Street. And off the Street as well. In particular, a large hedge fund in Greenwich, Connecticut put the trade on. And it put it on in the biggest size imaginable. It borrowed many times its capital to buy literally billions of dollars' worth of European government bonds.

At first, all went well. Partly as a result of the weight of money, nice capital gains soon emerged, for Chris, for the hedge fund, for everybody. But then, while they were all off on their summer holidays, Russia defaulted on its debt, causing a tremor of fear to spread around the world's financial markets. This had no direct bearing on the chances of monetary union being disrupted, but it caused what the markets call 'a flight to quality'. Nervous investors switched into what they considered to be the safest investments. They bought German bonds. They didn't buy Italian, Spanish, Portuguese or even French bonds.

The unrealized capital gains became unrealized capital losses.

In theory, this shouldn't have been a problem: as the jitters subsided the old unstoppable move towards convergence would continue. But Chris was nervous. He wanted to take his loss, and buy in again when things had settled down. Now, Chris had a big position, and the loss would be several million dollars. Effectively he would be giving back all of his profits for the year. So he spoke to Herbie Exler first.

Herbie was furious. He had just told his own boss, Larry Stewart, that Chris's profits to date were in the bag, and that he could be relied upon for as much again in the remaining months of the year. Herbie's bonus depended on Chris meeting those figures. And the two-million-pound house that Mrs Exler had set her heart on in Kensington depended on that bonus.

Herbie suggested doubling up. Convergence was inevitable, profits were inevitable, doubling up would double these, and double the bonus. To Herbie, this was a no-brainer.

Chris's position was already huge. He wanted to sell, not buy. Herbie and Chris had a series of vigorous discussions, where Herbie accused Chris of being a wimp, and Chris sounded like one. Afterwards Chris asked himself over and over again why he had given in. At the time, there were good reasons. Herbie was Chris's boss. Although Chris was sure there was a chance that the trade could go against them, Herbie was undoubtedly correct that there was a chance the trade would work. But there was another reason that Chris caved in, and one that he couldn't forgive himself for. Despite his impressive track record as a trader, Chris still saw himself as the Polish upstart from Halifax, the boy who scraped into school and university and investment banking, the boy who was lucky just to be doing what he was doing. Herbie Exler was a streetwise New York bond trader, a Bloomfield Weiss man through and through, a king of the market. At the final moment, Chris's confidence defeated him. There was never any risk of that happening to Herbie. So they doubled up.

Things swiftly fell apart. While the rest of the Street were unanimous that the trade would come back their way, they had no choice but to cut their losses. Investment banks had spent hundreds of millions on computer systems that could tell their managements instantaneously what unrealized losses their traders were sitting on, and as these losses grew, the word came down to the trading floors to sell.

So they sold. Of course, this drove prices further against Chris. And against the large Greenwich hedge fund. It had bet everything on this trade; it couldn't afford to quit. But the brokers that had fallen over themselves to lend money to it now fell over themselves to get their money back. So eventually the hedge fund had to sell.

But everyone else was selling. There were no buyers. The most liquid markets in the world, those for government bonds, dried up. There was a global crisis, which was only prevented from spinning completely out of control by the US Federal Reserve who encouraged a bail out of the hedge fund by the big international investment banks.

Those were terrible days for Chris. His losses had become astronomical, and there was absolutely nothing he could do about it. He couldn't have sold even if Herbie had let him; the market could never have absorbed the size of his positions. He was stuck with them.

Every day was like a nightmare, each worse than the last. Every evening he would check the unrealized loss before he went home. He would try not to think about the position overnight, but with no success. He couldn't concentrate on a book or a television programme for more than ten minutes without the horror of his losses encroaching. He tried getting drunk a couple of times, but that didn't work either. It just made the morning worse. He would arrive at his desk to see that while he had been asleep the market had added another few million to the already enormous negative figure on his position report.

It was the loss of control that he found hardest to deal with.

The market had gone against him before, but he had always been able to cut and start again. This was different. It was as though he was driving a fast car on a mountain road and had skidded on ice. The car was in a spin, the tyres wouldn't grip, and the cliff edge was coming nearer and nearer. Except that it was taking him days, not milliseconds, to reach it.

Chris tried to take it professionally. He kept a straight stony face from seven in the morning until eight at night. He struggled to produce a smile for anyone who cracked a joke, or even said hello. But there were few of those. Everyone knew what was happening. They all knew he was being killed. And they avoided him, as though his disastrous luck was contagious.

Herbie felt the pressure even worse than Chris. He spent most of the day locked in his office, literally staring at the screens in the hope that the little figures would move his way. He had some friends at the Greenwich hedge fund whom he called several times a day, and who consistently said that the trade would come back their way imminently. Herbie would tell Chris this at great length, along with Herbie's assessment of how smart these guys were. If Chris raised doubts about the position, Herbie would growl at him that it was a great trade, and he should believe in it. Any of the other traders who tried to talk to Herbie about anything else got nowhere. He was irascible and dangerous.

Chris couldn't work out why Bloomfield Weiss's management hadn't followed the other firms on the Street and ordered Herbie to cut the position. It was true that Bloomfield Weiss had the reputation for having bigger balls than anyone else. Chris assumed he must be living through the proof. Yet another mistake.

Then a piece appeared in the *Wall Street Journal* that Bloomfield Weiss was sitting on a loss of five hundred million dollars. As Chris read this early in the morning at his desk, he knew that it was inaccurate. His losses were actually six hundred and twelve million dollars. The phones were soon ringing from brokers, clients, journalists. The answers were all the same. No comment. No comment. No comment.

Herbie came in, paced around Chris for a few minutes, and then was hauled off to talk to his bosses. Chris spent a miserable couple of hours at his desk. There was nothing he could do. Nothing he could say. No comment.

Then at twelve o'clock he was summoned to see Simon Bibby, the head of the London office. With Bibby were Larry Stewart, the American head of fixed income in Europe, and Herbie. Needless to say, they all looked like men who had lost more than half a billion dollars.

Bibby was English, forty-five, and ruthless. Larry was usually friendly to Chris, but he didn't appear so now. And Herbie had a look in his eyes. A look that said to Chris: 'I'm going to screw you, and you're not going to escape, so don't even try.'

Bibby did the talking. He said that he had spoken to Sidney Stahl, the chairman, who had demanded immediate action to come clean and clear up the mess. Then Bibby asked Chris why he had misled them over the revaluation of his position. At first, Chris didn't understand. Then it became clear that Bibby had been told that the losses that were showing up on their reports weren't real, and were offset by understated profits on derivatives positions. This was incorrect, and Chris began to explain why. Herbie interrupted. He looked Chris straight in the eye and told him that he had been misled by Chris, and had therefore unwittingly misled his superiors.

Chris protested, but Herbie was implacable. He recalled conversations that never existed that buried Chris. Then, when Chris looked at the other two, he understood. Bibby was glaring at Chris as though he were a criminal, but Larry, whom Chris liked and trusted, was looking at his hands, at the table in front of him, anywhere but at Chris. One of the four people in that room would have to take the blame for what had happened. The other three had decided that it would be Chris. Believing Herbie's story was the easiest way to achieve this.

Chris protested for a further quarter of an hour, until the in-house lawyer came in with a two-page letter. Bibby told Chris that he was fired with immediate effect, but that he would receive six months' salary, and Bloomfield Weiss would not seek to prosecute, as long as he signed the letter. Chris read it through carefully. Under it, he promised not to discuss the disaster with the press or anyone else, and not to take legal action against Bloomfield Weiss. Bibby handed Chris a pen, and said that if he didn't sign the letter immediately, Bibby would be forced to call in the SFA, the City watchdogs.

Suddenly, Chris felt crushed. It was as though he had expected this moment ever since he had joined Bloomfield Weiss. He wasn't an investment banker and he had been found out. Like it or not, he had put the trade on. He had acquiesced to Herbie's demand that he double up. Of course he hadn't misled Herbie, or Bibby, or anyone else, but it was his word against Herbie's and he knew Herbie would win. Herbie was a ruthless street fighter. If there wasn't evidence against Chris, he would fabricate it. And Bibby and Larry would believe Herbie. They didn't want to believe the truth; they wanted to believe a lie, their careers depended on it. Chris now knew what he had long suspected: he wasn't cut out for investment banking. He had no business to be in the room at all. He signed.

Bloomfield Weiss didn't come right out and say that he had lost them six hundred million dollars. But they did say he had been dismissed. His name appeared in all the British press. Journalists wanted to interview him, his home phone rang constantly, people took photographs. He stood by the agreement he had signed; he didn't talk to any of them. But he was famous. Famous as the man who had dropped over half a billion.

Ironically, the trade did come right in the end, monetary union happened and the government bonds converged. Some people made a lot of money. But not Bloomfield Weiss. Under Sidney Stahl's insistence, they bared their chest, took their losses and moved on.

Chris tried to do the same. He called back the headhunters who had been calling him every week for a year. They didn't want to know. Nobody wanted to know. He couldn't get a job. He could probably have tried harder, but he didn't have it in him. He didn't want to be an investment banker anyway. So he gave up.

In time, Lenka pulled him out of it. They set up Carpathian together and everything went well, until suddenly, at the crucial moment, that loss came back to kick him in the balls again.

Except that this time, he wouldn't just take it. He owed Lenka that much, if not himself.

He straightened up and lengthened his stride as he made his way down Harley Street back towards the office. He would try to talk Rudy out of his decision. But if that didn't work, he would figure out a way to keeping going. He was determined to.

Back at the office, he examined the portfolio. The fund was set up so that there were two choices when an investor wanted to redeem: either find a new investor to take his place, or sell assets to raise the cash needed. Finding a new investor was out of the question without Lenka. She had the contacts, and it would be impossible for Chris to persuade someone he didn't know to invest ten million euros with him when half the management team had been murdered.

So he would have to sell some bonds. Which ones?

Although they only had fifty-five million euros of funds available to them, their portfolio was much bigger. They had borrowed money and used the mysteries of the repo market to build up much larger positions. In fact, most of the portfolio in volume was made up of a new convergence trade, which was managed by Chris. The theory was that most of the Central European countries would be admitted to the European Union. So Chris had bought the government bonds of countries like the Czech Republic, Poland, Estonia, Hungary and Slovenia. He dabbled in some of the second-tier countries as well. At first he had balked at putting himself in such a familiar position, but

Lenka had encouraged him, saying he was the best person she knew in the market to manage such a trade, and promising him that whenever he wanted to cut and run, she wouldn't get in his way. He had taken a deep breath and started buying.

The resignation of the Russian Finance Minister had shaken all these positions, but Chris was convinced of their fundamental strength, and wanted to hold on.

The rest of the portfolio was made up of high-yield bonds, otherwise known as junk. Lenka had learned about these in the United States, and the idea was that she would use her experience to analyse the small but growing number of junk bonds issued in Eastern Europe. By far the largest of these junk-bond positions was Eureka Telecom. It was also the position that was performing worst, and the one Chris trusted the least.

Eureka Telecom it would be, then.

It might take a while to sell the bonds, so Chris decided to start the process immediately. If he succeeded in persuading Rudy to maintain his investment in Carpathian, then Chris could always reinvest the money elsewhere. He called Ian.

'Where's Eureka Telecom trading?' he asked, dispensing with any small talk.

'I think we're making them ninety-five to ninety-seven,' Ian answered.

'Ninety-five! But Lenka bought them at par last week, didn't she?'

'I know,' said Ian sounding uncomfortable. 'But the market's spooked by this Russian news. And the latest subscriber numbers came out on Monday. They were, er, disappointing.'

'Bad news the week after the bond was issued!' said Chris. 'Wasn't that in the prospectus?'

'It was a complete surprise to everybody,' said Ian. 'That's why my trader has marked the bonds down.'

In theory, that meant that Bloomfield Weiss would be prepared to buy Chris's bonds at a price of ninety-five, and sell him more at a price of ninety-seven. Lenka had bought her twenty-five million bonds at a price of par, or a hundred. So, in theory, Chris could sell ten million of them for a five per cent loss, which was half a million euros. Not great, but not a total disaster. He had a bad feeling about this one. He wanted to get out straight away.

The trouble was, the junk bond market was illiquid. What this meant was that as soon as Chris said he wanted to sell the entire position, Bloomfield Weiss would drop their price. By how much, Chris would have to see.

'What would you pay me for ten?' asked Chris.

There was a pause on the phone. 'Ninety-five was only good for a million,' said Ian.

'OK, I understand,' said Chris. 'Now, where can I sell ten million?'

There was a long pause. Eventually Ian returned. 'My trader would like to work an order on that. Say at ninety-three?'

Chris wasn't having any of that. Bloomfield Weiss wanted to tout his bonds around the market at no risk to themselves to try to find a buyer. Chris wanted out, and he wanted out immediately.

'No, Ian. I want a bid for the ten million.'

'I think we'd prefer to work an order.'

'Ian, you sold us twenty-five million euros of this bond last week. You have to be willing to buy ten million back.'

Ian hesitated. 'Chris,' he said. 'You're not familiar with the way this market works. These aren't government bonds. The high-yield market is illiquid; everyone knows that. Let us work the order.'

'Don't patronize me, Ian. Ask your trader where he would buy ten million. Now.'

'But, Chris . . .'

'Ask him.'

'OK.'

Chris was left hanging on the phone for several minutes. Ian was right, Chris wasn't as familiar with the junk market as the government bond market, but he wasn't going to let Bloomfield Weiss take advantage of that. They sold Carpathian the bonds; they'd have to buy them back.

'Chris?' It was Ian. He sounded hesitant, nervous. Chris steeled himself.

'Yes?'

'If you want to sell the bonds on the wire, we'll pay seventy.'

'Seventy!' Chris almost screamed. 'That's absurd. How can you pretend the price is ninety-five when you'll only pay seventy?'

'We've nowhere to go with them, Chris. The market looks bad and the subscriber numbers spooked everyone. If we buy them from you, we're wearing them.'

Chris did the sums. At a price of seventy, the loss he would realize on the sale of ten million would be three million euros. The unrealized loss on the rest of the Eureka Telecom position would be another five. Basically, the value of Carpathian was eight million euros lower than it had been a week before.

'Listen,' Ian was whispering now. 'Don't sell them, Chris. Trust me. They're worth hanging on to.'

'Why?' Chris asked.

'Just trust me.'

Trust Ian! No way. Chris had a real problem, but trusting Ian wasn't the best way out of it. 'Send me the press release on the subscriber numbers. I need to look at this deal a bit more closely. We'll speak again tomorrow.'

Chris slammed down the phone and put his head in his hands. This was a problem. A big problem.

He spent the rest of the afternoon going through the information in Lenka's files on Eureka Telecom. It was a dog. Sure, it was an ambitious idea, to set up a mobile telephone network in Hungary, Poland, the Czech Republic and Slovakia, with the possibility of extending it to Romania and the Baltic States later. The networking agreements and licences were in place. But there was no cash, and precious few subscribers. Investment requirements over the next five years were huge. That was what the junk bond was for. But Eureka would get through the cash raised from that in eighteen months. Where the further money for investment would come from was a mystery.

Ian sent details of the subscriber information by e-mail. It was disappointing. For a company that was supposed to be entering a dramatic growth phase over the next few years, a five per cent increase in subscribers over a six-month period was pitiful. No wonder Bloomfield Weiss's trader was worried.

Chris put down the prospectus and stared at Lenka's empty desk. Why had she bought it? She was no fool. She could see this was a bad deal. He was surprised she had bought any, let alone twenty-five million, nearly half the value of the fund.

Oh, Lenka, Lenka. Chris felt a flash of anger. Not only had she gone and left him, but she'd left him with an enormous screw-up to deal with. He smashed his fist down on his desk with a crash that caused Ollie to look up in fright.

Chris put his head in his hands. Why was Lenka gone? How could such a horrible thing have happened to her? He wanted her back. Now.

'Are you all right?' said Ollie.

Chris looked up and forced a smile. 'Not really, but thank you.' He glanced back at the papers in front of him. 'Ollie?'

'Yes?'

'Lenka didn't tell you *why* she bought this Eureka Telecom deal, did she?'

'No. I asked her. She just said she had a good feeling about it.'

'You didn't hear her discussing it with Ian?'

'Not really. They did have a few conversations before the deal came out. He's been calling quite a lot recently, hasn't he? And then at the end of last week, Lenka said she didn't want to take any more of his calls. It was a bit embarrassing, really. I had to take messages for her.'

'Huh,' said Chris thoughtfully. 'Did she say why she didn't want to talk to him?'

'No. She was quite off-hand about it.'

Chris thought about that. Lenka being off-hand often meant that Lenka was angry. Angry because she had been sold a dog, perhaps.

'There is something else I've been meaning to mention to you, though. About Lenka.'

'Oh, yes? What is it?'

'Well, one day last week, when you were away, someone came round here to speak to her.'

'Uh-huh.' People always came round to speak to Lenka, or Chris for that matter.

'Yes. He wasn't a broker or anything like that. He didn't look like he worked in an office at all. Tall thin guy, in jeans. Big long coat. American accent.'

'Young?'

'Oh, no,' said Ollie. 'Old. Thirty-five, something like that.' Ollie saw the look on Chris's face. 'Well, not exactly old, but not young either. You know.'

'OK, OK, I know,' said Chris. 'What did they talk about?'

'No idea. Lenka took him into the boardroom and shut the door. They were in there about an hour. When he left, he looked angry. And she looked really upset. She went off to the loo for ages.'

'Interesting. Did Tina see this bloke?'

'No. She was out, I think. I remember I was the only one here, apart from Lenka of course.'

Pity, Chris thought. Tina would have been able to give him a much more accurate description of what had happened.

'And Lenka didn't say anything afterwards?'

'No. I tried to talk to her, to see if she was all right, but she told me to go away. So I went off and did some photo-copying.'

The photocopier was Ollie's equivalent of the gooseberry bushes. It was where he always liked to go when Lenka shouted at him.

'Can you be more precise about this guy? Hair colour, eyes, nose, face?'

Ollie screwed up his face, thinking. 'It's hard to remember. Eyes? Brown, I think. Although they could have been blue. Brown hair. Yes, definitely brown. Longish. Stubble – I don't think he'd shaved.'

'That's very helpful,' said Chris. 'But we've no idea who this man is.' He tapped his fingers on the desk. 'Can you remember what day it was?'

'Monday, I think. Maybe Tuesday.'

'Let's have a look.' Chris turned on Lenka's computer and opened it at her diary. There was only one entry that was not easily explainable. Against two o'clock on Tuesday 15 February was the word 'Marcus'. That was all, just 'Marcus'.

'Know who that might be?' Chris asked Ollie.

Ollie shrugged. 'There's a Marcus Neale at Harrison Brothers. But it definitely wasn't him.'

'I wonder who it was,' said Chris.

3

It was eight o'clock and Ollie and Tina had already gone, when Chris was disturbed by a loud buzz. The security guard had left at six; after that time, visitors had to use the buzzer out on the street.

'Who is it?'

He couldn't quite make out the reply, beyond identifying the voice as belonging to a woman, but he pressed the button to unlock the entrance to the building, and told whomever it was to come up to the fifth floor.

He opened the door to a young woman with long dark curly hair tied back behind the nape of her neck, blue eyes, freckles and a turned-up nose. She was dressed in jeans and was carrying two large bags. She looked familiar, but Chris couldn't place her.

'Chris?'

The voice was familiar as well. From a long time ago.

'Chris? It's Megan. Megan Brook. Eric's friend?'

'Oh, yes, I'm sorry. Of course.'

He recognized her now. She hadn't changed much. She looked older – perhaps twenty-five rather than eighteen, although he realized she must be closer to his own age of thirty-two. He didn't understand what she was doing there.

She marched into the reception area and dropped her bags. 'Very nice,' she said, nodding towards the swirling mural. 'So, where is she?'

Chris couldn't answer.

'Don't tell me she's not here! We agreed we'd meet here at seven thirty. I know I'm a bit late, but she could have waited.'

'No, she's not here.'

Megan heard the tone of his voice, saw his face. 'Oh, God,' she said. 'What's happened?'

'She . . . she's dead.' Chris said.

'No.' Megan slumped back into a chair. 'But I only spoke to her last week. When? What happened?'

'Monday. She was murdered. In Prague.'

'Murdered? Oh, how awful.' Megan's face reddened. Tears appeared in her eyes. She covered her face with her hands.

Chris didn't know what to do. He stood awkwardly in front of her for a few moments, and then touched her arm.

'I'm sorry,' said Megan, sniffing. She took a deep breath. 'It's just such a shock.'

'Yes, it is,' said Chris. 'For everyone.'

'How did it happen?'

'We were walking through an alley. Someone came up with a knife. It was very quick.'

'How horrible. Oh, my God.'

'You were meant to be meeting her now?' Chris asked.

'Yes. I'm supposed to be staying with her for a few days. I've just gotten in from Paris.'

She looked exhausted, slumped in the chair. Chris glanced down at her luggage. 'What are you going to do now?'

'I don't know. I guess I'll find a hotel.'

'Come back to my place,' said Chris. 'I have a spare room. You don't want to spend the evening tramping round looking for a place to stay.'

Megan hesitated, and then smiled. 'No. I guess I don't. Thanks.'

Chris locked up, and they took a taxi from outside the office to Chris's flat in Hampstead. Megan stared out of the window of the cab at the London streets.

Chris felt awkward. He wondered whether he had been right to invite her to stay with him. The offer had been honestly made, and Megan had accepted in the spirit it had been intended, but they hardly knew each other. Perhaps she was having second thoughts now, as she gazed blankly out of the window. Perhaps he should give her a way out: he could help her find a hotel that evening. Then he realized that would be even worse. He was being too English: an American would have had no hesitation in doing the hospitable thing.

The traffic was light, and they soon arrived at his flat. He carried her luggage to her room and she followed him into the kitchen.

'Wine?' he asked.

'I'd love some.'

He opened a bottle of Australian red and poured out two large glasses.

'Pasta OK for dinner?'

'You don't have to cook for me.'

'Are you hungry?'

Megan smiled and nodded.

'Well, then?'

'Pasta would be great. Thanks.'

Chris put a pan of water on to boil. Megan sipped her glass of wine and examined his flat.

'Nice place.'

'Thank you. You're lucky. The cleaner came today.'

'Did you do all this?'

'Yes. Or at least I paid for someone else to do it. It was a few years ago now.' Emboldened by his first big bonus at Bloomfield Weiss, Chris had spent a considerable sum on doing up the flat. Interior walls knocked down, blondwood floorboards laid, rooms remodelled, walls repainted. He had been very proud of it until the day he had been fired, since when it had become just a place to live. In fact, in the last year or so, he had become faintly embarrassed by it. It was taste that had been purchased: much more stylish than its owner.

'Where's that?' Megan asked, pointing to an eerie black and white photograph of factory chimneys clinging to an impossibly steep hillside.

'Halifax. Where I grew up.'

'Wow. Now I know what they mean by "dark satanic mills".'

'They're not satanic any more,' said Chris. 'They stopped working long ago. But I like them. They're dramatic in their own way.'

'Alex would have appreciated it.'

Chris smiled. 'Yes, he would. I thought of him when I bought it.'

She sat at his small kitchen table with her glass of wine.

'Sorry I didn't recognize you,' said Chris.

'It was ten years ago.'

'But you recognized me.'

'I was expecting you to be there.'

'Of course. Lenka didn't say anything to me about you coming to stay with her.'

'I only asked her last week. A grant just came through for me to study for my dissertation at Cambridge for six months. I thought I'd take a week's vacation first: spend a few days in Paris and then stay with her in London.'

Chris took scissors to plastic packaging. 'This won't be the greatest home-cooked meal you've ever tasted,' he said.

'I don't care,' Megan replied. 'I'm starving.'

'Good. I'd forgotten that you and Lenka were friends. But, come to think of it, didn't you go on holiday together a couple of years ago?'

'That's right. To Brazil. That was some vacation.'

'I can imagine a vacation with Lenka would be fun.'

'It was.' Megan sighed. 'We haven't seen each other much since then. The last time was in Chicago about six months ago. I'm doing my PhD at the University of Chicago. She was seeing some investors in her fund. We met at a Thai restaurant downtown. It was only for a couple of hours . . .' She tailed off, remembering.

'How did you two become friends? I didn't realize you knew each other on the programme.'

'It was afterwards. After what happened with Alex. As you know, Lenka felt responsible. She felt guilty about leading Alex on. All she wanted was for Duncan to give up on her. She never thought Alex would be hurt, let alone killed. She needed to talk to someone. You guys had all gone back to England, so that left Eric and me.'

'She must have been a mess.'

'She was.' Megan paused, remembering. 'Then, after George-town, I went to Columbia for a couple of years. I had fixed that up so that I could be with Eric in New York, but we split up a month before I got there. Lenka was still working on Wall Street and we saw quite a lot of each other. We got on well. We were very different, but we were good for each other.'

'I know what you mean.'

'She said she thought you and she would make a good team,' Megan said.

'We did, I think. We had different strengths and weaknesses. But we respected each other. She was right. A good team.'

'Lenka always liked to play the extrovert. But she seemed to prefer being around quieter people. Perhaps so she would shine next to them.'

'She was quite a serious person in her own way, too,' said Chris.

'You knew her well,' said Megan.

'So did you, by the sound of it,' said Chris, with a smile.

Chris served the pasta and the sauce, poured some more wine, and they sat down.

'So, are you still studying medieval history?' he asked.

'Yes,' said Megan. 'You studied history, didn't you? I can remember boring you about it on the boat.'

'You have a good memory,' said Chris. 'But I don't. I doubt if I can remember much more than the date of the Battle of Hastings.'

'Well, my field was the Carolingian Renaissance. I spent some time in France a few years ago. But I'm writing my dissertation on the effect that had on monastic reform in tenth-century England. That's why I'm going to Cambridge.'

That was all medieval gobbledygook to Chris. 'Are you still enjoying it?' he asked.

'I have good days and bad days. Teaching I like, if the students are interested. And I'm still fascinated by the history itself. But I've got my dissertation to finish before I can get my PhD. There's so much pressure to be original, you wind up having to study some tiny subject simply because it's so obscure no one else can be bothered to write about it.'

'No job's perfect,' said Chris.

'At least in this six months at Cambridge I'll get some time to do some proper thinking. I've been looking forward to that.'

Megan was tucking into the pasta with gusto. She was hungry. When they had finished, Chris offered coffee, or more wine. Megan went for the wine, and Chris opened another bottle.

'I don't usually drink this much,' she said. 'But I need it.'

'I know what you mean,' said Chris. As they began the second bottle, he felt some of the pressure of the last few days lifting off him. It was cheap solace, and he would pay for it the next day, but he needed it too.

'She was a special woman,' said Megan.

'She was,' said Chris. He took a gulp of wine. 'She saved me.'

'Saved you?'

Chris nodded.

'What do you mean?'

Chris stared into the deep red liquid before answering. It was painful bringing back what had happened, but he wanted to do it. He wanted to talk about Lenka.

'Did you know I was fired from Bloomfield Weiss?'

'No.'

'You obviously don't read the financial sections of the newspapers.'

'I have much better things to do with my time.'

Chris smiled. It was true. There were millions of people who had never heard of him, or had never even heard of Bloomfield Weiss. The trouble was, they were never the ones he was asking for a job.

'Well, I was fired for losing six hundred million dollars.'

Megan blinked. 'Wow.'

'Yes. Precisely. Wow. It was written up in all the papers. It wasn't my fault, but no one believed me.'

'I believe you.'

Chris smiled. 'Thanks. I wish I'd known you then, or people like you. But I didn't. Everyone I knew assumed it was my fault.' He took a deep breath. 'I tried to get another job as a trader. I was good at it, and I thought everyone realized that. But they didn't. Then, two weeks after I'd been fired, Tamara left me. Do you remember Tamara?'

Megan shook her head.

'You met her once. At Eric's party. Actually, it's probably a good thing you don't remember her. Anyway, at the time I thought she was wonderful. I thought I was lucky to be going out with her. When she rejected me, after the City had rejected me, I thought I was just a fraud. I gave up.' Chris glanced at Megan to see if she was listening. She was. He had thought he was going to talk about Lenka, but now he found he was talking about himself. He also found he wanted to.

'I moped around here for a few weeks, not seeing anyone, except perhaps Duncan, reading the newspapers, watching TV, sleeping. I slept a lot. Then I decided I'd travel the world. I had quite a lot of money saved, and I thought I just had to get away. So I bought a one-way ticket to India.

'I thought I'd always wanted to travel to India, although I'd never quite thought through exactly why. I hoped that going to a strange country might help me to find myself. If I wasn't really a young successful investment banker, what was I?

'India was a total disaster. It's a stupid place to go to when you're alone and miserable. I barely spoke to anyone the whole time I was there. I saw the Taj Mahal on a cloudy day, and all I can remember is how crowded it was and how difficult it was to get a bottle of mineral water. I got stuck in some godforsaken town in Rajasthan where it seemed to be impossible to get a seat on the train out no matter how long I stood in a queue. I got sick. I think I can remember the Coke that did it. It was in a place called Jaipur. You weren't supposed to drink anything with ice in it, because it could have been made from contaminated water. I was really ill. I couldn't eat, I had barely the strength to drink, and I spent days holed up in a dusty, decrepit hotel. Somehow, I managed to get myself to Delhi and a flight home.

'I was still ill when I got back to England. I came back here, saw a doctor, had some tests, took some medicine and lay in bed. My mother kept calling; she was worried about me, but I told her I was all right. She didn't believe me. One day she just showed up on my doorstep. We had an enormous fight. She wanted to take me back with her to Halifax so she could nurse me better, but I refused to go. She drove back by herself in tears.'

'Why didn't you go with her?' Megan asked.

'Stubbornness. Stupidity. I have nothing against my mother. Usually, we get on well. She's a strong woman, and I owe her a lot. She brought me up believing I could do something in the world. I suppose that was my problem. I had spent my entire youth planning my escape from Halifax, with her encouragement. Going back would have been an admission that I'd failed, not just myself, but also her. Although I was in a bad way, I didn't quite want to do that yet. So I stayed, and festered.

'Then Lenka called. She said she knew I was a good trader. She asked what had happened when I'd been fired from Bloomfield Weiss, and when I told her, she said she thought it must have been something like that. She said I was her first choice as a partner to set up a hedge fund. She wasn't just being kind; she needed me. Of course, I did my best to refuse, to condemn myself to perpetual failure. But you know Lenka. What she wants, she gets.' Chris stopped to correct himself. 'I mean, what she wanted . . .'

'You don't look like a failure to me,' said Megan.

'No, I'm not. Not now. Provided I can keep Carpathian going.'

'Are there problems?'

Chris took a deep breath. 'Let's just say that Lenka's death brought some complications. Nothing I can't sort out. I'd rather not think about it now.'

'Well, good luck, with that.' Megan stood up. 'And now, I'd better get to bed if I'm not going to get totally drunk.'

'That's a good idea,' said Chris, standing up as well. 'Look, I've got to go to Lenka's flat tomorrow evening and sort some stuff out for her parents. Would you like to come? You can stay here again tomorrow night if you want.'

'I can find a hotel,' said Megan.

'Are you sure? You're welcome to stay.'

She looked at him and smiled. 'OK. That would be good. Now I must get to bed.'

4

It made no sense. Chris sipped his coffee as he stared at the Eureka Telecom papers in front of him. The first thing he had done when he had arrived at the office that morning was go through them one more time in the hope that the reason Lenka had bought the bonds would become obvious. It hadn't. In fact, he found it difficult to believe that she had bought them at all.

But she had. Carpathian owned them. And they had no means of selling them.

The phone rang. It was Duncan.

'You remember you gave me some junk bond recommendations the other day?' he began.

'Yes.'

'Well, my client checked them out. He said they seemed to make more sense than anything anyone else had told him.'

'Good.'

'Do you think you could have lunch with him?'

'Duncan! There's a lot going on here, and only me to do it now Lenka's gone.'

'Come on, Chris. This guy's my best client. He's stuck with me since United Arab International. I know you'd give him an honest idea of what's going on out there. I'll pay.'

'Oh, all right,' Chris said. 'Who is he, anyway?'

'His name is Khalid. Royal Bank of Kuwait. Smart guy. Don't underestimate him. How are you placed next week?'

Reluctantly, Chris agreed a date. He put down the phone, reflecting that Duncan couldn't be that useless a salesman: he seemed to possess that essential ability to make people do things they didn't really want to do.

Now what the hell was he going to do about the Eureka Telecom bonds?

He stared across at Lenka's desk. Tina had put some fresh flowers in her vase, delphiniums or something. But they didn't know the answer.

If only he had been there the previous week. Although they trusted each other, he and Lenka always discussed major investment decisions. She would certainly have gone over this one with him. He had given her his phone number in Courchevel before he went skiing, but she had refused to use it, saying he needed a complete break from the office. If only he could at least have listened in to her end of the phone conversation with Ian when she had bought the bonds.

At Bloomfield Weiss, that would have been possible. All phone conversations were taped to resolve any disputed trades. But they hadn't installed any recording equipment at Carpathian. The firm was too small, and both Lenka and Chris hadn't liked the Big Brother aspect of bugging phones. Besides, if there was a problem they could always rely on the broker's recordings.

That was it!

Chris hit the number for Bloomfield Weiss.

Ian answered. 'Where are the Eurekas trading this morning?' Chris asked without preamble.

'One tick.' Chris waited. He knew the Bloomfield Weiss trader would have to think about this one. Eventually Ian returned. 'He's indicating ninety to ninety-two. But that's only good in a million.'

'That's down five points!' protested Chris.

'What can I say? There's a big seller out there.'

'I can't believe this market!'

'I told you it was different from trading govvies,' said Ian, with little sympathy in his voice.

Chris didn't bother to ask where the bid for his ten million block would be. He knew the answer would be below yesterday's price of seventy and he didn't want to hear it. There was no point going to any other houses in the market, either. Eureka Telecom was a Bloomfield Weiss deal, and if Bloomfield Weiss were moving the price down sharply no other dealer in his right mind would want to buy the bonds. They might pretend to make a price, but if Chris tried to hit the bid it would fade immediately. No, he'd have to argue this one out.

'Ian, why did Lenka buy this deal?'

'It looked great last week, before the numbers came out.'

'No, it didn't. I've looked at the prospectus. It was a dog. It's not the kind of deal she'd do. And certainly not in twenty-five million.'

'I don't know. It yields three per cent more than Buck Telecom.'

'Yeah, but Buck has a network already in place. And a market cap of three billion quid. This is a totally different deal. Didn't she say anything about why she liked it?'

Ian didn't reply.

'Come on, Ian. Help me here. This is a major headache for me. Lenka's dead, it's not as if she and I can talk about it.' Chris had no compunction in using Lenka's death as a means of getting what he wanted. It was her company's survival that was at stake; he was sure she wouldn't mind.

'Sorry, Chris. I've no idea.'

Although Ian was an experienced salesman, he couldn't keep the guilt from his voice. Chris knew him too well. And he knew he was lying.

'I'd like to listen to the tapes,' Chris said.

'What?'

'I'd like to listen to the tapes of Lenka buying the bonds.'

'Come on, Chris. There's no need for that.'

'Yes, there is. There's something funny about this and I want to find out what.'

'But you can't listen to the tapes unless you query the trade.'

'Then I'm querying the trade.'

'But it's already settled.'

'Ian. These are special circumstances. The person who did the trade is dead, and I have reason to believe that the deal was never done.'

'What reason?'

'It doesn't make sense.'

'What kind of reason is that? If everybody who bought a bond argued about it when the price went down, the market would grind to a halt.'

Ian was right. Chris didn't have any evidence. But his suspicions were growing.

'Look, Ian,' he said, trying to take on a more conciliatory tone. 'If there's nothing wrong with the trade, then it won't do you any harm if I listen to the tapes, will it?'

'I told you, there's no need.'

'I demand to listen to them.'

'No.'

Ian was hiding something. Chris was now certain of that.

'Put me on to Larry Stewart,' Chris said. He wasn't exactly sure how the reporting lines worked at Bloomfield Weiss, but he knew Larry would be somewhere up above Ian.

'Do you think he'd listen to you?' said Ian, with something close to a sneer.

For a moment, Chris's confidence nearly deserted him. Ian knew Chris's reputation. If it was his word against Chris's at Bloomfield Weiss, Ian was pretty confident that his would be believed. Then Chris pulled himself together. Larry knew Chris had done nothing wrong three years before. Chris was willing to gamble that Larry had at least a scrap of humanity left in him somewhere.

'Yes, Ian. I think Larry would listen to me.'

There was silence at the other end of the phone as Ian tried to decide what to do. Chris had got him!

'Chris, I really don't think it would be a good idea for you to listen to those tapes.'

'Put me through to Larry, or I'll hang up and dial him direct.'

'I can explain.'

'Go ahead.'

'Not here,' said Ian in a whisper. 'Let's talk about it later. Out of the office.'

'Let's talk about it now.'

Chris could hear Ian exhaling down the phone. 'OK. There's a café at the bottom end of Liverpool Street. Ponti's. I'll meet you there in half an hour?'

'See you there,' said Chris.

It took Chris twenty minutes to get there, but Ian was already waiting. The ten years since the programme showed. Lines had begun to etch his face, in particular a frown crease between his eyebrows. He was still trim; in fact, he exercised at the gym three times a week. His suits were tailor-made, his shirts hand-made, his ties the latest fashion from the latest fashionable house. His hair was cut rakishly and frequently. He looked older than his thirty-three years, and more experienced. The only clue that belied the veneer of elegant self-confidence was his fingernails, which were still bitten down to the quick.

Chris fetched a black coffee and joined him. 'Well?'

Ian played with the froth on his cappuccino with a spoon. He stirred the bubbly cream for several moments before replying. Finally, he looked up, straight at Chris.

'Lenka and I were seeing each other,' he said simply. 'That's why I don't want you to hear the tape.'

'Seeing each other? What, sleeping together?'

'Call it what you like. We were doing it.'

'I can't believe it,' said Chris.

Ian shrugged.

'But why would Lenka . . . ?'

Ian frowned. 'Come on Chris. There are a lot of women who don't find me that unattractive.'

'Yes, but Lenka?'

'You know I always liked her. Turns out she liked me too.'

'No.'

'Stop saying that!' snapped Ian. 'She and I were seeing each other, OK? Now we're not, because she's dead. Do you understand that?'

'Sorry,' said Chris. 'How long had this been going on for?'

'Not long. Remember we had that European High Yield Conference in Barcelona last month? We both got a bit drunk. That's when it started.'

'Was it serious?'

'Not really. But it wasn't totally meaningless either. It was just fun. I knew there was no point in getting serious with Lenka.'

'No,' said Chris. Lenka never got serious with anyone. He tried to remember any clue that Lenka had given that she and Ian had had a relationship. Nothing. Ian had been phoning her more frequently over recent weeks, but Chris had always assumed that was the flow of business. It had obviously been something more.

'And this comes out on the tape?'

'Probably. I haven't listened to that particular conversation, but there's probably something there that would suggest we had more than a business relationship.'

'OK. Let's listen to it then,' said Chris. 'Just you and me.'

'We can't do that,' said Ian. 'An IT geek needs to be there as well. To make sure no one messes with the recording.'

'All right. We'll have the IT geek as well.'

'Please, Chris.'

'I understand why you wanted to warn me. And I certainly understand why you don't want anyone else to hear. But I want to listen to the tapes. Now more than ever. I want to know why Lenka bought those bonds, and the fact that you and she had something going just makes me more suspicious.'

Ian sighed. 'I guessed you say that. Just stay here for twenty minutes, while I dig them out.'

'No,' said Chris. 'Call whoever you need to call on your mobile. We'll go and listen together.'

'Don't you trust me?' asked Ian.

'No,' said Chris. 'I don't.'

Chris followed Ian through Broadgate Circle to the entrance of Bloomfield Weiss. They passed the twenty-foot iron phallus standing at an angle outside, rusting. It seemed exactly right for the firm. Chris felt a shiver as he entered the squat, marble-clad building; he hadn't set foot in there since that awful day three years before.

They took the lift to the third floor, passed quickly through the deceptively sedate reception area, and entered one of the largest trading rooms in Europe. Chris tried to look straight ahead as he followed Ian weaving his way through the desks, but he couldn't help noticing the activity around him. The familiar cries, the bustle, the oaths, the screens, and the paper. Paper everywhere. There were some faces he recognized, but most he didn't. Turnover at investment banks is high; traders come and traders go. He spotted his own desk, occupied now by a youth who didn't look a day over twenty, lolling back in his chair, cradling the phone. Near the far wall of the room, he spied Herbie Exler. Their eyes met. A rush of pure disgust coursed through Chris's veins, taking him by surprise, and he was gripped by an urge to vault the desks, grab the little American's head, and ram it into a screen.

'Come on,' said Ian. 'Don't make a spectacle of yourself. Let's get this over with.' He steered him towards a conference room in the far corner.

'This is Barry,' said Ian, introducing Chris to a skinny man with a shaved head who was facing a computer screen. 'Things have changed since your day. All the tapes are voice activated now, and they're not actually tapes. We record to disk. Barry will have to listen to everything that's said, but don't worry, he'll keep it all confidential, won't you, Barry?'

Ian managed to lace these last words with a heavy dose of threat.

Barry seemed unconcerned. 'That's right, Ian,' he said.

Barry handed Ian a log to sign, and then tapped commands into the computer. Barry and Ian put on headphones and listened, searching backwards and forwards until they found the conversation. Chris couldn't complain about this. It would be unthinkable that Ian could let him listen to a conversation with another client.

After about five minutes, in which Chris fidgeted uncomfortably, Ian held up his hand. 'I think I've got it.'

'OK,' said Chris. 'Let's hear it. But I want the whole conversation, mind.'

'All right, all right,' said Ian. He took off his headphones and flicked a switch. The conference room was filled with the sound of Lenka's voice. Ian hurriedly turned the volume down, and checked that the door was closed.

'Hi, babe, how are you?'

Babe! She called him 'babe'. For the first time, Chris realized how difficult this was going to be. Lenka had been able to say what she liked to Ian without fear of being overheard. Chris had been away on holiday, and Ollie and Tina would have been too far away and too busy to hear.

'I'm OK,' drawled Ian. 'I'm really feeling pretty good.'

'After last night I'm surprised you made it into work,' said Lenka, with the wicked laugh that Chris knew so well. He flashed a glance at Ian.

Ian shrugged. Barry stared fixedly at the computer screen. Although he was trying not to look it, Ian was clearly embarrassed. 'You asked for it,' he said.

Chris had. He took a deep breath and listened.

'I've got more stamina than you think,' Ian said from the speaker.

'Oh, please!' said Chris, rolling his eyes in a mixture of embarrassment and fury.

Ian ignored him. But on the tape he said: 'Have you thought any more about the Eureka Telecom?'

'Yeah. I think I'll go for twenty-five. Will I have any problem getting them?'

For you, anything,' said Ian.

'Seriously. Is there a chance that I'll be cut back?'

'No. This deal isn't going terribly well.'

'What about the takeover play?' Chris's ears perked up. Ian saw his reaction.

'No one else knows anything about it.'

'But it's an obvious fit, isn't it?'

'I think so,' said Ian. 'Radaphone needs to fill in its Central European network. Eureka has all the agreements in place. All Radaphone has to do is buy them.'

'And then I'll own Radaphone credit risk at a yield of twelve per cent.'

'Precisely.'

'And you're sure this takeover is going to happen?'

'I spent a week with these guys doing the road shows. You get to know people. They think it's going to happen, and soon. Don't you trust me?'

'Of course I trust you,' said Lenka. 'Do you want to know why?' The wicked tinge had crept back into her voice.

'Why?'

'Because if you lie to me I will personally see to it that your Little Jan will never be any use for anything again.'

Although this was meant to be a threat, the way Lenka said it, it sounded more like an invitation. And Chris could guess what Ian's 'Little Jan' was.

'Well, that's something I would hate to happen,' said Ian. 'So I think you're safe.'

'All right,' said Lenka, suddenly businesslike. 'Put me down for twenty-five.'

'OK. We're pricing tomorrow afternoon. I'll confirm you've got the full twenty-five then. Any chance of seeing you tonight?'

'Greedy,' said Lenka. 'I'm busy.'

'Busy? What are you doing?' asked Ian, a tinge of something that sounded like jealousy creeping into his voice.

'Wouldn't you just love to know,' said Lenka, and rang off.

Chris and Ian exchanged glances. Hearing Lenka talk like that had been tough for both of them. But it was what she had said that interested Chris. No wonder Ian hadn't wanted him to hear the tapes. It wasn't just that it revealed their relationship. It also revealed that Ian had been effectively giving Lenka inside information.

Radaphone was one of the big three European mobile telephone networks. If they bought Eureka Telecom, the bonds would shoot up in price. Carpathian would make a nice quick return on twenty-five million euros. As Lenka had said to him when he had phoned her in Prague, there was a story.

Chris glanced at Barry. His ears had progressively reddened throughout the conversation. Chris remembered him vaguely. He was an IT guy through and through. He might have picked up the possibility that Ian had given away too much information to Lenka, but he would be much more interested in the nature of the relationship between her and Ian. The Bloomfield Weiss gossip machine would have plenty of new material before the day was out. Tough.

'Well?' said Chris, after Barry had left the room.

'What can I say? I'm embarrassed.'

'Not that. Radaphone.'

'Oh. Radaphone.'

'Will Radaphone take over Eureka Telecom?'

Ian paused for a long time before answering. In the end, he seemed to make up his mind. 'It's possible.'

'But no signs yet?'

'None at all.'

'Do you have any concrete evidence of a takeover?'

'You heard the recording,' said Ian. 'It's just guesswork.'

'You didn't see Radaphone executives talking to anyone from Eureka Telecom?'

Ian shook his head.

'What about any of your corporate finance boys?'

'I wouldn't know about it if they did, would I? Chinese walls, and so on.'

'She just trusted your hunch, didn't she?'

Ian smiled. 'Looks like it.'

Chris had had enough. Lenka's death, Rudy's demand for his money back, the collapse of Eureka Telecom's bond price, his presence in the Bloomfield Weiss trading room and now the discovery that Ian and Lenka were having an affair, all combined in some cavity deep within him to produce a surge of disgust.

'You lied to her, didn't you?' he muttered through clenched teeth.

'What do you mean?'

'Because she was sleeping with you, you sold her a pile of crap and took the sales credits. And now that she's dead, you think there'll be no comeback.'

'That's just not true.'

'What's going on here?' A sharp voice barked behind Chris. He recognized it. Herbie Exler.

The feeling of disgust became overwhelming.

Chris turned to face his old boss. 'You probably put him up to this,' he said, getting to his feet. 'Well, you can take the Eureka Telecoms and shove them up your arse. Both of you.'

'Get out!' hissed Exler. 'Get out now. I don't ever want to see you in this building again.'

'I'm going,' said Chris, and he left the conference room, passing the stares of a hundred salesmen and traders as he made his way to the lift.

5

Megan was waiting for him in the Drayton Arms, a pint of bitter in front of her. Chris liked the way American women ordered pints; they thought it was English and it didn't seem to worry them that it might look unladylike.

'Sorry I'm late,' he said. 'Have you been here long?'

'Ten minutes.'

'Here, let me get myself one of those.'

Chris returned from the bar with a pint and took a long drink. 'I needed that.'

'It tastes good,' said Megan.

'I'm glad you like it. Did you have a good day?'

'Oh yeah. I went to the Tate Modern. And the Wallace Collection. And the ICA.'

'All in one day?'

'What can I say? I like art. You have a lot of it in London. How about you?'

'Jesus,' Chris said, shaking his head. 'I had a pretty awful day. I lost it with someone, and I think I've blown my only chance of getting rid of a disastrous bond position.'

'Oh,' said Megan.

'Sorry,' Chris smiled. 'I don't mean to burden you with my work problems. But you might find it interesting. Do you remember Ian Darwent?'

'He was with us on the boat, wasn't he? He jumped into the sea after Alex. English. Quiet. Quite good-looking.'

Chris winced. 'I wouldn't know about that. But that seemed to be Lenka's opinion.' He explained what he had found out.

Much to his disappointment, Megan didn't seem surprised.

'Don't you think it strange that she and Ian were sleeping together?' he asked her.

'Not really. You know Lenka,' Megan said. 'And I do remember Ian.'

'Actually, I don't know much about that side of her life. She didn't talk to me about it. I didn't ask.'

'Probably wise.'

But now Chris couldn't restrain his curiosity. 'So she slept around, did she?'

'That would be unfair,' said Megan. 'We did talk about men sometimes, especially when we went on vacation to Brazil. She said she often went for months without sex, then she would see two or three men in succession. She liked men, and she liked sex, but she hated the idea of tying herself down. I guess you could say she was confused. And she sometimes chose the strangest guys. Ian isn't nearly as weird as some of them, I'm sure.'

Chris shook his head. 'I'm glad I didn't know about all that.'

Megan looked at him closely over her pint. 'What about you and Lenka?'

'What do you mean?'

'I'm sorry,' said Megan. 'I didn't mean to suggest anything. It's just you obviously liked each other, and . . .'

'That's OK. We did like each other. And I can't deny she was an attractive woman. But somehow I never considered it. She was too good a friend, I suppose. I always assumed she was out of my league. If I had tried something, and she'd rejected me, it would have been awful. And even worse, if we had gone out together it wouldn't have lasted long and then I'd have lost a good friend. No, we were much better as we were.'

'Perhaps.' Megan looked at Chris steadily.

'Did Lenka say anything to you about her relationship with Ian?' he asked, uncomfortable under her gaze.

'No. I only had that one conversation last week. It didn't come up. She did sound a bit stressed out, though.'

'Stressed out?'

'She said that something had happened that she wanted to talk to me about when I came to stay. She didn't say what it was.'

'No clue at all? Was it something to do with work?'

'I don't know. I was curious, of course, but I thought I'd find out all about it when I got here.'

'Hmm. Did she mention Eureka Telecom to you?'

'No.'

'Or a man called Marcus?'

'Marcus? No. Who's he?'

'A tall thin American man came to see her in our office last week. Apparently, he upset Lenka pretty badly. But I've no idea who he is.'

'Neither have I.'

Chris stared thoughtfully into his pint. 'Something was going on,' he said. He glanced over to Megan's glass. It was almost empty. 'Come on,' he said. 'We'd better go and check out her flat.'

Lenka had lived on the first floor of an elegant white-stuccoed building guarded by twin pillars in Onslow Gardens. The Czech police had recovered the key from her bag, and her parents had asked Chris to sort through her things and send them any personal belongings. There was going to be a lot to do. Chris was counting on a helpful neighbour.

He let himself and Megan into the building. There was a pile of mail for Lenka neatly stacked on a windowsill in the hallway. Chris carried it upstairs with him. Her door opened easily. It was as though she had been away for a day, not a week. The heating was still on. The flat was untidy, but not a total mess. Her bed was made. There was a note from 'Adriana' to Miss Lenka saying she was owed twenty pounds for Wednesday. The cleaning lady, no doubt. The flat was a mishmash of furnishings, things she had seen around the world that she just had to buy. They formed a pleasing jumble, and some of them, like a set of two-foot-high wooden carvings of elephants from Africa and a large intricately decorated table from somewhere in Asia, were quite dramatic.

Then there were her clothes. What seemed like miles of them, in wardrobes, chests of drawers, walk-in cupboards, trunks. Many years' bonuses from Bloomfield Weiss had been pumped into the world's fashion industry. And shoes. There must have been a hundred pairs. It was a staggering sight.

'Makes my closet look like a thrift shop,' said Megan.

Chris went through to her desk, which was in a kind of den just off the living room. It was a large pine affair, covered with papers and a computer. Chris took a deep breath. He would have to sort through this lot. He didn't want to. Going into Lenka's flat hadn't felt like an intrusion, neither did gaping at her massive collection of clothes. But going through her papers? He wanted to leave them there, undisturbed.

But something would have to be done with them. There would be the Czech equivalent of probate. Someone would have to sort out her assets. God, perhaps there was a will in there somewhere. Then there would be bills, rent, credit cards, bank accounts. Chris's heart sank. Perhaps he could get away with dumping it all in a box and sending it over to the Czech Republic.

'Would you mind helping me with this?' asked Chris.

'OK,' said Megan. 'I'll sort the papers into piles. You read them.'

They worked for two hours, getting progressively more depressed. They didn't find a will, or any evidence of investments, but there was a massive balance in a current account at US Commerce Bank. Like many investment bankers, Lenka would fight tooth and nail over a hundredth of a basis point at work, but leave a hundred thousand pounds of her own money in a low-interest account.

At ten o'clock, Chris stretched. 'Look, why don't we stop now? We can't do all this. I'll write a letter to her parents saying what we've found so far, and suggesting they get a solicitor to sort it all out.'

'Don't you think we should look in there?' Megan said, nodding towards the computer.

'But that's private,' said Chris.

'What do you think all that lot is?' asked Megan, pointing to the piles of papers, now neatly stacked.

'I suppose you're right. Go on then. Let's have a look.'

Megan turned on the machine. She expertly skimmed through the folders. There was very little there. Quite a few word-processed documents, many of them in Czech. No other software, no games, no personal finance packages, no will-making programs. But there was e-mail.

'Let's have a look.'

Megan seemed to have no trouble navigating the Internet software and downloading Lenka's mail. She came up with a list of the most recent e-mail correspondence. The names were fascinating. There were some to Ian. And one to 'Marcus'.

'There!' Chris cried, pointing to it. 'Open that one!'

'No. Let's do this in chronological order. It'll make more sense.'

Impatiently, they skimmed a dozen e-mails, half of them in Czech, until they came to one from Lenka to Ian:

> Ian
> I couldn't sleep last night. I think I have to tell Marcus about Alex. He has a right to know. And I've got to talk to Duncan.
> L

The reply from Ian was terse:

> Don't do that! We have to talk. For God's sake don't do anything stupid.
> Ian

Then, immediately following that, there was an e-mail to the mysterious Marcus. The subject line read simply *Alex*.

> Marcus
> I'm sorry I was rude to you yesterday. As you can imagine, it is a difficult subject for me. I have something important I need to tell you about Alex's death. It is complicated and needs

explanation, so I would like to tell you in person. I am
travelling to New York at the beginning of next month, so
perhaps we can meet then.
Best wishes
Lenka

There was a reply, short and simple:

I will call you.
Marcus

'Let's print those off,' said Chris.

As the small printer next to Lenka's machine chugged away,
Megan clicked on the last e-mail Lenka had received. She opened
it:

Lenka
See you Thursday at seven thirty. Can't wait. We're going to
have some fun!
Megan

'I wrote that last Sunday. It seems like a whole life ago.' She
blinked back a tear.

'It was,' said Chris.

Megan sniffed and dabbed her eyes. 'So, who can this Marcus be?'

Chris shook his head. 'You can't tell much from the e-mail
address. He could be from anywhere. I wonder what she wanted
to tell him about Alex?'

'The truth, presumably,' said Megan. 'That Duncan knocked
him into the sea. But I wonder why she'd want to do that. We
all agreed to keep it quiet, and I thought everyone had.' She gave
Chris an enquiring glance.

'They have, as far as I know,' he said. 'I thought that was all
buried. And I thought Lenka was as keen as anyone on burying
it. It's strange that she's the one who wants to tell, and Ian's the
one who wants to keep it quiet. I'd have thought he wouldn't
mind risking getting Duncan into trouble.'

'We'd all be in trouble,' said Megan. 'We lied to the police. That's against the law.' She frowned. 'Big trouble.'

Chris sighed. 'Well, whoever this Marcus is, he needs to know what happened.'

He sat down in front of the keyboard and began to write:

> Marcus
> I am a colleague of Lenka's. I have some very bad news. Lenka was murdered in Prague last Monday. I may be able to help you with Alex's death. Please contact me at chrissz@interserve.net
> Regards
> Chris Szczypiorski

He glanced at Megan, who nodded, and then he clicked on *Send*. 'There. He should identify himself now.' He yawned, and stretched. 'Let's go. I think we've done all we can here.'

He turned off the computer, took the small bundle of papers they had sorted, turned down the thermostat for the heating, and switched off the light. They left the flat.

Chris looked at his watch. Twenty past ten. 'Damn,' he said. 'I wanted to talk to one of her neighbours. It's too late to disturb them now.'

But they were lucky. Just as they were about to reach the front door, it opened, and a bespectacled man in a smart overcoat and suit came in, bringing with him the waft of alcohol. He glanced at them with curiosity.

'Hello,' said Chris.

'Hi.'

'Do you live here?'

'Yes, I do. Can I help you?'

He was American, about thirty-five, slightly overweight with a friendly face.

'Did you know Lenka Němečková?'

'Sure. I live in the apartment above hers.' Then his eyes narrowed. He had caught the tense Chris had used. 'What's wrong?'

'I'm afraid she's been murdered. In Prague. We're friends of hers.' Chris introduced himself and Megan.

As so many other people had been when Chris had told them the news, the American was stunned.

'Her parents asked me to take care of her stuff,' Chris said. 'They gave me the key. Can you keep an eye on her flat for me? Give me a call if there's anything wrong.'

Chris handed him his card. The American took it, and looked dully at the writing on it. 'I can't believe it,' he said.

'Perhaps I can take your number?' Chris asked.

'Oh, sure,' said the American, giving Chris a card in return. *Richard H. Storebrand, Vice President.* He worked for one of the large US investment management companies.

'Thanks. Oh, by the way, you didn't see anything odd last week, did you? Any strange visitors, anything like that?'

'No, I don't think so,' he said. Then he furrowed his brow. 'There was a guy who used to hang around here. He used to lean against the lamppost on the other side of the street. He was kind of creepy. Anyway, I was coming back here a couple of weeks ago and I bumped into Lenka. He crossed the street toward her. She saw him, pushed me into the building, and shut the door behind us. The guy rang the doorbell and shouted after her. She told me to ignore him and went up the stairs to her apartment. I haven't seen him around since then.'

'Did she look frightened?' Chris asked.

'No. More pissed off. But I guess a girl like that gets used to men hanging around her.'

'Was this man American?'

'No, I don't think so. But he did have some kind of accent. Irish or Scottish, I think. I'm not real good on those.'

'What did he look like?'

'Big guy. Red hair, kind of messy. Wore a suit. He looked respectable, he didn't really look like a weirdo, but he was just hanging out.'

Duncan.

'Thanks,' Chris said, smiling. 'Let's keep in touch, OK?'

The man nodded absently. 'Lenka. I can't believe it.'

And Chris and Megan left Richard H. Storebrand, Vice President, shaking his head at the horrors of the world.

When they returned to Chris's flat the light on the answer machine was blinking. Chris pressed the button.

'Hi, Chris, this is Eric. I heard about Lenka. I'm very sorry. I'm going to be in London for a couple of days early next week. I'm getting in Sunday. Would you like to meet me for a drink at my hotel Sunday evening? Say seven o'clock? I'm staying at the Lanesborough. Just leave a message there if you can make it. Hope to see you then.'

Chris glanced at Megan. She was standing very still, looking at the machine.

'A voice from the past,' said Chris.

'Yes,' Megan answered, almost in a whisper.

'Do you want to come with me? I'm sure Eric wouldn't mind.'

Megan took a moment to answer. 'No, no. I'd better not. Anyway, I should be going to Cambridge tomorrow.'

'OK,' said Chris.

'I'm sorry,' said Megan. 'It's just weird to hear his voice again. Look, er . . . I'd better be going to bed.'

'All right. Good night.'

'Good night.'

6

'Come here, bloody dog!'

The angry grey-haired man puffed past them in an attempt to catch up with his dog, a red setter that was streaking up the hill in pursuit of a spry fox terrier.

'Algy!' he screamed, and then the dog was out of sight.

It was a lovely morning: cold, crisp and clear. The northern slope of Parliament Hill was still brushed with frost, but the sun had warmed the southern side into freshly glistening dew. To their right stretched London, in the great grey bowl of the Thames, streaks of mists still lingering amongst the tall towers of the City. The low winter sun reflected in a bright orange triangle off the roof of Canary Wharf.

They paused when they reached the summit. The young setter was heading full speed for the Highgate duck ponds, leaving his master striding rapidly down the hill after him.

'I wonder who is taking who for a walk,' said Megan.

'The dog's certainly having fun,' Chris said.

The setter stopped abruptly, and turned back towards his master, at a lope, tongue hanging out, tail wagging, oblivious of the curses raining down on him.

'This must be dog heaven,' said Megan, looking round at the four-legged creatures of all shapes and sizes going about their Saturday-morning business.

'Did you ever have one?' Chris asked.

'Yes,' Megan smiled. 'He was a very fat basset-hound called Beau. Hills weren't really his thing. His two favourite pastimes were eating and lying in front of the TV with his eyes shut. I loved him, though. He died when I was twelve. I cried and cried.'

They made their way down the northern slope of the hill towards the centre of Hampstead Heath, their shoes crunching through the dusting of ice.

'Did the Czech police have any idea who might have killed Lenka?' Megan asked.

'Funny, I was just thinking about that,' said Chris. 'They hadn't much of a clue when I first spoke to them, but that was right after it had happened. I haven't heard anything from them since.'

'Do you think this man Marcus might have had anything to do with it?'

'Possible, I suppose. It's hard to say when we don't know who he is or what Lenka wanted to say to him.'

'It's odd that in the week Alex's death resurfaces Lenka should be killed.'

'Yes,' said Chris. 'It is.' They walked on in silence together, both thinking. 'Let's say that you were right and Lenka was telling this man Marcus what really happened. Why would he want to know?'

'Perhaps he's a cop?'

'Doesn't sound like one,' said Chris. 'If he was, you'd expect him to be waving a badge around. And he wouldn't use his Christian name. If it is his Christian name.'

'Private investigator? Maybe he was hired by Bloomfield Weiss?'

'Possible. Or perhaps he's a journalist?'

Megan winced. 'That would be bad. The last thing we need is all that dredged up in the papers.'

'It would make a good story though. "Investment Bankers Cover Up Ten-Year-Old Murder on Boat."'

'It wasn't a murder.'

'It would be after the newspapers got at it.'

'I think what Lenka's neighbour said about Duncan sounds pretty creepy,' Megan said.

'That's nothing,' Chris said. 'That's just Duncan.'

'Hanging around women's apartments isn't nothing,' Megan replied fiercely.

'But Duncan has always had a thing about Lenka.'

'Yeah. And now she's dead.'

'What are you suggesting?'

'I'm just saying. It sounds pretty creepy.'

Chris had to admit she had a point. 'OK. Let's say it does. But I know Duncan. He might follow Lenka, he might even pester her, but she would be the last person in the world he would kill. When I told him about her he was devastated.'

Megan sighed. 'I'm not accusing him of killing her. But someone did.'

'Yes, someone did.'

'Do you think we should tell the police about this?' Megan said.

'About Duncan?'

'Maybe.'

'No. He's a friend of mine and I don't want to get him into trouble needlessly.'

'What about the mysterious Marcus?'

'Hmm.' Chris thought it over. 'The problem is, if we tell them about Marcus, we have to tell them about the e-mail, and about Alex. And I don't think that's a good idea. We could still get into a lot of trouble about it all. Besides, perhaps the Czech police have some good leads in Prague. Who knows, maybe they've arrested someone.'

'I doubt it, don't you?'

'Yes,' said Chris. 'I do. I was planning to call Lenka's parents this afternoon. I'll ask if they've heard anything from the police. But I think if anyone is going to find out why Lenka died, it has to be us.'

'But what can we do?' asked Megan.

'Try to find out who this Marcus is. Talk to him. Find out what Ian knows.'

'And check up on Duncan.'

'And check up on Duncan,' Chris repeated. 'I can also ask Eric whether he has any ideas when I see him tomorrow evening. He usually has a good take on things.'

'He does,' said Megan.

They walked on.

'What happened between you and him?' Chris asked.

Megan glanced at Chris, as though she were trying to decide whether to tell him. In the end, she seemed to make up her mind. 'We split up. A year after your training programme.'

'Why?'

'I still don't know,' Megan replied. 'Or at least, I probably do know, but I don't want to believe it. At first he said it just wasn't practical living so far apart, which was why I arranged to move to New York. Then he said we were becoming different people: he had his life, and I had mine. I didn't understand that. I was devastated. I tried to change his mind, but I knew there was no point. If Eric decides he wants to do something, he does it, and there's not much you can do about it.'

'A bit like Lenka,' Chris said.

'I suppose. The thing is, two months later he met another woman. Cassie.'

'She's some high-society type, isn't she?'

'Yes. She's also beautiful and intelligent, and very charming. I was as jealous as hell of her. They got married a year later, as you probably know.'

'I heard.'

'I think I just wasn't good enough for Eric.'

'That's a bit harsh, isn't it?'

Megan shot Chris an angry glance. This was clearly something she had been thinking about a lot over the years. 'My father ran the five-and-dime in Oneonta, upstate New York. This town is small. Fourteen thousand people and fifty-four churches. You have to drive seventy miles to Albany for your thrills. I have no money, no influence. I'd be no use to Eric. But Cassie ... Cassie's different.'

'I'm sure Eric wouldn't be bothered by someone's background,' said Chris. Eric had always struck him as too sensible to spend the rest of his life with someone just because of how rich they were. Besides, Eric was quite capable of making his own money.

'Oh, no?' said Megan. 'It's not just that Cassie knows everyone. Nor that she's the perfect successful banker's wife. Do you know who her father is?'

'No,' said Chris, regretting now that he had contradicted Megan on such a sensitive subject.

'He's a Republican Senator. As was her grandfather. And her uncle was in the Reagan Administration.'

'Ah.'

'So, when Eric makes his move into politics, the whole family will be there to smooth the way for him.'

'I see. But do you think Eric will do that? I mean, he's doing so well at Bloomfield Weiss, why would he want to pack it in?'

'Oh, I'm sure Eric wants to do that. He's wanted to all his life. It's the kind of ambition that doesn't go away. I'd bet on it. He'll make his move one day, probably one day soon.'

'Do you still see him?'

'I tried for a few months. You know, we were "just good friends". He did a good job of it too, which infuriated me. But I couldn't stand it. I hated him. And I hated her. She was always so damned *nice* all the time. Every time I saw him for a normal social occasion I'd come back mad, and it would take me a week to recover. So I stopped. I was invited to the wedding, but I didn't go. I haven't seen him for eight years now.'

They walked on. They were in a quiet part of the Heath now, amongst gnarled old oak trees, whose bare branches intertwined like old women's fingers over their heads.

'He was a fool, you know,' said Chris. 'To let you go.'

Megan glanced at him. 'Thank you,' she said.

*

Chris waited in the bar of the Lanesborough, drinking a gin and tonic. It didn't quite seem the place for a pint of bitter. Book-lined walls, dark wood, leather chairs and sofas, crystal glasses, a fire: the place oozed wealth and comfort. It was heaving with aged American tourists, cigar-smoking businessmen, and a group of men in black tie there for some function or other. Chris was glad he had changed out of his jeans into trousers and a sports jacket. But he still felt underdressed.

He had taken Megan to King's Cross the day before and said goodbye to her. He also called Lenka's parents, and in a slow stilted conversation, he suggested that they should get a solicitor to sort out Lenka's affairs in London since her estate could certainly afford one. He asked them how the police investigation was going. They said that the police had questioned a local criminal with ties to the Ukrainian mafia, but that they had had to let him go again. Or at least that's what Chris thought Lenka's father had said; it was difficult to be sure. One thing he was sure of was that Lenka's funeral would be on Wednesday. Chris planned to go, and so did Megan. He called Duncan, who said he would come. A Czech funeral in February promised to be a grim affair. But at least Megan would be there.

He thought about Marcus. Who could he be? Lenka had said that he had a 'right' to know the truth about Alex's death. Who could have a 'right' to know? That didn't fit policemen or private investigators and it especially didn't fit journalists. It had to be someone with a closer link to Alex. Friend? Relation?

Suddenly, Chris knew the answer. It should be easy enough to check: Eric would be able to confirm it.

'Hey, Chris, how are you?'

It was the man himself, wearing a blazer, shirt and tie, and looking totally at ease in the surroundings. Like Ian, he gave the impression of experience and authority beyond his years, but unlike Ian, he wore it in a relaxed, self-confident way.

'I'm all right. And you?'

Eric perched on a stool next to Chris. 'It's crazy. But it's always crazy. I've just done my calculations for the IRS. Do you know I spent one hundred and forty-three days out of the country last year?'

'All on business?'

'All but four of them. We were supposed to have a vacation in Bermuda for a week, but I got called back early. Cassie was mad as hell, and I don't blame her. But I guess I like things this way.' He ordered a kir from the barman. 'It's been what? Over a year?'

'Almost. It was just after Lenka and I had started Carpathian. We all met up for dinner at that place in Chelsea.'

'I remember,' said Eric, smiling. Then the smile disappeared. 'I'm very sorry about Lenka. You were there when it happened, I hear?'

Chris sighed. 'That's right. I still dream about it at night. I don't think I'll forget about it for a long time.' Involuntarily he looked down at his hands. Eric noticed.

'Messy, was it?'

Chris nodded. For some reason, at that moment, he almost fell apart. He had spent so long telling people about Lenka in as dispassionate a way as he could, that he had almost succeeded in persuading himself that he hadn't really been there. But now, with Eric, he knew he had, and it all rushed back at him. He felt his eyes sting.

He swallowed. 'I'm sorry,' he said.

'That's OK,' said Eric softly. 'I can't imagine what it was like.'

'It's not an experience I'd want to repeat,' said Chris. 'How did you hear about it?'

'It's all over Bloomfield Weiss. Did they catch the guy who did it?'

'Apparently not. The police questioned someone in Prague last week, but they had to let him go. I'm not sure whether they've got any other leads.'

'Lenka was an extraordinary woman,' Eric said. 'I'll never forget her on the training programme. She added something, don't you think? Colour. Spontaneity. Spirit. Do you remember when she took on Waldern, after he'd bullied that Italian woman, what was her name?'

'Carla. Yes, I remember.'

'First Alex and now Lenka.' Eric shuddered.

'Speaking of Alex,' Chris said. 'He had a brother, didn't he? Do you remember his name?'

'As a matter of fact I do. Marcus.'

'I thought so!' said Chris in triumph.

'In fact, he tried to get in touch with me in New York a few weeks ago. He said he wanted to talk to me about Alex's death. I wouldn't see him. He was pretty upset about it, according to my assistant, but I thought it would be hard to talk to him without giving anything away.'

'That was probably wise,' said Chris.

'Have you spoken to him?'

'No, but Lenka did.' Chris told Eric all about Lenka's meeting with Marcus, and her subsequent e-mails to him.

'God,' said Eric. 'Do you know what she said? Do you think she told him what really happened?'

'I don't know,' said Chris. 'But if she didn't, it certainly sounds as though she meant to.'

'That could be awkward if he goes to the police.'

'I know,' said Chris. He was struck by an unpleasant thought. 'Christ, what will we do if the police ask questions?'

Eric thought for a second. 'If the police ask, don't say anything. It was a US crime, so it will be American jurisdiction. I don't know how it is in this country, but in the States they can't force you to incriminate yourself. In fact, better yet, give me a call, and I'll get you a good American lawyer. You'd better tell Ian and Duncan that as well.'

'And Megan,' said Chris.

'Megan?' said Eric in surprise. 'Have you seen Megan?'

'Yes. She came to our office last week. She was supposed to be staying with Lenka. They'd become good friends, apparently.'

'Really?' said Eric. 'How is she? I always liked that woman, you know.'

'I think she liked you too,' said Chris.

'Yes, well.' For a moment Eric looked uncharacteristically flustered. 'Actually, I haven't seen her for years. What's she doing now?'

'She's studying medieval history at the University of Chicago. She's spending the next six months at Cambridge researching her dissertation for her PhD, I think.'

'Good. Well, say hi to her from me if you see her again.'

'I will.'

Eric frowned. 'I think we did the right thing about Alex. I mean, Duncan would have been prosecuted, I'm sure, and that would have been wrong. Provided we all stick together and don't admit to anything, we'll be OK. It's a long time ago.'

'I think we did the right thing, too. Besides, we don't know what Lenka said to Marcus, let alone how he'll react to it. I'm going to the States next week and I'd like to get in touch with him. Do you have his phone number, or address or anything? I've only got his e-mail address.'

'I don't know,' said Eric. 'I doubt it. I can check when I get back to New York, if you like. But I suspect my assistant jotted his number down on a scrap of paper and threw it away when I told her I didn't want to talk to him. He shouldn't be too difficult to find, though. Marcus Lubron can't be a common name.'

'Did you ever meet him when Alex was alive?'

'No. If you remember, he was travelling. Skiing in the winter, and sailing in the summer, I think. He didn't even come back for Alex's funeral. I don't think Alex's mother could get hold of him in time. By the way, did you know she died a month later?'

'No, I didn't. I do remember she was awfully ill.'

'Poor Alex.'

They both drank in silence.

'Anyway, how's your fund doing?' Eric asked. 'What's it called again? Carpathian?'

'That's right. We had a solid start. Twenty-nine per cent return in the first nine months.'

Eric raised his eyebrows. 'That's more than solid. That's damn good.'

Chris smiled. He lapped up the praise. Eric was one of the few people he wanted to impress, and he was proud of what he and Lenka had achieved.

'But we've run into one or two problems since Lenka died.'

'Oh.'

'Do you remember Rudy Moss?'

'Rudy Moss. I certainly do. The fat guy with the pointy nose. Didn't he leave Bloomfield Weiss a few years ago?'

'Yeah. He joined Amalgamated Veterans Life. Where he invested in our fund. Until last week. He said he'd take his money out now Lenka was gone.'

'No? I always knew he was a jerk.'

'He is,' Chris confirmed. 'The problem is the market's down and Lenka took a big position in a Bloomfield Weiss deal that turns out to be a dog.'

'Let me guess . . . Eureka Telecom?'

'That's the one. You didn't have anything to do with that deal, did you?' asked Chris.

'Oh, no. It's my group, though. I do international telecoms M&A. It's a hot area. But Eureka Telecom is a bit small for me.'

'Really?' said Chris. 'I knew you were in M&A, but I'd forgotten which sector. Maybe you can help.'

Eric stiffened. 'I don't know about that.'

'You see, Ian told Lenka something quite interesting before she bought the bonds. He said there was a good chance that Eureka Telecom would be taken over by Radaphone. Since then, the deal has crapped out. Is there any chance that might be true?'

'Whoa, Chris,' said Eric. 'That question blasts through about fifteen internal procedures, half a dozen regulations and a couple of Chinese walls.'

'But Eric. As a mate. I really need the help. Just a clue.'

'No, Chris. These rules apply especially to mates. And definitely no clues. And don't assume from that that I know anything, OK? Also, Ian was way out of line telling Lenka that, whether it's true or not.'

'Sorry,' said Chris. 'I suppose I shouldn't have asked you. Forget it. It's just that it does worry me.'

'Forgotten,' said Eric. 'But I suggest we stay well clear of the topic in future.'

'Agreed. So how's your business going?'

'Pretty good,' said Eric. 'We did the Luxtel–Morrison Infotainment deal last year. And the Deutsche Mobilcom–Cablefrance deal. In fact, we're number one in telecoms advisory worldwide. And as I said, it's a hot place to be.'

'You're one of the top producers, I take it?'

'I took over the group at the beginning of last year.'

'Oh.' Chris thought about that. At thirty-three, Eric was running probably the most profitable Mergers and Acquisitions group in the world. He must have got a good bonus last year. A bonus in the tens of millions of dollars. Chris was so tempted to ask, but decided against it.

Eric was watching him. He knew what he was thinking. He gave a tiny smile.

'I always thought you'd do well,' said Chris. 'So well, that I think you can afford to buy me another drink.'

'I'd like to, but I'm supposed to be going out to dinner with some clients in a couple of minutes. But look, you said you were coming to the States soon?'

'I'm going to Hartford to see Rudy bloody Moss a week on Monday.'

'Why don't you come to dinner? I should be in New York that week, although the way things are going I can't guarantee it. You haven't met Cassie yet, have you?'

'No. I'd like to do that. Thank you.'

'Great. See you then.'

Eric slipped away, and approached a group of three Italian-looking businessmen in the lobby. Another big deal.

7

'Bloomfield Weiss.'

'Ian? It's Chris.'

'Oh.'

'Where are you making Eureka Telecom?'

'Do you want to deal?'

'No. Just a level.'

'One tick.'

Chris waited. He was expecting bad news, and he got it.

'Eighty-eight to ninety.' Ian's voice was tense. Ready for an argument.

Chris didn't give him one. 'Ian, we need to talk.'

Ian sighed. 'After Friday, I don't think that's necessary, do you?'

'It's about Lenka.'

'We talked about Lenka.'

'I went to her flat on Friday night. I saw her e-mails. Including one to you. And one to Marcus.'

'To Marcus! What did it say?'

'I don't think we should talk about that on the phone, do you? I'll see you in half an hour at Ponti's.'

'But Chris, I've got to talk to my clients!'

'No, Ian. You've got to talk to me.'

This time it took Chris the full half hour to get there. The café was quiet at nine thirty on a Monday morning. Those who were going to work were already there, and it was too early for the loiterers to emerge. Ian was sitting at a table over a cappuccino and a cigarette, flirting with a striking six-foot tall waitress. His smile disappeared when he saw Chris. The waitress gave Chris a black look for interrupting them, and drifted off. Chris ignored her and sat down opposite Ian.

'So, tell me about Marcus.'

Ian took a long drag on his cigarette and carefully flicked the ash into an ashtray before replying. 'As you probably know, he's Alex's brother. He came to see Lenka about Alex's death.'

'And what did she tell him?'

'I don't know. You saw her e-mail to him. What did it say?' Ian couldn't hide his anxiety as he asked the question.

'What do you think it said?'

'I don't know! That's why I'm asking you!' Ian's impatience was growing.

Chris paused for a moment, enjoying Ian's discomfort. 'It said that she had something important she wanted to tell him about Alex's death.'

'But she didn't say what it was?'

'No. She said she wanted to see Marcus in person to explain it.' As Chris said this, Ian relaxed. But only for a moment. 'There's a reply from Marcus. It says he'll phone her.'

'And you don't know whether he did?'

'No.'

Ian's tension had returned.

'There was also an e-mail from her to you saying she had to tell him about something. You begged her not to.'

'That's right.'

'What was it?'

Ian thought for a moment. 'What really happened, of course. That Duncan hit Alex and he fell in the sea. That Duncan was responsible for his death.'

'And why should this bother you? You don't care much about Duncan, do you?'

'It's not that. We'd all get in trouble, wouldn't we? It was stupid of Lenka to even think of talking about it.'

'Do you think that's why she was murdered?'

Ian looked at him with derision. 'Of course not. Are you suggesting I killed her? I was sleeping with her, for God's sake!'

'Ollie says that Lenka wouldn't take your calls for a couple of days before she died.'

'That's true. I was angry about Marcus. She was angry with me. But there's nothing odd about that. You know Lenka. She could lose her temper pretty easily.'

'Her funeral is on Wednesday. Are you coming?'

Ian closed his eyes, and shook his head.

'Why not?'

'I can't get away,' Ian said wearily.

Chris stood up with contempt in his voice. 'You weren't really much of a friend to her, were you?'

Ian pursed his lips, anger flaring in his eyes. 'Fuck off, Chris,' he said.

Chris was still angry when he got back to the office. There was something about Ian that made him lose his temper every time. He knew it was stupid: his only chance of getting out of that bloody Eureka Telecom position was to persuade Bloomfield Weiss to buy the bonds. Well, if he hadn't blown that on Friday, he definitely had now.

But what was it that was getting to him?

Obviously, the discovery of Ian's relationship with Lenka had rattled him more than he had realized. Could he be jealous, as Megan had hinted? Did he regret that Ian had succeeded where he hadn't dared to try?

He tried to think about that objectively. He was pretty sure the answer was no. He was very fond of Lenka, but he had never thought of her sexually. Right from the beginning, when he was still going out with Tamara, he had placed her off limits and kept her there ever since. That was the secret of their friendship. Lenka liked men. All her other relationships with males had deteriorated into sex and then breakup. But not with Chris. They felt safe with each other, they trusted each other, they were very good friends.

In which case, what was it about Ian that upset him so much?

He had always assumed Lenka had torrid relationships with men, and although he had never known the details, he had accepted it as part of who she was: if anything, it made her more colourful. But to see Ian treating her as just another casual relationship, a hot babe to bonk for a few weeks, made him crazy. Why didn't Ian recognize that she was so much more than that? He wasn't even going to her funeral, for God's sake! And the way he had used their relationship so cynically to sell her the Eureka Telecom bonds disgusted Chris. He didn't believe for one moment that there was anything in the Radaphone rumour. It was just a product of Ian's imagination, aimed at dumping twenty-five million euros of a difficult position. That should be good for a few grand on his bonus at the end of the year.

Could Ian have killed her to prevent her from telling Marcus about Duncan?

Chris had to admit that the answer was probably not. It wouldn't make sense. Certainly, the police would cause trouble if they asked questions. But Eric was right; as long as all the witnesses on the boat stuck together, they would all be safe. The police couldn't prove anything. With a shiver, Chris realized that Ian could even try to cut a deal if he agreed to tell the police what really happened in return for immunity from prosecution. That would be bloody typical. Either way, Ian would survive.

No. As much as he liked to think the contrary, Ian was probably not responsible for Lenka's death.

Chris wished he could talk to Megan about all this. She would be able to add some objectivity. He wondered how she was getting on at Cambridge. Would she even have a telephone? He desperately wanted to call her.

What about Duncan? Megan had suggested that he should find out a bit more about Duncan and Lenka's recent relationship. But before confronting him, there was someone else he wanted to talk to first.

He looked up the number for United Arab International Bank, dialled it, and asked to speak to Phillippa Gemmel.

'Securities Trading,' came the voice, bright and breezy.

'Pippa? It's Chris Szczypiorski.'

'Chris. How are you?' She wasn't rude, but she didn't sound exactly pleased to hear from him.

'Look, Pippa, do you think we could meet for a few minutes after work? It won't take long. There's something I want to discuss with you.'

'If Duncan wants to talk to me, he can speak to me himself,' Pippa said.

'It's true, I do want to talk to you about Duncan. But he doesn't know I'm calling you. Please. It won't take long.'

Pippa was silent for a moment. 'OK. But I'm leaving at five thirty. Can you meet me downstairs in the lobby?'

'Fine. I'll see you there at half past five.'

He hung up. Next, he pulled out the card of the English-speaking Czech policeman who had interviewed him after the murder. *Poručík Petr Karásek*. Presumably, *poručík* was his rank. He dialled, and eventually got through to him. Chris asked whether he had made any progress.

'We have had some success,' the policeman replied. His English was careful and clear. 'We found a woman who said she saw a man with a moustache running out of the street where Miss Němečková was killed. We showed her photographs and she identified a criminal we know here who uses a knife. He is Czech, but he works for the Ukrainian mafia. We arrested him. But there are problems. She was not sure of the identification when we put him in a line, and he has a – what do you say? Ah, yes. Alibi, I think?'

'Yes, alibi,' said Chris.

'It may be false. We are still working on that line of inquiry.'

'So you think the murderer is a local criminal?' Chris asked.

'From the way he used the knife, we think he was a professional. Unfortunately, we do have some professional killers in Prague. It is likely it is one of them. Do you have any idea of a motive?'

Chris knew that Karásek was thinking about Carpathian's investments. 'No,' he answered.

'You are sure Miss Němečková had no business deals in the Czech Republic?'

'We own two million euros of a CEZ bond and a lot of bonds issued by your government.' CEZ was the national electricity company, hardly likely to be the centre of an organized crime conspiracy. 'Besides that, we were planning to open an office in Prague, but I can't see why that would upset anyone. Have you spoken to Jan Pavlík?'

'Yes, we have, but with no luck.' There was a pause. 'Have you any other ideas for us, Mr Szczypiorski?'

Marcus and Alex was a can of worms that Chris didn't want to open at that moment.

'No. Nothing.'

Karásek didn't sound surprised. 'OK. Thank you for keeping in contact. Goodbye.'

Chris put down the phone. Nowhere. They were getting nowhere. Chris wasn't convinced by the identification. The more he thought about it, the more he suspected that the key to Lenka's murder lay in London, or possibly New York, rather than the Ukrainian mafia in Prague.

He stared down at the papers in front of him. There was his portfolio, mocking him. If Amalgamated Veterans did want to withdraw their money, what would he liquidate?

It would be next to impossible to sell the Eureka Telecom position to Bloomfield Weiss now that he had pissed off Ian so comprehensively. He checked the prices with other brokers. They were all floating around the Bloomfield Weiss level, apart from Leipziger Gurney Kroheim who were making the bonds ninety-one to ninety-two. But he knew he'd never be able to offload the whole ten million with them. The truth was Bloomfield Weiss were the market in these bonds, and Bloomfield Weiss didn't want to buy them.

So what else could he sell?

There were four other relatively small positions in junk bonds that Lenka had bought, plus a couple of better quality issuers like CEZ. All of them were good companies with good prospects. He considered his own large government bond position. This had moved against him following the wobble from Russia, but he was sure it would come back. Now was the wrong time to sell. It would be against all his principles to get rid of his good positions and be left with his bad one.

Then there was the problem of valuation. The fund was revalued once a month, and the February reval was the following day. Technically, he might be able to get away with a price of eighty-eight for the twenty-five million euro position. But he knew that the real price, the price at which he could actually sell the bonds, was more like seventy. That was a seven and a half million loss. Chris winced. The investors would not like that one bit.

But he would have to use that price. He knew what could happen if you didn't disclose your losses immediately, and he didn't want to find himself in a similar position again. Besides, allowing Rudy to sell out of the fund at a higher price would be unfair on the other investors who remained in. If Rudy was determined to sell, he would just have to take his loss and lump it. And Chris would have to pray that the fund survived the consequences.

Chris leaned back in his chair and exhaled. This was getting all too familiar. A big position spinning out of control, taking everything else down with it. He could tell himself that it wasn't his fault of course, just like it hadn't been his fault last time. But he should face reality. He couldn't handle this kind of thing. Somehow, it always went wrong, and he could never figure out why.

Perhaps trading really was like chess. People assumed that the secret to chess was the ability to plan precisely several moves ahead, just as they assumed that good traders were those who could calculate precisely what was going to happen next in the markets. But both chess and trading were much more imprecise than that. Good chess players developed a feel for a position. They would plan many moves ahead to achieve a position that they felt was strong: an unassailable knight, a bishop attacking the opponent's centre, a crushing pawn attack on the queen's side. For them, chess was as much an art as a science.

Chris had been good at chess. His father had taught him young, and taught him well. He had never pushed him to work hard at it, but had shown a quiet satisfaction whenever Chris played well. Chris played for his school, he played for his club, he beat players several years older than himself. After his father died, he tried even harder, with some success. At eleven, he could beat the average adult club player. He won a junior county chess championship. People expected great things of him; everywhere he was compared to his father.

And then, when he reached thirteen or fourteen, things changed. As he played in higher circles, his opponents improved. He lost matches. Once he even lost to a precocious twelve-year-old. He became even more competitive, he spent hours reading chess books, perfecting his openings, trying to understand the deeper subtleties of strategy, but none of this seemed to help. He lost to better players, and he didn't understand why. He came to realize that they had a better feel for a position than he did, that he could be pottering along quite happily through the game, while his opponent was consolidating a winning position that Chris hadn't even recognized. If his father had still been around, he might have explained what was going on. But his father wasn't around. It came to him that he was never going to be as good a player as his father. There would always be thousands of chess players better than him. The memory of his father's quiet smile of satisfaction as he made a good move, a memory that had sustained him through so many games in the years since his father's death, began to fade. It was no longer fun to play chess. He gave up.

He had done similarly well as a trader. For a few years, while he was trading so successfully at Bloomfield Weiss, he had thought he'd sussed it. He developed a feel for a good position and a bad one. He knew when to buy more of a good position, to have the courage to be a pig, as George Soros would say, and when to cut a bad one. The profits rolled in, until that disastrous summer when, thanks to Herbie Exler, he had dropped six hundred million. Eventually, with Lenka's help, he had managed to tell himself that that really wasn't his fault, that it wouldn't happen again.

And now it was happening again. Sure, he wasn't going to lose six hundred million dollars, but he could lose Carpathian's reputation, and with it its investors. And that mattered.

Once again, none of this seemed to be his fault. But perhaps there was something he just couldn't see, something about how to deal with the people he worked with, that meant that he found himself in these disastrous positions. Lenka could have helped him. But Lenka, like his father, wasn't there.

As he sat at his desk, he felt the icy fingers of panic slowly grip at his chest. He was afraid. Not just afraid of losing money on the Eureka Telecom position, or even of losing Carpathian, but afraid of losing the shreds of his self-esteem that he had fought so hard to regain. The market was battering him, and he was hurting.

The phone rang. He picked it up.

'Carpathian.'

'Chris? It's Megan.'

'Oh, hi. How are you?'

'I'm fine. What about you? You sound sort of tense. Or do you traders always answer the phone like that?'

'I suppose we do,' said Chris, although he was impressed and pleased that Megan had managed to pick up his mood. 'But it's true, I'm not having the world's greatest day.'

'Are the markets going against you?' she asked.

'You could say that,' said Chris. 'Never mind. How's Cambridge?'

'Great. They've given me some really nice rooms in college in a building that must be three hundred years old. And I've met my supervisor and found the library. I'm really quite excited by it all.'

'That's good.'

'I was calling because I've booked a flight to Prague with Czech Airlines from Stansted Airport for Wednesday morning, coming back that night. I thought we could go together.'

'That's a good idea. Give me the details. By the way, I think Duncan will be coming with us.'

'OK,' said Megan, unenthusiastically.

'Look at it this way, it'll give me a chance to find out what he was doing hanging around Lenka's place.'

'I'd have thought that was pretty obvious,' Megan said disapprovingly. But she gave Chris the flight information.

'By the way, I've worked out who Marcus is,' Chris said.

'And?'

'Alex's brother.'

'Of course!'

'I checked with Eric, who confirmed it. Apparently, Marcus tried to speak to him too, but Eric avoided him. And Eric told me to say "hi" to you, whatever that means.'

'OK,' said Megan. 'How is he?'

'Doing formidably well. He must be earning millions in bonuses.'

'That doesn't surprise me,' said Megan. 'Well, I'd better go now.'

'OK. Oh, Megan?'

'Yes.'

'Thanks for ringing. It has been a bad day, and it was very nice to hear from you.'

'Good,' said Megan, and she was gone.

Chris waited for ten minutes in the cool glass-clad atrium of United Arab International's office in Bishopsgate, watching suited bankers come and go. At last, Pippa emerged from the bank of lifts. She was a small woman with curly blonde hair and a bright smile. Quite pretty.

Chris kissed her on the cheek. 'Let's go to Williams. It's close.'

'Isn't that where you and Duncan used to meet?' Pippa asked.

'That's right.'

'Well, I hope he won't be there now.'

'I don't think he will,' said Chris.

They reached the dark pub in five minutes. Duncan wasn't there. Chris bought himself a pint of bitter, and Pippa a glass of white wine, and they sat down in the same dark corner he and Duncan had occupied the week before.

'I haven't got long,' Pippa said. 'I'm supposed to be meeting someone later in Covent Garden.'

'OK,' said Chris. 'I'll be quick. It's about Lenka.'

Pippa's face clouded over. 'Oh God, not that woman. What's Duncan done now?'

Chris was taken aback by her reply. It was clear she hadn't heard. It would be unfair to ask her any more questions until he had told her.

'Lenka's dead. Murdered.'

Pippa was shocked. 'Oh, my God. It wasn't Duncan was it?' Then she looked confused. 'Sorry, I shouldn't have said that. But that's why you're here, isn't it? It must have something to do with Duncan.'

'I have no reason to think that it has,' said Chris, although in truth Pippa's initial response had alarmed him. 'It happened in Prague. The Czech police think it was a local who did it.'

'Whew,' said Pippa. 'Duncan must be in a state.'

'He is.' Chris took a sip of his beer. 'I take it that you knew about Duncan's feelings towards Lenka?'

Pippa snorted. 'Knew about them? Yes, I knew about them. At first, she just had the status of old girlfriend to be wary of. But then, pretty soon after we were married, I realized she was much more than that.'

'How did you find out?'

'From Duncan. He told me. It was mad. He began to talk about her occasionally, and then more and more often. You know how frank Duncan can be. I used to think it was cute. Now I think it's just plain stupid. Once he came back from somewhere drunk and he went on about how Lenka was the only woman he'd ever really loved. To his wife, for God's sake! He wanted to go and see her for lunch or a drink. I told him not to, but I'm sure he must have gone anyway. Not that I think he did anything. I think she had more sense than that.'

'I don't think they "did anything", either, if that helps,' said Chris.

'I couldn't give a shit one way or another, now,' said Pippa. 'Probably better if they had, quite frankly.'

'Was that why you split up?' Chris asked. 'Duncan never said.'

Pippa sighed. 'That's probably the reason, but I wouldn't want to put all the blame on Duncan. At first, I thought he was great. He's cute, and he seemed to think I was the most wonderful person he'd ever met. He had that adoring puppy-dog look.' She scowled. 'I really fell for it. Then we got married, things changed, and it turned out Lenka was the most wonderful woman he'd ever met.'

'Difficult,' said Chris.

'Yeah. But I said it wasn't all his fault. Has Duncan told you about Tony?'

Chris shook his head.

'He's a guy at work. I'd been seeing him. Duncan found out about it. He was quite good about it, really. Things just fell apart from there.'

'Oh.'

'Yes. The whole marriage was a right cock-up. Thank God there weren't any kids.'

'Is it Tony you're going to see now?'

Pippa reddened. 'No,' she said. 'That ended pretty quickly. It turns out I'm not the world expert on relationships, either.'

Chris had to summon up his courage to ask the next question. 'Do you think Duncan could have killed Lenka?'

'Um, no. No, I don't.' But Chris noticed the hesitation in her voice.

'Isn't that what you seemed to think when I mentioned Lenka had been murdered?'

'Yeah.' Pippa looked down into her glass. 'I'm sorry about that. It was just that I assumed you wanted to see me because Duncan had got himself into some kind of trouble, and when you said she'd been killed, my first thought was that was it. But even in his weirdest moments, Duncan wouldn't do something like that.'

'A neighbour said that Duncan had been hanging around Lenka's flat.'

'That doesn't surprise me.'

'It also seems that Lenka had been avoiding him.'

'Neither does that. I never got any impression that Lenka felt the same way about Duncan that he did about her. She obviously had more sense.'

'So, if she rejected him, wouldn't Duncan have been upset?'

'Yes. He'd have been devastated.' Pippa downed her wine. 'Look. He drove me crazy, but for a while I loved the stupid bugger. He's not a killer. I know that.' She looked at her watch. 'I've got to go. Thanks for the drink. Oh, and I am sorry about Lenka. I know she was a good friend of yours, too.'

With that, Pippa disappeared, leaving Chris even more confused.

As Chris opened the door to his flat, he heard the phone ringing. He picked it up. It was his mother.

'Chris. How are you? Are you all right?'

How the hell did she know there was something wrong? Chris had avoided talking to her about Lenka. It was something he wanted to sort out by himself; the last thing he wanted to deal with then was his mother's panicking.

'Chris? Are you there? I've been ever so worried.'

'Why, Mum?'

'Because you haven't telephoned me for two weeks, that's why.'

'But I don't have to call you every week, do I?'

'You don't have to, no, dear. But you always do.'

Chris closed his eyes. There was no escaping his family. It was the same with all the Poles in Halifax. Even when you were an adult, you couldn't escape your parents. He knew a close family was supposed to be a good thing, but sometimes, no, most of the time, he just wanted to grow up and get away from it.

'There is something wrong, isn't there?' said his mother, worried now, rather than nagging.

'Yes, Mum, there is.' Chris took a deep breath. 'Lenka has been killed.'

'Oh, no!'

'I'm afraid so.'

'What was it? A car crash?'

'No.' Chris explained what had happened in some detail. To his surprise, he could hear his mother sobbing on the phone. She was a strong woman, his mother. She scarcely ever wept. It caught Chris unawares.

'Mum, don't cry.'

'She was a lovely girl,' said his mother. 'She did so much for you.'

'Yes, she did.'

'I got the most wonderful letter from her after you and she started your business together. I wrote to her thanking her for helping you out –'

'You did what?'

'I wrote her a letter.' Chris's heart sank. Not for the first time he was mortified by his mother. 'And she wrote me one back. She said you were her first choice for a partner. She said you were extremely good at your job, but that wasn't the important thing. She said you were totally trustworthy, and she knew she

179

could always rely on you if things went wrong. I kept the letter. I'll show it to you if you like.'

'That was nice of her,' said Chris.

'Oh, she meant it, dear. I know she meant it.'

Chris felt his eyes pricking. He knew she meant it, too.

'How are you coping without her?' his mother asked.

'Struggling, to be honest.'

'Ah, well. Never mind. I'm sure you'll sort it out. I know you won't let Lenka down now.'

'No, Mum, I won't.'

'Can you come up and visit us next weekend? Anna will be here with Vic and the boys. And your granddad would love to see you.'

Anna was his sister. He supposed that it would be nice to see her, but they had drifted apart since her marriage to Vic at the age of twenty. And he wasn't at all convinced about his grandfather. As a boy, Chris had idolized the crotchety old war hero, but as they had both grown older, they seemed to inhabit different worlds. His grandfather was suspicious of international banking, feeling it was a suitable profession for a Jew or a German rather than a good Polish Catholic, and Chris found the old man's increasingly extreme political opinions hard to take. He could get by without seeing his grandfather.

'Sorry, Mum, I can't. As you can imagine, there's a lot to sort out down here. And I've got to be in America on Monday.'

'You're always off somewhere or other, aren't you? All right, dear. Have a good trip. And I am so sorry about Lenka.'

Chris said goodbye, and put down the phone. He slumped back in his chair and thought about his mother. He cringed as he imagined her writing to Lenka about him. But Lenka hadn't cringed. She had understood a mother's concern for her son, and her pride in him. Chris smiled to himself. Despite their very different styles, Lenka and his mother would probably have got on very well. It was a shame they had never had the chance to meet.

A twinge of guilt nagged at him. It wasn't the usual guilt he felt about his efforts to distance himself from his family, about disappointing his mother and grandfather. For the first time he had an inkling that his desire to keep away from them was not a sign of maturity, but rather the opposite. His mother was a good woman, who truly loved him, and would do anything for him. If he really was an independent adult, there should be nothing in that to threaten him. Once he had truly established his own identity away from his family then there would be no shame or danger in seeing them. Lenka was a strong, independent person who had immediately seen the goodness in his mother. He was ashamed that he hadn't the strength to do that too.

Lenka.

He glanced across the room at his computer, and wondered whether the mysterious Marcus had anything more to say about her. He switched on the machine and checked his e-mail, as he had done at frequent intervals throughout the weekend.

There was something. Between *Hot Russian Babes Download* and *How to make $2,000 per week from home* was a message entitled simply *Lenka*. It was from Marcus.

Chris opened it.

> I was horrified to learn of Lenka's murder. It makes me concerned for my own safety. I know that you were one of the people on the boat when my brother died. Will you tell me what really happened?
> Marcus

Chris stared at the message. He had promised Marcus information about Alex's death. What could he tell him?

The problem was that he couldn't be sure what Marcus already knew. Megan had guessed that Lenka had told him about Duncan knocking Alex into the sea, and Ian had confirmed that that was what Lenka intended to do, but Chris couldn't be sure what she had actually said to him. And even if Lenka had told Marcus about Duncan, what if Marcus had decided to go to the police?

With Lenka dead, he would have no evidence, unless Chris gave it to him now. That didn't seem to Chris a good idea.

He started tapping the keyboard.

> Marcus
> I can't tell you precisely what happened. What I can say is that your brother's death was a genuine accident. Can you tell me what Lenka told you before she died? I'd like to talk to you directly, if I can, so please give me your phone number and address. Or you can contact me on one of the numbers below.

Chris signed off giving a handful of phone numbers: home, work, fax, mobile, and his address, and sent the e-mail. He had to know what Marcus had discovered, and what he was planning to do with the information.

8

Wednesday was horrible. Since it was possible to fly to Prague, attend Lenka's funeral, and fly back in one day, that was what they had done. Duncan was ostentatiously miserable the whole time. Chris's pleasure at seeing Megan again was tempered by her distracted manner. It was clear that she didn't like Duncan's presence. And, of course, she too was upset by the occasion. Most of the long day's travelling was passed in silence, or desultory small talk.

They took a taxi from Ruzyně airport to Mělník, about thirty kilometres north of Prague. It was an ancient medieval town situated at the meeting point of two large rivers, the Vltava and the Elbe, dominated by an impressive castle, and surrounded by vine-clad slopes. But the crematorium was functional and depressing, the many mourners, most of them Lenka's contemporaries, raised no more than a hushed greeting to each other, and her parents were devastated. There was no religious service, just music, and a eulogy from one of Lenka's friends. Although Chris couldn't understand a word of what she said, he could understand the sorrow.

Apart from that moment, Chris was surprised by how little he felt during the ceremony. It was hard to imagine Lenka growing up in this pretty little town, much harder than it was to be aware of her presence in the office in London, or even on the streets of Prague. Although he knew that the coffin must contain her body, he didn't feel that the Lenka he knew was there. He didn't know quite where she was, but he knew she wasn't there.

The ceremony, such as it was, ended, and, after a few sad words with Lenka's parents during which Chris managed to tell them that he had instructed Carpathian's solicitors to take care of Lenka's affairs in London, the three of them gratefully climbed back into the waiting taxi.

At Stansted, Megan took a train back to Cambridge and Chris and Duncan took one in the opposite direction to Liverpool Street. They sat opposite each other and stared out at the Essex night rushing by, their reflections interrupted by the flash of station lights.

'Thanks for agreeing to have lunch with Khalid tomorrow,' Duncan said.

'No problem.'

'I'm sorry, but I don't think I can make it. Something's come up.'

'That's OK,' said Chris, although in truth he was a little annoyed that he could be bothered to see Duncan's client and Duncan couldn't.

'Have you ever heard of someone called Marcus?' Chris asked.

'Marcus? I don't think so. Wait, isn't there a Marcus Neale who works for Harrison Brothers?'

'No. Not him. This man's American. Tall, thin, longish hair.'

Duncan shook his head. 'No.'

'Oh.' There was a pause. Chris noticed that Duncan was wary. Well he might be. 'I went round to Lenka's flat last week.'

Duncan grunted.

'I met one of her neighbours. He said he'd seen you hanging around.'

'Me?'

'It sounded a lot like you from his description. He said that you'd approached Lenka and she'd ignored you.'

Duncan didn't answer. He turned to face the night. Chris waited.

Eventually, Duncan answered. 'It's true. When things went wrong with Pippa, I tried to get in touch with Lenka. She didn't want to see me. But I didn't give up. She was too important to me to give up on.'

'So you hassled her?'

'No. I did watch her from a distance, sometimes, but I don't think she saw me. I wrote to her. And I approached her a couple of times, like that one you mentioned. But I didn't "hassle" her. I didn't force myself on her, if that's what you mean.' He smiled. 'It's funny. The week before she died, she called me. She wanted to see me. She said she had something important to tell me. We met in a bar somewhere near your office.'

'What was it?'

Duncan sighed. 'I don't know. I think I screwed it up. There was so much I wanted to tell her. She tried to stop me, but I needed to say it. I think I must have gone over the top. She left.'

'Before she told you anything?'

'Oh, she told me there was absolutely no chance of us ever getting together again,' muttered Duncan bitterly. 'The last time I saw her, and that was the last thing she said to me.' Tears were forming in the corners of his eyes.

'Bloody hell, Duncan, don't you realize that she must have had something quite important to say? Why didn't you listen to her, for God's sake?'

For a moment, Duncan looked surprised at the vehemence in Chris's voice. Then the resigned expression returned. 'I don't care now. It's too late.'

Chris leaned forward. 'Listen to me, Duncan. I know who Marcus is, even if you say you don't. He's Alex Lubron's brother. Lenka sent him an e-mail saying she wanted to tell him something, and she wanted to talk to you.' Chris was careful not to mention Ian in all of this. If Duncan found out about his relationship with Lenka, it might seriously unbalance him. And Chris wanted Duncan to be as balanced as possible. 'I think it was something to do with Alex's death. Now, do you have *any* idea at all what Lenka was going to say to Marcus?'

Duncan sighed and closed his eyes. 'I do know who Marcus is. In fact, he came to see me. He'd just seen Lenka in your office that afternoon. She'd told him that I'd hit Alex on the boat, and that was how he fell in the sea. Marcus waited for me outside the office. He got me on the way home. We were shouting at each other in the street.'

'What did he say?'

'He asked if it was true that I'd killed Alex. He asked why. He asked why I'd kept quiet about it. Then he gave me a lot of abuse.'

'And what did you do?'

Duncan sighed. 'I took it. You know I never felt comfortable about keeping it all quiet. I mean, it was very good of you all to do it, and I know I could have ended up behind bars, but Marcus had a point. It was unfair to him not to know what really happened.'

Chris grunted. 'Perhaps.'

'Then he ran out of steam. He stood there, sort of shifting from foot to foot. I thought he was going to leave me alone, when he took a swing at me. I just covered my face. He kept on trying to hit me, until some passers-by pulled him off. I turned and legged it. I didn't want to fight him.'

'What do you think he'll do?' asked Chris. 'Do you think he'll go to the police?'

Duncan shrugged. 'Maybe. I don't know.'

'Why didn't you tell me this before? Why did you pretend you didn't know who he was?'

Duncan sighed. 'After everything all of you had done to keep things quiet, I didn't want to admit that I'd let you down. That I'd let out what had really happened. I just hoped that Marcus would go away and I could forget about him.'

'But why didn't you deny it?'

'It was too late. Lenka had already told him. Besides, he had a right to know.'

He had a right to know. Lenka's words. Well, he knew now. And Chris had no idea what he would do with that knowledge.

*

Chris spent all the next day at the office, with only a break at midday to have lunch with Duncan's client, Khalid, at a restaurant in Devonshire Square in the City. Khalid was twenty minutes late, but was all smiles when he finally arrived. He seemed to be about Chris's age, neatly dressed with a small black moustache, warm brown eyes and a ready grin. They indulged in the typical market small talk. It turned out that Khalid was a friend of Faisal, the Saudi on Chris's training programme who was now apparently in charge of a large pan-Gulf investment fund. The waitress came, and Khalid flirted expertly with her before ordering his sole done in a very particular way. No wine.

Khalid asked about the Central European high-yield bond market, and Chris answered him as best he could. The problem was that there weren't yet many issues to choose from, and only three that Chris could strongly recommend.

The sole came, and it was prepared to Khalid's liking. 'But you don't just invest in high yield, do you?' he asked.

Chris told him about his government bond trades: about the forints, zlotys, korunas, kroons and lats he dealt in every day. Khalid was intrigued, and asked intelligent questions. He, too, had been involved in trading the Continental European bond markets before the euro, and from the sound of it, he was probably quite good at it. As Chris talked, he realized that after a couple of years of thorough immersion, he really did know these markets well.

They had finished the coffee, and Khalid insisted on paying the bill. 'That was fascinating,' he said. 'And thank you for steering me away from Eureka Telecom.'

'No problem. I think that's wise, at the moment. I wouldn't trust Bloomfield Weiss an inch on that kind of stuff.'

'I know what you mean,' said Khalid. 'Do you know Herbie Exler?'

'I used to work for him.'

'Ah,' said Khalid carefully.

'Don't worry. He screwed me.'

'He screwed me, too,' said Khalid. 'Several times. I think he thinks I'm just a dumb Arab who he can leg over whenever he feels like it. What did he do to you?'

'Remember that big convergence trade Bloomfield Weiss were involved with a couple of years ago?'

Khalid nodded. 'How could I forget it?'

'Well, that was me. But when I wanted to get out of it, Herbie wanted to double up. We did, we lost, I got the blame, I was on the street.'

Khalid watched Chris carefully as he said this, as though trying to judge whether Chris was spinning a convenient cover story. He could probably tell he wasn't. There was no need: Chris had no reason to try to impress him.

'He's an asshole,' Khalid said matter-of-factly.

Chris smiled. 'I wouldn't argue with that.' It was late by the time Chris got back to his flat from the office that night. He checked his e-mail before he went to bed. There was one from Marcus.

> You say Alex's drowning was an accident, but I only have your word for that. If you won't trust me by telling me what happened on the boat, then I can't tell you what Lenka told me. I am still worried by her death. I don't think I can trust any of the people who were on the boat that night. So I won't give you my phone number or address.
> Marcus

Damn! Chris quickly typed out a reply.

> Marcus
> I am flying to America on Sunday. I am going to New York, and Hartford, Connecticut. I would very much like to meet you. You name the time and the place, and I will be there.
> Chris

He sent the e-mail, and went to bed.

There was an answer waiting for him the next morning. One word.

No.

Chris sighed. Still, Eric was right. It couldn't be that hard to track down someone with a name like Marcus Lubron. He'd never heard the name Lubron before he'd met Alex. He'd allow himself some time while he was in New York to find him. Perhaps Eric could help.

Chris leaned against the wall by the porter's lodge and watched the children go by. He remembered how infuriated he had been when he was at Oxford to read an article by a graduate about how young all the undergraduates looked to him. Well, twelve years on he knew it was true. Surely, Chris thought, he had never looked quite like these kids?

Then he saw her, striding across the quad, or whatever they called it in Cambridge, in jeans, jersey and a denim jacket. He was relieved to see that she looked a couple of years older than most of the spotty inhabitants of the college. She brightened when she saw him. He kissed her cheek, already cold in the March air.

'Hi, it's great to see you,' she said.

'And you. Thanks for inviting me up here.'

'It seemed the least I could do after your hospitality last week. Do you mind if we just walk? I'd like to explore the town a bit.'

'That's fine with me,' said Chris.

'Do you know Cambridge?' Megan asked. 'You didn't go here, did you?'

'I went to the other place,' said Chris. 'I spent a couple of drunken evenings here ten years ago seeing friends from school. I'm afraid I don't remember it very clearly.'

They walked. Chris hadn't been back to Oxford for years, and he was surprised by how different Cambridge felt from the way he remembered university. There were few tourists around at this time of year. People were walking to and fro with quiet purpose. Although he knew, because he could remember, that students had their own problems, their own worries, their own crises, the atmosphere seemed to be one of calm serenity. Traffic had been banished from the centre of Cambridge and at times the loudest noise he could hear was the sound of footsteps around him, or the rattle of an old bicycle. He felt like a grubby outsider from the materialistic bustle of another world, from the world of pay cheques, commuting on the underground, suits, mortgages.

'What's the University of Chicago like?' he asked Megan.

'Nothing like this,' she said. 'At least, not physically. The oldest buildings are only about a hundred years old. But it's a good school. There are some good historians there: people even these guys respect.'

'I'm sure you're one of them,' Chris said.

Megan smiled. 'We'll see. What I really like about Cambridge is that it seems like a place where history happens. My kind of history.'

'You mean all the old buildings?'

'Yes, but it's more than that. You can imagine people studying here for centuries, reading and writing Latin, arguing about theology. It somehow makes the study of, I don't know, manuscript illumination in the tenth century, more real. In Chicago, I felt as if I was on a different planet. In fact, Mars seemed to be closer and more real than St Dunstan and his friends.'

'It seems an awfully long time ago to me.'

'Not to me,' said Megan. 'I remember the first time I became interested in all this stuff. I was an exchange student at a high school in France, in Orléans. The girl I was staying with couldn't care about anything that happened before about nineteen seventy, but her father was fascinated by history. He took me to this tiny little church in a place called Germigny-des-Prés. There was a blind curate who showed us round. Most of it was standard grey gothic, but one part of it, the apse at one end, was decorated with the most gorgeous frescos. I can still remember the curate describing them from memory. I couldn't believe that something

190

so beautiful could have been created a thousand years ago, in the so-called "dark ages". Ever since then, I've been trying to understand what it was like to live then, how mysterious and dangerous the world must have seemed, and how people tried to make sense of it.'

'And I thought all they did in Chicago was trade pork-bellies.'

Megan smiled. 'I know. I must sound pretty weird to you.'

'No,' said Chris. 'Not at all. You must show me some of this stuff.'

'I'll take you to see The Benedictional of St Aethelwold in the British Library. It's completely beautiful.'

'Do that.'

'All right,' Megan smiled. 'I will.' She pointed down a narrow alley. 'Shall we try this way?'

They wandered down the small road. Along one side was a row of cottages washed in varying shades of pink and grey, along the other was the back of a college, Chris had no idea which one. He was lost.

'The funeral was pretty grim, wasn't it?' he said.

Megan shuddered. 'Yes. But I'm glad I went.'

'I'm sorry we didn't talk much.'

'It was difficult with Duncan there. Did you get a chance to speak to him?'

'Yes, I did,' said Chris.

'And?'

'Although he wouldn't admit it at first, he did say Marcus had been to see him. Apparently, you were right: Lenka did tell Marcus what really happened on the boat. Marcus asked Duncan whether this was all true, and threatened him.'

'Threatened him?' said Megan in alarm.

'Yes. Nothing specific. But it seemed to rattle Duncan.'

'So why didn't he mention this to you before?'

'He said he didn't want to admit that he'd given away what really happened, after all we'd done to keep it quiet.'

'Yeah, right,' said Megan.

'I believe him,' said Chris.

'Did you ask him where he was the day Lenka was killed?'

'No, I didn't.'

'Why not?'

Chris took a deep breath. 'It was the day of her funeral. He was upset. I'm sure that was genuine. I think he would have been pretty angry if I'd suggested he was responsible.'

Megan looked at Chris disapprovingly.

'He's my friend. I know him,' said Chris. 'And I'm sure he didn't kill Lenka.'

They had reached the river, swollen by the recent rain. Wisps of fog still hung eerily over the fields towards Grantchester. A solitary, cold-looking student was propelling a punt downstream.

'What a stupid way to drive a boat,' said Megan. 'Can you do that?'

'Not in March,' Chris said, shivering.

They walked on. 'At least we now know what Lenka told Marcus,' Megan said.

'Yes,' said Chris. Then he stopped in his tracks. 'Wait a moment!'

'What is it?'

'We don't know what Lenka was going to tell Marcus. We don't know at all.'

'What do you mean?'

'Well, we know Marcus came to see Lenka on the Tuesday. We also know, because Duncan told us, that that is when Lenka told him that Duncan knocked Alex into the sea. Marcus went straight off to wait for Duncan coming out of work that afternoon.'

'OK.'

'But the e-mail Lenka sent to Marcus was written twenty-four hours later.'

'Are you sure?'

'Yes. Hang on, let me check.' Chris dug the e-mail out of the breast pocket of his leather jacket. 'Yes, here it is. It was sent on Wednesday the sixteenth of February.'

'That doesn't make sense,' Megan said.

'It does. It means that there was *something else* that Marcus had a right to know.'

'Something else?'

'Must be.'

'But what?'

'I've no idea.'

They crossed the river and walked along towards the Backs.

'There is one possibility,' Megan said. 'Did you hear Alex was in trouble over drugs?'

'No,' said Chris. He furrowed his brow. 'I don't remember anything like that.'

'Oh, yes. He was very worried about it. There had been some kind of sneaky random drug test and he'd been caught with traces of cocaine in his sample. It was a big deal. Bloomfield Weiss was threatening to make an example of him.'

'A random drug test? I don't remember a random drug test.' Chris thought hard. 'Oh, yes. I think there was some kind of medical for the American trainees after the final examination. The rest of us were allowed to leave. That must have been it.' He shook his head. 'Wow. He kept that quiet.'

'Yes. Eric knew, of course, and therefore so did I. But you can imagine it's not the sort of thing he wanted to broadcast.'

'I didn't realize Alex did drugs.'

'A lot of people did back then,' said Megan.

Chris grunted. 'I'm a complete innocent when it comes to drugs. You read in the press that it's going on all round you, but I've hardly ever seen any. Although I did catch Ian once.' He remembered Tamara barging into Ian's bedroom, and the look of embarrassment on Ian's face as he looked up from the white line of coke. But then he remembered his own discomfort when Tamara had taken some. 'Ian was very lucky he wasn't tested.'

'Perhaps Lenka knew about Alex getting caught,' Megan said. 'Perhaps that's what she wanted to tell Marcus.'

'But why? I hardly think that it was something Marcus had a "right to know".'

Megan shook her head. 'I suppose not. But it's another reason to look for him. Have you heard any more from him?'

'He's scared,' said Chris. 'He won't give me his address. He doesn't want me to find him.'

Megan looked at Chris. 'That's worrying.'

For the first time, Chris wondered whether Marcus had reason to be scared. And if so, whether he should be scared also.

They walked miles that afternoon, criss-crossing the town and its parks and meadows. They were dawdling by the river, surrounded by waterlogged stretches of grass, when darkness crept in around them. They made their way through the gloom to a pub, the Fort St George, standing alone by the bank of the river, and ate in front of a glowing fire.

Later, they walked back to Megan's college. Chris had intended to drive back to London that evening, but she invited him back to her room for a cup of coffee. They cut through two courtyards, past an ancient tree, a tangle of bare branches looming out of the darkness, to her building. Her room was warm and cosy, and it was cold and damp outside. He and Megan talked late into the night, and Chris didn't want the evening to end. Neither did Megan.

He stayed.

9

Chris tried to edge his left elbow on to the armrest beside him, but the large man reading a computer magazine wouldn't have any of it. On Chris's other side, a much smaller, skinny boy was playing a frantic game of cards with his brother. The research piece on macroeconomic adjustment in the Baltic States that lay on his lap was not making any sense. Chris cursed himself for travelling Economy. Lenka refused to do it, and became quite upset if Chris ever tried to travel that way. But with Carpathian in so much difficulty, Chris had felt guilty about shelling out the enormous fare for Business Class. Stupid. A thousand pounds here or there would make no difference to whether Carpathian survived. In any case, he had had to buy an expensive open ticket. The trip out to Hartford to see Rudy Moss should be straightforward. But he didn't know how long it would take him to find Marcus Lubron, or to discover more about Alex's drug problem.

Chris gave up on the Baltic States, leaned back, closed his eyes, and thought of Megan. He had said goodbye to her in Cambridge before driving back to London to get his stuff ready for America. It had been a great day, a great night. He remembered her smell, the softness of her skin, her hair against his face. She had awakened something in him that he had not experienced for a long time. Since Tamara. No, it was different from the way he had felt with Tamara. It was something new, something much better. There was so much more he wanted to know about her, and yet he felt he knew her well already. Spending time with her seemed so natural. He hoped that he would see a lot more of her; he was determined that he would see a lot more of her.

He thought about her and Eric, and wondered for a moment how he and Eric compared. But only for a moment. Rivalry with Eric was pointless: Eric was always a winner at everything, and it was best just to accept that as a fact of life. He winced at the only stupid remark he could remember making during the night. Sometime in the small hours, after they had made love for the second time, he had mentioned Eric. She had stiffened, and then asked him whether no one had ever told him not to discuss old lovers with new ones. He thought of Duncan and Pippa and felt like an idiot. His transgression had soon been forgotten, but it was clear that Eric was a taboo subject with Megan.

He smiled as he thought about seeing her again. Then the kid on his right whacked him in the ribs with a sharp elbow.

Rudy Moss's arrogance had matured. He used to be cocky or sycophantic, depending on whom he was with. Ten years had given him a certain authority. His pudginess had transformed into prematurely middle-aged flab. He used his long nose to great effect, holding his head at exactly the right angle to be able to look down it at whomever he was talking to. He was an expert too at the weighty silence, the pause that implied that he alone knew the right answer and was debating whether to divulge it. Chris couldn't stand him.

But he had to sit there and beg, a process that he found very difficult, but that Rudy seemed to be enjoying greatly.

The meeting started off promisingly.

'I got a call from Eric Astle about you last week,' Rudy began. 'He was quite complimentary.'

'Good,' said Chris.

'Yeah. He's done well,' said Rudy. 'Did you see that piece in *Business Week* a couple of months back? "Dealmakers of the Twenty-first Century" it was called. Something like that.'

'No, I didn't.'

'It seems that Eric is quite the M&A star.'

'It does.'

'It's a shame he couldn't do quite as well as me on the programme,' Rudy said, with a smile.

Chris's recollection was that Eric had just pipped Rudy for top place at the end, but he let it rest. Chris looked around Rudy's office. Small, but at least he had his own. He had a nice view of other tall buildings housing insurance companies. Amalgamated Veterans Life was a respected institution, and Rudy obviously had some responsibility. But he was hardly 'dealmaker of the twenty-first century'. Chris smiled to himself.

Mistake. Rudy saw him and frowned. He was probably all too aware that he hadn't fulfilled the promise of the training programme.

'I'm impressed by what Eric says, but I need to make up my own mind on this. I told you the reservations I have now you've lost Lenka. Why should I keep my funds with you?'

Chris launched into an explanation of the opportunities for Central Europe, of the rapid integration of the countries there into the European economy, and of how the hiccups on the way provided opportunities for the fund to trade its way to a stronger return. He focused on how he proposed to recruit a high-yield bond expert to replace Lenka. Chris convinced himself. He didn't know about Rudy.

'What do you think about Latvia?' Rudy asked. 'Do you think it will make the second wave of candidates for the European Union?'

Typical of Rudy to ask a technical question out of the blue that he had probably mugged up beforehand. But Chris knew his stuff, and, aided by what he had read on the plane, gave a convincing answer.

It seemed to satisfy Rudy. 'Do you have a current valuation for the fund?' he asked.

This was it. The moment Chris had been dreading, but that he couldn't avoid. He handed Rudy the February revaluation. Rudy scanned it.

'But this says the price is one hundred and fifteen euros.

Wasn't it a hundred and twenty-nine last month? What happened?'

'It's the Eureka Telecom position we bought recently. It was a new issue, but we would only get a price of seventy if we were to sell it today.'

Rudy grimaced. 'Nightmare. So the fund's down, what, ten per cent in a month?' he said, with the hint of a mocking smile. 'That's not very good is it?'

'No. It's our worst month to date,' Chris admitted. 'But remember you invested at a hundred. You've still made good money.'

'We might have made it in the past, but we're losing it now, aren't we?'

'The Eureka Telecom was Lenka's position.' Chris hated to say it, but it was true.

Rudy raised his eyebrows. 'That's not very gentlemanly, is it? Blaming your partner when she's not here to defend herself.'

He was getting to Chris. Chris took a deep breath, counted to three, and replied. 'Lenka has made some very good investments. She's half the reason that the fund has performed so well overall. But her last one doesn't seem to be working out.'

'Do you know why she bought it?' Rudy asked.

It was a good question, testing the level of communication between them and, by implication, how much Chris knew about what Lenka did. A good question that Chris couldn't answer. 'She bought it while I was away on holiday.'

'So it's fair to say that you know nothing about the fund's biggest position. The position that's giving you most trouble?'

'I'm finding out,' said Chris.

Rudy shook his head. 'Finding out. I'm not sure Amalgamated Veterans should be financing your learning curve.'

'Trust me, Rudy. I will make you money,' Chris said.

Rudy chuckled. 'Like you made Bloomfield Weiss money?'

Suddenly it all became clear to Chris. He was here so Rudy could enjoy rubbing his nose in the fact that his future was in

Rudy's hands. Rudy would toy with him, then go in for the kill. He could draw out the process for quite a while before he said no. Well, Chris had insisted on the meeting, so in a way it was his own fault. But his pride couldn't let Rudy get away with it.

He stood up and held out his hand. 'Thank you for investing with us, Rudy. But I think from now on the Carpathian Fund will get on better without you.'

Rudy, looking disappointed, shook the outstretched hand.

'I'll see myself out,' Chris said, leaving the office.

A waste of time.

Chris sat on the Amtrak from Hartford to New York, fuming. He had travelled thousands of miles to see Rudy, only to be abused and humiliated. He should have known. After all, Rudy had made clear his lack of enthusiasm to see him. But he had had to try. It was only by seeing Rudy face-to-face that he could be absolutely sure there was no hope of getting him to change his mind.

What now? Sell bonds at the bottom of the market? Give up? Close down Carpathian? Perhaps the market would bail him out this time. Perhaps, when he got back to London, there would be a rally in the junk market, a big buyer of Eureka Telecom bonds, or an announcement on the expansion of the European Union.

Once again, he was relying on the fickleness of the markets to survive: he hated that.

Once again, he felt helpless. But this time, his mind didn't go back to the disaster at Bloomfield Weiss, but to another time, twenty years before.

He was eleven. His father had been dead for nine months. The lives of his mother, his younger sister and himself had changed dramatically. They had moved house, from a semi-detached in a nice cul-de-sac, to a flat on the seventh floor of a tough tower block. His mother went out to work in the local VG Stores during the day and had taken on night-shift work at a warehouse three days a week. Although she was proud of him for getting into grammar school, even that would bring more expense. But despite the lack of sleep, the worry about money, the red-rimmed, fatigue-darkened eyes, he never saw her cry. She always had time for him and Anna, to listen to their fears, to comfort them. At eleven, Chris had found that he once again needed to feel the warmth of his mother's arms, and they were always there.

Until one evening, when he left school late, and met her outside the shop. Anna was playing at a friend's house. They walked home rapidly, chattering together, and took the stinking lift daubed with graffiti up to the seventh floor. Their flat was at the end of the walkway. As they approached, his mother suddenly quickened her pace and then broke into a run. Chris followed. The front door was swinging open. Inside, the flat was trashed. Chris's mother ran to the chest of drawers where he knew she kept a lot of his dad's stuff. The drawers were open. She stood silently staring at the mess inside. Tentatively, Chris joined her. His dad's watch was gone. So was his wedding ring. So were several chess medals, worth nothing to anyone but Chris's mum. Their wedding photograph lay on the floor, the glass broken, the print ripped.

Her shoulders heaved, and she let out a kind of animal howl. Then she began to sob. Scared, and unsure what to do, Chris grabbed hold of her and led her back to the bed. She began to bawl like a child, tears streaming down her face. Chris's eyes stung, but he was determined to hold back the tears, be the one to support her for once. He clung tightly to her shoulders, hoping she would quieten down. She pressed her face into his chest and wept.

Eventually, much later, she stopped. She lay still for several minutes, Chris unwilling to disturb her. Then she sat up on the bed and turned to him, her face puffy and damp with tears, her dark curly hair, usually so carefully tamed, a mess.

'You know what, Chris?' she said.

'Yes, Mum?'

'Things can't get any worse than they are right now, can they? It's just not possible.' She sniffed, and from somewhere she summoned a quivering smile. 'As long as you and me and Anna stick together and help each other, they can only get better. So come on. Let's get this mess tidied up.'

And she was right. Eventually things had got better. The flat was cleared up. The pain of the loss of his father became a persistent ache. She found a better-paying job in a travel agency, and was able eventually to afford a small house for them. Anna married and had two kids. Chris went to university. She'd done it. She'd pulled through.

So would he.

The train drew into Penn Station and Chris took a taxi downtown to Bloomfield Weiss. He remembered the thrill of anticipation he had felt that morning ten years before when he had first entered the building with Duncan and Ian. He took the lift up to the forty-fifth floor. And, just like that first day, Abby Hollis was waiting for him.

She had changed little. She was wearing a white blouse and her blonde hair was tied severely back. But she was chewing gum, and she smiled when she saw Chris.

'Well, how are you doing? Good to see you.' She held out her hand, and Chris shook it. 'Come through to the floor. It's quiet enough at the moment. We can talk there.'

She led Chris through the clutter of desks, chairs, bins, jackets, papers and people towards the far corner of the room.

Chris looked around him. 'This hasn't changed much,' he said.

'Management keep on talking about getting a new one, but there's not much point. This is still where it all happens on Wall Street.'

If that was true, then there was nothing happening on Wall Street at that particular moment, which wasn't too surprising for four o'clock on a Monday afternoon. The room was crowded, but those on the phone looked casual and unhurried, and most people were staring at their screens, the newspaper, or simply into space. There was the odd cluster of large men in white shirts goofing off. Somehow, it all seemed less intimidating than it had ten years before. Chris no longer expected someone to scream at him at any second to go and get a pizza. In fact, he saw a couple of frightened trainees squatting at the edge of a row of desks that he could scream at himself if he felt like it. He didn't.

Abby worked in Muni sales, not the most glamorous of departments at Bloomfield Weiss. As they reached her desk, Chris recognized Latasha James, wearing a smart black suit.

'Hello, Chris! It's been a long time.' She gave him a hug. 'I'm so sorry to hear about Lenka.'

'Yes, it was terrible,' Chris said. 'I see they still haven't let you out of Municipal Finance.'

Latasha rolled her eyes. 'I guess not. I work upstairs in origination. But it's not so bad. Some of these cities need the cash we can get them, you know what I'm saying? I guess I'm doing more good here than I would in many places.'

'Doing good at Bloomfield Weiss. Now there's a thought!'

'Isn't it just? I've got to run,' Latasha said. 'See you around.'

'She's really good,' said Abby, sitting down at her desk. 'She wins us more deals than the rest of the guys upstairs put together. The public officials love her. And not just the black ones.'

'I'm very glad to hear it,' Chris said, pulling up a chair, and glancing at the familiar screens on Abby's desk. 'How long have you been doing this?'

'Nine years,' Abby said. 'I eventually escaped from George Calhoun's clutches. It's OK. I keep my head down, I'm nice to my customers, I put up with shit from my boss, they keep me around.'

'An achievement these days,' Chris said.

Abby smiled. 'I heard it was Herbie Exler who screwed you on the convergence trade. They should have gotten rid of him, not you.'

Chris raised his eyebrows. 'I didn't realize other people knew.'

'Oh, yeah. They all know,' Abby said. 'They're not about to mention it, though. Herbie is not someone you want as an enemy. Nor is Simon Bibby. He's head of Fixed Income in New York now.'

'Well, I'm glad I'm out of it.'

Abby chewed her gum contemplatively. 'I'm sorry I was such a bitch on the training programme.'

Chris was startled. 'You weren't a bitch.'

Abby smiled. 'Oh, yes I was. I wanted to be the meanest programme coordinator Calhoun had ever seen. I know that's what he wanted, and I thought that was the only way I was ever going to make it in an investment bank. I was so uptight about everything.'

'They get you like that, don't they?' Chris said.

'They sure do. I was just as bad here, at first. Then, it dawned on me that it was possible to have a quiet life and work at Bloomfield Weiss. You just have to know how. Excuse me.'

One of the lights on a panel flashed and Abby answered it. She chatted amiably with someone on the other line, and ended up selling him three million dollars of a New Jersey Turnpike bond.

She hung up. 'Where was I?'

'Reliving the good old days.'

'Oh yeah,' Abby laughed. 'Now, how can I help you?'

'I wanted to ask you something about the programme. I think it might be related to Lenka's death.'

'Go ahead.'

'It's about Alex Lubron.'

Abby raised her eyebrows. 'Alex Lubron? Now that's a subject that I thought you had all the answers to, not me.'

Chris ignored the dig. He knew he would have to be careful. 'Actually, I wanted to talk to you about what happened a little before he died.'

'I'll see if I can remember.'

'I understand he tested positive for drugs?'

Abby nodded. 'I do remember that. We were supposed to have a crackdown on drug abuse in the firm. You might recall that a couple of salesmen had been caught supplying clients. Well, the idea was to fire one or two employees quite publicly to show that the firm was coming down hard on the issue. But they didn't want to fire real employees that were making real money. So they had the idea that they would pick on a couple of trainees. No one would miss them, right?'

Chris smiled.

'As you can imagine, Calhoun loved this idea. So he set up a fake medical exam, which would be taken without warning right after the final examination. The Frankfurt and London offices objected that their trainees were going to be sacrificed as well, so Calhoun was forced to restrict things to the American hires.

'So, they took the samples, and much to their surprise only one trainee tested positive.'

'Alex?'

'That's right. Alex. And what's more, he had some kind of mentor in mortgage trading who raised hell. Calhoun spent a lot of time with Alex; I'm not sure what the deal was, exactly. Anyway, after Alex died it was all forgotten. Bloomfield Weiss wanted a quick and easy sacking of someone who'd never been heard of again. Once Alex had drowned, he became entirely the wrong person to be found with drugs.'

'Did the police know?' Chris asked.

'I'm not sure what the police knew,' Abby said. 'They seemed suspicious about Alex's death for a week or so, and then they dropped the whole thing. But I'm sure you remember that.'

'I do,' said Chris. 'I definitely do.'

'Now, whether Bloomfield Weiss put some kind of pressure on them, I don't know.'

'Can Bloomfield Weiss do that?'

Abby looked around her. 'What do you think we do here?

We're one of the top three firms on the Street for raising municipal finance. We know a lot of public officials.'

'Hmm.'

Abby leaned forward. 'So tell me,' she said, a twinkle in her eye. 'What did happen on that boat?'

Chris sighed. 'Alex got drunk. The boat was going fast. The sea was choppy. He fell in. Ian, Eric and Duncan jumped in to try to find him. They couldn't. We were lucky to find them, quite honestly. Alex drowned.' Chris's voice was flat as he recited this. All of it was true, even if it wasn't the whole truth.

'I'm sorry,' said Abby, her curiosity punctured by Chris's tone. 'Sometimes you forget that disasters involve real people.'

'Yeah,' said Chris. 'You do.'

'There were rumours afterwards. That it hadn't been an accident.'

'I'm sure.'

'It was a big deal in HR. You see, they'd been trying a new approach to recruitment for a couple of years. Do you remember doing some psychometric tests when you joined?'

'Vaguely.'

'Well, one of the things they were looking for was extreme competitiveness, aggression, even ruthlessness. The theory was that investment bankers need to be predators, kings of the jungle, some crap like that.'

'Sounds just like George Calhoun,' Chris said.

'Exactly. In fact, I think the whole thing might have been his idea. Well, a lot of the people produced by this process were your average nasty red-blooded investment banker. But one or two of them were borderline psychotic.'

'And Bloomfield Weiss recruited them anyway?'

'You got it. With open arms. One of the psychologists who did the tests kicked up a fuss about it. In the end we stopped them.'

'Do you know who these "borderline psychotics" were?'

'I found out who one of them was later. A guy called Steve

Matzley was convicted for rape a few months after he left Bloomfield Weiss. I don't think he was on your programme. But he was recruited about that time. The rumour is that the psychologist's report flagged him as being a dangerous person.'

'And they took him anyway?'

'You got it. He was a great government bond trader. It was pure luck he wasn't working here when he committed the rape.'

'Jesus. So was the rumour that one of us on the boat had a similar profile?'

'That was the rumour. After Steve Matzley, it made some kind of sense. But it was pure speculation. The files were strictly locked up and confidential. Besides, you just told me it was an accident, didn't you?'

Chris didn't respond to her question. 'Did you know the name of the psychologist who complained about the tests?'

'No. Sorry. But you should ask George Calhoun about all this. He'd be able to tell you more.'

'Is he still in Human Resources?'

'They fired him about a year ago.'

'Oh, what a shame. Couldn't have happened to a nicer guy.'

'Especially after all he did for us,' said Abby, grinning.

'Do you know how I can get hold of him?'

'I don't know if he got another job,' said Abby. 'And in case you're wondering, I don't have his home number.'

'Never mind. I'll track him down. Thanks for your help.'

'No problem,' said Abby, picking up her phone.

I O

Chris took the elevator up a couple of floors. The doors opened on a large, hushed reception area, guarded by a beautifully groomed young woman, who asked Chris to take a seat, offered him a cup of tea, and promised that Mr Astle would be with him shortly.

Of course he wasn't, but Chris didn't mind waiting. He watched people come and go through a heavy smoked-glass door, waving their passes at a blinking green eye on a black panel each time. He thought about the police investigation into Alex's death.

It had been tense. The first set of questions was quick and easy. They had all agreed to describe what actually happened, including Duncan's argument with Alex, but to miss out the fight. Only Lenka and Duncan were to admit to actually seeing Alex go overboard, the rest of them were up on the bridge looking the other way. But a couple of days after the initial questioning, they were all interviewed again, by a pair of detectives who were much more probing. They seemed to think there was something wrong about the story, but they didn't know quite what. One of them had asked Chris if there had been a fight, and Chris had said that if there had been, he hadn't seen it. Afterwards, everyone's nerves were on edge, but they all felt they had succeeded in keeping to their stories. Duncan wobbled and said he was going to tell the truth, but Eric and Chris persuaded him that since they had lied this far, they may as well see it through. Eventually, Duncan had agreed.

Ian, Duncan and Chris had been asked to stay in New York for an extra week, so that they would be available for further questioning. It also gave them a chance to attend Alex's funeral.

They spent a lot of time together, with Lenka and Eric. Both Lenka and Duncan were distraught, blaming themselves for what had happened. Ian was moody, talking little, and brooding often. Lenka got herself hopelessly drunk twice in that week. She and Duncan were careful not to talk to each other, and it was always awkward when they were in the same room.

Eric, and to a lesser extent Chris himself, had been a calming force on all of them, although Alex was a closer friend of Eric's than any of the others. Then, after a week, the police had closed the case, and with a great feeling of relief the three Brits flew home.

'Hi, Chris, thanks for waiting.' It was Eric. 'I hoped I could get away early this evening, and I think I still can, but something's come up. I'll be another twenty minutes or so.'

'Can I wait in your office?'

'Sorry,' Eric said. 'You're not allowed beyond those doors. Security is everything in M&A these days.'

'I understand,' Chris said. 'But I wonder if I could ask you a quick favour. I thought I'd try to track down George Calhoun tomorrow. I know he got the boot from here a year ago, but I don't know where he is. Who can I ask?'

'George Calhoun, eh?' said Eric. 'Don't worry. I'll get someone to find out,' and with that he disappeared back behind the mysterious glass doors.

Chris spotted a phone in a quiet corner of the reception area, and asked the woman behind the desk whether he could use it. No problem. Chris dialled Carpathian's office. Ollie was still there, and he was agitated.

'Bad news.'

Chris's heart sank. 'What now?'

'It's Melville Capital Management. They want out.'

Chris closed his eyes. Melville was a small firm, based in Princeton, that managed the endowment funds of half a dozen private colleges across the United States. They were a relatively small investor in the fund, at three million euros. But after his disastrous meeting with Rudy, the withdrawal of another three million was the last thing the fund needed. And two investors jumping ship could be enough to scare the rest of them.

'Did they give any reason?'

'No. Just that they wanted to give their thirty days' notice.'

Although Lenka was the main point of contact with all of the investors, Chris had met most of them a couple of times. But not Melville. He remembered his phone call to them to inform them of her death. 'Who's the man there? Something Zissky, isn't it?'

'Dr Martin Zizka,' said Ollie.

'Give me his number.'

Ollie read out the digits.

'Thanks.'

'What are you going to do?' asked Ollie.

'Tell him he's staying in the fund.'

'Good luck.' Then, in a tentative voice. 'How did it go with Amalgamated Veterans?'

'You don't want to know.'

Chris hung up, and punched out the number Ollie had given him.

'Zizka,' a voice answered, so quietly Chris could barely hear it.

'Dr Zizka?'

'Yes?'

'This is Chris Szczypiorski of the Carpathian Fund.'

'Ah, yes.' Zizka didn't sound exactly pleased to hear from him.

'I understand you are thinking of withdrawing your investment.'

'That is correct.'

'Melville Capital is a very important investor to us, and we'd be sorry to lose you. I wonder if it would be possible to meet you to discuss this further.'

As Chris had expected, Zizka didn't sound thrilled with this proposal. 'Aren't you based in London?'

'I'm in New York at the moment. I could come and see you tomorrow.'

'Oh, I see. I'm very busy all day tomorrow. I'm not sure I have any free time.'

'Dr Zizka. All I need is half an hour. As I said, you are an important investor to me. And I know you were important to Lenka as well.' Chris winced as he said this, but he knew he had to use Lenka's name all he could if he were to keep Carpathian intact.

Zizka sighed. 'All right. Four o'clock. But it really will be half an hour. I have a meeting at four thirty.'

'That's fine, Dr Zizka. I'll see you then.'

Chris was just putting the phone down when Eric returned. 'What's up?' he asked, noticing the expression on Chris's face.

'Don't ask. It serves me right for checking in with the office.'

Eric smiled sympathetically. 'Always a mistake. Now let's get out of here before someone else grabs me.'

They swept out of the building, and just as Chris was wondering whether Eric would insist on taking a taxi to the train station rather than the subway, a black limo swept up, leaving half a dozen similar vehicles behind it. A driver leapt out and opened the door for Chris and then Eric.

'This is Terry,' Eric said. 'He'll take you to see George Calhoun tomorrow morning. You are staying the night, aren't you?'

'If you don't mind.'

'That's great. You don't want to come all the way back into the city late at night.'

'So where do you live?' asked Chris, as the limo, which was really just a large saloon car, pulled away from the front of the Bloomfield Weiss building.

'On Long Island. A place called Mill Neck. It's right near Oyster Bay.'

It was rush hour, and it took them over an hour to fight through the traffic. Eric spent most of his time on the phone. It wasn't for show, there seemed to be two live deals going on at the same time. Chris pretended not to listen, but of course he did. Eric was frustratingly vague, and kept on telling people he 'couldn't talk now', although he did mention Rome, Munich and Dallas a lot. He was talking to someone called Sergio about someone else called Jim. Some big Italian deal, perhaps with a US company based in Texas?

After a particularly obscure session, Eric turned to Chris. 'Do me a favour. Don't try to guess what's going on.'

'Of course not,' said Chris.

Eric sighed. 'You'd think just one night I'd be able to leave at five o'clock, wouldn't you?' Then his phone chirped its tune again.

Eventually they were on a small country road that wound its way through woods, past mansions surrounded by high walls and snatches of sea shifting darkly in the moonlight. After a couple of miles, they rounded a bend; Terry pressed a remote control, a set of iron gates swung open, and the car pulled up in front of a rectangular white house bathed in a soft light from the lamps placed strategically around it.

'We're here,' said Eric.

'Is this the place you showed me on the boat? The place you said you always wanted to buy? Wasn't it designed by some fancy architect?'

'Meier. That's right. I'd forgotten I'd shown you that. You have a good memory.'

'I remember that night, at least.'

'Yeah. Well, come inside.'

They got out of the car, and Terry drove off. Chris was almost expecting a footman, but it turned out that Eric had his own set of house keys, and was capable of using them himself. 'Hi!' he shouted, as they entered a huge hallway, with a wide set of stairs heading upwards.

A slender woman in jeans and socks, with her fair hair tied back, appeared and gave Eric an affectionate kiss.

'Chris, this is Cassie.'

'Hi,' she said with a friendly smile, and held out her hand to be shaken. There was a cry of 'Dad!' and a small boy with blond curly hair, who looked very much like his mother, hurtled into the hallway and grabbed his father's leg.

'And this is Wilson.'

'Howdeedodee,' said the boy, from between Eric's legs.

'Hello,' said Chris.

Eric heaved the boy up into his arms. 'Do you mind if I go up and read him his story?'

'No, go ahead,' said Chris, and followed Cassie into a huge kitchen. He passed an Hispanic woman who was putting on her coat.

'Good night, Mrs Cassie.'

'Good night, Juanita. Thank you.'

Cassie poured Chris some white wine and attended to the cooker, set on a kind of marble island in the middle of the vast room. 'Wilson's thrilled to have his dad home in time to put him to bed,' she said. 'He won't be long.'

'Are you working at the moment?' Chris asked.

'Part time. Since Wilson was born and we bought this place, it seemed a shame to spend the whole time in the city. I have a PR company. Fortunately, my partners are extremely good, but there are lots of evening functions that I still have to go to, which are kind of a drag.'

'This is a nice house.'

'We like it. Eric's family comes from round here.'

'I know. What about you?'

'Philadelphia. The Main Line. It's handy for Washington, which seems to be where all my family end up.'

'Including Eric?'

Cassie smiled. 'Probably. He can tell you about that himself. Now, how do you know Eric? He did tell me, but I find it difficult to keep track of all his friends.'

'We were on the Bloomfield Weiss training programme together. Ten years ago.'

'Do you still work there?'

Chris smiled. 'No, thank God.'

Cassie laughed. 'They all say that. I don't know how Eric survives.'

'He seems to be doing rather well.'

'I don't believe it,' said Cassie. 'I'm convinced he works in the mailroom. Have you seen his office?'

'No.'

'Precisely. Nobody has. And he calls his horoscope line every few minutes on his cell phone so that I'll think he's important.'

'And then the horoscope line rings him back?'

'Maybe it's got callback. I don't know. Eric would. He does seem to know about telephones.'

Chris laughed. Megan was right: Cassie was a nice woman. And attractive.

'He says he spends a lot of time out of the country,' Chris said.

'Tell me about it.' Cassie rolled her eyes. 'But I think he genuinely does try to get back here whenever he can. Here, help yourself to another glass if you like.'

After twenty minutes or so, Eric joined them, and they all carried dinner through to the dining room. The table, chairs and cutlery were over-designed modern stuff, and didn't look as though they were meant to be used for a real dinner at all. But Chris's attention was grabbed by a painting on one wall. It was the picture of the petrochemical plant in the Saudi Arabian desert that he knew so well.

'I recognize that,' he said.

'Yeah,' said Eric. 'I think it was Alex's best. His mother gave it to me.'

'I'm glad you've kept it.'

They sat down. Another wall of the room was entirely glass, and it gave a terrific view of the bay and lights twinkling in the distance.

'Is that Oyster Bay?' Chris asked.

213

'That's right,' said Eric.

'Do your parents still live there?'

'Not any more. Five years ago, my father ran off to California with some awful woman twenty years younger than him. My mother was so ashamed she moved out of town as well.'

'I'm sorry,' Chris said.

Eric sighed. 'That kind of thing happens in families, these days. I've got to say, it was quite a shock. Dad never struck me as that kind of man.'

Chris changed the subject. 'This is delicious,' he said, digging in to the exotic salad Cassie had made. And it was. So was the main course, tuna steaks in a pineapple salsa sauce, and there was crème brûlée afterwards. The evening passed very pleasantly, and then Cassie announced she was going up to bed.

'Would you like a cognac, Chris?' Eric asked.

'Here, I'll help you with the dishes first,' Chris said.

'Oh, don't worry about them,' said Eric. 'Juanita will deal with them in the morning.'

Chris paused for a second, thinking how nice it would be never to have to do the washing up after dinner parties, then followed Eric through to a large living room, with very little furniture and acres of empty floor space. Embers were glowing in a large open fireplace. It all looked good, but Chris suspected that Wilson spent very little time in there. Eric poured two brandies from a smooth curvilinear decanter.

'Thanks for putting in a good word about me to Rudy Moss.'

'No problem. How did it go?'

'Waste of time,' said Chris. 'I had to try it, and I thought that I'd be able to persuade him, but he wasn't having any of it. I reckon he just wanted to demonstrate his power over me. Gave him some kind of kicks I suppose. Nasty little man.'

Eric smiled. 'It's a shame someone so bright could be such a jerk.'

'The fund's in real trouble now. I'm going to have to sell some bonds to raise the cash to pay Rudy out, and the market timing is all wrong. Bloomfield Weiss won't give me a decent bid for that stupid Eureka Telecom position Ian Darwent stuffed us with. And now another investor wants out. I don't know what I'm going to do.'

'You'll figure it out,' said Eric.

'I wish I had your confidence. I'd hate to let Lenka down.'

'Don't take it so personally. She'd understand.'

No, she wouldn't, Chris thought. She would fight tooth and nail to save Carpathian. And so should he.

'Have you tracked down Marcus Lubron yet?' Eric asked.

'Not yet. That's tomorrow's task. Once I've seen George Calhoun.'

'Oh, yes. What on earth do you want to see him for? That really is a bad memory I'd like to keep in the past.'

Chris told Eric all about his discussion with Abby Hollis. Eric listened closely. When he had finished, Chris asked him about Alex taking drugs.

'I knew he did some drugs occasionally,' said Eric. 'But it was no big deal. It's not like he had a problem or anything. We didn't talk about it much.'

'Until he got caught.'

'Even then. Of course, he was really worried about it, and when I asked him, he eventually told me what was wrong. But he didn't want to discuss it.'

'Abby said that Calhoun was threatening him.'

'Probably. Something was going on. But as I said, he didn't want my help. I respected that. He and I were good friends, I knew him well. The thing with Alex was, sometimes he just wanted to be left alone. And that was one of those times.'

'So you don't know specifically what was going on?'

Eric shook his head.

'And you didn't say anything about it afterwards to any of us?'

'No way,' said Eric. 'It just didn't seem the right thing to talk about. Especially after what happened to him. Whatever his problems were, they died with him.'

'I'm trying to think how this might be related to Lenka's death,' Chris said.

Eric looked blank. 'I can't see how. Why should it be?'

'Well, I know Lenka wanted to tell Marcus something before she died. I'm pretty sure now that it was more than just Duncan knocking Alex into the sea. I thought maybe it had something to do with Alex getting caught with drugs.'

Eric frowned. 'I can't see a possible connection.'

Chris sighed. 'Maybe Marcus can tell me. If I can find him.'

'Perhaps,' said Eric. 'Let me know.'

Chris leaned back in his chair by the warm fire, and sipped his brandy. He looked across at Eric. Although he had a glittering future, indeed, was already living one, in many ways he was the most straightforward of Chris's friends from the programme. Duncan was an emotional wreck, Ian had become cynical and selfish as his career had progressed, but Eric was still basically a friend. He didn't have anything to prove to Chris, and there was no point in Chris trying to compete with him. He was glad it was Eric, not Ian, who had done so well.

'What is it?' asked Eric.

'Oh, nothing,' said Chris. 'Are you still intending to go into politics?'

Eric smiled. 'I guess so.'

'Everything seems to be going according to plan so far.'

'Partly. I'm making good money at Bloomfield Weiss, and I've also made some lucky investments. You can make excellent contacts in this business; it's amazing how grateful a big company boss can be if you help him make the biggest acquisition of his career. The problem is I never have any time for all the schmoozing. I'm going to have to figure out how to make more time. But yes, I'm still interested.'

'And you'd be following in the family tradition.'

Eric looked at Chris sharply. 'You mean Cassie's family? Wilson's a good man. I respect him. I can learn a lot from him.'

It took a moment for Chris to realize that he was talking about his father-in-law. Eric had even named his son after Cassie's father! But perhaps Chris was being too cynical: some American families did that, he supposed. Chris could see Eric felt sensitive about the whole subject.

'I'm sorry,' he said. 'Good luck with it. You deserve to go far.'

'We'll see,' said Eric. But he didn't smile. His tone was surprisingly serious. This was clearly more than an idle fancy. Suddenly the edge of Eric's ambition, which he kept well hidden, but which Megan had spoken about, showed through. But what was wrong with that? They were all ambitious, Chris included. That was, after all, why they had been so enthusiastically swept up by Bloomfield Weiss.

Eric's driver Terry opened the door of the limo, and Chris climbed in. It was nine o'clock: Terry had already driven Eric into Manhattan several hours earlier, and Cassie had left at eight, leaving Juanita in charge of the house and Wilson.

'You know where we're going, I hope,' said Chris to the closely cropped blond hair at the back of the driver's head.

'Westchester,' Terry replied. 'Home of a Mr George Calhoun. Don't worry. I know the way.'

'It's good of you to take me,' said Chris.

'Whatever the boss says.'

'I didn't know Bloomfield Weiss ran to limos for managing directors.'

Terry laughed. 'I don't think they do. This is more of a private arrangement. I drive for Mr Astle when I don't have any other work.'

'I see. And what is that work?'

'Personal bodyguard. That's how we met. I got Mr Astle out of a tough situation in Kazakhstan a couple years back. I've done quite a bit for him since then.'

This surprised and intrigued Chris. 'I didn't realize Eric needed a bodyguard. What happened?'

'Attempted kidnapping. We got away.'

'Wow. Investment banking must be getting more dangerous than in my day.'

'Not really. I only accompany clients to particularly trouble-some parts of the world. Or to meet particularly dangerous people. Even then, ninety-five per cent of my job is just watching and waiting. But occasionally I need to put my training into action. I haven't lost a client yet.'

'So I'll make it to Westchester?'

Terry laughed. 'You'll make it to Westchester, sir.'

They pulled into the lines of traffic on the Long Island Expressway.

'Pardon me for asking, but are you related to Stanislaw Szczypiorski?' Terry asked.

'I am. I'm his son. But you're about the first person I've ever come across who's heard of him. Do you play chess?'

'Sure. And I like reading the books, going through the old matches. I have an old book on the King's Indian Defence that features a lot of his games. They even have a variation named after him.'

'That's right. It was his favourite opening as black.'

'Do you play?'

'Not any more,' Chris said. 'I played a lot as a boy, but I was never going to be as good as my father.'

They chatted about chess until they reached the leafy county of Westchester. George Calhoun lived in a classic American suburban house: wooden, white-painted, with a large patch of grass in front of it running down to a mailbox and the sidewalk. Terry waited in the car, while Chris rang the doorbell.

Calhoun answered. He was greyer, balder and fatter, with a few more wrinkles. His hatchet face had become both softer and more bitter. He didn't recognize Chris.

'Chris Szczypiorski,' Chris said, holding out his hand. 'From the Bloomfield Weiss training programme.'

'Ah, yes. I remember,' said Calhoun. 'I remember quite well. What do you want?'

'I want to talk to you about Alex Lubron.'

'Alex Lubron, eh? Another one. Well, you'd better come in.' He led Chris into a living room. The TV was on. Adverts for laxatives or something. 'Sit down. Have you come to tell me what really happened?'

'No,' said Chris. 'I've come to find out what really happened.'

Calhoun snorted. 'You were there. You ought to know. It

would sure be interesting if you could let the rest of us in on it.'

'I know what happened on the boat,' said Chris. 'Alex fell in and drowned. But what interests me is what happened beforehand.'

'Beforehand?'

'Yes. Wasn't Alex in some kind of trouble with drugs?'

Calhoun looked at Chris suspiciously. 'That's all very confidential.'

Chris returned his stare. 'I'm sure it is,' he said, after a moment's thought. 'And I'm sure that after all your years of loyal service to Bloomfield Weiss the last thing you would want to do is discuss something confidential that happened ten years ago to someone who is now dead.'

It was the right thing to say. Calhoun laughed. Or at least Chris thought it was a laugh. It actually sounded more like a bark.

'I still can't believe it. Twenty-six years. Six months short of my fiftieth birthday, and they give me the pink slip. What chance have I of finding another job at my age?'

Chris smiled in what he hoped could be mistaken for sympathy. He enjoyed the irony. Calhoun had loved firing people. He had made it a personal business philosophy. If ever an ego needed to be downsized, it was his.

'All right. I'll tell you. We tested all the American trainees after the final examination. Alex Lubron was the only one who tested positive. I wanted to have him out of the firm the next day, but the head of mortgage trading, Tom Risman, wouldn't let him go without a fight. So I thought I'd try to get him to finger whoever had supplied him. He had the weekend to think about it. I think he would have told us, too. His mother was very ill, and he had loans and big medical bills to pay off. Also, he seemed worried about what effect a public dismissal and a conviction would have on her. He asked us to keep it quiet.' Calhoun smiled to himself. 'Big mistake. I said I'd make it as public as I could. Press release, the works. I had him. I'm sure he would have talked.'

'But wouldn't that have been bad publicity for Bloomfield Weiss?'

'No. That was the whole point. We'd gotten some PR consultants in after those salesmen were convicted for supplying drugs. They said it was vital for Bloomfield Weiss to be seen to be cleaning up its act.'

'So who was it who was supplying Alex?'

Calhoun sighed. 'We never found out. He died before he could tell us.'

'Do you know if it was anyone in the firm?'

'Not for sure. It could have been anyone from his doorman to Sidney Stahl. But somehow I think if it was his doorman he'd have been quick to tell us all about it.'

Chris nodded. 'Did you pursue the investigation after he died?'

'Certainly not,' said Calhoun. 'Once he was dead, we just wanted to hush everything up as quickly as possible. Especially once the police started getting suspicious.'

'I remember they were asking us lots of questions.'

Calhoun smiled. 'The thing is, they didn't believe you. That was a problem. We had to apply pressure.'

'How did you do that?'

'I don't know,' said Calhoun. 'That was done at a very high level. But one day they were asking a whole lot of questions. The next day they stopped.'

Thank God, thought Chris. 'I wonder if you could tell me something about the psychometric testing programme?' he asked.

Calhoun seemed surprised at the change of tack. But he answered the question. 'It was very successful. Psychometric tests are often used to measure what kind of a team player someone is, leadership, that kind of thing. I realized that wasn't really what Bloomfield Weiss wanted. Sure, we said we did, just like every other corporation in America, but we were just kidding ourselves. We wanted winners. People who were determined to come out on top, no matter what the cost. It's not like we used the psychometric tests alone to hire people, but they were a useful pointer.'

'Didn't they show up some people as borderline psychotic?'

'No. I mean not really. Everyone has psychological problems. You could argue that the truly successful have them more than most. Most driven people are driven by something, if you see what I mean. And that something may be ugly. But we weren't interested in their personal problems. We just cared about how they performed at work.'

'What about Steve Matzley?'

'A case in point. He did an excellent job for us before he moved on.'

'But then he raped someone?'

Calhoun's eyes flared up. 'That's not my fault! That's his responsibility.'

'Didn't the psychological assessment point out a high risk?'

'Who told you that?' Calhoun snapped.

Chris shrugged. 'It's just a rumour.'

Calhoun sighed. 'If you read the report with hindsight, it is just possible that you could have identified pointers to what happened. But you can do that with anything with hindsight.'

'I suppose so,' said Chris, trying to sound sympathetic. He didn't want to alienate Calhoun. He still had more he wanted to find out from him. 'Were there any others who had similar concerns raised in their reports?'

'I really don't remember,' said Calhoun.

'People on the boat the night Alex was killed? Alex himself, perhaps?'

Calhoun glared at Chris. 'I told you, I don't remember.'

'After Alex died, you checked the files, didn't you?'

'I have no idea.'

'What do you mean, you have no idea? We're not talking about some routine personnel matter, here. This was a big deal. You must remember whether you did check the files or you didn't.'

'I don't remember,' Calhoun growled through gritted teeth. 'And if I did remember, I wouldn't tell you. Those files are personal and very confidential.'

Chris was sure that there was something in those reports that had been of great interest to George Calhoun. He was equally sure Calhoun wouldn't tell him. There was no point in pushing it.

'OK, I understand,' he said. 'What about the psychologists who did the tests? Wasn't there one who was unhappy about it?'

Calhoun snorted. 'Marcia Horwath. I remember her. She was the one who persuaded the firm to drop the programme.'

'Did she test Steve Matzley?'

'She did.'

'And anyone else she was worried about?'

'Possibly. I really don't remember.'

Chris realized that he had got as far as he was going to go. 'Thank you very much, Mr Calhoun.'

'So you're not going to tell me what really happened?' asked Calhoun with a leer.

'I already have.' Somehow, Chris had no difficulties lying to him.

'Come on. All these questions about whether any of your friends on the boat were psychos. Something must have happened.'

'Alex Lubron fell in the water and drowned,' said Chris.

'OK,' said Calhoun. 'Have it your way.'

Chris got up to go. Then he paused. 'When I came in, you said "another one". Has someone else been asking about Alex?'

'Yes. His brother. Or at least he said he was his brother.'

'Marcus Lubron. Tall thin guy?'

'That's him. Scruffy. Probably hadn't had a bath in a week. He was on some kind of mission to discover the truth about his brother's death.'

'What did you tell him?'

'Not much. A guy like that, you know.' He wrinkled his nose in something close to a sneer.

'He didn't give you an address or anything?'

'No. I don't think he liked me much, either. But his car had Vermont plates.'

'Vermont plates? Thank you.' That might make finding him easier. 'Well goodbye, George,' Chris said, extending his hand. Calhoun shook it. Once he had left the house and was walking down the drive, Chris wiped his hand on his trousers. He hoped George Calhoun never got another job.

Terry drove Chris back to the city and dropped him off at a bland business hotel midtown. After Chris had checked in, he powered up his laptop, logged on to the Internet and started to look for Marcus Lubron.

It wasn't quite as easy as he had hoped. There wasn't a Marcus Lubron listed in the phone records anywhere in America. There were two M. Lubrons, one in Washington State, and one in Texas. Chris called them. A Matthew and a Mike. Marcus must be ex-directory.

He looked up 'Lubron' on one of the search engines, and discovered that it was the name of an anti-creasing solution for textiles. More promisingly, there was a mention of furniture made by a Marcus Lubron in the apartment of a wealthy Manhattan family named Farmiloe. Theirs was an easier number to find. Mrs Farmiloe was delighted that Chris had read about her apartment, but hadn't dealt with Marcus Lubron directly, although she knew he came from Vermont. She gave Chris the number of her interior designer, who was uncooperative at first, but, when Chris convinced her that he was an old friend from England desperate to catch up with Marcus after ten years, she relented and gave him the name and address. Chris looked it up on a map. Marcus lived in a small town in the mountains in the middle of nowhere, Vermont.

He decided not to call him. The chances of Marcus talking to him on the phone, or agreeing to meet him, were slim, and there was no point in alerting him that Chris was looking for him. Much better to surprise him. So, Chris called a travel agent, and booked a seat on a plane to Burlington the next day.

It was much easier to locate Dr Marcia Horwath. She had an office on the West Side, and said she could spare Chris fifteen minutes at a quarter to nine the next morning. Pleased that he finally seemed to be making some progress, he took a taxi to Penn Station and a train to Princeton.

Melville Capital took up the first floor of a neatly painted wooden building that looked more like a house than an office block, the ground floor of which was occupied by an upmarket stock-broker. Chris arrived at a couple of minutes before four, and was ushered by an overweight middle-aged woman into Dr Zizka's office. Large and airy with a couple of comfortable sofas, pleasant prints of college buildings on the walls, shelves stuffed with books and academic journals, and only one computer in the whole room, it seemed a very pleasant place to spend the day untroubled by the turmoil of the markets. The late afternoon sunshine streamed through the window, gleaming softly off the polished wood of the desk, and the bald head of the man sitting behind it reading a journal of some kind through half-moon glasses.

It was a few seconds before the man put his text to one side and looked up. He smiled, leapt to his feet, and scurried round the desk, extending his hand. 'I'm Martin Zizka.'

'Chris Szczypiorski.'

'Come, come. Sit down,' Zizka said, indicating one of the sofas. He was a small man in his fifties, with bright blue eyes twinkling out of a round face. 'I'm very sorry we only have thirty minutes, but it's been crazy round here,' he said, waving vaguely at his serene office.

'I understand,' said Chris. 'The markets are never quiet.'

'Never,' said Zizka, shaking his head.

'You manage money for a number of colleges, I believe?'

'That's right,' Zizka said. 'I used to be an economics professor at Melville College in Ohio. They were very disappointed by the attitude of the firms advising them on their endowment fund. Conflicts of interest, poor performance, lack of personal attention. So I offered to manage their money for them. I had a good couple of years, I have many contacts in the academic world, and now I advise on the funds of five more similar institutions.

'And you do that from here?' Chris said, glancing round the office.

Zizka smiled. 'Oh, I don't trade myself any more. I did to start with, but now I find it's not necessary. I parcel the money out to others to do that, such as yourself. I take the major strategic decisions. I find if you get those right, the returns take care of themselves. What I can never seem to get enough of, even here, is peace and quiet to read and think.'

There was something in that, Chris thought. He realized he was in danger of underestimating Dr Zizka.

'And presumably that was why you invested in Carpathian. It seemed the right strategic decision?'

'Partly.'

'Partly?'

'Partly that. Mostly Lenka.'

'You've known her for a long time?'

'Yes. When I started in this business, I got involved in the high-yield bond market. That was when I was still buying individual securities myself. I dealt with all the big brokers, including Bloomfield Weiss. While the others seemed happy to sell me any deal as long as it was one of theirs, Lenka only sold me bonds that worked. Although I was only a small client, she looked after me. I ended up giving her all my business. The returns were good, and she never abused my trust. We got on well: my parents were from a small town outside of Prague, you know. So, when she told me she was setting up Carpathian, I thought, why not support her? She deserves it. And so far it's worked out fine. The problem is that some of the trustees keep asking questions about it. It sort of sticks out on our list of investments.'

Zizka paused, and took off his little spectacles. 'I was shocked to hear what happened to her. A terrible thing.' He shook his head and rubbed his eyes. Then he looked up at Chris. 'But now she's gone, it seems the right time to get out, given all the other factors. I'm sure you understand.'

Chris did understand. But he couldn't allow himself to agree. 'Do you still think the strategic argument makes sense? That as the Central European economies become integrated with Europe there will be opportunities for making money?'

'Yes, I do, but . . .' Zizka shrugged.

Chris launched into his spiel on the opportunities in Central Europe, his view of the economic prospects there, the track record of the fund since inception, how the current market jitters provided a chance to make more money. Zizka listened politely, but Chris could see he wasn't getting anywhere. Zizka had invested to support Lenka. Now Lenka was gone, there was no reason for him to stay involved. His mind had been made up.

The minutes were ticking away. His half hour was nearly up. Chris stood up to go.

'Thank you for listening to me, Dr Zizka.'

'It's the least I could do,' he said. 'You were Lenka's partner, after all.'

'I was.' Chris shook Zizka's hand. A decent man. A fair man. A far cry from Rudy Moss. 'You know, I feel like I still am her partner. That she's still there, looking over my shoulder. Carpathian is still her firm. She trusted me and I won't let her down.'

Zizka's eyes flicked over Chris, examining him closely. 'I'm sure.'

'Will you reconsider?' Chris asked. 'If not for me, then for her?'

Zizka hesitated. He looked as if he was about to say something, but then he walked over to the door and opened it.

'Goodbye,' he said. 'And good luck.'

Chris arrived back at his hotel depressed. Zizka hadn't actually said he still wanted to withdraw his money. But he hadn't said he had changed his mind, either. Chris called Ollie at home. It was nearly midnight his time but Ollie was happy to talk. The market was weaker; prices were down. A miraculous bid for Eureka Telecom had not materialized. Ollie was enthusiastic, though. He thought that the latest news about the Slovakian economy was encouraging, and that investors hadn't picked up on it yet. Chris's first instinct was to tell Ollie to wait until he returned. But Ollie was convincing, and with Lenka gone Chris would have to start trusting him soon. So why not now? He told Ollie to buy Slovakian bonds in the morning. Ollie didn't ask about Melville, so Chris didn't tell him.

Chris put down the phone and looked around his sterile hotel room. He couldn't face moping the evening away in there, so he changed out of his suit, grabbed his wallet and headed out into the street. He was hungry. He made his way up the East Side, looking for his old haunts. He found a place that he, Duncan and Ian used to go to on Seventy-First Street and Second Avenue, and spent a pleasant hour drinking a couple of beers, devouring a chunky cheeseburger and remembering the good times of that summer in New York ten years before.

He wished that he had somehow got to know Megan better back then. In retrospect, all that time he had spent with Tamara was a total waste. Of course, it could never have happened, he would never have been able to prise her away from Eric. But it was a nice thought. He would see her again soon. That was a nice thought too.

He wandered back haphazardly and finally found himself on the cross street near his hotel. It was cold in New York in March and it began to rain. The temperature could only just have been above freezing and the cold hard drops of water bit into his face. He was glad he had been sent on the second training programme of the year: spending five months in the dark and cold and rain would not have been nearly so much fun. Now, it was hard to imagine the sweltering heat and humidity of the New York he had experienced. The rain intensified. He stared down at the sidewalk and quickened his pace, hands deep in his coat pockets, eager now to get back to the warmth of his hotel, only a block away.

Suddenly, a sharp jolt against his back propelled him into a doorway. He lost his balance and crashed into a metal door. As he tried to turn, he felt cold steel on his cheek. The flat of the blade of a knife pressed his face against the door. He tried to move his head to get a look at his attacker but the knife cut into his cheek. He did catch a glimpse of a black scarf, moustache, dark glasses and woollen hat, with long dark hair curling out beneath its rim. The man was a few inches shorter than him, but he was strong and determined.

'Stay still,' hissed a hoarse voice. 'And listen.'

Chris's cheek stung. He could feel blood trickling down to his jaw. He kept still.

'I'm gonna tell you this once,' whispered the voice in a good imitation of Marlon Brando. 'You're not gonna ask any more questions. You're gonna get on the next plane home. You're gonna forget all about Lenka. Got that?'

'Yes,' Chris said, through clenched teeth.

'You sure, now?'

'I'm sure.'

'OK. I'll be watching you.' Then the knife lifted from Chris's skin and he felt a blow to his ribs that doubled him up. He gasped for breath and turned to see a figure running off. He looked around him. He caught the eye of a woman who had watched the whole thing open mouthed from the other side of the street. She ducked and hurried off in the opposite direction. There were no other witnesses.

Chris picked himself up off the pavement and felt his cheek, which was bleeding quite badly. He set off at a jog to the entrance of the hotel.

The concierge was shocked to see him, and swiftly found a first-aid pack. He offered to call the police, but Chris said that since he wasn't badly hurt and nothing was taken there was no point. So he took the first-aid kit up to his room, breathing heavily and shaking.

He headed straight for the bathroom, holding his handkerchief to his cheek.

He looked into the mirror and froze. There, written on the glass in blood, were the words *I killed Lenka.*

He staggered back into the bedroom and slammed the bathroom door. He slumped down on the bed and put his face in his hands. He was shaking all over now. Who was this guy? Where was he? Was he still in the room?

He leapt to his feet and checked the room, behind the curtains, in the wardrobe, and in the bathroom behind the shower curtain. There was no one there, of course. He sat down on the bed and tried to get a grip of himself. After five minutes, when the worst of the shaking had stopped, he called the hotel manager.

The manager came, followed swiftly by two uniformed policemen. They were big men, who seemed even bigger with all the hardware they carried around their waists. Their toughness was both intimidating and comforting. They took notes. Their interest perked up considerably when they heard that Lenka was a murder victim and then subsided when they heard that the crime had taken place in the Czech Republic, which Chris had to spell.

They asked him whether the man who had attacked Lenka was the same one who had attacked him that evening.

Chris thought hard before answering. The clothes, although similar, were different. The moustache could have been the same. He couldn't remember seeing long curly hair in Prague.

But the run was familiar. He had seen both men run away and they were the same man.

The policemen were not convinced that this counted as positive identification but they wrote it down anyway. Then their radio crackled, calling them to a shooting somewhere or other, and they were gone.

The manager fussed over Chris. He said he had no idea how anyone could possibly have got past the front desk and into his room. Chris suspected it was easy. The manager gave him a new room, and Chris requested that the hotel be particularly careful not to divulge his new room number to anyone. The manager made lots of assurances and then left him alone.

Chris had a bath and went to bed. He couldn't sleep. The warning was as clear as could be. Someone wanted Chris to stop asking questions. If he didn't, he would be killed. And whoever had made the threat seemed perfectly capable of carrying it out. So what should Chris do?

The obvious answer was give up and go home. Chris resolved to cancel his ticket to Vermont and fly back to London the next day.

Having made that decision, he hoped that his brain, relieved, would shut down in sleep. But it didn't. A voice somewhere, deep down inside, protested. It called him a coward. Spineless. It whispered Lenka's name. Chris tried not to listen, but the voice wouldn't leave him alone. It pointed out that if someone wanted to stop Chris that badly, then Chris must be on the verge of discovering something important. Something about Lenka's murder. If he persisted, he would find out who had killed Lenka and perhaps do something about it.

But why should he? He wasn't a hero. It wasn't his job to solve crimes. Lenka was dead; there was nothing he could do to bring her back to life.

He knew what his grandfather would do. He would risk his life to find out what had happened to Lenka, just as he had risked his life so many times fifty years before.

But his grandfather was a bloody-minded bigot. A pain in the arse.

What about his father, the voice asked. That quiet man of steady principles also wouldn't quit. It had taken courage to defect when he had. And it had taken courage to stick with his ideals amongst his more conservative compatriots in Halifax. And what of his mother? The woman who had battled through so much hardship to give him and his sister every advantage she could. She would never give up and fly home.

He had left these people behind when he had gone to university, and then into investment banking. He had intended to become someone else, someone better, more successful, wealthier, and yes, more English. But it hadn't quite worked out like that. He had come close: he had proved to himself at least that he was a good trader, he could earn good money, he could turn a blind eye to the everyday deceptions of people like Ian Darwent or Herbie Exler. But then he had been spurned by the system, unjustly ejected on to the scrap heap of burned-out, toxic traders, ignored, left to rot.

He saw that he had a choice. He could remain in the world of Bloomfield Weiss and George Calhoun, or he could do what his parents, his grandfather and Lenka would do in his place.

If he was going to live with himself, however short that life would be, there was only one choice. He made it and swiftly fell asleep.

I 2

He awoke afraid. He still knew he had made the right decision, but he was scared of the consequences. Chris prided himself on his ability to assess risk. And he knew he was right to be scared.

But he had some leeway. He was safe until whoever was after him realized that he had decided not to be deterred. The longer whoever it was thought that he might have given up, the more grace he had.

He ate breakfast in the safety of his room, and packed. He caught a cab outside the hotel, and it crawled across town towards the Lincoln Tunnel. Then, as the cab drove through a light changing from green to red, Chris asked the driver to turn north. He looked over his shoulder. The streets were crowded with cars going in every direction. If someone was following, he might have lost him. Or he might not. He directed the cab left and right, along a few cross streets, before barrelling up Tenth Avenue towards the Upper West Side. It was impossible to tell whether he was being followed. The Indian driver thought he was crazy, but didn't care.

Dr Marcia Horwath's office was in a five-storey building in a quiet cross street. Chris leapt out of the cab, overpaid the driver and, quickly scanning the empty street, rushed into the building. It was ten minutes to nine and Dr Horwath was waiting for him.

She was in her fifties with short grey hair and an air of authority. Her office was an office, not a consulting room. No leather couch, no potted plants. Filing cabinets, charts on the walls, a computer, an expensive but businesslike desk. It looked more like the place of work of a management consultant than a psychologist.

She didn't have much time, and she let him know it. 'How can I help you, Mr, er . . . ?'

'Szczypiorski. I would like to talk to you about Bloomfield Weiss.'

'I see. Bloomfield Weiss used to be a client of mine. Even though our relationship terminated many years ago, my duty of confidentiality still stands.'

'I understand,' said Chris. 'So perhaps I'll talk and then you can decide how much you can tell me.'

'Go ahead.'

'I was recruited by Bloomfield Weiss as a graduate trainee ten years ago. As part of the recruitment process I was given some psychometric tests. I never found out the results, and quite frankly I forgot all about them. But my understanding is that Bloomfield Weiss used these tests to screen for particularly aggressive individuals.'

'That's true.'

'And you were one of the psychologists that they used to conduct the tests?'

'That's true also.'

'What did you think of their approach?'

At last, Dr Horwath smiled, and some of the caginess left her. 'At first I was intrigued. There has always seemed to me to be some hypocrisy in the way companies claim they are look-ing for all the noble virtues in their employees. One of the strengths of psychometric testing is that it doesn't necessarily show that people are good or bad. You don't pass or fail. Different people have different strengths and weaknesses that mean they are more or less suitable for different roles. Bloomfield Weiss realized that many of the successful people in their organ-ization had traits that were often looked upon negatively by recruiters.'

'Such as?'

'If you worked there, I'm sure you saw them. Aggression. The desire to win at any cost. The ability to lie and deceive. The ability to manipulate other people. A certain recklessness. Even a propensity to violence.'

'Violence?'

'Many traders are violent people, wouldn't you say?'

'Some,' said Chris.

'Civilized society sublimates the tendency towards violence in a number of ways. The most obvious is playing sport, or watching it. But trading the financial markets seems to be another way. Come on, don't tell me you haven't seen the macho language, the posturing, the desire to dominate on the trading floor?'

'I suppose I have,' Chris admitted.

'Well, that was what we were looking for.'

'So what went wrong?'

'I'm afraid I can't say.'

Dr Horwath looked at Chris neutrally. He could read nothing from her expression.

'My understanding is that one of the psychologists responsible for the testing, yourself, raised some concerns about some of the trainees you tested. You were afraid they might turn out to be dangerous. Your warnings were ignored and the candidates were recruited anyway. One of these, Steve Matzley, was subsequently convicted of rape. I'm concerned whether there were any others that troubled you.'

'There may have been,' said Dr Horwath. 'But I couldn't possibly discuss them with you if there were. And I'm not sure what your interest in this is. You don't still work for Bloomfield Weiss do you?'

'No, I left two years ago. But I witnessed the death of one of the trainees on my programme, Alex Lubron. He fell off a boat and was drowned. Did you hear about it?'

'Yes, I did,' said Dr Horwath. 'Weren't the circumstances suspicious?'

Chris had to be cautious here. Dr Horwath owed no duty of confidentiality to him, so he had to be careful not to say anything that could be used against him, or Duncan, or any of them later.

'I thought the circumstances were straightforward at the time,' he said. 'But now I'm not so sure. One of the other trainees on the boat, Lenka Němečková, was murdered in Prague a couple of weeks ago.' Dr Horwath's eyebrows shot up at this. 'I believe there may be some connection with what happened on that boat.'

'What kind of connection?'

Chris sighed. 'I don't know.'

'So what do you want from me?'

'If I give you the names of the people on the boat, can you tell me whether you were worried about any of them?'

'The short answer, Mr, er, . . . is no. For reasons I have already explained.'

Chris went on regardless. 'There were seven of us. Myself, Lenka, Alex, Duncan Gemmel, Ian Darwent, Eric Astle and one other woman whom you wouldn't know.' Chris listed these names slowly, watching Dr Horwath's face very closely as he did so. Nothing. Not a blink of an eyelid. 'Do any of those names ring a bell?'

'All of those people told me or my associates personal details in the strictest confidence. As did you, yourself. While I didn't approve of Bloomfield Weiss's approach to this programme, I do have to respect that confidentiality.'

'But Dr Horwath. A friend of mine has been killed already. I myself was attacked by a man with a knife last night.' Chris touched the cut on his face. 'Please. At least tell me if nothing showed up in the tests of any of us.'

Dr Horwath looked up at the ceiling for a long moment, and then returned her gaze very deliberately to Chris. She said nothing.

'You can't tell me that, can you?'

Still nothing.

Chris leaned forward, eager to pin her down. 'There was something wrong with one of them. Which one? You didn't have to look the names up in a file. One of them means something to you, doesn't it? One of them you remember, ten years later.'

Dr Horwath looked at her watch. 'I do appreciate the serious-ness of your enquiry. But I cannot help you. I absolutely cannot. Now, I have an appointment at nine.'

Chris realized that was as much as he was going to get. But he had got something, he was sure of it.

'Thank you, Dr Horwath. If you do change your mind, here's my card. And,' he paused. What he wanted to say was melodram-atic, but it needed to be said. 'If, sometime in the next few weeks, you learn that something has happened to me, please remember this conversation and pass it on.'

Dr Horwath's eyes flashed at him. He knew he sounded paranoid, but he hoped that she would be able to tell he wasn't crazy. 'I'll do that,' she said.

Chris left the room and, as he was putting on his coat outside her office, he saw Dr Horwath looking through a drawer of her filing cabinet.

The rented four-wheel drive ground up the hill, the tyres some-how gripping to the compacted snow under the wheels. Chris knew he wasn't being followed. All he had to do was look behind him down the ravine to the highway two miles behind and several hundred feet below him. He had taken a cab to Newark Airport, hung around International Departures, and then taken the monorail to the terminal for Burlington. So far, no one knew where he was.

There was snow in Vermont. The valley would have looked pretty on a sunny day, but the skies were leaden, the dark clouds hugged the mountainside only a couple of hundred feet above him, and Chris was pushing the four-wheel drive well beyond the limits of a normal car. So far, no skids. Which was fortunate, because there was a hundred-foot drop to his left.

What kept him going were the clear tracks of another vehicle along the road in front of him. Someone else had been along here since it had last snowed. If they had made it, so could he.

About four miles from the highway, he rounded a bend and came to a high meadow. The trees were cleared for about half a mile up a gentle slope to a white-painted house. Near it was a big red barn. Smoke trickled out of a chimney. A four-wheel drive similar to his own stood outside. Relieved that he had arrived intact, Chris parked his vehicle next to it, and got out. After the warmth of the car the cold engulfed him, making him catch his breath. He glanced up at the sky. He was no expert, but it looked to him like snow.

He approached the front door. It opened when he was still a couple of steps away. A tall woman with long greying hair eyed him suspiciously.

'Hi,' he said. 'Can I come in? It's freezing out here.'

'What do you want?'

'To see Marcus.'

The woman hesitated. Finally, her sympathy overcame her suspicion, and she let him in. She led him through to a warm living room and asked him to take a seat. He did so, on a strange-looking squat wooden chair that was surprisingly comfortable. The woman sat on the floor near a stove. The room was adorned with wild Indian-style fabrics. There were other pieces of furniture in a similar style to the chair Chris was sitting on, and at least a dozen pots of various sizes and shapes, all decorated in primitive browns and greens. And no TV.

'One of Marcus's?' Chris asked, tapping the chair.

The woman nodded. She had a smooth face, serene. Despite her grey hair, she didn't seem to be much older than Chris.

'Is he here?'

'He's out back. He'll be here in a moment.'

Chris heard a metallic click, and looked up. A tall man wearing a long coat was standing in the doorway. In his hands was a rifle. The rifle was pointing straight at Chris.

Chris slowly rose to his feet, holding up his hands in a placating gesture. He knew it would be difficult to talk to Marcus. The barrel of the gun didn't make it any easier.

'There's no need for that,' Chris said gently.

'I think there is,' Marcus growled. He sounded like Alex. He looked like him, too, only much taller. He had the same thin face and dark eyebrows. The stubble on his cheeks reminded Chris of Alex on a Sunday evening. But of course Marcus looked older, more than ten years older, and he lacked Alex's sense of humour. At least while he was holding a gun.

'Marcus, please,' the woman said.

'Be quiet, Angie. I don't trust this guy.'

'Put the gun down,' she said.

'No. I'm keeping hold of the gun. Now, what's your name?'

'Chris. Chris Szczypiorski.'

'I thought so. Didn't I tell you I didn't want to talk to you?'

'Yes, you did. But I want to talk to you. And I'm here now.'

'Well, just turn around and go right out the way you came in.'

Chris took a deep breath. 'Please, Marcus. I've travelled a long way to see you. Give me ten minutes.'

Marcus thought this over. His eyebrows knitted together in a frown. 'Since you're here,' he said. 'Talk.'

Chris returned to his chair, and Marcus sat opposite him. Angie watched carefully from her position on the floor. The gun rested on Marcus's knees, pointing at Chris.

'Tell me what happened on the boat.'

'Right.' Chris found it impossible to take his eyes off the rifle, and very difficult to get his thoughts in order. But having come this far, there was no point in prevaricating. He told Marcus about the evening on the boat in some detail. Marcus's intense brown eyes hung on every word. When he had finished, Chris fell silent.

'And that's it?' Marcus asked.

'That's it.'

'You haven't left anything out?'

Chris shook his head.

'If that's what happened, why didn't you tell the police?'

'We didn't want Duncan to get into trouble.'

'Why not? He killed my brother didn't he?'

'It was an accident. He didn't mean to knock Alex into the sea. He was drunk, and provoked.'

'So you covered it up. I thought Alex was a friend of yours.' The anger and contempt seethed in Marcus's voice.

'He was,' said Chris. 'That's why three of us, including Duncan, risked their lives to try to save him. It was very lucky they weren't all drowned. I thought we weren't going to find Ian in the end.'

'Shame you did,' Marcus muttered.

Chris ignored the comment.

'Trouble is,' said Marcus slowly. 'That's not what happened.'

Chris shrugged. He had told Marcus the truth. There was nothing more he could do.

'You investment bankers never quit lying, do you?'

'I'm not lying, Marcus.'

'How am I supposed to believe you? You lied to the police, didn't you?' A contemptuous smile flickered on his face. 'I know about the police investigation. A few months ago I was going through some of my mother's old stuff and there was a letter to her from my aunt talking about how the police suspected Alex's death was murder. I called my aunt, who said that there were all kinds of suspicions right after the death, but nothing ever came of them. I go to New York from time to time to sell my furniture, so the next time I was there I tracked down a detective who worked on the case. He said he was suspicious. There was bruising on Alex's jaw that was consistent with a blow. He thought you guys were all lying. Then suddenly his boss told him to forget all about it. So he forgot it. But I haven't.'

'That's why you went looking for Lenka?'

'That's right. I tried Eric Astle first, but he wouldn't even see me. And the guy who ran the training programme wasn't much help either. Pretty soon, I realized that most of the people on that boat were in London, so I went over there to find them. You were out of the country somewhere, but I spoke to the Czech woman. Lenka.'

'Who told you the same as I just have,' Chris said.

'More or less.'

'And then you found Duncan and screamed at him?'

'Yes.'

'So what's the problem?'

'I'm not sure,' said Marcus. 'But there is one.'

'Is it something Lenka told you?'

Marcus didn't answer.

'I know Lenka sent you an e-mail saying she had something important to tell you. You said you'd phone her. Did you?'

Marcus nodded.

'What did she say?'

'She said she was planning a trip to America in a couple of weeks, and she wanted to come out here to see me. We agreed on a day.'

'Did she say what she wanted to talk to you about?'

'I asked her. She said it was something to do with Alex's death. But she'd only tell me the details when we met.'

'Did she say why?'

'I asked her that, too. She said she had something to tell me that I had a right to know, but that she was worried about what I might do with the information. She said it would be better to discuss it face-to-face.'

'So you have no idea what this "something" was?'

'All she would say was that what she had told me happened, didn't happen. I asked her whether Duncan knocked Alex into the sea or not. I mean that seems a pretty difficult thing to get wrong. Lenka said he had, but that wasn't how Alex had died.'

Chris was stunned. 'What could she mean?'

'I don't know. I asked her, but she wouldn't tell me more. But you tell me.'

'What?' said Chris.

'How did my brother die?'

'I've no idea.'

'You were there. What happened? Did you all throw him in together? Is that what happened? Did you beat him senseless and toss him into the sea?' Marcus raised his voice. 'Tell me, for God's sake!'

'I don't know,' said Chris. 'If what Lenka originally told you is wrong, I just don't know.'

'How can that be?' said Marcus. 'You were there.'

Chris shrugged.

'You're all going to cover this up, aren't you? And then one of you is going to come out here and kill me too.' His eyes lit up as the thought took hold. 'Is that what you're doing here? Stand up!'

Chris didn't move.

'I said, stand up.' The end of Marcus's rifle twitched.

This time Chris did as he was told.

'Frisk him, Angie.'

'What?' Angie looked at him as if he was mad.

'He might have a gun.'

'I haven't got a gun,' Chris said.

'Frisk him. I can't. I want to keep him covered.'

'OK.' Angie gently ran her hands over Chris's legs and then inside his coat. She checked his pockets. 'Nothing,' she said.

'Check the car!'

Angie looked at Marcus, and then at Chris. 'Keys?'

'It's unlocked,' Chris said.

Chris sat down again. He and Marcus waited for Angie, staring at each other, Marcus's brown eyes simmering with anger.

'You look like him, you know,' Chris said.

'No, I don't.'

'I think you do.'

'He's dead.'

'Oh, come on,' said Chris in frustration. 'You know what I mean.'

'I don't know how you guys could do it,' said Marcus. 'Lie about him. You all say he was a friend of yours. Why don't you act like it?'

Chris felt a surge of anger rise in his chest. 'What do you mean, "why don't we act like it"? You have no idea how we felt about Alex's death. We'd all become good friends that summer. We all liked Alex, and with reason. He was a good person in a place where good people were thin on the ground. He lightened the whole place up a bit. He was fun.'

Marcus was listening grudgingly. The door shut as Angie returned from the car, shaking her head.

'It just about destroyed Duncan,' Chris continued in a lower voice. 'And Lenka, although she did a better job of getting over it. That evening comes back to me all the time, even now. Especially now. I'm sure it must be bad to lose a brother. But it's not much fun to lose a friend, especially when it happens right in front of your eyes and there's nothing you can do about it.'

'You know,' Marcus said. 'I was so disappointed when he became an investment banker. He was a good artist. See that painting over there?' He pointed over Chris's shoulder to a painting of a petrochemical plant at night: looming metal curves, orange glows, and bright halogen flashes. It wasn't one Chris recognized. It was out of the line of sight of the doorway, so Chris hadn't noticed it when he came in. It looked totally out of place in that room, but it had obviously been hung with pride.

'He did that. It won him a prize at college. He'd begun to sell some of his work, and then he gave it all up to go on Wall Street. It's good, isn't it?'

Chris nodded, and was surprised to feel the prick of tears in his eyes at such a tangible sign of Alex. He blinked, and looked directly at Marcus. 'Did you ever forgive him?'

'What? What do you mean?'

'Sorry. I shouldn't have said that.' But Chris could tell from Marcus's suspicious glance that he had guessed correctly.

'You're right: I didn't forgive him. I was a couple of years older than him. It was the end of the eighties, all anybody wanted to do was get a big job and make big money. It made me sick. I wanted to travel. See the world. Stay in touch with myself. Develop into a creative human being. Alex was my kid brother, and he thought the same way I did.'

Chris sensed that a powerful urge to talk about his brother was bottled up within Marcus, and now he had the opportunity to release it, it was overcoming his distrust. Chris tried to encourage it.

'What about your mother?'

'She didn't understand any of this. Since our dad died, she had become obsessed with us both getting a good job. Nothing exciting, just something that would guarantee us a pay cheque for the rest of our lives. And when I left college, it got worse. You see, I didn't even apply for any jobs; I just went bumming around the Caribbean, crewing on sailboats. Mom couldn't stand it. So I took off completely. Went to Europe. Australia. The Philippines.'

'And you lost touch with Alex?'

'Not at first. I came back, occasionally; spent time with both of them. But it was an ugly time, especially with my mother. I remember I came home one Christmas and she said she'd contracted breast cancer. Of course that shook me up, but then it turned out she had it beat. Or at least that's what she thought. Then Alex took his job at Bloomfield Weiss, and I thought, screw them, and I stayed out of touch for nearly a year.'

He sighed. 'The cancer came back. Later, I think I discovered the reason Alex took the job.'

'What was that?'

Marcus took a moment to answer. He was breathing heavily, trying to control himself. Chris saw the concerned look on Angie's face as she watched him.

'Mom wasn't properly covered. For healthcare. After Alex died, I found out he'd taken out some large loans. And I found Mom's healthcare bills. They were pretty big.'

'Alex did spend quite a lot of time with her,' Chris said. 'He got a couple of warnings for it. He looked after her.'

'Yeah. And I guess I'm grateful. Although sometimes it makes me so angry. I get angry with him and her for not telling me what was going on. But of course I realize it's me that I'm really angry with. I was so stupid, so selfish.' Marcus shook his head. 'You know, I only found out two months after Mom died. I kept calling her and getting no reply, and then I called my aunt and found out what had happened to the two of them. I missed their funerals, everything.

'I came right home. Sorted through all their stuff, tidied up, and moved up to Vermont.' He looked around at the small cabin. 'I like it here. It's quiet. Sometimes here I can feel peace. And finally I'm beginning to make some money out of the furniture. But I still miss Alex. Mom, too, sometimes, but it's mostly Alex.' He took a deep breath. 'And believe me if I find that someone, one of your friends, did kill him on purpose, did *murder* him, I'll, I'll . . .'

Chris kept quiet. He didn't want to know what Marcus would do. But Marcus told him anyway.

'I'll kill him.'

I 3

Chris was not prepared for what confronted him at the office. He had arrived straight from Heathrow after a lousy night with no sleep. The German stock market had wobbled the night before, and was now in full retreat. There were doubts about the strength of the German recovery, which meant that there were severe doubts about the prospects for Eastern Europe, which meant that most of Carpathian's government bond holdings had fallen. Ironically, German and other euro zone countries' bond prices had actually risen on the expectation of lower interest rates. This was the worst possible combination for Chris's positions. And, of course, Bloomfield Weiss had taken the opportunity to mark Eureka Telecom down by another five points.

Ollie was despondent. The Slovakian bonds he had bought had fallen with the rest of the market, and he seemed to blame himself for Germany's economic jitters. Chris tried to be supportive, as he knew he must, but it was difficult. He knew that in a month or two things would sort themselves out, but he didn't have a month or two. Rudy Moss would want his money back in two weeks, and Chris would be faced with either trying to sell his Eureka Telecom bonds at a huge loss, or unwinding his fundamentally strong government bond positions at exactly the wrong moment. Carpathian's performance would be severely damaged either way, possibly terminally.

And there was no message from Melville Capital. Chris had been half-hoping that Dr Zizka would change his mind. But he hadn't.

Chris spent the day with Ollie ineffectually wrestling with the markets. There was really nothing they could do. They didn't want to sell yet if they could possibly help it. Although there were bonds out there worth buying, they had no spare cash with which to buy them. All they could do was listen to the doom and gloom of a bearish market on a cold grey Friday afternoon.

There was definitely no chance of getting Rudy back into the fund. But Chris still had hopes for Dr Zizka. At the very end of their meeting, he had had a strong feeling he was finally getting through to him. There was nothing to be gained by waiting for Zizka to change his mind. Either he would, or he wouldn't. Chris needed to find out which. He picked up the phone.

'Zizka.' The voice was little more than a murmur.

'Dr Zizka? It's Chris Szczypiorski, Lenka's partner.'

For a moment, Chris thought Zizka had fled, leaving his phone dangling, but Chris could feel, as much as hear, gentle breathing down the line.

'Dr Zizka?'

'Yes, yes,' he replied at last. 'How are you?'

'I'm fine. Look, I was wondering whether you had decided to change your mind about pulling out of Carpathian.'

'Ah.'

'Have you?'

'It's difficult,' Zizka said. 'I have a meeting with some trustees next week. I'd like to be able to say we've gotten rid of this investment.'

'The markets are jumpy at the moment. I'm convinced you'll get a better price if you hang on for a couple of months. Lenka got you into the fund with the promise of good returns, and I'd hate you to come out without them.'

Silence again. Chris could feel his heart beating. He wanted to jump into the void, to fill the silence with persuasive talk, but he kept quiet. Zizka was thinking. And Chris knew who he was thinking about. Lenka.

'All right,' Zizka said, at last. 'Why not? Personally, I believe these worries about Germany are all overdone, anyway. It won't do any harm to wait a couple of months. I'll stay in. We'll review the situation in May, shall we?'

'Excellent. We'll talk then. Thank you very much, Dr Zizka.'

Chris put down the phone with a whoop. They were still going to lose the Amalgamated Veterans money, but keeping Melville Capital in the fund was a psychological boost both he and Ollie needed.

After that minor victory, there was nothing more they could do at the office late on a Friday afternoon, so Chris told Ollie to go home. He took the tube to King's Cross station and the train up to Cambridge, looking over his shoulder every few minutes to see whether he was being followed. To his relief, he didn't spot anyone.

On the train, he thought through his conversation with Marcus yet again. Assuming Lenka was telling the truth and not just trying to confuse Marcus, his conclusions were inescapable. She had said that Duncan had knocked Alex into the sea, *but that wasn't how Alex had died*. Alex was fine before Duncan hit him. So he must have died as a result of what happened afterwards.

Someone had drowned him. And that someone must have been one of the three people who dived into the sea after him. Eric, Ian or Duncan. One of Chris's friends. Someone he had known for ten years.

But which one?

Duncan was too shaken at the time to do anything. Eric was possible. But Ian seemed the most likely. For a start, he was in the water the longest. Also, he was most obviously linked to Lenka's death. From his e-mails to her, it was clear Ian had had problems with Lenka just before she was killed. Or rather, she had had problems with him. Ian knew Lenka was in touch with Marcus, he knew she was going to tell him something, and he wanted to stop her.

Perhaps he was afraid that Lenka was about to tell Marcus that he had drowned Alex ten years before. So he went to Prague to shut her up. Or paid someone else to.

The idea revolted Chris. But whichever way he looked at it, it was the only one that made sense.

It was dark by the time the train pulled into Cambridge station. Chris took a taxi to Megan's college. His spirits lifted as he walked through the ancient college gates into the quiet First Court and then passed the sprawling plane tree in front of her building. He looked up: the lights were on in her rooms.

'It's so good to see you!' Megan said when she opened her door to him. Before he had a chance to say anything, she gave him a long, warm kiss. He held her and thought it was good to see her, too.

'You look a wreck,' she said. 'Did you sleep on the plane?'

'No. Sleep is pretty difficult at the moment.'

'Come here,' Megan led Chris to the sofa, and nestled under his arm. Chris liked her room. It had white walls and large windows overlooking the court below. Black painted wooden beams ran across the ceiling. She had done her best to scatter the few possessions she had been able to bring to England about the place. On the mantelpiece were two photographs: one of Megan's parents sitting on the porch of a yellow clapboard house, and another of a much younger Megan lying on the grass next to her grandmother, hugging an overweight basset-hound. Framed posters of exhibitions long gone by adorned the walls. Next door was a tiny bedroom with a single bed. Cramped, but Chris wasn't complaining.

'Tell me what happened,' Megan said. 'Did you find Marcus?'

Chris told her all about his conversations with Abby Hollis, George Calhoun, and Dr Marcia Horwath. He told her in detail about his trip to Vermont to see Marcus. But he only gave his visit to Eric's house a brief mention, and said nothing at all about the double threat he had received in New York. He didn't want to scare Megan. Having made his decision to continue the search for Lenka's killer, he didn't want Megan to talk him out of it.

She listened attentively, interrupting only once or twice for clarification. When Chris had finished, she asked the obvious question. 'What was Lenka going to tell Marcus?'

Chris gave her his answer.

Megan didn't say anything for several seconds. Her face was pale. 'That's horrible. I just can't believe it. Do you really think Ian would do something like that?'

'It was either him or Eric,' Chris said. 'I don't believe Duncan was in any state to drown someone that night.'

'I'm sure it wasn't Eric,' said Megan. 'I know him too well. It must have been Ian. Yuk.' She recoiled. 'And you think he killed Lenka as well?'

Chris nodded.

'Oh, my God!' She shook her head. 'But why? Why would Ian want to drown Alex? They weren't enemies.'

'No, they weren't,' said Chris. 'There's only one reason I can think of. Did I ever tell you I caught Ian taking cocaine on the training programme?'

'Yes, I think so.'

'I only saw him do it the once. But what if he was a regular user? What if he was the one who supplied Alex? Remember, only the American trainees were tested. Ian could have had a lucky escape. But what if Alex was planning to tell Calhoun all about Ian?'

'So Ian drowned Alex to keep him quiet.' Megan shuddered. 'Are you absolutely sure that's what happened? I still can't believe it.'

'No, I'm not sure. It's my best guess. But remember, we were out of sight of all three of them. It could have been Eric, or perhaps even Duncan himself.'

'It wasn't Eric.'

There was something about Megan's certainty on that score that irritated Chris. He knew it was jealousy on his part, and he wasn't proud of it. But although he agreed with Megan, he couldn't stop himself from arguing. 'We shouldn't rule him out.'

'You don't have to rule him out if you don't want to,' said Megan. 'But I know it was Ian. What do we do now?'

Chris slumped back on Megan's sofa. He suddenly felt very tired. 'I don't know.'

'Can we go to the police?' Megan asked.

'I thought about that,' Chris said. 'And the question is, which police? There's no point in going to the police in this country; no crime has been committed here. We could go to the police on Long Island and try to get them to reopen the investigation into Alex's death. But we have no hard evidence. Just hearsay and deduction. And as soon as we start explaining what really happened, we'll have to admit that we all lied to them ten years ago. All that will do is get us arrested for obstructing the course of justice. They might decide to get Duncan on a murder or manslaughter charge as well.'

'What about the Czech police? If we're right and Ian murdered Lenka, then they can go after him.'

'True. But we have no real evidence at all linking Lenka's death to Ian. The Czechs would have to go through all the evidence about Alex's death, which would get us back to square one with the American police. And then they'd have to extradite Ian. It's unlikely to stand up.'

'I see,' said Megan.

There was one further reason why Chris didn't want to go to the police. He knew it wasn't Ian who had accosted him on the street in New York. If Ian was behind the killings of Alex and Lenka, then he had an accomplice. A dangerous accomplice. And once Chris went to the police, that accomplice would know that he had ignored his threat. Unless the police moved very fast, which given the evidence available was extremely unlikely, Chris could wind up dead.

'What about talking to Ian?' he suggested.

'That's a bit dangerous, isn't it?' said Megan. 'What if we're right and he did kill Alex and Lenka? He might just kill us too. Chris, this is beginning to scare me.'

'He can't carry on killing everyone,' said Chris. 'I could talk to him and tell him that you'll go to the police immediately if he tries anything stupid. Murdering someone in England in those circumstances would be just plain dumb. And Ian isn't dumb.'

'I don't know. It still sounds dangerous to me.' Doubt and fear were written all over Megan's face as she looked to Chris for reassurance.

'I don't think so,' Chris said, as convincingly as he could. He knew Megan was right: it was dangerous. But at least they would be taking the initiative. It was probably less dangerous than allowing Ian to pick them both off at his convenience.

'What will you say?'

'I'll talk it through with him. Ian's smooth, but he's not that smooth. Even if he denies everything, which I'm sure he will, I'll know.'

Megan took a deep breath. 'All right,' she said, nodding towards her phone. 'Call him.'

Chris hesitated. Was he sure about what he was doing? It still wasn't too late to bury his head in the sand, to pretend that he had stopped asking questions, that he didn't care that Alex and Lenka had died.

But he did care.

He looked up Ian's home number and dialled it. He told Ian simply that he had discovered some things in America that he wanted to talk to him about, and persuaded him to meet him at lunch-time in a pub in Hampstead the next day, which was a Saturday. At that time it should be crowded and, from Chris's point of view, safe.

Or at least he hoped it would be.

Lovemaking with Megan that night was both tender and intense. The fear they felt for themselves and for each other drew them together. Afterwards, they held each other tightly in the darkness, neither one of them willing to give words to what they felt. Outside, beyond the comforting walls of the college, beyond the winter dawn only a few hours away, lay uncertainty, danger, and, quite possibly, death.

As Chris left the college before breakfast the next morning, he saw an indistinct figure in a car parked a few yards up the road put down a newspaper and drive off. Why would anyone want to read a newspaper in a car at half past seven in the morning, Chris thought. He shuddered, and walked through the damp morning gloom towards the station, unable to shake the feeling that he was running out of time.

PART FOUR

I

Eric looked over the top of his *Wall Street Journal* as his car slowed towards the rear of the yellow taxi in front. He checked his watch. It was still only five forty. He was due at the lawyers' midtown offices at five forty-five. He was going to be late. Since this was a Friday evening and they were only half way there, probably very late. Tough. It was only a rinky-dink deal, anyway. Some company called Net Cop that made switches for the Internet was up for sale. The only reason he hadn't been able to palm the deal off on to a junior was that Sidney Stahl had invested in the company himself. Sidney would be pleased if Eric could get a good price for Net Cop. And Eric would. It was what he did. Three big telecoms equipment manufacturers were interested. One had offered four hundred million dollars, but Eric was confident he could achieve at least double that, maybe even a billion if he could get them all scared enough of each other.

The car lurched forward twenty feet. 'Is there any way we can get around this?' he asked.

'Nuttin' we can do,' said the massively overweight driver, who seemed perfectly content to spend his Friday evening slouched in Manhattan gridlock.

Eric sighed, but decided not to argue. Terry would have done something. But just then, Terry wasn't available.

He turned back to the legal documents on his knee. It was beginning to get dark and the dense print blurred together. He rubbed his eyes and switched on the interior light in the car. Eric could work hard, he liked to work hard, but it was getting so he was working all the time. And there was this other business to worry about.

His cell phone chirped. Eric sighed. The damn phone never stopped.

'Eric Astle.'

'Eric, it's Ian.'

Eric put down his papers. Ian sounded shaken.

'What is it?'

'Chris wants to see me.'

'So?'

'He said he found out something in America he wants to talk to me about.'

Eric's pulse quickened. 'Did he say what?'

'No. Did you see him while he was there? Did he tell you he'd discovered anything?'

'I did see him,' said Eric. 'He hadn't found out much. He knows about Alex and the drugs. But when I saw him he hadn't made any connection with what happened to Alex, let alone Lenka.'

'Did he talk to Marcus Lubron?'

'I don't know. He was intending to. But I was hoping he might have changed his mind.'

'Perhaps he did talk to Marcus,' Ian was sounding agitated. 'Perhaps Marcus told him everything.'

'Relax, Ian,' said Eric. 'We don't know what Lenka told Marcus. We don't know whether Chris even saw Marcus. And if he did, we don't know what Marcus said.' He paused to think. He could hear Ian's panicked breathing on the phone. 'When did Chris call you?'

'A few hours ago.'

'And when are you supposed to meet him?'

'Tomorrow lunch-time.'

'I think it would be best if you didn't see him.'

'But if I don't show, he'll find me.'

'Then go away somewhere.'

'Go away somewhere?'

'Yeah. Go abroad. Frankfurt. Paris. Somewhere like that.

Say you'll see him when you get back. That'll buy us some time.'

'But tomorrow's a Saturday!'

Eric closed his eyes. Boy, did this guy whine. 'Ian. Real men work Saturdays. Just tell him.'

'What are you going to do?'

'I don't know,' said Eric. 'But I'll figure something out.'

'Eric. Don't do anything rash.'

'I said, I'll figure it out. You know what? Go to Paris. Call me when you get there. Better yet, I'll meet you there.' He paused for a few moments, putting together a schedule in his head. 'We'll have breakfast in the George Cinq on Sunday.' With that, Eric hit the red button on his phone and Ian was gone.

Eric stared out at the crowds and the cars and thought. Despite that carefully cultivated British arrogance, Ian was weak. And Chris was determined. Eric would have to act. Again.

He hit a number from his phone's memory. It took a few moments to connect. He glanced up at the thick neck of the driver. He was stupid, but Eric didn't want to take any chances. He might already have said more than he intended in his conversation with Ian. He would be more careful this time.

The call was answered on the first ring.

'Yes?'

'Terry?'

'Yes.'

'Where are you?'

'Cambridge.'

'Where's our man?'

'With our girl.'

If Eric caught a slight note of mockery in Terry's voice, he ignored it. 'OK. I don't think he's got the message. So go ahead and do what you have to do. Then get yourself on a plane to Paris. I'll see you there Sunday.'

'Understood.'

More calls. To his secretary to book a flight to Paris. To one of his more ambitious vice presidents to tell him he was now working on the Net Cop deal, and should get his ass up to the lawyers' offices immediately. The guy couldn't wait. Great visibility with Sidney. Then the call to Sidney Stahl himself, explaining that Eric had got the whiff of a big European telecoms merger and needed to be there immediately. Stahl was clearly pissed off, but couldn't say anything. The conflict of interest would be too obvious if he made Eric drop that for a deal in which Stahl had a personal investment. Eric winced as he made the call. It was never a good idea to bullshit Stahl. But he had no choice.

Finally, he called Cassie, once again blowing their weekend plans out of the water. Cassie took it well. Eric smiled to himself. She was a wonderful woman.

Chris took the tube from King's Cross to Hampstead and walked the half mile to his flat. He lugged his bag up the hill, thinking nervously about his meeting with Ian in just over an hour's time. He tried to ignore the fear. There was nothing Ian could do in a crowded pub. In fact, it was hard to take Ian seriously as a physical threat. As a manipulator, certainly. As a devious, lying, conniving bastard. But not as a cold-blooded killer.

But Alex and Lenka were both dead. And Chris had been warned.

Chris checked the street both ways before unlocking the front door of his building. Nothing suspicious, just a man in his fifties walking his dog, and a harassed mother dragging two reluctant children towards the Heath. No one was waiting for him on the stairs and his flat was locked just as he had left it. He entered, dumped his stuff, put the kettle on to boil, and listened to the messages on his machine. There was one from Ian.

'Sorry, I can't make lunch. Something's come up. Got to go to Paris. I'll call you next week.'

Chris looked up Ian's mobile number and dialled it. It was answered.

'Hello?'

'Ian? It's Chris.'

'Oh, hi, Chris.'

'Where are you?'

'Heathrow.'

'Look, I've got to see you.'

'Yes. I'm sorry about lunch today. But we can catch up at the end of next week. I'll give you a ring as soon as I get back.'

'But why the sudden rush to Paris?'

'Big deal. We've got to move fast. I only heard about it after you called me yesterday.'

'But it's a Saturday!'

'What can I say? It's a live deal. They say jump, I jump.'

This didn't sound right. Corporate Finance people like Eric might work all weekend but Ian was basically a salesperson. They worked Monday to Friday. Or they certainly had when Chris was at Bloomfield Weiss.

'I have to talk to you Ian. I can drive out to Heathrow now.'

'My flight's in twenty minutes.'

'Can't you get a later one?'

'No. I've got a meeting in Paris. It's going to be tight as it is.'

Damn, thought Chris. 'When will you be back?'

'Can't say. Depends on how the deal goes. End of next week at the earliest. I'll call you.'

'Ian –'

'Got to go, now. Bye.'

Chris put down the phone, thinking that he didn't believe a single word Ian had told him.

Ian had a horrible flight to Paris. He was sweating: the heating on the plane must be too high, or something. Eric was right: he would be safer in Paris. It was unlikely that Chris would come looking for him there. He had no idea what he was going to tell the office on Monday. There was, of course, no big deal in France for him to be working on. But there were deals in London that he was supposed to be doing something about. He would have to develop quite a story to justify his presence in Paris. But at least he had two days to think of it.

He was scared. He had been scared for ten years. He had done his best to hide it, to forget it, to rationalize it away, but the fear had always been lingering under the surface. And now, since Lenka had died, it had forced itself very much into the open.

He felt for the little package in his jacket pocket. It was the first time he had taken any abroad with him. Until now, he had always made it a rule never to carry drugs over international borders. But these days London to Paris didn't count. The only guys he had ever seen checked were swarthy men with moustaches wearing leather jackets who practically had 'smuggler' tattooed on their foreheads. He'd be OK. And he'd brought enough to last him until the end of next week.

He could certainly use some now. He knew his consumption had gone up in the last few weeks, since Lenka died. That was hardly surprising. These were exceptional circumstances. Besides, he knew he could give up any time. He'd gone cold turkey many times over the last ten years, hadn't he?

Ian fidgeted in his seat. He didn't underestimate Chris. Chris was smart and determined, and he would discover the truth eventually. Unless Eric stopped him first. Ian shuddered. Chris had become a pain in the arse, but he didn't want another killing. The killing had to stop.

He wished that he had told people what he knew when he had the chance, ten years ago. Now he had no choice. He had to keep quiet and trust Eric.

It was too much. Ian stood up, pushed past the man in the aisle seat, and headed for the toilets.

Terry's feet hit the damp soil with the barest of sounds. It was a ten-foot drop from the wall of the college: no problem. Terry smiled to himself. These old colleges might look like fortresses from the outside, but they were a cinch to get into. And once inside the walls there were all kinds of bushes, staircases and corridors to lurk in. Plus everyone he had seen wandering around the place during the day looked as weird as hell, so he doubted anyone would think anything strange if they did see him.

It was one thirty. There was only a slither of a moon, which cast the palest of light on the spreading tangle of branches of the ancient tree outside the building. Terry waited for ten minutes, stroking the moustache he had attached for the exercise. He was getting to like it. Perhaps he should grow a real one when this was all over. But the wig irritated him. The long greasy hair tickled his neck. It made him feel scruffy, not the neat, well-trimmed man of action that he liked to think himself to be. It was necessary though, enough to mislead anyone who caught a brief glimpse of him. He grinned to himself as he thought how it had fooled Szczypiorski in New York.

He waited while a loaded kid made his unsteady way across the grass to bed, and then crept along the shadow of the wall until he came to the building. He straightened up and walked up to the staircase and through the doors. Nothing was locked. Up two flights of stairs and there was the thick wooden door with the number eight painted on the wall above it. This door was locked, but it was only a Yale, and within a few seconds Terry was inside.

He found himself in a sitting room. No bed, but a door in one corner. He opened it and slipped into a much smaller room. There was a narrow bed here, and a figure huddled under the covers, dark hair splayed over the pillow. Terry smiled to himself, slid his gloved hand into his jacket and gently pulled out a six-inch knife.

Two hours later, he was in an all-night Internet café in London, typing out a brief message. Three hours after that, his moustache and wig now removed, he was at Heathrow's Terminal Four, waiting for an early flight to Paris.

2

Chris woke up early on Sunday morning. There was no chance of him indulging in his traditional Sunday morning lie-in, so he rose and made himself a cup of tea in the kitchen. The thoughts that had been tumbling about incoherently in his sleep coalesced into the questions he needed to answer. Marcus, Ian, Alex, Lenka. How were they all connected? What had happened in the water off Long Island Sound ten years ago? What had happened in Prague two weeks before? And what was Ian doing in Paris?

Chris wandered into his sitting room with the cup of tea. He glanced at the blank screen of his PC. Perhaps there was an e-mail from Marcus. Or George Calhoun. Or someone else that could shed some light on the whole mess. He knew it was probably a waste of time, but he turned on the machine and checked his e-mails.

There was one. From 'A concerned friend'. The subject line was 'I told you once'.

The message read:

> Chris
> I warned you in New York, and I'm warning you again. Stop asking questions about Alex. Forget him. Otherwise it is not just you who will die. So will Megan.

Chris stared at the message open mouthed. It was too early in the morning to take it in. He checked the address of the sender: a chain of Internet cafés he had vaguely heard of.

The phone rang. He picked it up.

'Chris! Chris, it's Megan!' She sounded close to hysteria.

'Did you get one too?' Chris asked.

'One what? I've just woken up. I rolled over, and on my pillow was . . . God, it was horrible.' She sobbed.

'Was what? Slow down, Megan. It's OK. Slow down.'

'A knife, Chris. A great big long knife. With blood on it. There was blood all over my pillow. It's horrible.'

She broke off into wild sobs.

'Oh, no, Megan! Are you hurt?'

'No,' she sniffed. 'Someone must have broken in and done this inches from my face, while I was asleep. I didn't hear a thing.'

'Thank God they didn't harm you. It must have been terrifying.'

'It was. It truly was. But who would do this? And why?'

'They were trying to scare you. And me.'

'Well, they succeeded,' said Megan. 'I've never been so scared in all my life.'

'I'm sure.' Chris said. He wished he could hold her, comfort her, try to make her feel better. Then he felt the guilt creep over him. 'I'm so sorry.'

'Sorry? There's nothing for you to feel sorry about.'

Chris swallowed. 'I got an e-mail this morning.' He read it off the computer screen in front of him. 'And I got a warning myself when I was in New York. Someone pulled a knife on me and wrote in blood all over the mirror in my hotel bedroom.'

'Jesus, why didn't you tell me?'

'I didn't want to frighten you,' said Chris. 'I thought you might try to talk me out of going to see Marcus. I didn't think that you were in danger as well.'

'Well, next time someone tries to kill you, let me know, OK?' Megan sounded angry. As well she might.

'OK, OK. I'm sorry.'

Megan was silent on the phone for a while. 'They are serious, aren't they?' she said at last.

'Yes.'

'Do you think it could have been Ian?'

'Possibly. Perhaps he went to Cambridge instead of Paris. But it definitely wasn't Ian who attacked me in New York. If he is behind it, he must be working with somebody else.'

'What shall we do?'

'You can tell the college authorities, if you want. They'll contact the police. I'm not sure it'll do much good: I haven't heard anything from the New York cops since I told them what happened to me. But I can't make you hush it up.'

Megan sighed. 'There's no point. It would hardly go down well with the college. And whoever did this must be a professional. It's unlikely the police will catch him. I'll put the pillowcase and the knife in a plastic bag and throw them away.'

'Keep the knife. We might need it for evidence later.'

'Oh, God. OK.'

They were silent for a moment.

'Chris?'

'Yes?'

'I'm scared.'

'I know. So am I.'

'I think maybe this is getting out of hand.'

Chris didn't answer for a moment. He had decided to take risks on his own behalf. But he couldn't risk Megan's life as well.

'Maybe it is,' he said. 'I'll lie low for a bit. Not ask any more questions. Keep quiet.'

'I'm sorry, Chris. I think you should.'

'You must be feeling terrible. I hate the idea of you being alone up there. Can I come up and see you today?'

'That would be great if you could. I was planning to spend most of the day in the library, but if you came up this evening, I'd love to see you.'

'I'll be there,' said Chris.

'Thanks,' said Megan. 'Now I'd better go clean up this mess.'

Ian looked around him at the ostentation of the dining room of the George V. Normally he would have relished a breakfast meeting in these ornate surroundings, playing the international investment banker with like-minded people. But not that morning. What he craved was a strong cup of coffee and a ciggy in a corner café. Of course, with Eric, there was no chance of that.

He had been skulking in Paris for nearly a day, now. It had started to rain from the moment his taxi had hit the Périphérique, and it had continued to rain all night. It took him an age to find a hotel room at short notice on a Saturday night, and he spent much of the day avoiding boisterous men in red jerseys there to cheer on their country in a rugby match. Finally he found a scruffy hotel near the Gare du Nord, dumped his bags, walked around in the rain for a bit, and then went to see a bad American film dubbed into French at a cinema on the Champs-Élysées.

He felt foul. He had overdone the drink the night before. And the coke. It had made him feel better for a bit. But now he felt like shit. He pulled out a cigarette and lit it. Ah, that tasted good.

'Ian, good to see you.'

Ian had missed Eric's entrance. He looked disgustingly bright and cheerful with his gleaming white shirt, and his tie tied so tightly that it seemed to leap straight forward out of his neck. Ian had an urge to pull it, but instead he just grunted, ignoring Eric's outstretched hand. Despite the surroundings, this wasn't a business meeting, and he didn't feel like pretending it was.

'Plane was half an hour late into Charles de Gaulle. But there was no traffic coming into the city. Have you ordered?'

Ian shook his head. Eric caught a hovering waiter's eye and ordered croissants and some coffee.

'How are you?' Eric asked.

'Shit,' Ian answered, and sniffed.

'You don't look too good.' Eric stared at him closely. Ian flinched. 'Are you on something?'

'I was,' he answered, deciding he had no need to lie for Eric's benefit.

'Is that wise? I think we all need clear heads at the moment.'

'What do you mean, is that wise?' Ian snapped. 'I'll do what I bloody well like. I seem to remember you did enough of that

267

stuff in the past. That's what got us into this mess in the first place.'

'That was a long time ago. I haven't touched anything for ten years,' said Eric.

'Well, aren't you the little saint?' Ian said. 'I haven't killed anyone for ten years. In fact, I've never killed anyone.'

'Keep your voice down,' said Eric calmly, with a smile.

'What the hell did you have to get Lenka killed for, anyway?' Ian said, more quietly this time.

'I had no choice. She was going to talk. First to Marcus Lubron, then to other people. You knew Lenka. There was only one way to shut her up.'

'But now Chris is on the trail. And your old girlfriend, Megan. And then Duncan. The whole thing's out of control.'

'Not quite,' said Eric calmly. 'I'm working on getting it back under control. And remember, if you hadn't told Lenka about Alex, none of this would have happened.'

Ian sighed. His head throbbed. He closed his eyes. Eric was right. He remembered the night when he had opened this whole can of worms. It was very late, at Lenka's flat. They had just had sex. Great sex. Lenka was talking about how she had met Marcus that day. Ian was a little tired, a little high; his brain wasn't working quite right. He had smiled and said it was funny that it wasn't even Duncan's fault that Alex had died. Lenka was suddenly wide awake. She wanted to know what he was talking about. Ian tried to deny that he had meant anything, but she knew he had. She pressed him hard, assaulting him with a barrage of questions. His resistance quickly broke down. He had wanted to tell someone for years, and Lenka suddenly seemed the right person. So he told her he had seen Eric drown Alex. It turned out Lenka was not the right person at all. She exploded. Within ten minutes, Ian found himself outside in the Old Brompton Road looking for a cab.

Lenka told Ian that she was going to tell Marcus. Ian told Eric. And then Lenka was dead.

'We both screwed up,' said Ian. 'But there's no need to make things worse.'

'You're right, there isn't,' said Eric. 'I think it's very important that you keep quiet. Because you know what will happen to you if you don't.'

'Is that a threat?'

'Of course,' said Eric quietly. 'And you know I'll carry it out if necessary.'

Ian felt a surge of anger. Somehow, he had been under Eric's thumb ever since Alex had drowned. At the time, it had seemed smart to let Eric take control and sort things out. Eric, who always seemed to have an answer for everything. Well, it was clear now that that had been a mistake. Eric had more to lose than Ian. It was time Ian took the upper hand.

He lit another cigarette. 'Shouldn't I be the one threatening you?' he said, straining to make his voice sound calm and authoritative.

'I don't think that would be wise,' Eric answered coolly.

'Why not? You killed Alex. You had Lenka killed. Just get off my back, or I'll tell people what I know.'

Ian had hoped that this would rattle Eric. But it didn't.

Eric watched Ian for a long minute. Ian tried to smoke his cigarette calmly, but he couldn't help shifting in his chair. Eventually, his thumb drifted up to his lips, and he gnawed at the nail.

Eric smiled, a smug self-confident smile, a declaration of his superiority. 'Nobody threatens me,' he said, and left the table, just as the waiter was bringing the croissants.

Terry was waiting for Eric at Charles de Gaulle. Eric ushered him to one of those quiet dead spaces in airports that are not on the way from one place to another, nor outside anywhere important. They sat in a pair of isolated chairs. The only person in earshot was a cleaner.

'Well, boss?' Terry asked.

Eric sighed and puffed out his cheeks. 'Ian's unreliable. Deal with him.'

'Same bonus as last time?'

Eric nodded.

Terry smiled. Eric paid a very good bonus.

'All go well in Cambridge?' Eric asked.

'I got in OK. Left the knife. Got out. No one saw me.'

'Do you think it will scare her?'

'Oh, yes. It'll scare her,' said Terry. 'But are you sure that'll be enough?'

'We can't leave dead bodies all over the place,' Eric said. 'Every one increases the risk we'll get caught. I think it'll help that each is in a different country, but if some cop somewhere puts together the fact that they were all on the same boat ten years ago, we're in trouble.'

Terry nodded non-committally. But Eric picked up the implication. Terry thought Eric was being soft on Megan because she used to be his girlfriend. Well, he was right. Eric really didn't want to kill her if he could avoid it. In fact, he hadn't really wanted to kill any of them. But after Alex, one led to another.

And he had had to kill Alex. If he hadn't, he would have no chance of fulfilling his destiny. Eric had always known he was an exceptionally able person, he had known it ever since he was a small child. There was no class he couldn't come top of, no job he couldn't get, no competition he couldn't win. From childhood, he had assumed that he had been given this extraordinary talent for a purpose, and the purpose seemed to him to be to lead his country. He could do it. He had the talent. He could earn the money. Hell, he even had the luck. And he was certain that once he was in high office, or even the highest office, he would do the job well. Eric knew that his ambition was far beyond most mortals. But he was confident it wasn't beyond him.

Alex and a few grams of white powder would have put a stop to all that. He couldn't let it.

'Let's hope we've scared them off,' Eric said. 'But if that doesn't work, I have another idea.' He checked his watch. 'I've got to go. My flight leaves in twenty minutes. Good luck.'

'Thanks, boss,' said Terry, and they parted.

Eric passed through the security check and passport control, and made his way to the gate. The flight to London Heathrow had been called, but the queue was a long one, so he had a couple of minutes. He dialled a number on his mobile.

'Hello?'

He recognized the voice. It had changed little in the last nine years. 'Megan? It's Eric.'

There was silence for a second. Then he heard her voice. 'Eric?' It was little more than a whisper.

'That's right. How are you doing?'

'Er . . . OK. I guess.'

'Good. That's great. Look, I know we haven't seen each other in a long time, but I'm in London for a meeting tomorrow, and I've got some time this afternoon. I just thought it would be good to see you. After what happened to Lenka and everything.'

'Um, OK.' Megan sounded hesitant. 'Where are you?'

'At the airport.' Eric was careful not to say which airport. 'I've got one or two things to do, but I might be able to get up to Cambridge by three.'

'All right. Three o'clock is fine. Ask at the porter's lodge and they'll give you directions.'

'OK,' said Eric. 'See you then.'

Chris stared at the rings of white bubbles on the surface of his beer, oblivious of the growing noise around him as the Hampstead pub filled up with the Sunday lunch-time crowd. Duncan had rung him at about eleven that morning and suggested a pint, and Chris had been happy to agree. There was a lot he wanted to discuss with him.

But all Chris could think of was Megan. These people weren't messing around. Although he had been happy with his decision to risk his own neck, he couldn't risk hers: she was just too important to him. A flood of helplessness overwhelmed him. Keeping Megan safe implied sitting back and doing nothing, and he hated that idea. It meant letting Lenka's killer get away with it. But he had no choice.

He was jolted from his thoughts by the thud of a beer glass on his table. Duncan sat down on the small stool opposite him, bringing with him a blast of good cheer. 'Hi, Chris. How's the market been treating you?' he asked, by way of useless small talk.

'Crap,' said Chris.

'Oh. And how are you?'

'Crap also.'

'Well, never mind. I have some good news.'

'Impossible.'

'No. Very possible. Remember your lunch with Khalid?'

'I do,' said Chris, thinking he scarcely had the patience to tolerate Duncan freeloading more information off him.

'He said he's interested in all those weirdo government bond markets you trade in. Apparently, he was very impressed with you. He asked me if he can put money in your fund rather than into the market directly. He'd like to watch how you perform for a year or so, and then perhaps try it for himself.'

Chris sat up in his chair. 'You're not serious?'

'I am,' said Duncan. 'He checked you out with Faisal who apparently had good things to say about you. I told him you were a loser of course, but Khalid never listens to my opinion.' Duncan was grinning.

'But he knows how I was fired from Bloomfield Weiss. How I lost all that money.'

'Looks as though he doesn't care. A lot of the best people have been fired from Bloomfield Weiss: me, for example. Could you take another investor now? I don't know how the fund is structured.'

'As it happens, we could. How much are we talking about?'

'Fifteen million dollars. But he could do less.'

'No, fifteen million dollars would do nicely.' Fifteen million dollars was seventeen million euros, as near as damn it. That would be enough to buy out Rudy and leave seven million euros over. 'And I think the timing is perfect. For him and for us.'

Duncan smiled. 'Shall I tell him that after careful consideration you've decided you can squeeze him in?'

'You tell him that,' said Chris. 'Well done, Duncan! I owe you one.'

'No you don't,' said Duncan. 'It's good to be able to help you for a change.'

Chris smiled and raised his glass. 'To Khalid.' They both drank.

'Also,' said Duncan as he put down his beer, 'I think I've got you to thank for talking to Pippa.'

Chris hesitated for a moment. He had hoped that Duncan wouldn't find out about that conversation. But Duncan didn't seem to be angry. 'Perhaps,' Chris said carefully.

'I don't know what you said to her, but it seems to have worked.'

Chris was puzzled. 'As far as I can recall, she said you were a jerk and I agreed.'

'Well, she and I went out on Friday night, and I think we might be getting back together again.'

'Great,' said Chris. And then, 'Is that a good thing?'

'I think so. You're right, and so is she. I was a jerk. But, I don't intend to be from now on. We'll see. It's worth a try, anyway.'

Chris looked at Duncan and smiled. 'Yes, it is. Good luck.'

'What about you? Why are you in such a foul mood? The market's gone down before, hasn't it?'

'Let me tell you,' said Chris. He took a gulp of beer, and described all that had happened since he had left for America, including the threats to himself and Megan. Duncan listened open-mouthed.

When Chris had finished, Duncan rubbed his eyes and

slumped back in his chair. He exhaled. 'You mean I didn't kill Alex after all?'

'It doesn't look like it,' said Chris.

Duncan shook his head. 'For all these years I've been blaming myself. And Ian knew all along that it wasn't my fault?'

'Yep.'

Duncan reddened. He sat up and struck the table, spilling beer. 'The bastard!' The couple at the table next to theirs turned to stare. Duncan glanced at them and lowered his voice. 'So what did Lenka mean?'

'Megan and I have an idea, but tell me what you think first.'

'OK.' Duncan thought it over. 'We know Alex was drowned. So if I didn't kill him when I hit him and he fell in, then . . . someone else must have drowned him. After he was in the water.'

Chris nodded.

'It can only have been one of the people who dived in to save him. So apart from me, that was Ian and Eric.'

Chris nodded again.

'Well, it's got to be Ian, hasn't it?'

'That seems the most likely to us.'

'I can't believe it. The murdering bastard! And do you think he killed Lenka as well?'

'Yes. Or else he paid someone else to do it.'

'Jesus. What are you going to do about it?'

'It's difficult. I told you how I was attacked in New York. And about the knife on Megan's pillow last night.'

'Yes, but we can't just sit here and let him get away with it.'

'I think we have to. At least for the time being.'

'What do you mean?' Duncan looked aghast. 'That's just cowardice.'

'It's common sense.' Duncan frowned, but Chris continued. 'Look, when it was just me being threatened, I was willing to carry on. I owe Lenka a lot, and I was prepared to take risks to find out who killed her. But I can't risk Megan's life.'

Duncan's eyes narrowed. 'There's something going on between you and her, isn't there?'

'Yes,' Chris admitted. 'There is.'

Duncan snorted.

'Duncan. Be reasonable. Even if there wasn't, I wouldn't want to risk her life. And neither should you. Anyway, Ian is in Paris until later on this week.'

'You can do nothing if you want,' said Duncan. 'But that doesn't mean I have to.'

'What will you do?' Chris asked.

Duncan said nothing. He drained his pint and stood up to leave.

'For God's sake be careful,' Chris said, but Duncan ignored him, as he pushed his way through the crowd to the door.

Megan found it extremely difficult to concentrate on the book in front of her. It was an analysis of the work of the monks of Fleury, a Clunaic abbey on the Loire that had played host to a number of important English churchmen. It wasn't just that it was in French, or that the author seemed to have an aversion to sentences of fewer than thirty words. Megan could cope with that. Indeed, since she had arrived in Cambridge, she had found the library and its difficult texts a refuge from the madness of Lenka's death. It was only here that she could lose herself for a few hours. That was why she had been so eager to leave her rooms that morning, hoping to blot the horror of the knife on her pillow from her mind. But for once, it hadn't worked. And the reason for that was Eric.

After she had spoken to Chris that morning, she had put the knife in a plastic bag and hidden it at the back of one of her drawers. Then she had shoved the bloody pillowcase into another bag together with the contents of her wastepaper basket and dumped it in the college rubbish bins. She had been just about to leave for the library when Eric had called.

Perhaps she shouldn't have told him that he could come and

see her. For eight years now she had avoided him, and there was no doubt that that decision had helped her get over him. But surely, by now it was harmless. He was married, she seemed to be at the beginning of something with Chris, something that she hoped would develop. No, there couldn't be any harm in it.

Then why did her throat feel dry? Why couldn't she concentrate on the book in front of her? Why couldn't she stop thinking about his voice, his face, his eyes, his touch?

She knew she had to see him. It was probably a good thing. Closure, whatever that meant. He would be a podgy, greedy investment banker. They had had little in common when they were students: they would have nothing in common now. It would do her good to see Eric ten years on. She would finally realize she was better off without him.

By two o'clock, she gave up and walked back to the college. She shuddered as she entered her room. Only twelve hours before someone else had been prowling round her bed. It was going to be difficult to sleep there that evening. Locking the outside door hadn't made any difference. She looked over to the sofa: if she pushed that in front of the door before she went to bed, it should make it impossible for anyone to enter without waking her up. And then she would scream. There were probably a hundred people within earshot, at least. That should get rid of him.

She paced around her room. She brushed her hair. She dug out some lipstick, which she never wore, and then put it away. What was she thinking of? She had no need to look good for Eric.

She stood by the window and stared down at the court below. A carpet of snowdrops and crocuses lay beneath the old plane tree. She had never seen one so big, or so tangled. Presumably leaves would appear in a month or two, but it was difficult to imagine: the tree seemed too decrepit to be capable of it. She checked her watch. Three o'clock. No sign of Eric.

At five past three, there was a soft tap at her door. Somehow, she must have missed him cross the court. She forced herself to take her time to answer it.

He hadn't changed much. Same height. Same eyes. Same smile.

'Hi, Megan.'

Same voice.

'Hi.'

'Can I come in?'

'Oh, sure. But I thought we'd go out somewhere, if that's OK with you. Have a cup of tea?'

'And scones, I hope.'

'I'm sure that can be arranged.'

'This is lovely,' said Eric, walking around her sitting room.

'Yeah. It's nice. I was lucky to get it. Most graduate students are stuck outside college. And I've got a phone. That's a real luxury here, apparently.'

'I don't believe it! You still have that poster?'

He pointed to a black and white photograph of a dead tree haunting the Arizona desert. It was advertising an Ansel Adams exhibition dated 1989.

'I like that poster. Look, it's framed now.'

'So it is. Very nice. Well, shall we go?'

Megan took him to a tea shop she had been to once before. It was very quaint and English, and in the tourist season it would probably become a nightmare, but in March it was quiet and a good neutral ground.

'So how have you been?' Eric asked, after they had ordered tea and scones. 'Really?'

'Awful,' said Megan. She had intended to be cool about the last few weeks, but now Eric was here, she found herself launching into a long description of everything that had happened. She talked about how she felt about Lenka's death, about staying with Chris, about Chris's suspicions, about his investigations, about Duncan and Ian and Marcus Lubron. And then she told him about how she had found the knife on her pillow that morning, and how scared she had been and how Chris had been threatened in New York.

Eric was a sympathetic listener, coaxing fears and reservations out of Megan that she had had difficulty articulating to herself, let alone Chris. It felt good to Megan to talk to him, to release some of the tension of the last couple of weeks.

'It sounds like you've been seeing a lot of Chris,' said Eric.

'Yes,' said Megan, smiling shyly.

'He's a nice guy,' Eric said.

'He is.'

Eric returned her smile. 'That's good.'

Megan could feel herself blushing. But she was pleased that she had been able to make clear to Eric that she had her own relationship. It seemed to clear the way for a question she had been eager to ask him. 'How's married life?'

He paused, and seemed to frown for just a second before answering. 'Oh, good, good,' he said. 'It's been seven years now.'

'So it has. Do you have kids?'

'One. A little boy. Wilson. He's two. He's great.'

'I'm sure you make a good father.'

Eric sighed and shook his head. 'I'm never there. Or not there nearly as much as I'd like. Work is crazy. I spend half my life on a plane. More than half my life.'

'I'm sorry.'

'It's my own choice,' said Eric. 'You know what I'm like. Driven.'

Megan smiled. 'I remember.'

'It puts a strain on me and Cassie, though,' said Eric. 'And I do regret that. But you just can't do my kind of job at half speed.'

'Have you dipped your toe into the world of politics?'

'A bit. Help with fund raising. A bit of schmoozing. Some quiet advice to policy wonks on telecoms legislation.'

'But you haven't made your big move yet?'

Eric smiled. 'Not yet.'

'Somehow I doubt you've been converted to the Democrats since I last saw you.'

Eric shook his head. 'Sorry. But I'd put myself kind of centre-right, if that helps.'

'Not much,' said Megan. 'I don't think we were ever destined to have the same political views.'

'I guess not,' said Eric. He poured out the last of the tea. 'So what are you and Chris going to do about Lenka?'

'I don't know. After what happened today, I think we might just give up. But it makes me so angry. Whoever killed Lenka deserves to be caught. I'm pretty sure Ian had something to do with it. Have you seen him recently?'

'No,' said Eric. 'I bump into him sometimes when I'm in the London office. He still works at Bloomfield Weiss. But we're not really friends any more.'

'What do you think?' Megan asked. 'I've told you everything we've found out so far. You're a smart guy. What do you think we should do?'

Eric didn't answer at first. His blue eyes held hers. 'I think you should be very careful, Megan,' he said softly.

Something melted inside Megan. She felt herself begin to blush. Close to panic, she turned and waved at the waitress.

'We should get the check.'

Chris took the steps up Megan's staircase two at a time. He was eager to see her. All day he had been torn between his desire to take a personal risk to find Lenka's killer, and his fear of putting Megan in danger. His fear for Megan had won. He didn't want to be responsible for any more harm coming to her.

He knocked, and she opened the door. He pulled her into his arms, and she clung to him. He stroked her hair.

'I'm so sorry,' he said.

She broke away. 'It's not your fault. You're not the psycho who broke in here.'

'Yes, but I should have told you about what happened in New York.'

'Don't worry,' said Megan. 'Let's just make sure we tell each other about that kind of thing in future, OK?'

'OK. Did you go to the library?'

'I did. I couldn't stay here, and I thought it'd help me forget about the knife. Besides, I do have a lot to do.'

'Did it work?'

'Not really. I couldn't concentrate.'

'I'm not surprised.'

'Look,' said Megan. 'Do you mind if we go out? I don't want to hang around here.'

They went to a Café Rouge. Chris had steak frites, and Megan a goat's cheese salad. They polished off a bottle of red wine, and ordered another.

Megan seemed distracted. She didn't finish her food, and for the first time in their relationship, Chris found it difficult to make conversation. He would start a topic, and Megan would quickly let it trail off. Chris told her about his drink with Duncan, and how angry Duncan had been at the discovery that it was Ian who had probably killed Alex, and Lenka as well. But now Chris and Megan had decided to ease off their investigations, her enthusiasm for the subject seemed to have waned.

Chris wasn't surprised that a shock such as Megan had had would produce an unpredictable reaction, but he was nevertheless disappointed in the form it had taken. He had imagined himself comforting a distraught Megan. A distant one was not what he had expected.

At the end of the meal, after a particularly long silence, Chris spoke. 'Are you angry with me, Megan?'

'No,' she answered simply.

'Because I'd understand if you were.'

She smiled, for almost the first time that evening, and put her hand on his. 'It's not that Chris. Don't worry. It's just . . .'

'You need to get over last night?'

Megan glanced at him nervously. 'Yes. That's it. I just feel all over the place.'

'I can imagine. You must feel dreadful.'

'I do. Look, can we go?'

'Of course.' Chris tried to pay the bill, but she wouldn't let him. Chris didn't want to push it, and so they split it. They walked back to her college in silence. As they reached the college gate, she stopped.

'Chris, I'm sorry to ask you this, but do you think you could leave me alone tonight?'

'I'll do no such thing,' said Chris. 'After what happened last night, I'm staying with you. You shouldn't be by yourself.'

Megan touched his hand. 'You don't understand, I want to be alone.' Chris opened his mouth to protest, but she interrupted him. 'Wait. I'll be safe. They won't come back tonight. We've done what they wanted; we've backed off. I just need to be by myself for a bit.'

'But Megan –'

'Trust me, Chris. Please.'

Chris looked about him in frustration. This he did not understand. But Megan was watching him intently. She was serious. And he would do what she wanted.

'OK,' he said. 'But if you get scared, or you want to talk to me, just call me.'

'I will.' She kissed him on the cheek. 'Thank you,' and she was gone, leaving Chris to make his way back through the dark Cambridge streets to his car, and the drive back to London.

After Chris left, Megan couldn't sleep. At first, she didn't even try. She changed into a T-shirt, pushed the sofa against the door, balanced a lamp on the armrest that should fall off if the sofa was disturbed, opened her bedroom window so that she could be heard if she screamed, and climbed into bed.

She was confident that the intruder wouldn't return, at least that night. All she had to do was repeat that to herself and she wouldn't be scared.

But, tucked into her little fortress, she wanted to think.

The afternoon with Eric had not gone at all as she had planned. He wasn't a fat investment banker at all; in fact, the extra ten years had made him if anything better looking. He had been considerate to her, and kind. The memories of what it had been like to be totally, hopelessly in love with him flooded back. She had had boyfriends before at high school and at college, but he was the first man she had really loved. Possibly the only man she had ever really loved. She wondered now whether she had ever stopped loving him.

She had been awful to Chris to send him away like that. But she had to. She couldn't have slept with him in her current state of confusion. It would have been artificial, dishonest. And the last thing she wanted to do was to tell him the real reason she wanted to be alone that night. Chris had done nothing wrong, and she liked him. Eric was from the past, and she wanted to keep him there.

Didn't she? Eric had hinted that things weren't going well with Cassie. Megan was sure that he had married her for the wrong reasons, even if he had done it unconsciously. She was pretty, she was well connected, she probably appeared to be the perfect wife, but she couldn't have the same bond with Eric that Megan had had. Now, too late, perhaps he realized it.

Megan turned over, huddling under the duvet and blankets. A cold breeze blew in from the open window.

What was she thinking of? Eric was married, for God's sake! She knew she was an emotional mess, and for understandable reasons: the knife and Lenka. She was seeking stability by trying to re-create a happy period from her past. She was deluding herself.

She needed to talk to someone and she knew whom. Lenka. Lenka would have been able to understand how she was feeling and give her good advice. But Lenka was gone. The misery of that fact swept over Megan.

She opened her eyes. She might have slept, but not for long. She thought she heard a creaking sound from her sitting room. She jumped out of bed and crept to her bedroom door. She looked into the darkened sitting room. Nothing.

She tried to go back to sleep, but she couldn't. The blurred image of the unknown intruder inches from her face forced her eyes open every time she shut them. Eventually, she gave up and carried her pillow and duvet through to the sitting room. She removed the lamp, and curled up on the sofa. Now that she knew she would be instantly wakened by anyone trying to open the door, she felt safe enough to fall asleep.

3

Ian left the George V as soon as he could pay the bill, and found himself a seedy little café off the Avenue Marceau. He sat by a tiny table next to the window, savouring the combined smell of Gitanes and strong coffee, and tried to think.

He was angry with himself for losing the initiative, and angry with Eric for taking it. Right from the beginning, Eric had been calling the shots.

He remembered that night ten years before, the shock at seeing Alex pitch over the side, the drunken euphoric urge to heroism that had propelled him over the side after Alex, the shock of the cold water and the high waves. Ian wasn't a bad swimmer, but he could see nothing in the choppy waters apart from the stern of the boat speeding off towards Long Island, and in a moment even that was out of view. He had battled his way through the sea, shouting Alex's name, but he couldn't hear anything in response apart from the water boiling around his ears.

Then, after a few minutes of frantic swimming, he caught sight of an arm raised above the waves. He pulled towards it, and intermittently through the rising and falling water, caught sight of two bodies splashing frantically. At first, he thought one was struggling to save the other. Then, as he came closer, he saw a head emerge, and two hands push it firmly down beneath the water. Ian was tired, but he laboured nearer. It seemed to take an age. Then, when he bobbed over the crest of a wave, he could see just one head left above the water. Eric. He shouted his name, Eric turned, and then swam strongly off in the opposite direction.

Ian looked for Alex's body, but couldn't find it. Whether it had been submerged or swept out of sight, he didn't know. But after a couple of minutes, he began to worry about his own situation. He was tired and very cold. Where was that damn boat? He stopped flailing about, and trod water, trying to conserve energy.

His brain was numbed by the cold and the fatigue, and the shock of what he had just seen. What the hell was Eric doing with Alex? It made no sense. He didn't have the mental energy to make sense of it.

In the rough sea, it was hard work to keep his face safely out of the water. Whenever he lost concentration and a wave broke over him so that he swallowed a lungful of water, it took almost all of his remaining energy to cough it out and stay afloat.

Eventually, he heard the sound of the boat's engines, and then saw the hull edge towards him through the darkness. Voices he recognized called his name, and arms heaved him out of the water and on to the deck where he lay in a stunned heap.

Eric had whispered in his ear. 'Don't say anything. Alex was going to tell them about both of us. I had to do it.'

And Ian hadn't said anything. He was too tired to think straight then anyway, and so he went along with the cover-up suggested by Eric and Chris. Afterwards, what the hell? Eric seemed in control. If Ian tried to tell the police what he had really seen, he would just get himself into all kinds of trouble. It had nothing to do with him. All he had to do was keep quiet and forget it.

Of course, he couldn't forget it. Although he was in no way responsible for Alex's death, he felt guilty. And in a strange way, the guilt strengthened the bond between him and Eric. They both shared a secret. If they both kept quiet, they would be OK. And, in the ten years following Alex's death, Eric had most definitely done OK.

Ian knew now it had been a dreadful mistake. In retrospect, he realized he had had little to lose compared to Eric. It was Eric who had provided the drugs for Alex and Ian. None of them was more than an occasional weekend user, but in the eyes of Bloomfield Weiss and the police Eric would have been the supplier and Ian and Alex the customers. Eric had somehow got wind of the drugs test at the end of the final examination, and had left early. Ian wasn't tested, because he was a London-office hire. But Alex had been tested, and caught. He was worried about his job and his mother's medical bills, and Eric was convinced Alex was going to point the finger at Eric to get himself off. Eric wouldn't just have lost his job, but he would have done so publicly. If he were to run for political office in the future, any journalist who took the trouble to dig would find that he had been fired from a Wall Street firm for dealing drugs. It was that, Ian was sure, that had prompted Eric to kill.

The stakes were much lower for Ian. Sure he would have lost his job, but he would eventually have found something else. It was just that it was easier to go along with Eric's version of events, and once he had done so, it became increasingly difficult to change his mind.

He had been so stupid to tell Lenka about Eric. And he could never forgive Eric for killing her. Ian had always liked Lenka. They had had some very good times together in the weeks before she died. Until now, he had felt powerless even to protest at her death, because of his fear of Eric. Well, no longer.

Angrily, he left the café and walked towards the river. The rain had finally stopped and the streets were quiet on the Sunday morning, with the exception of the odd group of hung-over Welshmen lurching about after a long night's drinking. From the look of them, Ian assumed their team had lost.

What could he do? For an hour or so, he seriously toyed with the idea of killing Eric himself. It would be a just revenge for the murders of Alex and especially Lenka. And if Eric could so blithely murder his old friends, why couldn't Ian?

But he knew it wouldn't work. It wasn't that Ian had qualms. As far as he was concerned, the bastard deserved it. Ian just didn't have the guts. The practicalities of planning and carrying out a murder were beyond him.

He stopped at another café somewhere in the Marais for an early beer, a cigarette and a bite of lunch. The clouds began to divide, and thin snatches of watery sunshine broke through.

So, if he didn't kill Eric, what should he do? He couldn't continue to bury his head in the sand, pretending he didn't know anything. Chris was determined, and Ian didn't underestimate him. If Chris succeeded in exposing Eric, Ian wouldn't be able to claim he was an innocent bystander. He would be in deep trouble: he'd be lucky to escape prison. And even if Eric successfully managed to keep things quiet, it would be a messy process. More people would be hurt, or killed, possibly even Ian himself. Ian didn't want to spend the rest of his life under the shadow of that one event, which he had witnessed but for which he felt no responsibility.

He would do now what he ought to have done all those years ago. Talk. Crossing Eric would be dangerous. But things had reached the point where it was just as dangerous to do nothing.

He left the bar, and headed for the Île Saint-Louis. Swollen by the recent rain, the Seine rushed towards the sea, tugging at the feet of the bridges that obstructed its passage. There were more people out and about now, tempted by the feeble sunshine. Suddenly Ian felt better, better than he had for weeks. Possibly better than he had since the programme. Of course, it would be difficult to know whom to tell. He could try going into a police station in London. Or perhaps he should go to Prague, or New York. Maybe he should first get himself a lawyer. Or talk to a journalist. Actually, as he thought about it, the best person to talk to would be Chris. It was true that every time they had seen each other recently they had ended up swearing at each other, but Chris was basically a good guy. He was honest. He would do the right thing. They could give each other the moral support they would need to get through this.

The more Ian walked, the surer he became of his decision.

Eventually, he made his way back to his hotel to book a flight back to London the next day, have a nap, and keep an appointment with charlie.

Three hours later, invigorated by his decision, his rest, and in particular the white powder he had ingested, he set off for a last night on the town in Paris. He visited a few bars on the Left Bank and bumped into two Danish girls in a place near the Pont Saint-Michel. He pretended to be French, and he thought he did a very good job of it. His own French wasn't bad, and his French-accented English was good enough to fool the Danes. He was having a good time and so were they. The evening passed very pleasantly as they all drank more. Then one of them began to look at him suspiciously. This didn't bother Ian, because the other one, the one with the larger breasts, still seemed to think he was great. She was getting drunk and very friendly. Then the suspicious one took her friend off to the toilet and they never returned.

After waiting half an hour Ian shrugged, finished another beer, and left the bar, confident that if he could pull once, he could pull again.

He was now very drunk. He walked for a few minutes without knowing where he was going. Somehow, he had drifted away from the bars and was now in a quiet residential street.

'Ian!'

He turned, his brain too fuzzy to register surprise that someone should know his name.

The knife plunged deep into his chest between his third and fourth ribs, piercing his heart.

4

Chris had a busy Monday. It was good to lose himself in work; he had no time to worry about Megan or Ian or Duncan. Ollie was ecstatic to hear the news about Royal Bank of Kuwait. The market had sagged again, but they didn't care. It would mean Rudy's losses would be greater, but RBK would come into the fund at a lower price. Chris was relieved to get a call from Khalid; he had been worried that Duncan in all his agitation had forgotten. Khalid wanted to move immediately, so Chris and Ollie walked the quarter mile to RBK's office off Oxford Street, and made a presentation to Khalid and his Arab boss. Khalid asked some penetrating questions, but Chris was able to answer them. As the meeting progressed it was clear that Khalid and his boss had already made up their minds. They wanted to invest!

That afternoon, Chris made the call he had been looking forward to all day.

'Rudy Moss.'

'Morning, Rudy, it's Chris.'

'Yes?'

'Rudy, I'm afraid we have a problem,' said Chris, forcing the morning's euphoria from his voice.

'A problem? What kind of a problem?'

'It's the fund's price, Rudy. It's slipping badly. Eureka Telecom is still heading south. And these German jitters have seriously hurt our government bond positions. It doesn't look good.'

'It doesn't sound good.'

'I was wondering whether with these prices falling you wanted to reconsider your decision.'

'You know my decision,' Rudy snapped. He sounded angry. Good, thought Chris.

'If you can wait another month, maybe things will look better,' said Chris, ensuring that his voice carried no conviction.

'Wait a month?' protested Rudy. 'You've got to be crazy. I want out. I want out now!'

'But you still have another two weeks to go before the thirty-day notice period is up.'

'I don't care. I want you to get me out of this piece of crap now, do you hear me?'

'I'm not sure there's any way I can do that.'

'You'd better think of a way,' growled Rudy.

Chris let Rudy dangle on the line for a delicious few seconds. 'Well, there is one investor who I might be able to persuade to buy your stake,' he said at last. 'But I'd be surprised if they could move that quickly.'

'Try them,' snapped Rudy.

'If you're sure about this?'

'I'm sure. Now get on with it.'

Chris drummed his fingers for twenty minutes and then called Rudy back.

'We're in luck,' he said. 'I think I have found someone. And they might move quickly. If you can fax your instructions through this afternoon, you could be out by tomorrow.'

'Wait by the fax machine,' said Rudy, and hung up.

By five o'clock, Chris and Ollie had instructions from Amalgamated Veterans to sell their stake, with a matching order from the Royal Bank of Kuwait to buy it. The Kuwaitis were also committed to invest a further seven million euros. Zizka had sent a fax through that afternoon revoking his earlier instructions to withdraw from the fund. Eureka Telecom was still in the doldrums and the German economy didn't look too hot, but Carpathian would survive.

'I don't believe it,' said Ollie for the umpteenth time. 'I just don't believe it.'

Chris leaned back in his chair and smiled. He glanced over at Lenka's desk. She would be pleased with them, wherever she was.

'Ollie?'

'Yes?'

'Move your stuff over there, will you?'

'What, now?'

'No, not now. Tomorrow morning. I'm going to buy you and Tina a bottle of champagne now.'

Marcus sat in his truck sipping Royann's coffee. He watched the occasional car pull up into the parking lot. He recognized most of the customers. Even the ones he didn't recognise he knew weren't Eric Astle.

Eric had called him from Burlington Airport. That was better than the other guy, who had just shown up unannounced. Marcus had refused to meet him at his house. He had suggested Royann's Diner at three fifteen. He had been very specific about the three fifteen, even though it meant that Eric would have to wait a couple of hours. At three fifteen, Carl always dropped by for a cup of coffee and a doughnut. Regular as clockwork. And Marcus wanted Carl there when he met Eric.

At three ten, a bland car with Vermont plates drew up. A man wearing a businessman's tan raincoat climbed out, looked around and trod carefully through the snow and slush to the entrance of the diner. He paused, checked the parking lot again, and went inside. He was a few years younger than Marcus: about the age Alex would have been if he were still alive. Eric. Marcus waited and watched, fingering the hunting rifle on the seat beside him. But Eric was alone.

Five minutes later, the white police cruiser arrived. Marcus smiled to himself and jumped out of the truck. 'Hi there, Carl,' he called to the scrawny policeman as he got out of his vehicle.

'How're you doin', Marcus?' replied the policeman. Marcus was sure that Carl didn't really trust him, but having lived in the area for nine years, he was confident he rated a greeting. And if he got into an argument with an out-of-towner, he was quite sure whose side Carl would be on.

Eric was sitting at a booth at the back of the diner, a crisp suit surrounded by jeans, dungarees and grimy T-shirts. He glanced up as Marcus walked in and seemed to recognize him, bringing home to Marcus how much like his younger brother he must look, even after ten years. Marcus sat at a booth near the counter, within a few feet of Carl's favourite spot, but just out of earshot. He caught Eric's eye and nodded. Eric picked up his cup of coffee and joined him, just as Carl took his place at the counter. Carl ordered a doughnut and a cup of coffee, and began his daily chat with Royann, who knew how to flirt with a regular. As far as Marcus could tell, Carl spent his day eating his way around the county, yet he never seemed to put on an ounce of fat.

Eric's eyes darted between the policeman and Marcus and he smiled. 'That's fair.'

Marcus didn't smile back.

Eric held out his hand. 'Eric Astle.'

Marcus didn't shake it. 'What do you want?'

'To talk to you.'

'So talk.'

Marcus was doing his best to unsettle Eric, but it wasn't working. Eric seemed unconcerned by Marcus's rudeness.

'OK,' he said. And then sipped his coffee, looking steadily at Marcus.

'I said, talk!'

'I want to talk to you about your brother.'

'I figured as much.'

'He was a friend of mine.'

'Sure. Just like he was a friend of that other guy's. That Brit. Well, if you were all so damned friendly with him, how come he's dead?'

Eric ignored him, and continued in a low, steady voice. 'As I say, he was a friend of mine. We met in our first week at Bloomfield Weiss. We got on straight away; we had a different attitude from most of the others. We were both looking for apartments. He found one, he needed someone to share it with, he asked me, I said yes.'

'You were his room mate?'

'Yes. As I said, he and I got along real well. We had a ball. Two single guys can have a lot of fun in Manhattan.'

The waitress came by, and Marcus curtly ordered a coffee. Eric waited until she had gone off to fetch it before he continued. 'I was devastated when he was drowned. I did what I could to help his mom organize the funeral and everything; she was too sick to do it by herself. I spent quite a lot of time with his mom, your mom, afterwards. But as you know, once he was gone, she lost her will to fight.'

'I know,' said Marcus, swallowing. Of course, he didn't really know. He hadn't been there. He had been thousands of miles away.

'I only knew your brother for nine months or so, but he made a big impression. He was different from the others. He had a great sense of humour. I've tried to remember the way he never took anything that happened at Bloomfield Weiss too seriously. When everyone is uptight and the crap is flying, I sometimes try to think what Alex would do. It kind of keeps me human.'

Marcus was watching Eric all the time as he spoke. He seemed calm, almost wistful. Not nearly as uptight as the Brit had been.

'I saw some of his paintings: they were really good. I kept one after he died. Your mom said it would be OK. He was wasting his talent in an investment bank.'

Marcus held his tongue. He didn't want Eric to see that he was getting through to him. But he was. This was the kind of thing Marcus had wanted someone apart from himself to say about his brother ever since he had died. Until now, no one had.

Eric sipped at his coffee.

'Go on,' said Marcus eventually.

'I thought what had happened to Alex was all in the past. But over the last few weeks, I've realized that it isn't. It all started soon after you tried to see me in New York. I'm sorry I didn't meet with you then, by the way. I was busy on deals, and I guess . . . No, it doesn't matter.'

'You guess what?'

Eric looked Marcus straight in the eye. 'I guess I was still mad at you because you weren't there when Alex died. Nor his mother.'

Marcus felt a flash of anger. Who was this guy to criticize him? But Eric held up his hand in a calming gesture. 'I'm sorry. I know that's unfair. Especially since I now know how much you've been doing to find out what really happened to him.'

Marcus grunted. At least the guy understood that he was trying to do something now. But he was still suspicious of Eric. He was, after all, an investment banker in a suit.

The investment banker continued in his slow, reasonable voice. 'As I think you know, Alex's death wasn't straightforward. It wasn't an accident. Someone drowned him. And then someone killed Lenka, whom I think you've met. And last night, someone else was murdered. In Paris.'

'Someone else?'

Eric nodded. He pulled a folded piece of paper out of his pocket and passed it to Marcus. It was the printout of a Reuters report that Ian Darwent, a thirty-two-year-old British investment banker, had been found stabbed in the streets of Paris the night before.

Marcus hadn't met Ian, but of course he knew who he was. 'Do you know who did this?'

'I think so. And I do know who killed your brother.'

Marcus could feel his heart beating faster. He was about to find out what had been eluding him for so long.

'Who?'

'Duncan Gemmel.'

'Duncan Gemmel?' Marcus snapped in irritation. 'I know it wasn't him. Lenka told me. Someone drowned Alex after Duncan had knocked him into the sea.'

'Duncan did,' said Eric quietly.

'Duncan did?'

Eric nodded. 'When Alex fell in, Ian and I dived in right after him. Duncan saw us and then jumped in himself. The water was choppy and it was difficult to see anything. Ian and I lost your brother. But Duncan didn't. Duncan found him and drowned him.'

'How do you know?'

'Ian saw him,' Eric said.

'*Ian?*'

'Yes. He told me last week. I was in London and we met up to talk about what had happened to Lenka. He was a real mess. He said that he'd seen Duncan drown Alex ten years ago, but he had kept quiet. Then he'd let it slip by mistake to Lenka. Lenka said she was going to tell people, including you, which, by the way, I assume she didn't?'

Marcus was careful not to react to this question. 'Go on,' he said.

'So, Ian told Duncan, and before he knew it, Lenka was dead. By the time Ian saw me, he was scared. I mean, really scared. He thought he was next. He said he was going to Paris on business, and he didn't want to come back.'

'And then this?' Marcus nodded at the news report in front of him.

Eric nodded.

'So who killed Ian? Duncan?'

Eric frowned. 'Well, that's the thing. I don't think it was Duncan. I think it was Chris Szczypiorski.'

'The Brit who came to see me?'

'That's right.'

'Why do you think that?'

'Because when I was at the airport coming back here, I saw him at the check-in for flights to Paris. I would have gone over to say hi, but I didn't want to lose my place in line. By the time I'd checked in, he was on his way to his gate.'

'So he was on his way to Paris. So what's the big deal?'

'It could just be a coincidence. But I'd spoken to him on the phone that day, and he said that he was spending the weekend in London. So he lied to me. Why would he need to do that?'

Marcus looked doubtful. 'Look,' said Eric. 'I'm not sure about Chris. I don't know what his deal with Duncan is, and I can't be sure that he killed Ian. But I'm sure as hell suspicious.'

Marcus tried to take it all in. It all added up, apart from one thing. 'If Duncan did drown Alex on purpose, then why did Lenka tell me that he wasn't responsible for Alex's death?'

'I don't know,' said Eric. 'Perhaps she meant that Duncan didn't kill your brother by accident. But I do know what Ian told me. He saw Duncan push your brother under.'

Marcus leaned back and rubbed his temples. This was getting complicated. 'Do you have any proof?'

Eric sighed. 'No. If I did, I would go to the police. As it is . . .'

'So I'm supposed to just believe you?'

Eric smiled. 'You can believe me if you want. Or not, it's up to you. I just know you have a right to be told. But please don't tell anyone I told you. Especially don't tell Duncan or Chris. They don't know Ian spoke to me, so I hope I'm safe. But you're not.'

'I'm not?'

'Of course not. Not after Lenka spoke to you. I doubt they'll stop at Ian.'

'What are you going to do?' Marcus asked.

'There's not much I can do. Keep quiet. Pretend I know nothing. What about you?'

'Me?'

'Yes. You were the one who first suspected there was something going on. Now you've found out there was. What are you going to do?'

'I don't know. I need proof.'

'If I get proof, I'll let you have it,' said Eric. 'But I'm not going to go looking for it.'

'I don't know what I'm going to do,' said Marcus.

'Well, I've got to go back to London tomorrow. Another damned deal. If you do decide to go over there, give me a call on my cell phone. I might be able to help you. Discreetly. Here's my card.' Marcus took it and slid it in his pocket without looking at it. 'I do know somebody has got to do something. Think about it.'

With that, Eric took a five-dollar bill out of his pocket, left it on the table, and stood up to leave. 'Be careful,' he said, and pushed past Carl on his way to the exit.

Marcus followed him, unfocused, his brain trying to take in what he had just heard. Did it make sense?

Chris came into work early the next morning. He and Ollie had to revalue the portfolio. This revaluation was necessary to determine the price at which Amalgamated Veterans' investment would be transferred to Royal Bank of Kuwait. This was an easy task for the government bonds, but the junk bonds had much murkier prices, and Eureka Telecom had the murkiest of them all.

By nine thirty, they had all the prices bar Eureka Telecom. Exchanging glances with Ollie, Chris dialled Ian's number. Even though he knew Ian was in Paris, he still asked for him by name; that way he would make sure he spoke to whoever was covering for him. As he was put on hold, he wondered what number Bloomfield Weiss would come up with. He wanted as low a price as possible. The more Rudy lost, the happier Chris would be, and the more profits RBK would make when the market bounced back.

Eventually, the phone was answered. 'Chris? It's Mandy. Mandy Simpson.'

Chris remembered her as a junior salesperson when he had been at Bloomfield Weiss. She was probably a top producer by now.

'Hi, Mandy, how are you? I didn't know you were covering for Ian.'

297

'I'm not. I'm just talking to you because I know you.'

Chris recognized from her tone that something was very wrong.

'What is it, Mandy?'

'It's Ian. He was murdered the night before last. In Paris.'

Chris closed his eyes. He knew it. He just knew it.

'Chris?' Mandy said.

'Sorry. Any idea how it happened?'

'He was stabbed, apparently.'

Oh, Duncan, Duncan! 'Stabbed? Did the police catch who did it?'

'Not as far as we know. But we don't know much.'

'Jesus.'

'I'm sorry, Chris,' Mandy said. 'I know you two were friends.'

Some friend, Chris thought. But even though he was virtually certain that Ian was responsible for the deaths of two people, Chris was surprised to feel a wave of sadness sweep over him.

'OK, Mandy. Thanks for telling me,' and he hung up.

Ollie was listening in. He was white. 'Oh, my God,' he said.

Chris exhaled. 'Precisely.'

Duncan had killed him. The stupid bastard! The second Chris had told Duncan about Ian, Duncan had jumped on a plane, gone to Paris, found Ian and killed him. Knowing Duncan, he wouldn't have been too subtle about it either. He'd probably be in jail within twenty-four hours.

'Ollie, can you give me a moment? I need to make a phone call.'

Ollie scurried back to his desk, still in a state of shock. Chris called Megan and told her the news.

'It must have been Duncan,' she said.

'I'm afraid so.'

'That guy's a psycho. I knew it all along.' There was an undertone of 'I told you so' in her voice, but then Chris had to admit, she *had* told him so.

'You're right,' Chris said. 'I bet the stupid bastard will get caught.'

'I'm not covering for him again,' Megan said.

'No, not this time. Not if he did it.'

'Do you think we should go to the police first?'

Chris sighed. 'No. Let them come to us. This could all get very messy. They'll have to investigate Lenka's murder, and Alex's, and we could still get in trouble for the cover-up there. You're right, we shouldn't lie, but I think we should wait for them to ask us the questions before we answer them.'

'OK. I must say, I'm relieved.'

'Relieved?'

'Yeah. Now Ian's . . . gone. No more people creeping around my bedroom. No more dead bodies. And I hate to say it, but if he did kill Lenka, he got what he deserved.'

'Yes,' said Chris flatly.

'What is it? You don't sound convinced. You do think it was him who killed her?'

'Yes, I suppose so.'

'But you're not absolutely sure?'

'No. Are you?'

'I don't see how we can be. We'll just have to wait and see what the police dig up.'

'Megan?'

'Yes?'

'Can I come up and see you tonight? In Cambridge?'

Megan hesitated. 'Of course. That would be great.'

'See you, then,' said Chris. But he was anxious as he put down the phone. He had caught the hesitation in Megan's voice when he had asked to come and see her, and he didn't like it. And they couldn't be sure about Ian.

He thought of calling Duncan. There wasn't much point; he was almost certainly in Paris, very probably in a police cell. But he picked up the phone and tapped out the number of Honshu Bank. To Chris's surprise, he heard Duncan's soft Scottish accent answer.

'Duncan! I didn't think you'd be there!'

'Why not?' Duncan said. 'It's Tuesday morning. It's ten o'clock. Where else would I be? Did you sort out something with RBK?'

'Yes, I did. Look, I need to talk to you.'

'Go ahead.'

'Not on the phone,' Chris hissed. Honshu Bank's phones were recorded, of course, just like Bloomfield Weiss's.

Duncan lowered his voice, serious suddenly. 'Is it about Ian?'

'Yes.'

'OK. I've got to go into a meeting now. I'll be out about half twelve. We can meet then.'

'Duncan! This is important!'

'I'm sorry, Chris. I can't get out of this one.'

'OK. See you outside your office at twelve thirty.'

5

Honshu Bank's offices were in Finsbury Square at the northern edge of the City. Duncan was five minutes late.

'Where are we going?' he asked.

'For a walk,' said Chris, leading him out of the building.

'But it's freezing,' said Duncan shivering. And it was. A cold wind swept across the square. 'I haven't got my coat.'

'That's your problem,' said Chris, walking rapidly up City Road.

After a hundred yards or so, they came to Bunhill Fields, an old burial ground for the City of London. They passed inside the green-painted iron gates and along a pathway through tightly packed gravestones covered with moss and lichen, the inscriptions on most of them now unreadable. There was a group of benches in the middle, and Chris sat on one of them. In front of him lay John Bunyan, resting on a white stone slab, feet towards them.

'Why here?' said Duncan. 'I'm cold.'

'It's quiet,' said Chris. On a fine day it would be crowded with office workers enjoying their lunch. But in this March wind, they were all alone with the gravestones.

'What's up with you?' Duncan asked, shoving his hands deep in his pockets.

'Ian.'

'I thought I was the one who was supposed to be pissed off with Ian.'

'Nice trip to Paris, was it, Duncan? See the sights? Go up the Eiffel Tower?'

'I don't know what you're talking about. I haven't been to Paris.'

'Duncan, I'm not stupid. And I'm not going to cover for you again.'

'Cover for me? What do you mean?' And then he stopped. 'Something's happened to Ian, hasn't it? In Paris. And you think I'm responsible?'

'Too right, I think you're responsible,' Chris muttered.

'What happened? Is he dead?'

Chris looked at Duncan. His confusion seemed genuine. But then Chris had just said he wouldn't cover for him. There was no reason for Duncan to tell him the truth, and every reason for him to act surprised.

'He was stabbed in Paris on Sunday night. By you.'

'Hey, come on, Chris,' protested Duncan. 'You can't say that. I didn't kill him. I wasn't even in bloody Paris.'

'But you wanted to, didn't you?'

'No I didn't.'

'It certainly looked like it when I saw you in the pub at lunch-time.'

'I was angry, that's all,' said Duncan. 'You can hardly blame me.'

Chris shook his head. 'You've gone too far, Duncan. What Ian did was wrong, but what you've done is just as wrong. You shouldn't have killed him.'

'But I didn't kill him! For Christ's sake, I was in London then.'

'All tucked up in bed by yourself, no doubt?'

'Probably. No, let me think. I remember. Sunday was a bad day. I went out by myself for a drink or two in the evening. You're right, that stuff about Ian had shaken me. But then I went to see Pippa.'

'What, in the middle of the night?'

'About half eleven. I wanted to talk to her. She said I was drunk and told me to piss off.'

'And she'll back up your story?'

'I suppose so. I don't see why she shouldn't.'

Chris hesitated. 'You might have got her to lie for you. Like you got us to lie for you on the boat.'

Duncan's eyes flashed with anger. 'I never got you to lie for me! As I remember, it was your idea. I wish you'd have let me tell the truth now. All this might not have happened.' He ran his hands through his hair. 'Jesus. If the police come talking to you, are you going to tell them I killed him?'

'I'll tell them the truth. Nothing more,' said Chris.

'Well, the truth is I didn't kill him. And think about it for a second. If I didn't kill Ian, someone else did. And that doesn't make you very safe, does it?'

Chris looked at Duncan for a moment, and then stood up to go. As far as he was concerned, there was nothing more to be said. But Duncan grabbed his arm.

'Here,' he said, thrusting his mobile phone at Chris. 'Call her.'

Chris hesitated. Duncan punched out a number and handed the phone to him. Chris shrugged and put it to his ear. He heard it ringing, and then Pippa's voice.

'Phillippa Gemmel.'

'Pippa, it's Chris Szczypiorski.'

'Oh, hi, Chris. Look, I'm just going out.'

'This won't take a minute,' Chris said. Duncan was watching him intently. 'Have you seen Duncan in the last few days?'

'Why do you ask?'

'Answer my question, and I'll tell you.'

Pippa sighed. 'We went out for a meal together on Friday night.'

'And since then?'

'He came round to see me in the middle of the night. He was drunk. He wanted to moan at me. I told him to piss off.'

'Which night was that?'

'Sunday.'

'Are you sure?'

'Of course I'm sure. Why?'

'Ian Darwent was murdered on Sunday night in Paris.'

'Oh, my God.' There was silence for a moment. When Pippa

spoke again, the brusqueness had left her voice. She sounded weary. 'Not another one. Duncan was going on about him, but I couldn't make sense of what he was saying.'

'Duncan thought Ian had killed Lenka,' Chris said.

'And so you think Duncan might have killed Ian?'

'Yes,' Chris said curtly, glancing at Duncan sitting next to him.

'Don't trust your friends much, do you?' said Pippa scathingly. 'But with friends like yours, I'm not really surprised. No, Duncan was in London that night. I can vouch for him.'

Chris didn't say anything.

'What's the matter? Don't you believe me?'

Chris sighed. He knew Pippa wasn't covering for Duncan. Suddenly he felt ashamed of his lack of trust in her, and in Duncan. 'I believe you. Thanks, Pippa. Bye.'

He disconnected, and passed the phone back to Duncan. 'Sorry.'

Duncan slipped the phone back in his pocket. Then he smiled. 'It's OK. Weird things have been happening recently. It's difficult to know who to trust.'

'You're right there,' Chris said, putting his head in his hands. He leaned back against the bench. A magpie pecked amongst the worn gravestones.

'You know what this means?' said Chris eventually.

'What?'

'If you didn't kill Ian, then he must have been killed for the same reason Lenka was: because he knew who had drowned Alex.'

'Do you think so?'

'It seems the most likely to me. I can't think of any other reason.'

'So who did drown Alex?' Duncan asked.

'There's only one possibility,' Chris said. 'Three people dived into the sea. You, Ian, and Eric.'

'Eric.'

'Must be,' said Chris. Now he had made that assumption

everything slotted into place in his brain. 'Eric drowned Alex. Lenka found out about it and threatened to tell people. So Eric killed her. Ian knew about that, and now he's dead.'

'Jesus,' said Duncan.

'Of course, Eric didn't kill Lenka and Ian himself. Probably he hired the same man who scared Megan and me.' The man with the moustache and long hair. The man in New York whose run Chris had recognized from Prague.

A moustache and long hair could easily be faked. Suddenly, Chris knew who the man was.

'Terry,' he said. 'Eric's driver and part-time bodyguard. Terry.' Chris turned to Duncan. 'What do you think?'

Duncan blew air through his cheeks. 'It all hangs together,' he said. 'After getting so upset about Ian, I don't want to jump to the wrong conclusion this time, but I think you're right. Eric is the only one who makes sense. Apart from anything else, it would take some organization to do all that. I'm sure Eric could get someone like this Terry to jet all over the world doing his dirty work for him. But I'm not sure any of the rest of us could. Eric seems such a charming guy, but there's something cold about him underneath. He's always calculating, you know what I mean? Yeah, I think it fits.'

They stared at John Bunyan's grimy toes a few feet in front of them.

'Of course, you have no proof,' said Duncan.

'No.'

'What about that psychologist you saw in New York?'

'She wouldn't talk to me. Confidentiality issues.'

'Is there any point in trying again? Now we have a name?'

Chris considered this. 'I don't know. I don't see why not. Give me your phone.'

It was a quarter past one, eight fifteen New York time, but Dr Marcia Horwath was already in the office, even if her receptionist wasn't. She answered her own phone.

'Dr Horwath, this is Chris Szczypiorski.'

'Oh, yes?' Her voice was cool, but Chris thought he detected a trace of curiosity.

'We met last week. I asked you about the testing of Bloomfield Weiss trainees.'

'Of course.'

'Have you had a chance to think about whether you can give me any more information about the test results?'

'Yes, I have, and I'm afraid the answer is no. At the time, I decided it was my duty to tell Bloomfield Weiss about my concerns. Beyond that, I owe a duty of confidentiality to them, and to the trainees concerned.'

'I understand that,' said Chris, trying not to show his impatience. 'And I appreciate that this is a difficult ethical problem. But Ian Darwent was murdered two days ago. That means three of the seven people on that boat have been killed, probably all by the same person. It is very likely that person will kill again.'

'Then you should inform the police,' said Marcia. 'I would have to consider a request from them.'

'It's not that easy,' said Chris. 'Please.' Sod it. He let the desperation come through in his voice. 'The next person to be killed may well be me. This isn't some abstract ethical dilemma. If I die in the next few days because you didn't give me the information I need, you will remember this conversation for the rest of your life.'

There was silence at the end of the phone. Duncan gave Chris a thumbs up in encouragement.

'Dr Horwath?'

She answered him. 'One of the tests I used was the Minnesota Multiphasic Personality Inventory. This is more commonly used in diagnosing personality disorders than in recruitment, but it seemed appropriate, given Bloomfield Weiss's aims. During the period I used the test, two candidates' results suggested major psychopathology. I requested further interviews with both of them, and my fears were confirmed. I expressed my reservations each time in the strongest possible terms to Mr Calhoun at Bloomfield Weiss, who went ahead and hired them both anyway. One of them was Steven Matzley, who as you know was convicted of rape after he had left Bloomfield Weiss.'

There was a pause. Come on, thought Chris. The other one. The name. Give me the name.

'The other was recruited later. Mr Calhoun subsequently called me back to tell me that he had achieved first place in his training programme. I believe it was the same training programme you attended. Mr Calhoun seemed to think that this was a vindication of his decision to hire the candidate despite my protests.'

'Thank you very much, Dr Horwath.'

'No problem. You will keep me informed of developments, won't you?'

'I will,' said Chris.

He handed the phone back to Duncan.

'Well?' Duncan asked.

'Eric.' Eric had come top of his training programme. It was Eric who had displayed strong psychopathic tendencies. They were well hidden by his smoothness, his charm, his apparent frankness. But Dr Horwath had had no doubt. They were there. 'She said it was Eric.'

'That just about settles it.' Duncan exhaled. 'So what do we do now? Go to the police?'

'I don't know,' said Chris. 'It's difficult. In the first place, there's the problem of which police force to report it to. We're talking about three murders in three different countries, none of them Britain. Also, we don't have enough proof to get Eric arrested immediately. The police would have to start a long and complicated international investigation. Eric would hire the best lawyers in three countries to keep himself out of jail. And in the meantime you, me and Megan would all be in danger. The police might never get the evidence to convict him, and even if they did, we'd probably be dead by the time they locked him up.'

'I see what you mean,' said Duncan. 'But we can't sit around doing nothing, waiting for someone else to die. What about Lenka? And Ian and Alex? If Eric killed them, we can't let him get away with it.'

'I don't know what else we can do,' said Chris.

'I do,' said Duncan, determination in his voice.

'No, Duncan,' said Chris. 'I know I was wrong to think that you stabbed Ian, but I wasn't wrong that that would be a stupid thing to do. You'd get caught. Killing people is wrong, Duncan, even when it's someone like Eric.'

'I admire your moral scruples, Chris. But if we don't do something about it, he'll kill us all anyway.'

Chris knew Duncan was right. 'OK, OK. Perhaps we should go to the police. It's a risk, but as you say, so is doing nothing. I want to talk to Megan about it before we do, though. I'm seeing her this evening.'

'Why do you need to talk to her?'

'Because she's in just as much danger as we are if Eric finds out what we're doing.'

'OK,' said Duncan. 'We'll do it your way. Talk to her, and then we'll go to the police. But for God's sake, be careful about it.'

Marcus took the long run down to the lake smoothly, his cross-country skis sliding over the snow, freshly fallen from the night before. The sky was clear and blue, and he was surrounded by muffled silence, his favourite sound. He paused by the side of the frozen lake, which should hold his weight for a few weeks yet. The half-dozen summer cabins that ringed it were quiet, still in hibernation, the snow on their roofs and in their yards undisturbed. He struck out across the lake, moving easily over the thin layer of snow that covered the ice. This was where he liked to think, to recharge. It would be a long slog from the lake uphill back to his house, but it was worth it.

The cold air was invigorating. He had slept poorly the night before, and had felt imprisoned by the warm cabin, which he usually found so comforting. Angie, too, had been driving him crazy. He knew she was only trying to help, but he needed to sort this out by himself.

And sort this out he must. The guilt and sense of loss over the deaths of his brother and his mother had been festering inside him for ten years. When he had begun to ask questions about what had really happened to Alex, he had started a process that he could not reverse. He literally could not rest until he had ended it.

What that meant, he wasn't quite sure. Establish who had killed Alex, certainly. Ensure that person received retribution as well. But what form that retribution should take, he wasn't yet certain. He knew what he wanted to do. What he felt he had to do. But he wasn't yet ready to admit it to himself.

He played over for the umpteenth time in his head his conversation with Eric, and felt the rage re-emerge. How could Eric talk that way about helping his mother, about being angry that Marcus hadn't been there when Alex had died? He had no right to! It was hard enough for Marcus to deal with, without some fancy investment banker who claimed to be Alex's friend telling him what he should have done.

The trouble was, Marcus believed that Eric really had been Alex's friend. He understood Eric's anger; in fact, he shared it. He had let his brother and mother down. It had been good to hear Eric saying such complimentary things about Alex, but the criticism of himself still stung. And it would continue to sting until Marcus resolved the issue.

Marcus sped up along the lake, establishing a rapid rhythm. He used to be an excellent downhill skier, but it was only when he had moved up to Vermont that he had taken up cross-country. He was good: he had the physique and the temperament for it. Some weeks he would ski fifty miles, when the weather was good, and when he felt the urge.

Alex had never skied. But he was better at nearly everything else than Marcus. He was smarter, he was a better artist, he was more popular. Marcus had never held Alex's success against him: he had always been proud of his kid brother. And Alex never seemed to let any of it go to his head, or to take himself too seriously. Eric had been right about that.

Alex had deserved a friend like Eric. He had deserved a brother like Eric, too, but he hadn't got one.

Was Eric telling the truth about Duncan killing Alex? After all, he had no proof, and he was an investment banker. Marcus went over the conversation yet again, trying to be as objective as possible. The more he thought about it, the more convinced he became.

He wasn't so sure about the Brit with the Polish name, Chris whatever-it-was. He had been very different from Eric. More uptight. More cagey about divulging information. More eager to find stuff out from Marcus. Eric, he knew, had come in peace, told his story, and left. Marcus wasn't sure what Chris's agenda had been. But all that was too complicated. He didn't really care who had killed Ian Darwent. All he cared about was who had killed his brother. And he was sure, now, who that was.

Duncan.

He left the lake, and began thrusting his skis up the slope towards home. He knew he had to go to London and find him. He had no choice.

Eric flopped into the back seat of the hired Jaguar. He was exhausted. He was used to a punishing travel schedule, but this was ridiculous. Still, it had had to be done. As he had told Terry in Paris, there was a limit to the number of dead bodies that they could be directly responsible for, and with Ian, they had just about reached that limit. They needed a new recruit.

As Terry guided the car through the airport traffic and coasted towards the M4, Eric pulled out his mobile phone and listened to his messages. There were a dozen of them, all of them urgent. He ignored all but one, even the one from Cassie. But one message required an immediate reply. He looked up a number and punched it out. The conversation was brief, but he smiled as he disconnected.

'Good news, sir?' Terry asked from the front seat.

'Yes, I'd say it is,' Eric replied. 'That was nice work you did in Paris by the way, Terry. Your bonus should have gone through yesterday.'

'No problem. I'd be happy to do something similar again. Just ask.'

'No need for the time being,' said Eric. He settled back in his seat and closed his eyes. 'I'd say things are slotting together quite nicely just as they are.'

6

Chris was both eager and nervous as he climbed Megan's staircase. Eager because he wanted to tell Megan what he had
discovered. Nervous because he was still worried about her
coolness to him the previous Sunday and the note of hesitation
in her voice when he had invited himself up to see her.

He knocked on her door, a little out of breath from the stairs.

She opened it in an instant. 'Hi,' she said, smiling.

'Hi.'

'Come here.' She pulled him towards her and kissed him. All
his nervousness left him as he felt her hands run over his back.
She pulled away and began to unbutton his shirt.

'What's this?' Chris said.

'What does it look like? Do you have any objections?'

'None at all,' he smiled.

'Well, come on then,' she said, and led him through to her
bedroom.

Half an hour later they lay in each other's arms, naked in the
darkened room. Chris eased himself up on to his elbows and
watched the light from the college buildings opposite play on
Megan's skin.

'That was nice,' he said, running a finger along her thigh.

'Yes, it was. You deserved it after how mean I was to you.'

'That wasn't your fault,' Chris said. 'You were still in shock.'

'It was my fault,' Megan said earnestly. 'And I'm sorry.' She
kissed him gently on the lips.

'I found out something today,' he said.

'Oh, yes?' She sat up and hunched her legs up to her chest.
'Tell me.'

So Chris told her about his discussion with Duncan, about

Pippa backing up Duncan's story, and about what Dr Horwath had told him about Eric. She listened closely. When he'd finished, she didn't say anything.

'Well? What do you think?' he asked.

'I'm not sure you've drawn the right conclusion.'

'About Eric?'

'Yes. About Eric. I don't think he has anything to do with this.'

Chris was stunned. He stared at Megan, not sure what to say. He had been looking forward to her common sense to help him decide what to do, now they knew Eric was responsible for so many deaths.

'But don't you see? It must be him. He drowned Alex, he had Lenka murdered to shut her up, and then he had Ian killed. It's obvious.'

'Not to me,' said Megan.

'But why not?'

'You don't have any evidence, do you?' she said. 'I hate to say this, but I think you're losing perspective, trying to find a reason to let Duncan off the hook. I don't think that's smart. We were wrong to cover for him all those years ago, and it would be wrong to cover for him now.'

'But what about the psychometric tests?'

Megan laughed. 'Oh, come on! You can't convict someone on the basis of a bunch of multiple choice questions they answered ten years ago. That stuff's all bullshit anyway.'

'Dr Horwath was convinced.'

'Of course she was convinced. It's her job to be convinced by that psychocrap.'

'Well, we know Duncan wasn't in Paris that night.'

'According to his wife, who is very probably protecting him. Besides, we know Eric wasn't there, either.'

'Do we?' Chris asked, puzzled. 'Where was he, then?'

'He was in England that day,' Megan said quietly. 'He came up here to see me.'

'He what?'

'He came up to Cambridge. We went out for tea. We talked.'

'Why didn't you tell me this?' Chris demanded.

Megan shrugged. 'I don't have to tell you everything.'

'Megan!'

'Look, Chris, he was my old boyfriend. I feel uncomfortable talking about him with you; you know that. It was no big deal. But it does mean he wasn't in Paris.'

'But that doesn't matter. We know he gets someone else to do his dirty work.'

'Maybe Duncan does as well. Have you thought about that?'

Chris ran his hand through his hair in frustration. 'But the whole point is that we assumed Duncan had killed Ian in a fit of anger. If Eric did all this, it was carefully planned.'

'Maybe Duncan planned the whole thing,' Megan said. 'I've never trusted him. Whereas I do trust Eric.'

Chris looked at her. Just ten minutes ago, everything had seemed so simple. Now it was becoming complicated. Megan's readiness to defend Eric bothered Chris. It bothered him intensely. And if she had seen Eric on Sunday, then that, rather than the shock of discovering the knife on her pillow, might explain her coolness towards him that evening.

Megan was obviously following these thoughts. 'There's nothing between us now, you know. There's been nothing for years.' She touched his arm. 'You must believe me, Chris.'

'Must I?' he snapped.

'I'd like you to.'

Chris wanted to argue, but he bit his tongue. He knew Megan was trying not to make an issue of it and he wanted to try to do the same. 'OK,' he said, making his tone as conciliatory as possible. 'But do you mind if I ask you a couple of questions about Eric?'

'Sure.'

'We know that Alex and Ian took drugs when we were all in New York together. Did Eric?'

314

Megan looked uncomfortable. 'Yes, he did. A little. Cocaine. But he stopped when Alex was caught.'

Chris stared at her. 'Why didn't you tell me this before?'

'It didn't seem important. Everyone took drugs then.'

'Did you?'

'No,' Megan admitted. 'I'd tried it at college, of course. But I never really got into it.'

'But Eric did?'

'Yes. I was a bit worried about him at college. And again in New York. But, as I said, after Alex was caught he gave up. It might have interfered with his precious political ambitions.'

'I can see it might have,' Chris said. 'And who had the drugs?'

'What do you mean?'

'You know what I mean. Presumably, either Eric or Alex must have bought the drugs from someone. Which of them was it?'

'I don't know,' said Megan. 'I didn't ask. I didn't want to know about it.'

'OK, so who kept them safe?'

'Eric,' Megan said reluctantly.

'And when Alex wanted some, he would go to Eric?'

'I guess that's right.'

'So Alex could have told Bloomfield Weiss that Eric was his supplier?'

'No,' Megan protested, raising her voice for the first time. 'They were friends. What are you trying to say? Eric was the evil drug-dealer, and Alex was his innocent victim?'

'No. I'm trying to say that Alex was going to shop Eric to George Calhoun. That Eric knew this. And that when Eric saw he had a chance to shut Alex up for good, he took it.'

Megan snorted.

'Megan,' Chris said quietly. 'Duncan and I think we should go to the police.'

'About Eric?'

Chris nodded.

'Don't you think you should discuss that with me, first?'

'That's what I wanted to do this evening.'

'Oh, did you? Well, I think you'd be making a big mistake. You're just jealous of Eric because he and I were going out years ago, and you want to protect your stupid friend from the consequences of his own actions. I'm not going to go along with it.'

Chris had been trying to hold his temper, trying to avoid the confrontation that had been looming, but he lost it.

'Maybe I am jealous. Maybe I should be,' he said. 'There's a lot you haven't told me about Eric. You never mentioned the drugs before. You never told me he came to see you on Sunday. There's probably a lot else you haven't told me about him. You're the one who's losing perspective. The man's a killer, Megan! Don't you understand that? He's extremely dangerous. It's quite likely that he'll try to kill you or me or both of us. We should think hard about that. Do something, before it's too late.'

Megan glared at Chris. He suddenly felt cold and awkward in his nakedness. 'I think you'd better go,' she muttered through clenched teeth.

'But Megan –'

'Just get dressed and go!'

So Chris went.

Megan watched Chris as he strode across the court below, shoulders hunched. For a moment, she felt the urge to open the windows and shout down to him to come back. But she couldn't. Not without admitting that he was right about Eric. And that was something she could not do.

She had genuinely tried to put Eric behind her. Her warm welcome to Chris hadn't been entirely for his benefit. She had wanted to prove to herself that Eric was in the past, that it was Chris she cared about now.

But she had failed. Chris was right about her and Eric. Her head's battle with her heart had been lost. She, who was so proud of her self-control and her ability to analyse the most complicated problems dispassionately, wanted to see Eric – no, *had* to see Eric. She knew nothing would come of it. She knew it was pointless. But she had to do it; she wouldn't be able to forgive herself if she let the opportunity to see what would develop between them slip by. She knew now that she had never stopped loving him when they had split up. She might have told herself time and time again that she was over him, but she wasn't, she never had been. Now she would have to accept that fact and see what happened. The prospect frightened her, especially the likelihood that she would be rejected, but it also thrilled her. Remembering her afternoon with him that Sunday, she knew he still felt something for her. There had to be a chance.

Chris had sensed all that, and that had made her angry with him. She had denied what he could see was obvious, and she had been unfair to him. She liked him, liked him very much, and she didn't want to hurt him, but she felt that the situation was out of her control. Until that week, she hadn't believed in destiny. Now she felt destiny was taking hold of her life and her role was to let it.

She was sure that Chris was wrong about one thing, though: that Eric had killed all those people. She knew Eric, and she knew he would never do anything like that. She distrusted both Duncan and Ian and she was sure that one or other of them had been responsible for the deaths. Chris's jealousy had made him unable to see what was to her perfectly obvious.

She turned away from the window and began to work on her notes. She soon gave that up; she hadn't the concentration. So she pulled out an old, dog-eared volume of Emily Dickinson's poetry that Eric had given to her when they were at college. The familiarity of the poems gave her some comfort, like old friends, their rhythms stable, unchanging, reliable.

The phone rang. She lifted the receiver.

'Hello?'

'Megan?'

She felt a glow course through her body as she recognized the voice. 'Eric.'

'How are you?'

'Not too good, actually.'

'Have you heard about Ian?'

'Yes, I have. I can't believe it. Another one.'

'Yeah. I called because I'm worried about you.'

'Oh, yes?'

'Yes. I mean, I've no idea why Ian was killed, but after our conversation on Sunday, I wanted to make sure you were OK.'

'I'm fine. No more psychos creeping about my bedroom.'

'Good. I'm worried that whoever threatened you on Saturday night meant business. Don't do anything to provoke them, OK?'

'Don't worry. I won't. I just want to forget about the whole thing.'

'That's easier to say than to do, I'd guess. What about Chris?'

Megan couldn't bring herself to tell Eric about Chris's ridiculous suspicions of him. At least, not over the phone. She decided to keep it vague. 'I think he's decided to go to the police and tell them all he knows.'

'Isn't that dangerous?' Eric said. 'I mean, it's OK for him to put himself at risk. He knows what he's doing. But that knife was left on your pillow.'

'He seems to have made up his mind about it.' Megan sighed. 'We had a disagreement.' There was a pause. 'Where are you calling from now?' she asked.

'London. I've been in meetings all day.'

Megan's heart beat a little faster. 'I don't suppose you've got any free time while you're over here? It's just . . . it would be nice to see you, if you can manage it.'

'Sure,' said Eric. 'I'd like that. Hold on a second, let me look at my calendar.' Megan waited. She wanted to see him so badly. She had to see him. 'Yeah, OK. I can come up to Cambridge tomorrow evening, if you like.'

'All right.' She didn't want him to come to her rooms this

time. Somewhere more neutral. 'How about we meet at a pub?'

'OK. Which one?'

'There's one called the Fort St George. It's by the river. I'd give you directions, but I'm still a little confused where it is myself. But it's a nice place.'

'Don't worry,' Eric said. 'I'll find it. See you there at seven.'

'OK.' Megan smiled to herself as she replaced the receiver.

The early spring sunshine caressed Marcus's tired features as he sat on the bench in St James's Park. He was sure it was the right one, on the Mall side of the lake, by the footbridge, just as Eric had described it. He checked his watch. Five past eleven. Eric had said eleven o'clock.

He wasn't sure what to expect: whether Eric would meet him, or someone else would. He had considered not showing up at all, but in the end he had decided to go ahead with the rendezvous. He had nothing to lose and he could use any help he could get. He still wasn't sure what he would do once he found Duncan. But find him he must.

He hadn't slept at all on the flight over. In fact, he hadn't slept well for a couple of nights, since his conversation with Eric back in Vermont. He was tired, and he let his eyes close, lulled by the steady background traffic noise and the sound of ducks fussing on the water in front of him.

Suddenly he felt the pressure of something placed on his lap. He opened his eyes and saw a cheap black canvas sports bag. He glanced up from left to right. On one side, a couple were sauntering arm-in-arm towards Buckingham Palace. On the other, a man with dark hair creeping over the collar of his leather jacket was walking briskly away. Marcus shouted to him, but the man lengthened his stride. Marcus shrugged. It wasn't Eric, and the messenger didn't matter. What mattered was the bag.

He unzipped it. Inside were a single sheet of white paper and a dark blue plastic bag. He glanced at the paper. It contained two neatly typed addresses: Honshu Bank's London office, and Duncan Gemmel's home address.

He felt the plastic bag. It contained something small and heavy. He guessed what it was as he cautiously peered inside, keeping it all the while in the sports bag.

He was right. A handgun.

His heart beat rapidly and he zipped up the bag. He stared ahead, trying to decide what to do, oblivious of the tourists and office-workers strolling by.

There was no choice. He had known what he had to do since he had skied across the lake the day before; he just hadn't been able to admit it to himself. But now, with the means lying there on his lap, he took the decision. He stood up and walked purposefully down the Mall towards Trafalgar Square, gripping the handles of the sports bag tightly.

7

'Hey, Chris! Look at the screen! I don't believe it.'

Chris, jolted out of his reverie by Ollie's urgent cry, looked. On Bloomberg News was an announcement:

Radaphone in agreed €1.5 billion takeover of Eureka Telecom.

Chris scanned the details. It looked like a done deal. He dialled Bloomfield Weiss and got through to Mandy Simpson. 'Have you seen the Eureka Telecom news?' he asked.

'Yes.'

'What does it mean for the bonds?'

'Good news for you, Chris. And good news for Bloomfield Weiss too. We've got Radaphone debt paying a twelve per cent coupon.'

Chris smiled to himself. Radaphone was a good credit: its bonds would normally trade at half that yield. 'Where's your trader making them?'

'He says he'll bid one-oh-seven. But that's low. They'll go higher than that.'

'Excellent!' said Chris. 'Thanks, Mandy.'

'Looks like Ian sold you a good deal after all,' she said.

Chris thought about her words as he put down the phone. She was right. Ian had known all along that Eureka would be taken over. He had told Lenka when he probably shouldn't. She had bought the bonds when she probably shouldn't. Everything had gone according to plan. Except that neither Lenka nor Ian was alive to see it.

Ian had been right to be cagey with Chris. Chris had thought it was because Ian had deceived Lenka and was worried about being found out. In fact, Ian had told her the truth, but had been unwilling to admit as much to Chris. He was probably right to be careful. Ian would no doubt have argued that his guess that the takeover would happen was no more than a guess, but what he had done was close to passing on inside information. The fewer people who knew about that, the better.

For the first time Chris wondered whether he had been too cynical about Ian and Lenka. Perhaps she had meant more to Ian than Chris had given him credit for. After what had happened to them both, he hoped so.

This was good news for RBK. The price at which they had bought Amalgamated Veterans' position had been fixed the day before. It had just gone up at least fifteen per cent. Chris smiled to himself. Khalid's gain had been Rudy Moss's loss. Carpathian definitely had a future now.

Chris dialled Duncan's number.

'Did you see the news about Eureka Telecom?'

'Yes,' Duncan said. 'You had some of that, didn't you?'

'We had a lot of it.'

'Khalid will be ecstatic.'

'He was very lucky.'

'Not entirely,' said Duncan. 'He got the market timing right, and he picked the right fund manager. He deserves to make money.'

'And Rudy Moss deserves to lose it.'

Duncan laughed.

'Seriously, thanks, Duncan. RBK really bailed us out.'

'Don't worry about it. My client's happy. It makes me look good. In fact it makes me look bloody brilliant.' Duncan chuckled. Then his tone became serious. 'Did you talk to Megan?'

'Yes, I did.'

'And what did she say?'

'She thinks we've got the wrong end of the stick. She thinks Eric couldn't possibly have done it.'

'That's crazy. She went out with him, didn't she? Maybe she's biased. Maybe she still fancies him. Does she?'

'I think so,' said Chris, with difficulty.

Duncan picked up the tone in Chris's voice. 'Sore point, obviously. Hang on. If she thinks Eric's innocent, then who does she think killed everyone? Me?'

Chris didn't say anything.

'I thought so,' Duncan said. 'Look, I understand why you wanted to talk to her. But we have to do something now. If she can't see that she's wrong about Eric, that's her problem. You've told her everything you can.'

Chris sighed. 'You're right. We should do something. But, as I said earlier, it's not that simple. Who do we talk to? The cops on Long Island? Or in Prague? Or Paris? The only name I've got is some guy called Karásek in Prague, but he's going to have to do a lot of work to put it all together.'

'Jesus, Chris, we've got to do something!'

'I know.' Chris thought. 'What about a lawyer?'

'A lawyer?'

'Yes. If we get a good one, he might be able to help us make sure we protect our role in all this. And he'd know the best way round the international legal system. I think that's the safest way to go.'

'All right,' said Duncan. 'Find one. And let me know what happens.'

'I will.'

Chris stared at the receiver as he put it down. Duncan was right, there was no time to lose. They were all at risk as long as Eric was running around unchecked. He picked up the phone and called the Fund's lawyer. She recommended someone who recommended someone else, and within an hour he had an appointment to see a Mr Geoffrey Morris-Jones at his offices in Holborn at nine o'clock the next morning.

Duncan found it very difficult to concentrate. At 12:05 he grabbed his jacket and left the office. He hurried to a pub round the corner and ordered a pint. It tasted good.

Duncan felt better than he had in a long time. He had energy and he had focus. He knew what had to be done: Eric had to be stopped. If this could be done within the framework of the law, so much the better, but he wasn't at all sure Chris's plan would work. The police investigation would be slow and cumbersome. Eric would simply hire the best lawyers available and keep quiet. It would take months or years to put him in jail, if they ever succeeded at all. And in all that time, their own lives would be at risk.

Then Duncan thought of Lenka. Her death had to be avenged.

He finished his pint, left the pub and walked fifty yards down the road to a hardware shop. There he bought a large, sharp kitchen knife. If Chris's plan didn't work out, he would be ready.

Chris, too, was finding it hard to focus on his work. The Eureka Telecom bonds had risen to 109 and Ollie was in a jubilant mood. He and Chris discussed how they were going to invest RBK's extra seven million euros. Chris did his best to share Ollie's good spirits, but couldn't manage it.

He was worried about seeing the lawyer the next day. He was sure Megan was wrong to put her faith in Eric, but he hated to place her in a potentially dangerous situation without her consent. If Eric ever did find out that they had gone to the police, her life would be in real danger. That thought scared Chris. Perhaps she would be safer if she went back to America. The problem was that Eric seemed to have no trouble leaving dead bodies all round the world: America would be no safer than England. Chris resolved to talk to the lawyer the next day about what steps could be taken to ensure her safety; and his own, for that matter.

He had to speak to Megan again, to try to get her to see that what he was doing made sense. He stared at the phone for a whole minute, then he called her.

She sounded subdued when she heard his voice, but at least she would talk to him. He told her about his appointment the next day.

She was unimpressed. 'I don't know why you're telling me all this. You're wasting your time. You know I think Eric is completely innocent.'

'I know. And I respect that. But I wanted you to know what I'm doing. And I want to make sure that you're safe, just in case you're wrong.'

'If you want to keep me safe, don't talk to the police,' said Megan.

'But we have to do something! The riskiest thing is to sit back and do nothing.'

'OK. But what if I'm right? What if it's Duncan you should be worried about?'

'I talked to him again today,' Chris said. 'I really don't think there's any need to worry about him.'

'Oh, great,' said Megan. 'Well, I'm seeing Eric this evening, and I'll let you know what I think after I've spoken to him.'

'You what?'

'I said, I'm meeting Eric.'

'Where? When?'

'At the Fort St George. At seven.'

'You're crazy. Don't do it.' Chris could feel the panic rising in his voice.

'Look. I'll talk to him about your theory. See what he says. I know him. I'll be able to see if he's telling the truth.'

'But if you do that, he'll know we're still asking questions. He'll know I'm on to him. It'll put all of us in danger.'

'Oh, I see. So it's perfectly safe for you to talk to Duncan, but it's dangerous for me to talk to Eric, is it?' Megan's voice was rising.

'It's not that simple.'

'Isn't it? Well, I think it is. Anyway, I've already told him you're planning to speak to the police.'

'You what! Why did you do that?'

'I didn't say it was him you were suspicious of.'

'But he'll know! For God's sake, Megan. Don't see him this

325

evening. Please. It's too dangerous. I'm only asking you this because I care about you. I couldn't bear it if you were hurt.'

There was silence on the line for several seconds. When Megan spoke, her voice was softer. 'I know you mean that, Chris. And I know I've been unfair to you over the last few days. I am sorry about that, I really am. But you're right; it is to do with Eric. I just don't know where I am with him, and it's something I need to sort out. That's why I have to speak to him. Why I'm going to see him this evening.'

'Megan –'

'Sorry, Chris,' and she hung up.

Chris stared at the receiver in disbelief. He looked at his watch. Twenty past five. He could just make it to the Fort St George before seven. He wouldn't have time to go back to the flat and get his car, but if he caught a train from King's Cross, it should work. He had to get to her before she met Eric.

He dialled Duncan's number.

'Honshu.'

'Duncan, bad news. Megan is meeting Eric in a pub in Cambridge this evening. She's going to tell him everything I've discovered. I'm worried about her. I'm going up there right now. Do you want to come?'

'All right. How are you getting there?'

'Train from King's Cross. You can get one from Liverpool Street. We'll meet at Cambridge station, and then go to the pub. We should get there before Megan if we move.'

'OK. I'll call you from my mobile when I know what time my train gets in to Cambridge.'

Chris hung up, said goodbye to the bewildered Ollie, and headed for the door.

The Jaguar whispered up the M11 at just under eighty miles per hour, Terry driving, Eric in the back, composed, neat in a dark suit, white shirt and Ferragamo tie. He was feeling good.

'I think we're going to pull this off, Terry.'

'I hope so, sir.'

'All I need to do is convince Megan that she should keep her head down and forget about who killed Lenka. I think she's just about there as it is.'

'Are you sure you don't want me to deal with the other two? We don't want them going to the cops.'

'I think we'll leave them to our friend Marcus. He's primed and dangerous. And without them the police will get nowhere.'

'Don't you think there's a risk he'll rat on you when he gets caught?'

'No,' said Eric. 'There's no point. He'll think he's killed the man who murdered his brother. And the police will probably believe him, since there'll be no one left to contradict him. He'll have no reason to drag me down with him. Anyway, I'll just deny everything. A good lawyer will protect me, no problem.'

'So, it's just Megan, then?'

'Just Megan. Will you wait for me in the parking lot?'

'I can't do that. I checked the map and it looks like the pub isn't even on a road. We'll have to park on the other side of the river and you can walk over the footbridge.'

'Whatever. I'm not totally sure I'll be coming back with you this evening,' Eric said.

'No?'

Eric tried to ignore the curiosity in Terry's voice. 'We'll just have to see how things progress.'

'Yes, sir,' Terry replied, as he eased the Jaguar off the motorway and on to the road to Cambridge.

Chris took the tube to King's Cross direct from Oxford Circus; it was quicker than a taxi during the rush hour. He arrived at the station just in time to jump on the five forty-five, which was due to arrive at Cambridge at six thirty-six. That should just give him time to get a taxi to the Fort St George by seven.

The train was pulling out of the station when Chris's mobile phone rang. It was Duncan. He had caught a train from Liverpool

Street that would reach Cambridge at six forty-four. Chris said he would wait for him on the platform.

The train sped through the flat Hertfordshire countryside, past Stevenage and Royston, and into the even flatter Cambridgeshire fens. They were only ten minutes from Cambridge when it slowed to a stop. Chris drummed his fingers in frustration. He wasn't psychologically prepared for a delay. It was getting dark outside. The clear sky, now a light blue-grey, was shrinking, blotted out by inky black clouds rushing in from the fens to the west. The train didn't move. Raindrops spattered the carriage window for a few moments, and then what seemed to be a wall of water battered the glass. The whole carriage rocked in the wind.

Chris stared in frustration at the rain outside. They'd be late. There was no way now that they could reach the pub before Eric and Megan. What would Eric do to her? Chris couldn't stand the thought of him harming her in any way. But if she told him all that Chris had discovered, would Eric have any choice?

Unless . . . Unless Eric planned to seduce her. Surely, she wouldn't let him do that. Chris didn't know whether it was instinct or jealousy, but he feared she might. At that moment that was a thought almost as horrible for Chris to contemplate.

Chris's fears were interrupted by an announcement over the train's loudspeaker system that there was a problem at a level crossing just ahead of them, and the train would be moving shortly.

It didn't.

8

Megan was still a quarter of a mile from the Fort St George when the rain hit. She could see the pub standing next to the river, surrounded by the wide spaces of Midsummer Common and Jesus Green. As the rain turned into a torrent, she broke into a run, but she was soaking by the time she made it inside.

The pub was almost empty. There was no sign of Eric. She checked her watch: she was ten minutes early. She bought herself a pint of bitter and sat in a small bar with a fire glowing in one corner. She sniffed as she pushed the damp hair from her eyes.

She was nervous about seeing Eric, but she also felt the thrill of doing something foolhardy. She had no idea what she was going to say to him, but she did know what she wanted to learn: whether her future was in any way connected with his. Somehow, she was sure, she would find out that evening.

She heard the door to the pub slam shut, and a moment later Eric popped his head round the door, water dripping from his hair, his nose and his clothes. She smiled at him. He came over and kissed her on the cheek, bringing with him the cold of the wind and rain outside. They exchanged greetings, and he went off to get himself a pint. A minute later, he was sitting opposite her, next to the fire.

'Jesus, this weather is awful,' he said, shivering.

'You get used to it.'

'Where does that wind come from? The Arctic?'

'Probably.'

Eric took a long drink of his beer. 'Can you believe what happened to Ian?' he said.

'No. It was horrible.'

'First Lenka, and now him,' Eric shook his head. 'And that knife on your pillow. Things are getting seriously weird.'

'They are.'

'I'm worried about you, Megan. And I'm worried about Chris going to the police. I mean, whoever did this might not stop now. Please take care of yourself.'

Megan gave him a small smile. 'I will,' she said. She sipped her beer nervously. The time had come to ask him. It was something she would have to do if she was ever going to be sure of him. 'Chris thinks that you killed Ian. And Lenka. And Alex, for that matter.'

Eric closed his eyes. He shook his head slowly. 'I thought Chris knew me better than that.'

'Did you?' Megan asked, looking him directly in the eye.

'How can you ask that?' he said.

'Did you?' she repeated.

Eric's eyes met hers. 'No,' he said, barely audibly. 'No, I didn't.'

They sat for several seconds, just looking at each other. Memories of that time so many years before when Megan had been so desperately in love with Eric came flooding back to her.

'Do you believe me?' he asked eventually, still holding her eyes.

'Yes,' she said. 'Yes, I do.'

Eric smiled. 'Good. But why does Chris think I killed them? And how could I possibly have killed Alex? Surely Duncan did that, if anyone?'

Megan launched into an explanation of Chris's view of events. When she had finished, Eric looked thoughtful.

'But he doesn't have any evidence at all. It's all smoke. He's just freaked out by it all, and he's picked on me as the answer. That disappoints me. I always liked Chris: I thought he'd know better.'

'What about the psychometric tests?' Megan asked.

'Oh, that,' Eric smiled. 'I was the perfect interviewee. You must remember that. I got offered jobs by ten Wall Street firms

330

in my senior year in college. My secret was that I told them what they wanted to hear. And Bloomfield Weiss wanted to hear that I was a big, tough, nasty guy who ate babies for breakfast. So that's what I told them. I guess I went a bit over the top. But, as you know, they gave me the job.'

'So you lied?'

'Not exactly. But close. I embellished. Whenever there was a choice of helping a little old lady across the road or throwing her under a bus, I threw her under a bus. That kind of thing. But none of it was real. Once I got to Bloomfield Weiss I paid lip service to all the "it's a jungle out there" bullshit. I was always the predator, not the prey. But I think I behaved pretty decently. Ask Chris. He knows.'

Megan was relieved. Eric's explanation was totally believable. If this Dr Horwath woman had been any good, then she should have been able to detect Eric faking his answers, but Megan wasn't surprised that he had managed to mislead her.

'So who do you think killed Ian and Lenka?' Eric asked.

Megan sighed. 'I don't know. I try really hard not to think about it. It must be Duncan, I guess. But Chris is sure Duncan's innocent. I don't know what it is about those two, Chris always seems to be covering for him.'

'We all did on the boat, didn't we?' said Eric. 'Maybe that was a mistake. I don't know. Those kind of secrets have a habit of coming out eventually.'

'What do you think?' Megan asked.

Eric stared into his beer thoughtfully. 'I don't know, either. I guess it must be Duncan. But I think the most important thing for you to do is to forget all about it. If Duncan is a killer, or someone else who we don't even know, they're watching you. Chris can get himself into whatever kind of trouble he likes, but I'd hate for anything bad to happen to you.'

Megan blushed and looked up at Eric. The look of concern in his eyes was much more than worry about an old friend from a previous life. 'Thank you,' Megan said, and touched his hand.

Eric smiled at her. They sat like that, her hand touching his, for a moment that felt to Megan to last for ever.

'Let's talk about something else,' said Eric eventually. 'What are the famous Cambridge dons like? Are they all as crazy as they look? And what do they all do now they can't recruit spies for the KGB any more?'

Megan launched into a description of some of the eccentrics she had met in her college. That led on to exchanging memories of their professors at Amherst. Then the conversation became more personal. They discussed the major decisions they had taken in their lives, and why they had taken them.

Eric began to talk about Cassie. 'You met her, didn't you?' he asked.

'Yes. A couple of times, when you first went out with her.'

'What did you think of her?'

'She was nice. Very pretty, obviously. I can't say I liked her, but I was a bit biased at the time.'

'Sorry,' Eric said. 'Stupid question. But you're right. She seemed like the perfect woman. Beautiful, intelligent, charming.'

'And her father is a bigshot in the Republican Party.'

'That's unfair.'

'Sorry.' But Megan wasn't. She didn't like this listing of Cassie's charms.

Then Eric frowned. 'I don't know. Although I never admitted it to anyone, that probably was something else in her favour. In fact, she seemed perfect in every way. All my friends said so. And for the first couple of years they were probably right.'

Megan's pulse quickened. 'The first couple of years?'

'Yes,' Eric said, and fell silent.

'Why? What happened then?'

'I don't know. It was nothing she did; she's always been the perfect wife. It was more me. I came to realize that I needed something else from the person I was supposed to love for the rest of my life. Something that for some reason Cassie couldn't give me.'

'Something else? What do you mean?'

'I don't know. It's hard to describe.' Then he looked directly at Megan. 'Well, actually I do know. And so do you.'

Megan did her best to fight the surge of excitement within her. She knew it! Her feeling that there was a unique bond between them was confirmed. Eric knew it too, she was sure. 'That's a bit tough on Cassie, isn't it?' she said carefully.

Eric nodded. 'It is. And I feel so bad thinking it. So ungrateful for all she does for me. But I can't help it. And it's one of those ideas, that once you get it, it doesn't go away.'

'Are you going to do anything about it?' Megan asked. For a moment, she thought she had gone too far, but she had to know. She just had to know.

Eric looked confused. 'I don't know. The truth is, most of the time I'm thinking about work. And I love Wilson. No. I expect we'll just drift further and further apart. It's sad, though.'

Megan's throat felt dry. 'Yes, it is.'

She felt like throwing herself on him right there and then. But she knew that he was still married, and despite his unhappiness, from the sound of it there was no imminent bust-up likely. He gave no hint that he had ever been unfaithful; on the contrary, he gave the impression of being a dutiful, if occasionally absent, husband. She couldn't be responsible for breaking up a family, could she? And what about Chris? Starting something with Eric would be very cruel to him. And she didn't want to be cruel to Chris.

Eric glanced at their empty beer glasses. 'I think it might have stopped raining. How about we go find somewhere to have dinner?'

'Yes,' she said immediately. She couldn't have said otherwise: she had no choice.

Eventually, Chris's train began to move, and ten minutes later it pulled into Cambridge. Duncan had been delayed by the same level-crossing incident. Chris waited the couple of minutes for him to arrive, and after exchanging curses they jumped into a taxi. The rain had snarled up the traffic, and it was twenty minutes before the taxi reached a small residential road by the river.

Chris and Duncan ran over the footbridge to the Fort St George. They scoured the place, but no sign of Eric and Megan. Chris grabbed the barman's attention, a lanky boy with spots and an earring. 'Have you seen two Americans in here? A tall man and a girl with long dark curly hair?'

'Oh yeah,' he said. 'They left a couple of minutes ago.'

'Thanks.' Chris turned to Duncan. 'They've probably headed back across the green towards the town. Let's go.'

They ran out of the pub, and surveyed the acres of parkland surrounding them. It was very dark, and although streetlamps illuminated a road that crossed the green they couldn't see either of them.

'Come on,' said Chris, and he set out along a path that led to the lights of Jesus College and the centre of the town. He ran fast, praying that Megan was all right, that Eric hadn't touched her, that Eric wouldn't touch her.

Terry looked up from the portable chess set on the front seat beside him, and saw the two figures leaping out of the taxi and rushing over the bridge. He recognized them immediately. As the taxi drew away, he was just about to get out of his own car, when he saw another cab pull up. This time a tall man in a long coat appeared, looked over the bridge where the other two had disappeared, and followed them.

Terry went after the three of them, his senses alive. It looked like the boss was going to need some help.

9

Chris ran steadily, peering into the darkness of Jesus Green. He could hear Duncan puffing along behind him. Then he saw them: two figures walking slowly towards the town. He increased his speed to a sprint. They turned as they heard him approach. It was Eric and Megan.

Chris came to a halt beside them, out of breath. They were in the middle of the green, far from any buildings. No one else was near them.

'Chris! What the hell are you doing here?' Megan exclaimed. 'And why did you bring *him* with you?'

Duncan joined them, panting heavily.

'I need to talk to you,' Chris said between breaths.

'Well, we don't need to talk to you.'

'Please, Megan. This is important.'

Megan threw Chris an impatient look. But there was hesitation in it also.

'Come on, Megan,' Eric said, taking her arm.

'No, stay!' Chris's tone changed from pleading to a command.

'What is this, Chris?' Megan protested.

'I'm just trying to keep you alive, that's all. Keep us all alive.'

'That's ridiculous. Look, why don't you talk to Eric sensibly? He can help you.'

'Wait, Megan,' said Eric. 'I've kept out of this so far, and I want to stay out of it. As long as you're safe, that's all I care about. Chris can dream up all the wild theories he likes, but I'm having nothing to do with it. Now let's go.'

Chris glanced at Megan. She looked at him with a mixture of confusion and anger. He couldn't let Eric walk off with her.

'Stop!' he said, grabbing hold of Eric's arm.

Eric turned and glared at him. 'Get your hands off me!'

'Yeah, stop,' said Duncan. He stepped forward, brandishing the kitchen knife at Eric, a light sliver of grey in the darkness.

Eric froze. Megan let out a small scream.

Chris's first thought was to step back and let Duncan stick the knife into Eric. Maybe he could even help him. Then sense took over. 'Duncan. Hold on. Don't do it.'

'Why not? He killed my friends. He'll kill us if we let him. He deserves to die.'

'Don't, Duncan. It's wrong. And anyway, you'll get caught. You'll go to jail for a long time.'

'It'll be worth it.'

'No, it won't. Wait. I'll call the police.'

'No,' said Duncan grimly.

Chris glanced at Duncan's face. He knew there was no point in arguing further. And he couldn't try to restrain Duncan physically without letting Eric go. So he released Eric's arm and stood back. Megan was watching, horror-stricken. 'Stop him, Chris.'

At that moment, Chris heard a click behind him. They all turned towards the sound. There was Marcus in his long coat, unshaven and out of breath. He was holding a gun, and pointing it directly at them.

'Well, well, well. What do you call a group of investment bankers? A gaggle? A herd? Whatever. It looks like you all just can't get along with each other.'

They were silent, staring at the gun.

'Who are you?' Megan asked at last.

'Marcus Lubron. Alex was my brother. Until *he* killed him.' Marcus nodded towards Duncan.

'What do you mean?' Duncan objected.

'Put down the knife,' Marcus said, jerking the gun at him.

Duncan didn't move.

'I said, put it down.'

Duncan slowly laid the knife on the ground.

'You make me sick,' Marcus said. 'Not only do you kill my brother, but you start killing each other as well.'

'No, you don't understand,' said Duncan, moving towards Marcus.

'Stand still,' snapped Marcus. 'I know how to use this thing. It looks like I got here just in time to stop you killing another one.'

'But it's Eric who killed your brother!' Duncan protested. 'And the others.'

'I've had enough of this whining bullshit. Stand over there. And you,' Marcus waved the gun at Chris. 'Stand with him.'

Chris and Duncan stood to one side, next to each other, facing Marcus. His face was in shadow, but Chris could just make out the determined set of his mouth. He was serious. Deadly serious. Chris felt fear grab him.

'Marcus,' Chris said, in his best attempt at a reasonable voice. 'I think you've got this all wrong.'

'Shut up, or I'll blow your head off.'

'But Chris didn't do anything,' Megan protested.

'He killed your friend in Paris,' Marcus said.

'No he didn't. Tell him, Eric.'

She turned to Eric. He said nothing.

Marcus raised the gun and pointed it directly at Duncan. 'Alex may have meant nothing to you,' he said. 'But he was my kid brother. He would have had a great life ahead of him if you hadn't finished it. I wasn't there to protect him then. But I'm here now.'

'Marcus –' Duncan said, his voice cracking with panic.

'I said, be quiet,' Marcus snapped.

Megan watched all this with mounting horror. She was about to see someone shot in cold blood. She wanted to scream. She wanted to run. After the emotional turmoil of the last hour, and the strain of the previous month, she thought she was going to crack. It was all too much for her to take in. She looked at Duncan. Total fear. At Eric, impassive, with the hint of a small

337

satisfied smile. And at Chris, standing straight, tense, but facing his last few seconds with courage.

In those last moments before his death, he turned to her. His eyes met hers. Suddenly something snapped inside her, and she saw everything clearly. People were going to die here. The wrong people. This was so much more important than her stupid infatuation. She also saw that somebody loved her. And it wasn't Eric.

Slowly and deliberately, she stepped forward and placed herself in front of Duncan.

'Get out of the way!' Marcus growled.

'No,' Megan said calmly. 'Put the gun down.'

'Look, I don't care how many investment bankers I blow away here. Now, move!'

'I'm not an investment banker,' said Megan. 'And I don't think these people had anything to do with your brother's death. Even if they did, there has been too much killing. It must stop.'

A flicker of hesitation appeared in Marcus's eyes. Megan glanced quickly at Eric. 'Just tell me, how do you know who killed Alex? And why do you think Chris killed Ian?'

'He told me,' Marcus nodded towards Eric.

Then Megan knew. Eric had mentioned nothing to her about talking to Marcus. The attempt to implicate Chris was pure cynicism on his part. Eric had deceived her. About everything.

'He lied,' she said.

'Jesus,' Marcus said in frustration. 'OK. Then I'll shoot the lot of you. You all deserve it.'

'You won't shoot any of us,' Megan said, taking a step forward. 'You're not a killer. Alex wouldn't want you to kill us.'

'I will,' Marcus said, but Megan could see the doubt in his eyes.

'Well, if you do, you'll have to start with me. And you know I'm innocent.'

She took another step. The barrel of the gun was just inches from her chest. Marcus let it drop to his side.

Then Eric lunged. In one movement, he grabbed Marcus's arm and twisted it behind his back. Hard. Marcus let out a yelp of pain and dropped the gun. Eric shoved him forward and picked it up. He pointed it at Megan.

'Don't try that stunt with me,' he said coolly. 'Because I'll pull the trigger.'

'You bastard!' Megan said, her voice laden with contempt. 'I believed in you, and you lied to me. And you murdered all those people just because they threatened your precious little plans.'

'If you want something, you have to be prepared to do what it takes to get it.'

'I thought you were something special,' Megan said. 'But I was wrong. You think you're better than us, don't you? Better than all of us. You think it's OK for lesser people to die so that the great Eric Astle can realize his destiny. Well, let me tell you something. You're small. You're a nasty, lying, evil little low-life. You amount to nothing, Eric. You never were anything, and you never will be.'

'Bitch,' he said and raised the gun to take aim.

A few seconds earlier Chris had faced death and accepted it. He had felt fear and overcome it. Now he couldn't stand and watch Megan die in front of him. In that moment, the decision seemed easy. If he stood still, Megan would die. If he jumped, perhaps he would get shot, perhaps Duncan would, but perhaps Megan would live. His eyes darted to Duncan, and he saw his fear had gone. He too was ready to act.

They launched themselves at Eric simultaneously. The gun went off, and then they were on him, joined in a moment by Marcus. Chris went for Eric's right hand, still clasping the gun. He pinned it to the ground as it exploded again, this time the bullet speeding harmlessly off into the darkness. Eric writhed and kicked, but in a matter of seconds they had him pinned to the ground. Marcus prised the gun from his fingers, and held it to his ear. 'Don't move, fucker,' he growled.

Terry watched all this from his vantage point, twenty yards

away behind a tree. He knew this would happen sometime, that Eric would get himself in too deep. Well, Terry wasn't going to go down with him. He had over a million dollars stashed away in a Swiss bank account for just such an eventuality. Not enough to see him out for the rest of his life, perhaps, but enough to support him on an extended vacation somewhere. Time to go. He slipped off and headed quietly back to the Jaguar and Stansted Airport.

Chris got to his feet, and Megan ran to him. He held her tightly.

'I'm so sorry,' she said, looking up at him. 'Will you forgive me?'

'Of course,' Chris stroked her hair. 'Of course I will.'

She smiled, and buried her head in his chest.

He heard a curse on the ground beside him. Duncan was holding his shoulder.

'Are you OK?' Chris asked.

'I'm alive. But this hurts like hell. And it's bleeding.'

'Let me have a look.' Chris and Megan squatted beside him. There was blood, and Duncan's face was contorted in pain, but it didn't look life threatening.

'What shall I do with this asshole?' said Marcus, prodding Eric.

'Keep him there,' said Chris. He pulled out his mobile phone and dialled 999. The questions and explanations were about to begin. But the insanity had ended.